Red Wizards

You can't win.

You know what Red Wizards can do.

What they love to do to anyone who defies them.

You know the sort of creatures who fight for them.

*I'm only the first of many such beings
who stand in your way.*

*Choose now whether you mean to live or die,
or I'll choose for you.*

An arcane brotherhood at war with itself.

THE HAUNTED LANDS

Book I
Unclean

Book II
Undead

Book III
Unholy
March 2009

Anthology
Realms of the Dead
Early 2010

Also by Richard Lee Byers

R.A. Salvatore's War of the Spider Queen
Book I
Dissolution

The Year of Rogue Dragons

Book I
The Rage

Book II
The Rite

Book III
The Ruin

Sembia: Gateway to the Realms

The Halls of Stormweather

Shattered Mask

The Priests

Queen of the Depths

The Rogues

The Black Bouquet

FORGOTTEN REALMS

The Haunted Lands | Book II

undead

Richard Lee Byers

Wizards
OF THE COAST
®

The Haunted Lands, Book II
UNDEAD

©2008 Wizards of the Coast, Inc.

Cover art by Greg Ruth
Map by Rob Lazzaretti
First Printing: March 2008

9 8 7 6 5 4 3 2 1

ISBN: 978-0-7869-4783-6
620-21626740-001-EN

U.S., CANADA,	EUROPEAN HEADQUARTERS
ASIA, PACIFIC, & LATIN AMERICA	Hasbro UK Ltd
Wizards of the Coast, Inc.	Caswell Way
P.O. Box 707	Newport, Gwent NP9 0YH
Renton, WA 98057-0707	GREAT BRITAIN
+1-800-324-6496	Save this address for your records.

Visit our web site at www.wizards.com

For Lance

Acknowledgments

Thanks to Susan Morris and Phil Athans
for all their help and support

prologue

11 Hammer–16 Ches, the Year of Blue Fire (1385 DR)

Sometimes even archmages have to wait, and so it was for Szass Tam, standing on the wide, flat roof of the castle's highest tower. He passed the time gazing out at the chain of volcanic peaks his people called the Thaymount, at other fortresses perched on lofty crags, mining camps clustered around yawning pits and the black mouths of tunnels, and, here and there, leaping flame and trickling lava. The cold winter air smelled of ash.

Beyond the peaks lay farms and parklands, cloaked in snow. Except for the leaden overcast sky, which once would have seemed an aberration in a realm where sorcery managed the weather, the view was much as it had always been throughout Szass Tam's extended existence.

He smiled appreciatively at the geography, as one smiles at a favored pet. During the first two years of the war, his troops had fought savagely to dislodge his enemies from their estates on the plateau, and in the wake of his army's success, High Thay had become his secure redoubt. His foes were evidently sensible enough to deem it unassailable, for they'd never sought to clamber up the towering cliffs of the Second Escarpment to challenge him. Rather, they fought him on the tablelands beneath, and on the lowlands between the First Escarpment and the sea.

Footsteps roused him from his musings. He turned toward the doorway and four blue-bearded frost giants shambled forth from the shadows beyond. The grayish tinge of their ivory skins, the slack-jawed imbecility of their expressions, and the smell of rot surrounding them identified them as zombies.

They carried a platform of oak affixed to two long poles. Atop the square surface was a transparent, nine-sided pyramid composed of crystallized mystical energy. Within it rested Thakorsil's Seat, a high stone chair with arms carved in the shapes of dragons. Seated thereon was Yaphyll, a woman of youthful appearance, small for a member of the long-limbed Mulan aristocracy, with an impish face.

As the zombie giants set her down, Yaphyll shifted and adjusted her robe. "As litter bearers," she said, "your servants lack a certain delicacy of touch. Especially when carrying their passenger up flight after flight of stairs."

"I apologize," Szass Tam replied, "but I hoped you'd enjoy a change of scenery. Aren't fresh air and this magnificent vista worth a bit of bouncing around?"

"If you had only freed me from the pyramid," she said, "I would have been happy to walk up under my own power. After so much sitting, I would have enjoyed the exercise."

"I'm sure you would," he replied, "just as I'm sure that you would have found some way to turn the situation to your advantage. That's why I took the trouble to confine you in a prison built to hold an infernal prince."

"I appreciate the compliment. Someday I hope to show you how much."

"No doubt. Meanwhile, consider the view." He waved his hand at the mountains and the shadowed gorges between. "This is the highest point in all Thay. Legend has it that a person can gaze out from here and observe everything transpiring across the land. That's nonsense, of course, or at least it is for most of us. But I wonder what the eyes of the realm's greatest oracle can see."

"Burnt villages and plundered towns," Yaphyll said. "Fields returning to wilderness. Famine. Plague. Armies preparing for another season of ruinous war."

"I had hoped you'd grace me with a genuine exhibition of your skills, not a banal recitation of common knowledge."

"As you wish." She sketched a sign on the air. Her fingertip left a shimmering green trail. "Some of your troops are besieging a castle east of Sekelmur. A company of our raiders has attacked a caravan of supply wagons on the Sur Road. Neither action looks important, but then, they never are decisive, are they? Thus the game drags on and on and on."

"Perhaps if we work together, we can change that."

"I'm willing to try. That was why I forsook the other zulkirs and joined you. Anything to shift the balance of power, break the stalemate, and bring the war to an end before it cripples the realm beyond recovery."

"I had no idea your motives were so patriotic. I thought you simply decided I was going to prevail and preferred to be on the winning side."

Yaphyll grinned. "Perhaps there was a bit of that as well."

"Yet eventually you elected to turn your cloak again, and nearly succeeded in slipping away. Because you found my strategy and resources less impressive than expected?"

"Not exactly. But the stalemate endured, and in time I realized I'd rather stand with the living than the dead. With lords who, whatever their excesses, refrain from massacring their own subjects to turn them into ghoul and zombie soldiers."

Szass Tam shrugged. "It was scarcely indiscriminate slaughter. I only did it when necessary."

"If you say so. At any rate, now that you've made me your prisoner, such details no longer concern me. I need to look after myself. So please free me, and I promise to serve you loyally."

"And how could I possibly doubt your pledge, paragon of honesty and loyalty that you are?"

Yaphyll took a deep breath. "All right. If you feel that way about it, bind me into your service."

"I'm afraid the usual ritual wouldn't take, at least not permanently. It's one thing to shackle a common Red Wizard, but another to trammel the mind of the zulkir of the Order of Divination."

"Then turn me into a lich or one of your vampires, something your necromancy can control. Better that than to stay in this box!"

"I've considered that, but the passage from life into undeath alters the mind, sometimes subtly, sometimes significantly. I won't risk compromising the clarity of your vision. Not yet. We have a war to win."

"If you won't release me from the chair, I won't help you."

"Please, don't be childish. Of course you will."

He held out his hand and the Death Moon Orb appeared in his palm. Coils of black and purple swam on the surface of the sphere. The orb changed size from time to time. Currently, it was as big as a man's head, which made it seem an awkward burden in such a frail-looking hand. But despite their withered, mummified appearance—the only visible sign of his undead condition—Szass Tam's fingers were deft and strong, and he managed the sphere easily.

He lifted the orb to the level of Yaphyll's eyes. "Look at it," he said.

She did. The power of the orb had compelled her into Thakorsil's Seat, and she found it as irresistible as before.

"You will tell me," he said, "when and where to meet the legions of the other zulkirs in battle to win that decisive victory which has thus far eluded us all. I command you to cast the most powerful divination known to your order, no matter the peril to your body, mind, or soul."

"Curse you!" Yaphyll gasped.

"I'm sure you will if you ever get the chance. But for now, does the spell require arcane ingredients? I daresay my own stock contains whatever you may require."

"Panacolo." Yaphyll spat. "Haunspeir. Dreammist. Redflower leaves. The eyes of an eagle, a beholder, and a medusa. A mortar and pestle, and a goblet of clear water."

That combination of narcotics and poisons would kill any living woman under normal circumstances. Szass Tam wondered if it would kill her, too, or if her mastery of her art would enable her to survive. It would be interesting to see.

He sent a pair of apprentices to fetch the spell ingredients, then opened the pyramid long enough to hand them to her. Her features twisted with reluctance, she then proceeded with the ritual.

Gray fumes of dreammist twisted through the air. Yaphyll chanted as she pulped and powdered the other items one by one, then stirred them into her cup. When she'd mixed everything, she shouted a final rhyme, raised the cup, and drank the narcotic concoction.

She convulsed so violently that only the magic of Thakorsil's Seat kept her upright, thrashing against that invisible restraint. Her dainty fist clenched and the pewter goblet crumpled. Then her fingers relaxed and the ruined cup slipped from her grip to clank on the oak platform. Her body slumped and her head lolled to the side.

"Are you still conscious?" asked Szass Tam. "If so, tell me what you see."

Yaphyll blinked and sat up straighter. "I see . . ."

"What? I explained what I need."

She shuddered, bumping her head against the high back of the chair, and then the shaking subsided. "Come spring, send word to Hezass Nymar that you mean to march the legions of High Thay to lay siege to the Keep of Sorrows. Summon him and his legions to rendezvous with you there."

Szass Tam frowned. Hezass Nymar, the tharchion of the province of Lapendrar, had switched sides five times since the war for control of Thay had begun, which branded him as faithless and unreliable even by the shabby standards of this chaotic conflict. "Such an assault would put my strongest army deep in enemy territory, drawn up in front of a formidable fortress, with the River Lapendrar and the First Escarpment limiting our mobility. On first inspection, I don't see that idea's merit."

Yaphyll grinned, a flicker of her usual impudence shining through the daze induced by magic, drugs, and poison. "You're right to be skeptical, for Hezass Nymar is about to change sides again. He'll betray your intentions to the Council of Zulkirs, and if he opts to march his army to the battle, it will be to fight on their side."

Szass Tam nodded. "I doubt I would have blundered into this trap in the first place, but I appreciate the warning. Still, it isn't the answer to my question. When and where can I bring your peers to battle to tip the balance in my favor for good and all?"

Yaphyll's back arched, and she raised her trembling hands before her face as if she meant to claw at it. "You have your answer. The other zulkirs will leap at the chance to catch you. They'll field every soldier who can reach the Keep of Sorrows in time. But, knowing the situation is a snare, you can plan accordingly. You can turn it around against your enemies, and when you defeat such a large number, you'll cripple them."

"Interesting." It seemed a mad scheme altogether, and yet

Szass Tam knew that where augury was concerned, she was a better wizard than he was. He was also confident that, compelled by the Death Moon Orb, she couldn't lie. What if—

Yaphyll's laughter jarred him. Or perhaps she was sobbing.

"The white queen is troubled," she said, "but can't say why."

"What queen is that?" Szass Tam asked, without any sense of urgency. Since Thay didn't have kings or queens, the remark was cryptic, seemingly without relevance to his question. Now that Yaphyll had obeyed his command, he suspected her mystical sight had drifted to some unrelated matter.

"The black queen hates the white," Yaphyll continued, "and gives the assassin a black cloak. The assassin steals up on the white queen. She can't see him gliding through the shadows."

"Who are these people?" asked Szass Tam.

"The sword screams," Yaphyll continued. "The white queen falls. Her city falls. Stones fall in the cavern to crush the soothsayer."

"It sounds like a bad day all around."

"The tree burns," Yaphyll said, "and thrashes in agony. Branches break. Branches twist and grow togeth—"

Tendrils of blue flame erupted down the length of her body, from her hairless scalp to the tips of her toes. She screamed and thrashed.

Szass Tam took a step back. Had her spell escaped her control? He'd save her from the consequences if he could, in the hope she'd prove useful again. He spoke the word that dissolved the crystal pyramid into a fading shimmer, then prepared to conjure a splash of water.

The flames went out of their own accord, leaving behind spots where flesh, silk, and velvet had melted and flowed like wax. Indifferent to the bizarre injuries, Yaphyll giggled and rose from Thakorsil's Seat.

Szass Tam was astonished, but didn't delay. He thrust the Death Moon Orb at her. "Sit down."

"Thank you," she said, "but I'd rather stand. You bade me split myself in two, and send one half into tomorrow. Your silly globe can't touch that half."

She waved her hand and a gout of acid flew at him and splashed across his chest. But fortunately, he was never without his defenses, and although much of his robe sizzled and steamed away, he felt only a little stinging.

Which didn't mean he was inclined to let her try again. He lunged at her and grabbed her by the wrist.

When he willed it, his grip could paralyze, and she stiffened as he expected. But then, to his chagrin, he sensed the life vanish from her body like a blown-out candle flame. After the poison she'd already taken, the malignancy of a lich's touch had proved an unendurable strain. Such a waste.

He dropped her and turned to the zombie giants. "Return Thakorsil's Seat to its chamber," he said, "then take this corpse to Xingax."

For his part, Yaphyll had left him with a mystery to ponder—and, he supposed, a campaign to plan.

•• •• •• •• •• •• •• •• •• •• •• •• ••

"It knows we're coming," Brightwing said.

As he often did when they flew by night, Aoth Fezim had married his senses to the griffon's. Even so, he couldn't tell how she knew, but he didn't doubt her.

"Is it in the air, too?" he asked, adjusting his grip on the spear that served him as both warrior's weapon and wizard's staff.

"I can't tell yet," Brightwing said, then hissed when the base of her right wing gave her a twinge.

With their minds coupled, Aoth felt it too. "Are you all right?" he asked.

"Fine."

"Are you sure?" He'd almost lost her last autumn, when one of Szass Tam's undead champions drove its sword deep into her body, and he didn't want to take her into battle if she hadn't fully recovered.

"Yes! Now stop fretting like a senile old granny and tell your friends what I told you."

She was right—he needed to relay the information. His familiar spoke Mulhorandi, but with a beak and throat poorly shaped for human speech, and for the most part, only her master could understand her.

Flying on his own griffon, Bareris Anskuld acknowledged the warning with a curt nod. As the bard's fair complexion and lanky frame attested, he was of Mulan stock, but he sported a tangled mane of blond hair that shone bone white in the moonlight. He'd abandoned the habit of shaving his head during his travels abroad and had never taken it up again.

A dimly luminous shadow, Mirror floated on the other side of Bareris, far enough away to keep his presence from spooking the singer's mount. As it might well have done, for Mirror was a ghost. Because he lacked all memory of his mortal existence he tended to take on the appearance of anyone who happened to be near. Although sometimes he showed a murky, wavering semblance of what had been his own living face, a lean visage notable for a big, hooked nose and a drooping mustache. Occasionally, he even spoke.

Mounted on his flying horse, Malark Springhill acknowledged Brightwing's warning with a grin and a finger-flick of a salute. Compact of build, with pale green eyes and a wine red birthmark on his chin, Malark was an outlander, but he sported the usual Thayan hairless pate and collection of tattoos.

To some, they would appear an ominous trio. Bareris's bleak, obsessive nature revealed itself in his cold stare, gaunt face, somber dress, and indifference to personal hygiene. Mirror was one of the living dead. Malark's unfailing good cheer in the face of every hardship and horror the war could unleash sometimes verged on the demented. Yet Aoth felt a bond with them all. They'd all but been to the Hells and back together.

Aoth, Bareris, and even Mirror, in his inscrutable fashion, served as soldiers in the service of Nymia Focar, tharchion of Surthay. But Malark was spymaster to Dmitra Flass, governor of Eltabbar and zulkir of the Order of Illusion since Szass Tam slew her predecessor. Thus it was rare for all four of them to gather in the same place at the same time with the leisure to devote to any sort of reunion.

But it had happened a few days earlier, after some secret business brought Malark to Nymia's palace. When word came that the enemy in the north had sent another menace to stalk the countryside, Aoth had suggested that, in lieu of the usual patrol of griffon riders or horse archers, the foursome fly out and hunt down the threat themselves.

He'd hoped the diversion would lift him out of the brooding glumness that had afflicted him of late. But it seemed to have the opposite effect.

"Shake it off," Brightwing growled. She'd sensed the tenor of his thoughts. "This isn't the time to mope. A cluster of houses lies up ahead. The thing—or things—we're hunting could well be down there."

"I suspect you're right." He pointed his spear at the ground, signaling his companions to descend.

They made a wary, swooping pass over the village. "I smell fresh blood," Brightwing said, "but I don't see anything moving."

"We'll have to land to determine what's what," Aoth said.

"You could just throw spells and burn the whole place from the air." The griffon snorted. "But you won't. Not when there could be survivors."

"And not when there might be something to learn. Set down

in front of the biggest house. The one with the carvings on the corners of the eaves."

She did as he'd bade her, touching down lightly in the snow. His companions followed, although Malark's dappled mare was reluctant, whickering and tossing her head. After dismounting, he murmured to her, and she wasted no time galloping back up into the air.

"That's a bit reckless," said Aoth.

The spymaster shrugged. "If I kept her on the ground, she'd become more and more nervous, and less tractable. She'll come if I whistle. Now, how about a light?"

"Why not?" Aoth replied. "Since Brightwing says the enemy already knows we're here, I don't see much point in trying to sneak around." He exerted his will, and the head of his spear flared yellow. The radiance was as bright as sunlight, anathema to most undead, although it never troubled Mirror. He could move around even in real daylight without harm.

The glow revealed doors smashed open, and a confusion of marks and footprints in the snow.

•• •• •• •• •• •• •• •• •• •• •• •• •• ••

Bareris squatted to examine the signs. "Skeleton tracks."

"Well, then." Malark unsheathed the oak batons he wore strapped to each thigh. A blue gleaming flowed down the lengths of polished hardwood, a sign of the enchantments within. "I was hoping for something more interesting, some new creation from your old friend Xingax, but we'll have to make do."

The mention of Xingax gave Bareris a spasm of hatred and self-loathing, for it was the aborted demigod who'd transformed his beloved Tammith into a vampire. Not long after, he'd come face to face with the hideous fetal creature but had botched the job of killing him. But then, he'd always failed when it mattered most.

"It might be more than skeletons," said Aoth. His coat of mail clinked as he stooped to examine the ground. Most wizards found their spellcasting hindered by armor, but war mages like the swarthy, stocky Aoth, who looked like a humble Rashemi despite his claim to have come from Mulan stock, trained to overcome the limitation. "Look here. Some of the farmers ran out of their houses. They made it this far, then the tracks end in a great muddle, as if something magical sprang up and destroyed them."

"Or something big dived down on them from the air," Bareris said. "It's curious there are no corpses, just the occasional spatter of blood. It's likely the enemy carried its victims away, possibly for reanimation."

"I agree," Malark said. "Here's a spot where it looks as if a pair of skeletons hauled away a body."

"We don't know that it was a dead body," Aoth said. "They may be taking prisoners, and we may be in time to save them. Come on." Glowing spear at the ready, he stalked forward, following the trail Malark had indicated. His companions prowled after him. Brightwing and Vengeance, Bareris's griffon, padded out to guard the flanks of the procession. For a time, Mirror appeared as a wavering, murky parody of Malark, with a cudgel sketched in shadow in both fists, but then the weapons melted into a sword and targe.

The trail led to the hamlet's little cemetery. So did other sets of tracks. Nothing was moving there, but something had torn open all the graves, leaving black, ragged wounds in the frozen earth, toppling markers, and scattering bones.

"I guess," Malark said, "we need to look in the graves. Unless the skeletons and others have moved on, I don't know where else they could be."

They crept forward. Bareris realized his mouth had gone dry, and he swallowed hard to moisten it.

Several paces inside the desecrated space, slumped at the edge of an open grave, he discovered a mass of torn, bloody flesh clad in peasant clothing. At first glance, it looked like a farmer, but something was wrong with its mangled shape. Bareris lifted one of its arms, saw it flop and sag, and then he knew. Something had pulled out all its bones.

That might explain why so many bones were lying around, more than the open graves could have contained. But no, actually even the mutilation of all the locals couldn't account for it—bones lay everywhere. It had simply been difficult to mark their true plenitude amid the heaps of dislodged earth and snow.

Bareris frowned. He didn't understand what he was looking at, and that frequently meant he'd blundered into serious trouble. He drew breath, about to suggest that he and his companions withdraw, and then several skeletons scrambled up from the concealment afforded by the open graves.

Bareris shouted, and his thunderous bellow, charged with bard's magic, blasted one of the skeletons to scraps and splinters.

Aoth hurled a fan-shaped blast of fire from the head of his spear and burned an opponent to ash.

A skeleton swung a warhammer at Mirror, and the weapon passed harmlessly through his insubstantial form. Mirror struck back with his sword. His blade passed through the undead warrior's fleshless body without cleaving any bones, but the foxfire sheen in the creature's eye sockets guttered out, and its legs collapsed beneath it.

Malark positioned himself in front of a skeleton, inviting an attack. The creature swung its axe at his neck. He slipped out of the way, shifted in, and rapped the skeleton's skull with one of his batons. The yellowed cranium, naked except for a few lank strands of hair, shattered.

Beating their wings, the griffons pounced, each bearing a skeleton down beneath a snapping beak and slashing talons.

Clattering sounds reverberated across the cemetery. The loose bones leaped up from the ground and tangled themselves together into something not unlike a wicker sculpture. In a heartbeat, they became a colossal serpent, its tail looping around the perimeter of the graveyard as if to cage its prey.

It reared its head high, then struck down at Bareris.

He hurled himself to the side. His foot slid in a patch of snow and he fell. The serpent's fangs—blunt knobs of bone that would not pierce but would surely crush—clashed shut on empty air.

It swiveled its misshapen head and opened its jaws to bite again. Bareris scrambled to regain his feet, too slowly.

With an earsplitting screech, Vengeance plunged out of the air to land on the serpent's head. Pinions flapping, he hooked his talons into the spaces between the bones and caught a mass of them in his beak. His neck muscles bunched beneath his feathers as he strained to bite through.

The serpent tossed its head, shaking the griffon loose from his perch, and caught him in its jaws. The pressure burst Vengeance's body open as if he were a ripe piece of fruit. With a ghastly sucking sound, the bones slid out of his body, rattled down the serpent's gullet, and snapped into spaces along its body, adding to its mass.

Bareris's lips drew back in a snarl, for Vengeance had been a good mount, steady and loyal. The bard rose, readied his mace, and started singing.

•• •• •• •• •• •• •• •• •• •• •• •• •• ••

The slithering, clattering wall that was the serpent's body slid past Malark, and he considered how best to attack it. He despised the undead for the abominations they were and fought them at every opportunity, always hopeful that this time, his foe might kill him. Death was a gift—one he had long ago spurned by armoring himself against the ravages of age and becoming an abomination in his own right. Since that time, he sought to atone for his folly by honoring the greatest of all powers. One day, perhaps, the multiverse would deem his service sufficient. Then, despite the formidable combat arts he had learned from the Monks of the Long Death, a blade or arrow would slip past his defense, and he could pass into the darkness.

Striking with one hand, then the other, swinging his batons like a demented drummer, he battered the creature's flank. Bones cracked and snapped with every stroke, but he couldn't see if the creature was weakened. Sorcery might be the only thing that could destroy the snake. If so, the best tactic might be to hold the serpent's attention, buying Aoth and Bareris the chance to cast their spells without interference.

He scanned the wall of bone, found his bearings, and sprinted toward the creature's head, bounding over open graves on his way. Armed with a scythe, a surviving skeleton rushed in on his flank. Malark broke stride, leaped high into the air, and kicked to the side, driving his heel into the creature's neck. The attack shattered the skeleton's spine and its head tumbled free. Then the spindly figure fell to pieces, and its bones flew through the air to integrate into the snake. Malark ran on.

As he neared its head, he heard Bareris singing. The tune was mournful, dirgelike, but it sent a thrill of fresh vitality through Malark's limbs.

Bareris had managed to lay an enchantment on himself, and he flickered in and out of view. Malark knew his friend was solid one moment, but not the next. With luck, he'd be safely intangible if the snake's fangs slammed shut on him. But that was not a certainty, so he dodged when his colossal adversary struck at him, and pounded back with his mace.

Mirror was intermittently visible as well. Taking advantage of his lack of a solid foe, he was trying to attack the interior of the serpent's body, and was alternately inside and out as the creature's mass writhed back and forth.

Aoth chanted the words of an incantation, spun his glowing spear through mystic passes, and the snake's head swiveled toward him. Plainly it was intelligent, but then, Malark had already guessed that, because it had laid a trap for them. It had lured its foes into striking distance before manifesting, and had choosen ground where the yawning graves might keep them from maneuvering to their best advantage.

Aoth leaped backward, evading the attack and carefully preserving the precise cadence his chant required. A sphere of bright white light shot from the luminous head of his spear. It struck the snake on the snout and exploded into twisting, crackling arcs of lightning.

The attack charred the serpent's head, but caused no noticeable injuries. It reared for another strike.

Completing his dash, Malark interposed himself between the creature and Aoth. "Get up in the air," he called out. "Bareris, stay away from it. Mirror and I will keep it occupied."

Aoth shouted Brightwing's name, and the griffon, who'd already taken to the air and had been wheeling overhead, maneuvering to make an attack, furled her pinions and dived toward her master. Bareris scrambled backward, his head twisting as he sought to keep his eyes on his foe without falling into one of the graves.

Malark lost track of his allies after that, because the snake spread its jaws wide and lunged at him. He had to hold his attention on his adversary. It was his only hope of survival.

He forced himself to delay his dodge, lest the serpent adjust its aim. He waited until the last instant, then spun to the right. The creature's jaws smashed shut beside him.

Malark bellowed a war cry, slammed the serpent as hard as he could with a baton, and bashed a substantial breach in the weave of bones beneath the jagged-edged eye socket. Apparently, Aoth's lightning had weakened the tangled lattice, allowing the baton to inflict significant harm.

The serpent finally reacted almost like a living creature, jerking its head away as though the strike had caused actual pain.

"That's right!" Malark called. "I'm the one who can hurt you the worst! Fight *me!*"

The snake obliged him with a few more attacks, which gave Bareris time to sing a spell unhindered. A shuddering ran down the length of the snake, breaking certain bones and shaking others loose from the central mass.

The serpent's body twisted around as it oriented on Bareris. Malark had to move quickly to keep the bony coils from knocking him down and grinding him beneath them. The movement left him yards away from the creature's head, with little hope of diverting it from the bard.

Then Mirror flew up from the ground to hover right in front of the serpent's face. His ghostly sword sliced back and forth.

The snake tried to catch him in its teeth, while Bareris sent shudders and convulsions tearing through it, and Malark battered it with his cudgels. At first, Mirror either dodged the creature's bite or oozed free unharmed. But then the colossal jaws clamped down again, and the malignancy of the snake's own supernatural nature finally overcame the protection afforded by the ghost's phantasmal condition. Mirror fell from the gnashing teeth tattered, fading, dwindling, and incapable of continuing the fight. Bareris cried out in dismay.

Overhead, Aoth chanted words of power. For the first time,

Malark felt truly confident that he and his companions would prevail. War magic won battles more often than not, provided the war mage positioned himself out of reach of the foe and conjured unimpeded.

With a great clatter, the serpent arched itself and hurtled up into the air. Malark had forgotten their earlier guess that their quarry might be capable of flight.

Aoth and Brightwing had evidently lost sight of the possibility as well, for they were flying low, and the griffon took a heartbeat too long to start swooping out of the way. It looked to Malark as if the serpent would snag her in its jaws.

Bareris gave a thunderous shout. The noise jolted the snake, and its strike missed.

Aoth bellowed the final words of his incantation. An orb of mystical force, glowing a dull blue, flew from his outstretched hand. It struck the serpent like a stone from a trebuchet, and with a prodigious crack, broke it entirely in two. The sections collapsed, and Malark raised a hand to shield his head from the rain of bone.

He watched to see if the serpent would reassemble, but couldn't detect even a slight twitch. The thing looked utterly destroyed.

Aoth and Brightwing glided back to earth. The rents in Mirror's substance began to mend, and his vague form took on definition. He was going to be all right.

"What's the proper term for that thing?" Malark asked. "A living bone yard?"

"I don't know," said Aoth. "I've never heard of such a beast before. The necromancers' creations grow stranger every year."

"Well, the important thing is that we won."

Aoth's mouth twisted. "Did we? The peasants are dead. Will anyone else come and work this isolated, poorly protected patch of land and feed us in the coming year?"

"They'll dare it if someone in authority orders them to. What ails you, friend? I thought Bareris was the gloomy one." Malark gave the bard a wink, which he didn't bother to acknowledge.

"I just. . . ." Aoth shook his head. "Mirror isn't the only one. We're all ghosts. Ghosts of the men and lives that ought to have been."

"How do you mean that?"

"I don't know," said Aoth, "but sometimes I feel it."

chapter one

26–29 Ches, the Year of Blue Fire

Hezass Nymar, tharchion of Lapendrar and Eternal Flame of the temple of Kossuth in Escalant, drew breath to conjure, then hesitated. What, he thought, if the lich or his spies are watching me at this very moment? Or what if the lords of the south disbelieved his statements, or chose to kill him on sight, without even granting him a hearing?

He scowled and gave his head a shake, trying to dislodge his misgivings. Yes, it was dangerous to act, but it might well prove even more perilous not to. He wouldn't let fear delay him now.

He recited the incantation, the ruby ring on his left hand glowed like a hot coal, and the dancing flames in the massive marble fireplace roared up like a bonfire, completely filling their rectangular enclosure. Hezass walked into the blaze.

Without bothering to look back, he knew that the four archer golems would follow. Carved of brown Thayan oak with longbows permanently affixed in their left hands, the automatons were Hezass's favorite bodyguards, in part because they were incapable of tattling about his business no matter what persuasions were applied.

Beyond the gate he'd opened lay an entire world of flame. The air was full of cinders, the sky, nothing but swirling crimson smoke. Fires of every color hissed and crackled everywhere, some as tiny as blades of grass, some the size of shrubs or trees, and some as huge as castles or even mountains, without the need for fuel to feed them. The yellow ground was an endless glowing furnace with streams of magma running through it. Birds or something like them flew overhead, a herd of four-legged beasts stood on a rise in the distance, and even they were made of fire.

The extreme heat would have seared flesh and ignited oak instantly, except that Hezass's power protected him and the golems. Indeed, he found this realm exhilarating, and had to take care lest that excitement swell into a delirious joy that could make him forget his purpose.

He walked until the prompting of his spell pointed him toward a patch of blue-white fire the size of a cottage. He led the golems into it and out the other side.

As he'd expected, the other side was one of the scores of ceremonial fires burning behind the altars of the Flaming Brazier, the grandest temple of Kossuth in all Faerûn. Eyes glowing, shrouded in nimbuses of incendiary power, images of the god glared from the walls and the high vaulted ceiling.

Despite the lateness of the night, it didn't take long for a Disciple of the Salamander, a warrior monk performing sentry duty, to discover Hezass while making his rounds. In other circumstances, the exchange that followed might have been comical, for the poor fellow plainly didn't know whether to react with hostility or deference. Hezass was a supposed enemy of the Council of Zulkirs and all who gave it their allegiance, but he was also a hierophant of the church, decked out in all the pomp of his formal regalia.

Fortunately, it was easy for the disciple to resolve his dilemma. He only had to do as Hezass requested and fetch Iphegor Nath.

The High Flamelord arrived with a handful of monks in tow. He was a tall man with craggy, commanding features. His muscular physique, the uncanny glow of his orange eyes, and the tiny flames that crawled on his shaved scalp and shoulders all combined to make him resemble the traditional depiction of the deity he served. His simple attire stood in marked contrast to Hezass's gemmed and layered vestments, for, most likely roused from his bed, he'd only taken the time to pull on breeches, sandals, and a shirt.

Hezass dropped to his knees and lowered his eyes. Iphegor let him remain that way for a long time.

Finally, the High Flamelord broke the silence. "You realize, I'm going to drown you."

Inwardly, Hezass winced. "Drowning is the traditional punishment for an apostate, Your Omniscience, and thus inappropriate for me. I walked through the god's domain to come here. How could I do that if I'd renounced my priesthood?"

"You renounced the church," Iphegor growled. "You renounced me."

"With all respect, Your Omniscience, that is incorrect. I freely acknowledge your supreme authority . . . in matters of theology. The matter of who should govern Thay is a political question."

"And your answer is—the creature whose treachery slew scores of the Firelord's priests."

"I confess, I made an error. I've come here to rectify it."

"By sneaking an armed force into the temple."

"What, these?" Hezass waved his hand at the golems standing like statues behind him. "They have their uses, but it's laughable to think that four of them could prevail against all the magic and armed might protecting the Flaming Brazier. I simply wanted to present myself with the dignity an escort affords. Now, do you truly intend to keep me on my knees for the entire parley, and to conduct it in the hearing of these good monks? I'm sure they're pious and loyal, but even so, it would be indiscreet."

"Get up," Iphegor said. "We can talk in the chapel over there. Leave your puppet bowmen outside, and I'll do the same with the monks."

A statue of Kossuth bestowing the gift of fire on humanity dominated the shrine. The golden light of votive fires gleamed on the crimson marble. In the mosaic on the wall, the god presided over a court of red dragons, efreet, and other creatures whose natures partook of elemental flame.

"So," Iphegor said, seating himself on a bench, "how do you propose to atone for your sins?"

Since the High Flamelord hadn't given him leave to sit, Hezass remained standing as he explained his proposal.

When he finished, Iphegor stared at him for several heartbeats, until Hezass, who'd just negotiated the Plane of Fire without discomfort, felt sweat starting to ooze under his arms. Finally, the big man said, "You string words together as glibly as ever. But after all the lies you've told over the past ten years, how can you possibly expect anyone to believe you?"

"I've already explained that my link with our god remains intact. How could I not desire reconciliation with the head of my faith?"

Iphegor snorted. "How many times have I offered my forgiveness, only to have you wipe your arse on it by slinking back to Szass Tam? I've lost count."

"I confess. I've maneuvered for power and wealth. I've put my own welfare ahead of every other concern, doing whatever seemed necessary to survive amid a war of wizards. Which makes me no worse than many other nobles and officials in Thay. But I know that's not the man I want to be. I want to be steadfast and honorable and worthy of the god we serve."

"That would be inspiring if I thought you meant it."

Hezass sighed. "If you can't believe I've had a change of heart, perhaps you'll credit this. The Council currently occupies a goodly portion of eastern Lapendrar. I'd like those lands back, and in reasonable condition."

"And you doubt Szass Tam's ability to recover them?"

"He may succeed, or he may not. Even if he does, I don't approve of the way he's conducting the war. I understand the strategic points of causing flood and drought, slaughtering peasants, and poisoning the soil, rain, and streams. Since his legions are largely undead, the resulting scarcity of food hurts his enemies more than it injures him. But what will be left of the realm after he wins? I don't want to live out my days as the pauper governor of a ruined province. I want the old Thay back!"

Iphegor grimaced. "As do I. So I'll tell you what I'll do. I still don't trust you, but I will ask the Council to listen to your blandishments. They can make up their own minds about you."

•• •• •• •• •• •• •• •• •• •• •• •• •• ••

Aoth steeled himself for an ordeal. When convening for a council of war, the zulkirs sometimes commanded the attendance of their tharchions, whisking them to the site of the meeting by magical means. The military governors, in turn, made it a habit to bring a trusted lieutenant or two, which meant Nymia Focar occasionally dragged Aoth along.

He supposed he should be used to it, but after all these years, he never felt fully at ease in the presence of the notoriously cruel and capricious wizard lords. It didn't help that, of everyone in the hall, with its long red wooden table and jeweled crimson banners hanging from the rafters, he was the only person who didn't look like a proper Mulan.

Still, the zulkirs probably deserved commendation for possessing the prudence to seek advice, especially considering that the council was less than it once had been. Not that there was any real shortage of intelligence. The bloated Samas Kul, shrewish Lallara, clerkish Lauzoril, glowering Nevron with the brimstone stink emanating from his person, and the comely Dmitra Flass were as shrewd as anyone could wish. But Kumed Hahpret, who'd succeeded the murdered Aznar Thrul as zulkir of Evocation, and Zola Sethrakt, representing what little remained of the necromancers after Szass Tam suborned most of the order to fight on his behalf, had proved to be less impressive intellects than their predecessors. And the chair once occupied by the traitorous Yaphyll sat empty. The Order of Divination hadn't yet elected a leader to replace her.

Aoth stiffened when Iphegor Nath ushered Hezass Nymar into the chamber. The fire priest's faithlessness had, on more than one occasion, cost the Griffon Legion good men and mounts. But Aoth couldn't vent his anger in such an assembly, at least not yet. He had to sit quietly while Hezass spoke his piece.

When the whoreson finished, the zulkirs sent him out of the room under guard. "Well," said Dmitra, who often acted as presiding officer, to the extent that the other haughty zulkirs would tolerate, "what do you think?"

"Question him under torture until he dies of it," Lallara said. Powerful as her magic was, the zulkir of Abjuration could easily have erased the outward signs of advancing age, but had instead allowed time to cut lines and crow's feet and loosen the flesh beneath her chin. It made her bitter manner all the more intimidating.

Dmitra smiled. "That's my first impulse, also, but I wouldn't want to waste a genuine opportunity. Your Omniscience, what's your opinion? What game is Nymar playing this time?"

Iphegor frowned. "Your Omnipotence, I wish I knew. Much as it irks me to admit it, he hasn't lost his connection to the Lord of Flames. He's still a priest, and it's possible he wishes to mend his quarrel with me, just as he asserts. In addition, I find his claim that he only ever served Szass Tam to achieve a life of opulent wealth, and that he fears that such an existence is slipping forever beyond his reach, to be plausible. Still, there's no disputing the man's a treacherous worm. Who knows where his allegiance really lies, or where it will reside tomorrow?"

"Not I," said Samas Kul. If Hezass was in fact motivated by avarice, he ought to sympathize, for, taking full advantage of his position as Master of the Guild of Foreign Trade, he'd made himself the richest man in Thay even before his ascension to leadership of the transmuters. His red robes reflected the fact, for they glittered with more gems and precious metal than any of the other costly attire on display in the chamber. Unfortunately, even the finest raiment couldn't make his obese, sweaty, ruddy-faced form attractive.

Lauzoril pursed his lips and pressed the fingertips of his hands together to make a pyramid. "The important question," the zulkir of Enchantment said in his dry tenor, "isn't whether Hezass is a scoundrel, but whether his information is accurate. If so, then as Dmitra Flass observed, we may have a chance to win a meaningful victory at last."

"I concur," Nevron said, scowling so fiercely that anyone who hadn't heard his words might have assumed he disagreed. A number of his tattoos took the forms of hideous faces, the countenances of the demons and devils that, as a master conjurer, it was his particular art to command. "Szass Tam descends from the heights to lay siege to the Keep of Sorrows. We swing an army in behind him. They'll be the hammer, and the castle and the edge of the cliffs, the anvil. We'll pound the necromancers, and they won't be able to retreat."

"You can't count on Nymar to bring the troops he pledges," Samas said. "He'll keep them in their garrisons to protect the lands he still holds, and afterward, claim sickness in the ranks prevented them from marching. Or else, that his scouts reported Aglarondan troops maneuvering on the western border, and he had to leave his men in place to protect against a possible invasion. He's done it before."

"I remember," Dmitra said. "He doesn't much care to ride heroically into battle, does he? But if we can prevail on him to bring his army as far as the western bank of the River Lapendrar, to make certain Szass Tam can't maneuver in that direction, that in itself would be a help."

"Right," Nevron said. "We can do the real work ourselves, if we commit enough of our own strength."

Samas responded, as well as Lallara, in much the same vein. Before long, it became clear to Aoth that, without bothering to say so overtly, the zulkirs had decided on a strategy. Now they were discussing how best to implement it.

Aoth gnawed his lower lip. In theory, he and the zulkirs' other subordinates were present to provide their opinions, and he would have preferred to hold his tongue until someone specifically asked for his perspective. But it didn't seem that any of the mage lords meant to do so.

Wishing he were somewhere else, he cleared his throat. "Masters?"

The zulkirs all turned to regard him, some more coldly than others, but none with extraordinary warmth. "Yes, Captain?" Dmitra said.

"I think," said Aoth, "we should evaluate Hezass Nymar's claims carefully, and not just because he's a known traitor and liar. I realize that many of you have magic to determine whether a man is speaking the truth as he understands it, and I imagine you've applied those tests in this instance. But on the face of it, the scheme he's attributing to Szass Tam makes little sense."

"Why?" Nevron asked. "The Keep of Sorrows is an important fortress. If he takes it, it will be far easier for him to strike into Tyraturos, and if he's successful there, it opens the High Road for incursions into Priador."

"Yes, Your Omnipotence," said Aoth, "*if* he's successful. But the keep is generally considered impregnable, or nearly so. Until now, Szass Tam has only undertaken major battles and sieges under conditions advantageous to himself. Most of the time, he picks away at us, raiding, burning crops and granaries, killing a few folk here and there to raise as zombies and swell the ranks of his legions. He's been slowly tipping the balance in his favor, as if—as Hezass Nymar suggested—he doesn't care how long it takes to win, or what condition the realm is in when he does. Why, then, would he suddenly change tactics and commit his troops to such a reckless venture?"

"Because he's grown impatient," Lallara said, "and made a mistake. The wretch isn't infallible, whatever you and fools like you may imagine."

Aoth glanced at Nymia Focar in the forlorn hope that his superior would support him. She was an able warrior and capable of seeing the sense in what he was saying. But, as he expected, she gave him a tiny shake of her head, warning him to desist. The motion made the silver stud in her left nostril flash with a gleam of lamplight and the rings in her ears clink faintly.

He wished Malark were present. Dmitra often heeded his opinion, but hadn't seen fit to bring him. Perhaps he was busy with some other task.

Milsantos Daramos might also have spoken on Aoth's behalf, for the former tharchion of Thazalhar had been both the canniest and the bravest Thayan general in recent memory. Unfortunately, he'd succumbed to old age three years back.

In the absence of such men and the counsel they might have offered, Aoth stumbled on alone. "I understand that the lich is capable of miscalculating. Everybody is. But I still worry that there's something about this situation we don't understand."

Samas grunted. It made him seem even more swinish, if that was possible. "You realize, Captain, that if the lich marches on the Keep of Sorrows, we have no choice but to defend it. Unless you advocate simply opening the gates and surrendering."

Aoth clamped down hard to keep resentment from showing in his face or tone. "Of course not, Master. But the keep should be able to resist a siege for a considerable time. We needn't be in a hurry to commit the bulk of our forces to defend it, and we needn't look to Nymar for anything. We can proceed cautiously."

"And perhaps lose the castle as a result," Lallara rapped. "Perhaps even forfeit the opportunity to win the war."

"Which is something," Dmitra said, "we cannot afford. You said it yourself, Captain, more or less. Time is on Szass Tam's side. We must defeat him while we're still strong."

Aoth inclined his head. "Yes, Your Omnipotence. I understand."

.. ..

Tammith Iltazyarra winged her way through the night sky as a flock of bats, the lights of Escalant shining below. The sea reflected Selûne's crescent smile, and the haze of glittering tears that followed her, like an obsidian mirror. Tammith's inhuman senses registered the sea in somewhat the same way that a living person might discern the presence of a wall or cliff face looming close. She didn't merely see it, but felt it as a confining pressure. It exerted a force upon her, because no vampire could cross open water.

Once upon a time, her transformation into a swarm of leathery-winged beasts would have significantly altered her consciousness. The human—or quasi-human—Tammith was prey to shame and regret, and the bats were not. But it had been a long while since such feelings troubled her in any of her various guises. She supposed that meant she truly was dead now, and she was glad of it. Existence was easier this way.

Their shrill cries echoing from roofs and walls to guide them, the bats flew into an alley, checked a final time to make sure no one was watching, then swirled together. In a moment, they merged to become a petite, dark-haired woman in a plain cloak and gown. In other circumstances, she would have worn a sword and mail, but she didn't feel vulnerable without them. Her most formidable weapons were always with her. Xingax, curse him, had seen to that.

She walked onward, through streets that were busy even after dark, because Escalant was a thriving port. Though under Thayan governance, it was a colony, geographically removed from the realm proper, and as a result, the zulkirs' war had yet to blight it. In fact, the contented faces, well fed and unafraid, the music and laughter sounding from the taverns, and the scarcity of soldiers reminded her of Bezantur as it had been when she was alive. Something stirred inside her, some vague approximation of melancholy or nostalgia.

Then the temple of Kossuth came into view, and she quashed the feeling, whatever it was, to focus on the task at hand.

Like all the Firelord's houses of worship, this one was a ziggurat, built of blocks of cooled lava. Fires burned on either side of the door, on the terraces leading upward, and at the apex of the pyramid.

Tammith again felt a pressure, because the flames were the

sacred symbols of Kossuth, and although no priest was trying to use their power to repel her, there were plenty of them, and more holy force, concentrated inside the temple.

Still, since the ziggurat was a public place, it should be possible for her to enter. It would simply take spiritual strength and resolve.

As she advanced, Tammith fought the urge to lean forward as if she were struggling against a strong wind. Her skin grew hotter and hotter.

She stumbled as she climbed the steps to the entrance. Fortunately, the two warrior monks standing guard at the top didn't take any notice. Perhaps they were used to the sick and the lame hobbling up to pray to the god for healing.

Grimacing with effort, she forced herself across the threshold, and then the pressure and heat abated. Wherever she looked, more fires burned, altars stood piled with offerings, and images of Kossuth glowered at her, so the aversive sensations didn't vanish entirely. But it seemed that by coming this far and asserting her supremacy, she'd heightened her resistance. She should be able to bear the unpleasantness for a time.

She reached out with her mind, and the results were disappointing. The priests and monks evidently did a good job of waging war against rats, or perhaps the rodents simply found the pyramid with its hard stone walls and scores of open fires uncongenial. But every large structure provided a home for at least a few such vermin, and she summoned them to rendezvous with her as she prowled onward, doing her best to look like a worshiper heading for her favorite shrine or chapel.

The ruse lost its utility when she reached the staircase leading up. The higher reaches of the temple were closed to everyone but clerics and monks. Before continuing onward, another vampire might have become a bat or rodent to make himself less conspicuous. But Tammith could only transform into a cloud of bats or a scurrying carpet of rats. Those guises were more likely to attract attention than a single human figure, and the same was true of a hulking wolf, or billows of mist flowing along in the absence of a breeze. Best, then, simply to slink on two feet.

The rats she'd collected on the first story scurried behind her. The eyes of a few more gleamed from the shadows on the level above. Somewhere in the ziggurat, a choir commenced a hymn, the sound of the nocturnal ceremony echoing through the stone chambers.

Fortunately, most of the temple's occupants were asleep. That fact and her talent for stealth allowed Tammith to reach the highest level and the antechamber of Hezass Nymar's personal apartments undetected. Shelves stuffed with ledgers and documents lined the walls. During the day, clerks would be hunched over writing desks, quills scratching. Petitioners and underlings would lounge on the benches, awaiting the high priest's pleasure. But at this time of night, no one was around.

But no. She was mistaken. Perhaps no person was here, but something was. She couldn't see it, but she suddenly sensed its scrutiny, its watchful expectation.

Perhaps it was a guardian creature, or some sort of unliving but sentient ward. Since it hadn't attacked or raised an alarm immediately, it might be giving her a chance to prove she belonged there. By speaking a password, or something similar.

"Praise be to Kossuth," she said. The odds were slim that she'd guessed correctly, but she couldn't see that she had anything to lose by trying.

Heat exploded through the chamber. Something hissed and a wavering yellow brightness splashed the walls. Tammith pivoted and saw the creature that had emerged from nothingness to destroy her.

It was a spider as big as a pony, with a body made of glowing magma, with flame dripping from its gnashing mandibles. Its eight round eyes gave her a lidless, inscrutable stare.

This was bad. She'd spent the past decade battling every devil and elemental Nevron that the Order of Conjuration could raise, and had learned early on why it was difficult to fight entities like the spider. If she closed to striking distance, the heat emanating from its body would burn her to ashes.

Better to subdue the spider without fighting if she could. She stared into its row of eyes and willed it to cower before her.

Instead, it sprang. She leaped out of the way, snatched up one of the benches, and threw it. Tavern-style combat would make too much noise, but that couldn't be helped.

The bench smashed into the spider and clattered to the floor in burning pieces. One of the arachnid's legs dragged, twisted and useless. The injury didn't impair the creature's quick, scuttling agility, but it was a start.

Tammith scurried to grab another bench, keeping an eye on the spider lest it jump at her again. Instead, it reared onto its hind legs, exposing the underside of its body. Burning matter sprayed from an orifice in its abdomen.

The discharge spewed in a wide arc and expanded in flight to become a kind of net. Caught by surprise, Tammith tried to dodge, but was too slow. The heavy mesh fell over her and dragged her to her knees. Its blazing touch brought instant agony.

With burning, blackening hands, she struggled to rip the adhesive web away from her body. Another weight, far heavier than the mesh, slammed down on her and crushed her to the floor. Liquid fire dripping from its fangs, the spider lowered its head to bite.

She wasted a precious instant in desperate, agonized squirming, then realized what she needed to do. Focusing past the distractions of pain and fear, she asserted her mastery of her own mutable form.

Tammith dissolved into vapor. Even the lack of a solid body failed to quell the ache of her wounds, but the spider could no longer bite her, and its bulk and web couldn't hold her any longer. She billowed up around it and streamed to the other side of the room.

Given the choice, she might well have kept flowing right out the door. But although she was a captain in the legions of the north, she was also a slave, magically constrained to obey Xingax and Szass Tam. The latter had ordered her to accomplish her mission at any cost.

That would require slaying the spider, and she couldn't do it as a cloud of fog. She had to become tangible once again.

As she did so, she glanced at her charred hands and her arms where the sleeves had burned away. New skin was already growing, but not quickly enough. If the arachnid seized her again, it would likely hurt her so severely as to render her helpless.

She spun and scaled one of the bookcases, then released the shelves to cling to the ceiling. Intent on climbing up after her, her adversary raced across the floor.

She grabbed the bookcase and strained to heave it away from the wall. She could use only one hand and had no leverage, and for a moment, she feared that even her vampiric strength would prove insufficient. Then she felt the case's center of gravity shift, and it toppled.

It crashed down on top of the spider. She dropped after it, then jumped up and down to smash the arachnid's body. Layers of paper and wood insulated her from flames and the worst of the heat. At first, the wreckage rocked back and forth as the spider tried to drag itself out, but after several impacts, its struggles subsided.

Tammith grinned, and then something hit her like a giant's hammer. Her guts churned and her skin burned anew, glowing, on the brink of catching fire. She reeled back and Hezass

Nymar stepped from his apartments into the antechamber. She could barely make him out, for the man assailing her with the power of his priesthood stood shrouded from head to toe in Kossuth's fire.

Tammith ordinarily had a strong resistance to the divine abilities that most priests wielded against the undead. But Nymar was a high priest standing in his place of power, and she was already badly hurt. His righteous loathing ground at her flesh and mind.

She silently called to the rats, crouching in the shadows. She hadn't sought to use them against the spider. They would have burned to death in a heartbeat, most likely without the beast even noticing their presence. But maybe they could help her now.

The rodents charged Nymar and clambered up his bare feet and ankles, biting and clawing. He yelped, danced, and flailed, trying to dislodge them. It broke his concentration, and his nimbus of flame, along with Tammith's sickness and paralysis, vanished altogether.

Tammith rushed Nymar, grabbed him, and slammed him down on his back. The rats scurried away. She bashed the priest's head back and forth, pinned him, and showed him her fangs. She needed willpower to refrain from tearing her captive's throat out and guzzling him dry. She was still in pain, and such a meal would speed her healing.

"Please," he gasped, "this is a mistake. I'm on Szass Tam's side."

"No," she said. "You slipped away to betray him to the council. As he knew you would. As he intended."

"I . . . I don't understand."

"Since you were sincere, you were able to win a measure of their trust despite your history of treachery. But now that your task is accomplished, it's time to cement your allegiance where it belongs."

"I swear by the holy fire, from now on, I truly will be loyal."

"I know you will."

"You made too much noise! The monks are surely coming even now!"

"I know that, too. I can hear them. But by the time they arrive, I'll be gone, and you'll explain how an assassin tried to murder you, but you burned the dastard to ash. They'll have no reason to doubt you, as long as you hide the marks on your neck."

chapter two

16–29 Tarsakh, the Year of Blue Fire

The griffon rider came running to tell Bareris that some of the legionnaires were violating the patrol's standing orders. The soldier found his immediate superior in consultation with Aoth.

When the two comrades investigated, they discovered a griffon crouching outside the hut in question. No doubt its master had stationed it there to keep anyone from interfering with the mischief inside. Aoth brandished his spear at the beast and it screeched, lowered its white-feathered aquiline head, and slunk to the side.

Bareris tried the door. It was latched, so he booted it open.

The round dwelling was all one room, with a stove in the center, a loom to one side, and a bed on the far end. Their faces pulped and bloody, a man and a woman sprawled on the rush-strewn earthen floor. Two of the soldiers responsible were holding a sobbing, thrashing girl—Bareris put her age at twelve or thirteen—spread-eagled atop a table. The third was tearing off her clothes.

The door banged against the wall and all three jerked around. Aoth could have simply snapped orders at the men, but he was too angry to settle for mere words. He lunged at one and struck with the butt of his spear. The ash haft cracked against bone and the man fell, tatters of skirt in his hand. The other two released the child and scrambled out of reach.

Aoth took a deep breath. "You know the rules. No looting except for what an officer gives you permission to confiscate, no beatings, and no rape."

"But that's provided the rustics are friendly," said the soldier on the left. "Provided they cooperate. These didn't."

"What do you mean?" asked Aoth.

The warrior picked up a clay bowl from the table. Somehow, it remained unspilled and unbroken. The legionnaire overturned it, and a watery brown liquid spattered out.

"The villagers are supposed to give their best hospitality to the zulkirs' troops," he said. "Yet this is what they serve us. This slop! Isn't it plain they're holding the good food back?"

Aoth sighed. "No, idiot, it isn't. Last year's harvest was bad, the winter was long and harsh, and they've barely had time to begin the spring planting. They'll go hungry tomorrow for want of the gruel they offered you tonight."

The griffon rider blinked. "Well . . . I couldn't know, could I? And anyway, I'm almost certain I heard one of them insult the First Princess."

"Did you now?"

"Besides," the soldier continued, "they're just peasants. Just Rashe—" It dawned on him that he might not be taking a wise tactic in light of his commander's suspect ancestry, and the words caught in his throat.

"The two of you," said Aoth, "pick up your fellow imbecile

and get out of here. I'll deal with you shortly." They did as instructed, and then Aoth turned to Bareris. "I trust you know songs to calm this girl, and to ease her parents' hurts."

"Yes," Bareris said. He applied the remedies as best he could, even though charms of solace and healing no longer came to him as naturally as they once had.

With the parents back on their feet and the girl huddling in her mother's arms, Aoth offered his apologies and a handful of silver. The father seemed to think the coins were some sort of trap, for he proved reluctant to accept them. Aoth left the money on the table on his way out.

"What's the punishment?" Bareris asked. As the miscreants' immediate superior, he was the one responsible for administering discipline.

"Hang the bastards," Aoth replied.

"You don't mean that."

"They deserve it. But you're right. Nymia would string *me* up if I executed two of her griffon riders just for mistreating a family of farmers, especially on the eve of a major battle. So five lashes each, but not yet. Let them sweat while you and I have a talk."

"As you wish." They'd already been talking when the soldier came to fetch them, but Bareris inferred that Aoth had something more private in mind. Sure enough, the war mage led him all the way through the cluster of huts and cottages. The men-at-arms watched as their officers tramped by.

Beyond the farmhouses were fields and pastures, which gave way to rolling grasslands that made up the greater part of Tyraturos. Bareris scrutinized the landscape stretched out beneath the evening sky, still banded with gold where the sun had made its farewell, and charcoal gray high above.

Earlier that day, they'd ascertained that the bulk of Szass Tam's army was marching well to the northwest, and it was unlikely that even the lich's scouts and outriders had strayed this far from the main column. Still, it paid to be cautious.

Aoth led his friend to a pen made of split rails. It held no animals, only a scattering of leprous-looking toadstools. The war mage heaved himself up to sit on the fence, and Bareris climbed up beside him.

"Well," said Aoth. "Ten years since I discovered you and Mirror hiking out of the Sunrise Mountains."

Responding to his name, Mirror wavered into view. Maybe he'd been with them all along. For a moment, the phantom resembled the bard, then Aoth, and then settled into a blurred gray shadow that scarcely possessed a face at all. His presence chilled the air.

Aoth acknowledged the ghost with a nod. "Ten years since we started fighting Szass Tam."

"Yes," Bareris said.

"Have you ever thought it might be time to stop?"

Bareris cocked his head. A strand of hair spilled across his eye and he pushed it up, noticing in passing just how matted and greasy it was. "I don't know what you mean."

"A griffon rider could be out of Thay before anyone even realized he'd decided to leave, and then, well, Faerûn's a big place, with plenty of opportunities for a fellow who knows how to cast spells or swing a sword."

"This is just blather. You'd never abandon your men."

"We'll invite them to come along. Think how much a foreign prince will pay to employ an entire company of griffon riders."

"You must be tired if that unpleasantness back in the hut upset you as much as this."

"It wasn't that. At most, that was the last little weight that finally tipped the scale. Do you ever ask yourself why we're fighting?"

"To destroy Szass Tam, or at least to keep him from making himself overlord."

"And why is that important, when he has as much right to rule Thay as anyone? When the lords who oppose him are just as untrustworthy and indifferent to anything but their own interests?"

"Because they aren't. Not quite, anyway. Don't you remember? We made up our minds on the subject back in that grove, when the necromancer came to speak with us."

"Yes, but over the course of a decade, a man can change his opinion. Consider this. Samas Kul cast his lot with the lich for a season or two. Yaphyll's allied with him now. Half the tharchions jump back and forth like frogs. By the Abyss, I doubt that even Nymia would stay loyal if she thought she'd fare better on the other side, and then where would you and I be with our preferences and principles?"

"It's more sensible," Bareris said, "to consider where you actually are. Our mistress and the zulkirs have treated you well. They've given you command of the Griffon Legion and purses full of gold."

"Things I never wanted. I was happy as I was. If they want to reward me, I wish it could be with their respect. Respect for my judgment and experience." Aoth shifted slightly atop the fence.

"Now I see. They offended you by rejecting your advice. But I'll be honest with you. It isn't plain to me that you were right and they were wrong."

"It isn't plain to me, either, but I feel it, just as I've sensed such things once or twice before. We believe we've outthought the enemy, but we haven't. Something nasty is going to happen at the Keep of Sorrows, and I'd rather be far away when it does."

"You say that, but I know you're not a coward," Bareris said.

"You're right. I have my share of courage, or at least I hope I do. What I lack is a cause worth risking my life over. For a long while, I thought I was fighting to save the green, bountiful Thay of my boyhood, but look around you. That realm's already dead, trampled by armies and poisoned by battle sorcery. I'm not a necromancer, and I don't want to waste the rest of my days trying to animate the rotting husk that remains."

"And neither should you," Aoth continued. "I understand why you fight—to avenge Tammith. But from all you've told me, she'd weep to see what your compulsion has made of you—a bard who never sings except to kill. I think she'd want you to lay down your grief and hatred and start life anew."

He's made up his mind, Bareris realized. He's going to saddle Brightwing and disappear into the sky, even if I refuse to go with him.

And that would be a disaster. Aoth had matured into one of the most formidable champions in the south. The cause could ill afford to lose him, and it certainly couldn't manage without all the griffon riders, who might well follow where their captain led.

Bareris would have to stop him.

"You know me too well," he said, infusing his speech with enchantment. "It is hate that drives me, and I won't pretend otherwise. But your judgment is too pessimistic where our homeland is concerned. What sorcery has broken, it can mend. Given a chance, the old Thay will rise again, blue skies, thriving plantations, mile-long merchant caravans, and all."

Aoth's eyelids fluttered. He gave his head a shake as if it felt muddled and he needed to clear it. "Well, it's possible, I suppose. But for it to flower again in our lifetime—"

"We need to win the war quickly," Bareris said, "before it further fouls the earth, water, and air, and further depopulates the countryside. I agree, the zulkirs agree, and that's why they intend to strike hard at the opening Szass Tam is giving them. You see the sense in it, don't you?"

"Yes," Aoth admitted, his speech ever so slightly slurred. "I do understand, just as I understand that they're cunning, and mine is only one dissenting voice. It's just . . ." He seemed unable to complete his thought.

"If you understand, then help! Keep your oath. Stand with me and the rest of your friends. If we win, you'll share in the glory and all the good things that will follow. If we lose, at least you won't live out your life wracked with a betrayer's guilt, wondering whether your prowess might have meant the difference."

"Fastrin the Delver went mad," Mirror said in his hollow moan. Bareris jerked around, and Aoth did too, despite his light trance. Over the years, they'd grown used to the ghost hovering around, but he spoke so rarely that his utterances still tended to startle.

"He wanted to kill everyone," Mirror continued. "Some folk fought, some ran, and either way, it didn't matter. He got everyone in the end. But I'm glad I'm one who fought."

Bareris's mouth tightened in exasperation. The terse story agreed with the history Quickstrike the gravecrawler had once related, and almost certainly represented one of Mirror's rare glimmers of authentic memory, but that wasn't the point. Though the ghost appeared to be recommending courage, his story also implied that those who dared to cross archwizards like Szass Tam could anticipate only destruction. That moral seemed likely to bolster Aoth's doubts and so disrupt the influence Bareris was weaving.

But Aoth sighed and said, "I suppose I'd feel the same way. Death gets us all eventually, doesn't it? If not in the form of an ambitious lich or crazy warlock, then in some other guise. So you might as well stick by your comrades and follow the banner you've chosen no matter how ragged and faded it becomes."

Bareris's shoulders slumped with relief. Beneath that emotion was the hint of another—a vague, uncomfortable squirming that might have been shame—but it subsided quickly. "Now that's the Aoth I've known for all these years."

Aoth snorted. "Yes, Aoth the fool." His mail clinking, he slid off the fence. "Let's go back and get the flogging over with."

•• •• •• •• •• •• •• •• •• •• •• •• •• •• ••

Perched on a mound at the edge of the sheer drop that was the First Escarpment, girt with a double ring of walls, the Keep of Sorrows had never fallen, and wise men opined it never could. Still, as Nular Zurn, the castellan of the granite fortress, stood on the battlements and studied the advancing host through his spyglass, he felt tense anyway.

It wasn't just the size of the besieging force, though it was huge, darkening the plain like a vast stain and flying the standards of every tharch and order of Wizardry, since Szass Tam claimed dominion over them all. Nor was it the knowledge that the lich himself was down there somewhere. What troubled him was the nature of the troops under his command.

Throughout its history, Thay had employed undead troops, the Zombie Legion, dread warriors, and the like. During his thirty-five years of soldiering, Nular had, of necessity, grown accustomed to such creatures. But he'd never seen so many gathered together, rank upon rank of withered and sometimes eyeless faces, and enclosed wagons shrouded in pockets of unnatural gloom carrying entities that could only move around between sunset and dawn. Although the host was still some distance away, the wind already carried its carrion stink, and he wondered how the lich's companies of living warriors could stand marching in the thick of it.

Nular glanced up and down the walkway. Lacking spyglasses, his own soldiers couldn't see the advancing army as well as he could, but they could discern enough to discomfit them. He could read it in their faces.

"Where's our hospitality?" he said, raising his voice sufficiently to carry along the battlements. "Why do you stand mute when guests have come to call? Say hello!"

Its gray hide creased with scars and spittle flying from its mouth, a blood orc sergeant screamed an ear-splitting battle cry. In moments, all the orcs joined in and the human warriors too, although the latter couldn't compete with their pig-faced comrades. Their shouts were all but lost in the din.

As the noise subsided, the company looked steadier. The sergeant turned to Nular. "Lord! The closest ones are in catapult range."

"I believe so," said Nular, "but wait." The zulkirs promised a swift resolution to the siege, but in case they were mistaken, he intended to use catapult stones, ballista bolts, and all other resources with care.

"Look!" someone shouted.

Nular peered outward again. Riding in from the west, a dozen horsemen galloped into the open space between Szass Tam's army and the keep. From their course, it was plain they rode for their lives, hoping to reach the latter.

Szass Tam's archers reacted within a moment or two, and arrows arced through the air. Nular expected to see men and horses fall, but instead, they simply popped like soap bubbles until only a pair of riders remained. The others, Nular realized, had been illusions intended to draw the enemy's attack.

More shafts flew at the real horsemen and their mounts, but glanced harmlessly away. The riders had a second defensive enchantment in place. Nular realized the fools might actually reach the keep. "Open a sally port!" he shouted.

Voices bellowed, relaying his command. Then a huge shadow soared up from a patch of darkness in the midst of the enemy host and flew toward the riders.

Nular had difficulty making out its shape, but it resembled a giant bat. "Shoot the thing!" he shouted. "Where are our spellcasters?"

Bows creaked, crossbows snapped, and arrows droned through the air. Several found their mark, but failed to penetrate the bat-thing's hide. It raced ahead of the horsemen and whirled around to face them. Mystical energy, visible as ripplings in the air, streamed down at them from its head.

Nular winced in anticipation of the horsemen's destruction, but they had another trick to play. Riders and mounts vanished and reappeared several yards closer to the castle. The leap whisked them out of the way of the creature's blast, which covered the piece of ground they'd just vacated in ice.

The shadow bat wheeled, seeking its quarries once again. Twisting in the saddle, one of the riders pointed a wand. Fire streamed from the tip of the weapon and splashed against the creature's wing. It convulsed and began to fall.

Then the beast spread its wings, arrested its plummet, and swooped toward the riders again. But by that time, the men were pounding through the sally port. Nular heard the small gate slam shut after them.

The bat flew high enough to peer over the outer wall of the keep. But if it thought to continue the chase, the sight of so many soldiers standying ready and the wizards and priests scurrying to aid them, must have discouraged it, for it wheeled and retreated toward the rest of Szass Tam's army. Legionnaires cheered and howled derision after it.

Nular descended the stairs to the courtyard. By the time he arrived, the newcomers had already dismounted, thrown back their cloaks to reveal the crimson robes beneath, and started drinking the cups of wine the grooms had brought them. They set the goblets aside to greet Nular.

One rider was exceptionally pudgy for a Mulan, and a wand dangled from his belt. The other had sharp, haughty features and was missing the fingers on his right hand. Both were panting and sweat-soaked, with a gray cast to their skin.

"Masters," Nular said, "are you all right?"

"We will be," said the Red Wizard with the maimed hand. "The nightwing—the creature that chased us—moves in a kind of poison cloud, but now that it's flown away, the sickness will pass. My companion is So-Kehur, and I'm Muthoth. We're messengers from Hezass Nymar."

"He sent two," So-Kehur wheezed, "in the hope that at least one of us would make it past the enemy."

"What is your message?" Nular asked.

"The tharchion and his army have crossed the Lapendrar safely," Muthoth said, "less than a day's march to the north, and without the necromancers knowing about it. The governor will move in and strike when the time is right, in concert with the forces closing in from the north and east."

"I'm pleased to hear it," Nular said. In fact, he was astonished that the infamously unreliable Nymar had actually decided to commit his troops and person to battle. "And also honored to have you as my guests. Unless you're minded to try to slip past Szass Tam's army a second time."

"Thank you, no," Muthoth said. "We'll stay here where it's safe."

•• •• •• •• •• •• •• •• •• •• •• •• •• ••

Dmitra Flass knew she wasn't the most powerful illusionist in Thay. She had her skill at politics and intrigue and her primary role in the opposition to Szass Tam to thank for her election as zulkir in the wake of Mythrellan's demise. Or perhaps, knowing that whomever succeeded Mythrellan would likewise receive the lich's homicidal attentions, no one else with any brains had wanted the job.

In any case, Dmitra was zulkir whether her arcane capabilities justified it or not, and only the zulkir, by virtue of the rituals that had consecrated her ascension, could perform the task required of her now. Accordingly, she sat chanting in the dark, stuffy confines of the enormous rocking, creaking carriage—essentially a conjuration chamber on wheels—for bell after sleepless bell. A circle of her underlings recited with her, sending flickers of light, whispers and chiming, surges of heat and cold, baseless sensations and manifestations of unreality, dancing through the air. But those wizards were able to work in shifts. As the essential hub of a vast and intricate mechanism, Dmitra had to perform her function continuously.

That mechanism consisted of far more than the occupants of a single carriage. Other such coaches rolled among the marching legions of Eltabbar. Their positions would define a magical sigil if any flying creature gazing down from above had the knowledge and wit to connect them with imaginary lines. The entire fleet of wagons had its counterparts amid the armies of Tyraturos and Pyarados, all working as one to keep Szass Tam's scouts and soothsayers from discerning the foes advancing on their flank and rear.

Dmitra reached the conclusion of one lengthy incantation and drew breath to start another. Then someone touched her on the shoulder. She turned and saw Malark. For a moment, a stray wisp of illusion painted iridescent scales across his brow.

Careful not to unbalance the forces at play, she uncoupled her power from the structure she'd created. It could manage without her, but only for a little while. "Is it midday?" she asked, her throat raw and dry.

"Yes," Malark said, "just as you ordered." He offered her a goblet of water.

It was cold, a pleasant surprise given the army's current circumstances. Malark must have persuaded a wizard to chill it with conjured frost. She gulped it greedily.

"I also have food," the spymaster said. "Raisins, dried apricots, bread and honey—"

"I'll start with that." He proffered a silver tray. "Do we know," she continued after her initial bite, "whether all this effort is actually accomplishing anything?"

He shrugged. "My agents can't see any indication that Szass Tam knows we're creeping up on him, and the diviners say they can't, either. Since I don't practice their mysteries, I've little choice but to defer to their expertise. I imagine their opinion is reliable. After all, we have the entire Order of Illusion working in concert to do what you do best."

"You're right," she said, "that should suffice, but you don't know Szass Tam like I do. He's a genius, and a master of every school of wizardry. So can we really hide whole armies from him, or was that Rashemi griffon rider correct? Is this a feck-less plan?"

Malark smiled. "Captain Fezim would be gratified that you recall his opinion, though chagrined to hear you call him Rashemi. But in response to your question, I can only say that in war, nothing is certain, especially when facing an enemy like Szass Tam. But brilliant though he is, you've always proven his equal in guile whenever it truly counted. So I trust your judgment, and think you ought to trust it, too."

"Thank you," she said, and felt a swell of affection. Collecting and evaluating intelligence was a demanding task, especially in the midst of an army on the march. She hadn't required that Malark attend to it and also ride alongside her coach to guard her while she was vulnerable, fetch her food and drink, and soothe her frazzled nerves. He'd volunteered for the latter duties, as he always did his utmost to assist her, and without wheedling for lands and lucrative sinecures like so many courtiers.

"Once we destroy Szass Tam," she said, "I'll make you a tharchion, or whatever else you want."

"Some people might object to that, considering I'm not Mulan, nor even a Thayan."

"Then they'll just have to choke on it, because I mean it—whatever you want."

He inclined his head. "You honor me, but let's discuss it after the war is over. Right now, all I truly want is to kill a great many of your enemies."

•• •• •• •• •• •• •• •• •• •• •• •• •• •• ••

Aoth glanced around, making sure he knew where everyone was, as his command winged its way across a sky that was clear and blue for once. Bareris gave him a nod. Aoth felt a fleeting pang of hostility, and then wondered why.

"Because your eyes water every time he comes near," Brightwing said.

Aoth snorted. "You've been known to stink yourself."

"That's different. I'm an animal. I'm allowed. Do you resent him for persuading you not to desert?"

"No." A new thought struck him. "Do you? If I left, you'd enjoy a safer, more luxurious life, too. You could gorge on horse-flesh every day."

The griffon laughed her screeching laugh. "Now you tell me! But no. You raised me to fight, and I wouldn't want to miss a battle like this. Look at them down there."

They were soaring high enough that Aoth had called upon the magic in one of his tattoos to ward off the chill. High enough that he could gaze down on them all—the legions of Pyarados, Eltabbar, and Tyraturos converging on the foe. They were visible to him because the same spell of concealment that cloaked them enshrouded him.

When he contemplated them, he reflected on how difficult it could be for even two companies to coordinate once separated by any distance. It seemed little short of miraculous that, marching through spring rain and mud, all the diverse elements of this great host had managed to assemble in the right place at the right time to close the trap on Szass Tam. And on top of that, there was still no indication the lich knew they were coming.

As anticipated, the shield of illusion failed at the end. Aoth knew it when horns started blowing and living men and orcs began shouting amid the necromancers' army. That force had arranged itself to threaten the Keep of Sorrows, and now companies scrambled to defend against the enemies who'd suddenly appeared in the opposite direction.

The southerners meant to hit them before they had the chance to form ranks. Their own bugles blew, their blood orcs bellowed, and clouds of arrows blackened the air. Aoth brandished a spear, and the Griffon Legion hurtled forward.

A flat, leechlike undead known as a skin kite flew up at Aoth. Brightwing caught it in her talons and shredded it. Aoth rained lightning and flame on the massed foes on the ground, while Bareris sang noxious clouds of vapor and hypnotic patterns of light down into their midst. Their fellow riders shot arrows from the saddle.

"Beware!" Brightwing lifted one wing and dipped the other, turning, and then Aoth saw the danger—several yellowed, rattling horrors, reanimated skeletons of giant raptors, seeking to climb above them.

There were too many for the griffon to handle alone. Aoth pointed his spear at the closest and flung darts of emerald light from the point.

•• •• •• •• •• •• •• •• •• •• •• •• •• ••

The knight was undead, its face a rotting skull inside its open helm. Its flying steed, with its night black coat, blazing eyes and breath, and hooves shrouded in flame looked demonic, but nonetheless alive.

If so, Bareris thought, it should be susceptible to enchantments that couldn't affect its master. Murder, his new griffon, maneuvered to keep away from it while he sought to sing it blind.

When the horse balked, jolting the corpse-knight in the saddle, he knew he'd succeeded. He sent Murder streaking at it.

The undead knight spurred its mount and hauled on the reins, but couldn't induce the sightless, panicked creature to move in any way useful for defense. Abandoning the effort, it braced its lance in both gauntleted hands and aimed to impale Murder as he closed.

Bareris leaned forward, swung his spear, and knocked his adversary's weapon out of line. Murder's talons stabbed deep into the black horse's body, and for a moment, they all fell down the sky together. Then the griffon pulled his claws free, lashed his wings, and flew clear. The knight and his destrier smashed into the ground.

Bareris cast about to locate the next threat. He couldn't find one. For the moment, the patch of air in which he and Murder had been fighting was clear of foes.

Good. He and Murder needed a chance to catch their breath. While they did so, perhaps he could figure out how the battle was progressing.

When he surveyed the battlefield, he decided it was going well. Hammered by flights of arrows and quarrels, by the devils and elementals of the conjurors and the firestorms and hailstones of the evokers, by sword and mace and spear, Szass Tam's battle lines were buckling, and his warriors had nowhere to retreat. Yielding to the pressure only moved them closer to the walls of the Keep of Sorrows, where the defenders maintained their own barrages of missiles and spells.

Ten years we've been fighting, Bareris thought, and by dusk it could all be over.

It should have been cause for rejoicing, but he felt empty. He scowled and looked around for something else to kill.

•• •• •• •• •• •• •• •• •• •• •• •• ••

To So-Kehur's relief, the keep's temple, with its altars to Kossuth, Bane, and an assortment of other deities, was empty of priests. No doubt they were all outside tending the wounded and casting maledictions on the undead.

Of course, even had the clerics been in attendance, it was unlikely they would have objected to So-Kehur visiting the shrine. When the defenders of the keep learned that a siege was imminent, they'd surely started watching for spies and scrying. But by entering the castle despite the northern army's supposed efforts to stop them, and then delivering good news, he and Muthoth had diverted all suspicion from themselves. As the castellan had promised, they were honored guests.

Still, some busybody might have found it odd if one of the newcomers showed an interest in the crypts. So-Kehur appropriated a votive candle and hurried down the stone steps, getting himself out of sight before anyone wandered in.

The wavering yellow candlelight revealed massive sarcophagi, the lids sculpted into the likenesses of those who rested inside. Slabs of marble graven with names, titles, and dates, with mottos, coats-of-arms, and the sentiments of the bereaved were mortared into the surrounding walls. Apparently no aristocrat had died in a while, for dust lay thick and cobwebs choked the walkways. The air smelled of dampness and decay. So-Kehur extracted the scroll Szass Tam had given him, unrolled it, and hesitated.

He wasn't afraid of the act he was about to perform for its own sake. He sometimes thought that his necromancy and the entities it summoned were the only things that *didn't* frighten him. But once he cast the spells, everyone in the fortress would know him for the enemy he truly was. Everyone would do his or her utmost to slaughter him on sight.

But it didn't matter that he was afraid. He was mind-bound, and had no choice. The enchantment might not poison a man if he made an honest effort to carry out Szass Tam's orders and then gave up when the task proved impossible. The magic was subtler than that. But it would smite So-Kehur if he didn't even try.

He read the first trigger phrase on the vellum, releasing the spell contained therein. Stone grated and crashed as coffin lids slid open and marker stones fell away from the vaults behind them. So-Kehur winced at the racket, but doubted anyone would actually hear it. The battle raging outside the castle was even noisier.

He recited the second trigger. A cold breeze gusted, nearly blowing out his candle. The smell of decay thickened, and the spiders skittered in their webs.

A dead man sat up in his coffin. Another stuck his head out of a newly opened hole in the wall.

Some of the dead, more recently deceased or artfully embalmed, retained a goodly portion of their flesh. Others had deteriorated to mere rickety-looking skeletons, but it didn't matter. Infused with the power of necromancy, they could all fight, and many already carried swords and axes. As befitted knights and warriors, they'd been laid to rest with their weapons and armor.

Milky eyes fixed on So-Kehur. Empty, mold-encrusted orbits turned in his direction. The dead awaited his command.

"Range through the castle," he said, "and kill everyone you find, except for me and a man with the fingers missing on his right hand." The way Muthoth liked to insult and bully him, it would serve him right if the dead went after him as well. But however obnoxious, the other necromancer had been So-Kehur's partner in desperate endeavors for a long time, and he was the only ally who could stand with him now.

Or at least the only one who thought and spoke and breathed.

.. ..

Muthoth sat cross-legged on the floor of the bedchamber. He breathed slowly and deeply, from the belly. He sank deeper and deeper into his trance, deeper and deeper into himself, until he reached the cell or psychic cyst that caged the thing within.

So-Kehur had smuggled death into the Keep of Sorrows on a roll of parchment. Recognizing Muthoth as a more powerful necromancer and a stronger will, Szass Tam had chosen him to bring an even more terrible weapon to bear, and to carry it entombed in his own mind. At times the oppressive weight and the whisper of alien thought had nearly driven him mad, and he was eager to put an end to the torment.

Which didn't mean he could afford to rush. The entity was inimical to all life, but since it hadn't enjoyed being imprisoned any more than he'd enjoyed containing it, it now hated him more than anything else in the world. Accordingly, he recited the incantation of release, or rather, of transfer from one form of binding to another, with the utmost care.

The caller in darkness, as such abominations were known, howled up around him in that realm of concept and image they both occupied. The entity was a vortex of dark mist with anguished faces forming and dissolving inside it. Their shrieks pounded at him. They'd blast his mind apart if he let them, then tear the pieces out to add to the collective agony that was their source.

Steeling himself against the onslaught, Muthoth repeated the words of command he'd just recited. The caller recoiled from him, then vanished.

For an instant, Muthoth was confused, then he realized it had transferred itself to the physical plane. It hoped the surface of his mind would prove vulnerable to assault while his awareness was focused deep inside.

He hastily roused himself, suffered a fleeting illusion of extreme heaviness as his psyche fully meshed with his corporeal form. The demented ghost—or amalgam of ghosts—raved around him. It looked just as it had inside its quasi-imaginary dungeon, but its howls were silent now, albeit as palpable and hurtful as before.

He recited the spell a third time, and the caller flinched from him. Its power stopped beating at him, although the psychic howling didn't abate.

"Go forth," he panted, "and kill every living person you meet, unless I tell you otherwise." He intended to trail along behind the caller, where he'd be safe. He hoped that if the entity encountered So-Kehur, he'd spot his fellow necromancer in time to keep the thing from attacking. If not, well, the fat fool wouldn't be much of a loss.

Still, So-Kehur had a role to play. As the dead men he'd already roused proceeded with the work of slaughtering the garrison, he'd make new zombies of the fallen, just as Muthoth intended to reanimate the caller's victims. As the defenders' numbers dwindled, the ranks of their enemies would swell.

•• •• •• •• •• •• •• •• •• •• •• •• •• ••

Xingax liked to ride on the shoulders of a hill-giant zombie. It made folk assume that a being who resembled an oversized, leprous, and grossly deformed fetus couldn't get around by himself, and he liked being underestimated in that way. It gave him an edge when ill wishers sought to kill him.

Or rather, it had worked that way in the past, but he'd discovered that in the midst of a battle like this, his mount was a liability. Even at the center of the northern host, sticking up higher than the heads of the people around him increased the likelihood of being pierced by arrows or fried by flares of arcane energy. So now he simply floated in the air beside Szass Tam.

Xingax disliked the roaring, dangerous chaos that was warfare, and privately felt that he shouldn't have to endure it. He was an inventor, sage, and artist, not a brute. Thus, it galled him to recognize that he himself was responsible for his presence at the battle. After Bareris Anskuld had mutilated him, he'd repaired the damage with a hand and eye harvested from the body of the fallen nighthaunt Ysval, then learned to wield the abilities the grafts conferred. As a result, Szass Tam had incorporated him into his battle strategy.

The lich had created half a dozen hovering eyes, then sent them soaring up into the sky. Periodically he opened his mind to the sights the disembodied orbs beheld. It allowed him to oversee the progress of the battle as a whole. He signaled the end of such an interlude by pivoting toward Xingax.

"Is it time?" Xingax asked.

The lich smiled. "It is, indeed. Our enemies smell victory. They're pushing in hard, and that means they won't be able to disentangle themselves from us later on. So remember what I taught you, and use your power."

Xingax closed his natural, myopic eye so only Ysval's round white orb could see. He raised the nighthaunt's oversized, shadow black hand to the heavens, clenched the clawed fingers into a fist, and strained with all the considerable force of his will.

Responding to his summons, darkness streamed across the

sky. For the Keep of Sorrows, night fell early, and across the length and breadth of Szass Tam's army, wraiths and other fearsome entities exploded from the wagons, tents, and pools of shadow used to shield them from the light of day.

•• •• •• •• •• •• •• •• •• •• •• •• •• ••

Tammith looked around. The horses stood ready, but she couldn't see any clear path along which she and her command might ride to engage the enemy.

Fortunately, the vampires of the Silent Company, made up largely of progeny Tammith had created over the years, had other ways of reaching the foe.

"We fly!" she called, then dissolved into bats. Her warriors each transformed into a single such creature. None of them had inherited her trick of breaking apart into an entire swarm.

She led her spawn over clusters and lines of combatants to a company of mounted knights. By the looks of it, they'd just finished butchering a band of ghouls.

The Silent Company dived at the southerners. Midway through her plummet, Tammith yanked her bats back into a single human body. It was a difficult trick and it hurt, but it was necessary, because her target wore plate armor and had his visor down. The bats wouldn't be able to hurt him.

She crashed into the knight, swept him from the saddle, and hurled him to the ground beneath her. The impact prob-ably killed or at least crippled him, but she ripped the visor off his helm and drove her stiffened, mail-clad fingers deep into his head to be sure.

She sprang to her feet, found another target, and stared at his face. Addled by her hypnotic power, he faltered, giving her time to draw her sword. As she leaped up at him, his wits returned, and he swung his shield to fend her off. He was too slow, though, and the point of her sword punched through his breastplate into his vitals.

Meanwhile, the other vampires attacked like lethal shadows, until all the riders were dead. Tammith looked around for new foes and saw the griffon riders wheeling and swooping overhead.

Since the Silent Company could fly, it could engage the zulkirs' aerial warriors—but no. By all accounts, Bareris was still alive, and had joined the Griffon Legion.

Of course, she didn't love him anymore. The predator she'd become was incapable of loving anyone. Sometimes she even hated him for failing her as he had.

But still: no. Now that the battlefield was dark, Szass Tam had other warriors capable of fighting in the air, and the Silent Company could find plenty of work to do on the ground.

.. ..

Malark considered himself as able a combatant as any in Thay. He had, after all, had centuries of life to perfect his disciplines. But he couldn't use them to best effect standing in a shield wall or charging in a line. The philosopher-assassins of the Monks of the Long Death hadn't modeled themselves with those sorts of group endeavors in mind.

Thus he preferred to fight on the fringes of the battle, and found plenty of enemies to occupy him—skirmishers, warriors separated from their companies, and undead horrors so savage and erratic that even the necromancers mistrusted their ability to control them. Accordingly, they didn't even try, just shooed them off in the general direction of the zulkirs' army to rampage as they would.

He kicked an orc in the chest and burst its heart, then used his batons to shatter the skull of a yellow-eyed dread warrior. He dispatched foe after foe, all the while exulting in the slaughter. Until the ground began to shake.

The first jolt knocked some warriors to the ground. Malark took a quick step to keep his balance, then glanced around to see what was happening.

On the plain to the north, entities huge as dragons heaved up out of the earth. Dirt showered away to reveal forms akin to those of octopi, but shrouded in moldy cerements. Vast black eyes glaring, tentacles clutching and churning the soil, they dragged themselves toward the rear of the legions of Eltabbar.

As he stared dry-mouthed at the colossi, Malark wondered if Szass Tam and Xingax had created them or unearthed them from some forgotten menagerie of horrors, and wondered too how the enemy had managed to bury them in the field beforehand without anyone in the Keep of Sorrows noticing. Well, caverns riddled the earth hereabouts, and from the first days of the war, the necromancers had employed zombies with a supernatural ability to dig. So perhaps they'd tunneled up from underneath.

Not that it mattered. What did was that the squid-things were about to smash and crush their way into Dmitra's soldiery like boulders rolling over ants, and that meant Malark's place was at her side. He sprinted toward the spot where the standards of Eltabbar and the Order of Illusion, both infused with magical phosphorescence, glowed against the murky sky.

•• •• •• •• •• •• •• •• •• •• •• •• ••

Since the day he'd first sat on griffon-back, Aoth had loved to fly, but now, for an instant, he hated it and the perspective it afforded. He wished he didn't have such a perfect view of victory twisting into ruin.

Gigantic tentacles lashed and pounded, smashing the infantry and horsemen of Eltabbar to pulp. Those few warriors who survived the first touch of the kraken-things' arms collapsed moments later, flesh rotting and sloughing from their bones. Meanwhile, strengthened by the creatures that had emerged with the premature night, the army assembled before the Keep of Sorrows counterattacked ferociously and started to drive the southerners back.

By rights, the castle's defenders should have fought to hinder that. They should have kept up a barrage of arrows and magic from the battlements, or attempted a sortie beyond the walls. But they'd stopped doing anything. Plainly, the necromancers had found a way to kill or incapacitate them.

Aoth felt a sudden surge of hope when the legions of Lapendrar appeared in the northwest. Maybe, driving in on the kraken-things' flanks, Hezass Nymar's men would have better luck fighting the behemoths than the soldiers they were pounding flat by the moment.

But it soon became clear from their maneuvering that they weren't inclined to try. Rather, in a betrayal that seemed the crowning achievement of his life of opportunism and disloyalty, Nymar meant to attack the southern host.

The object of the zulkirs' strategy had been to surround and trap Szass Tam. Now, with the lich's soldiers on one side, the squid-things on another, and the legions of Lapendrar on a third, their army was the one boxed in.

"And I could have gorged on horseflesh every day," Brightwing said.

Aoth managed a laugh, though it felt like something was grinding in his chest. "It sounds pretty good right now, doesn't it?"

"The other riders are looking to you," the griffon said. "They need orders."

Why? Aoth thought. The day is lost whatever we do. Still, they had a duty to fight until Nymia Focar or one of the zulkirs gave them leave to retreat.

"We attack Nymar," he said. "If we hit hard before his men can form up properly, maybe it will do some good." He brandished his spear, waving his men in the proper direction, and they hurtled across the sky.

•• •• •• •• •• •• •• •• •• •• •• •• •• ••

Szass Tam knew he'd won the battle, and that meant he'd as good as won Thay, but it was no reason to let up. Any zulkirs who escaped might cause trouble later, delaying the start of his real work, to which all this fighting and conquering was merely the necessary prelude.

Of course, if they realized their cause was lost, it was possible they'd all whisked themselves to safety already. They certainly wouldn't tarry out of any misguided devotion to the doomed followers who lacked the same ability to make a magical retreat.

Still, he had nothing to lose by dropping his line in the water. He sent his magical eyes flying this way and that, swooping over the enemy army to locate his rivals.

And there was Dmitra, looking sweaty, pale, and exhausted. She'd wearied herself maintaining the shield of illusion that, she imagined, kept him from discerning the southern army's approach, and had cast many more enchantments during the battle. Nor was she done yet. Reciting hoarsely and whirling a staff, she meant to hurl fire at the undead kraken crawling in her direction.

Szass Tam summoned the Death Moon Orb into his hand. The jet and magenta sphere was the size of an apple this time, as small as it ever shrank, but fortunately, its potency didn't vary with its size. He focused his will to wake its magic, then hesitated.

Because, at the end, the Death Moon Orb hadn't worked on Yaphyll. And these days, Dmitra, too, was a zulkir.

He snorted his misgivings away. He still didn't understand everything that had passed between Yaphyll and himself, but he didn't regard her resistance to the orb as part of the mystery. No charm of domination succeeded every time. Still, in its way, the artifact was the most powerful weapon in all his arsenal, and he had nothing to lose by trying it. If Dmitra proved impervious to its magic, he'd simply change tactics.

With a gesture and a spell, he placed an image of himself, complete with the orb, before her. A lesser wizard couldn't have used the sphere at such a distance, but Szass Tam believed he could, and while doing so, he'd be less vulnerable than if he'd moved his physical body into the center of an enemy army, beleaguered and on the brink of rout though it was.

When she glimpsed his shadow from the corner of her eye, Dmitra pivoted to face him and continued her incantation. He, or his image, would be the target of the fire spell if he chose to let her complete it. He didn't. He held out the Death Moon Orb, and she staggered. Her staff slipped from her spastic fingers.

"It's all right," he said. "I should punish you for your betrayal, but I always liked you, and you were always useful. I'll make you a lich and then you can join the new circle of zulkirs I'm assembling to serve me. How does that sound?"

Her eyes rolled. Shuddering, she fumbled at her scarlet robe, seeking one of the hidden pockets and whatever talisman it contained. But she lacked the coordination to reach it.

Szass Tam concentrated, bearing down to crush what little capacity for defiance remained. "For now, you can help my leviathans slaughter your soldiers. Don't worry, the brutes won't strike at you if I don't want them to."

At that moment, squirming and shoving his way though the mass of panicky legionnaires, Malark Springhill lunged into view. Capitulating to Szass Tam's orders, Dmitra oriented on the spymaster and started chanting. Realizing she meant him harm,

Malark dropped into a fighting stance. He obviously hoped he'd be able to dodge whatever magic she was about to conjure.

Then, despite her skill and the coercive power of the orb, she faltered, botching the spell. Szass Tam didn't blame her. He, too, had frozen, as true wizards all across Faerûn undoubtedly had. They sensed what had happened, if not how or why. Mystra, goddess of magic, had just perished, and with her death, the Weave, the universal structure of arcane forces, convulsed.

Corrupted by sudden chaos, the Death Moon Orb exploded in Szass Tam's grasp.

•• •• •• •• •• •• •• •• •• •• •• •• •• ••

Aoth felt a shock so profound that for an instant it obliterated thought. He assumed, when he was once again capable of assuming anything, that some hostile priest or wizard had cast a spell on him. Yet he seemed unharmed. "Are you all right?" he asked his mount.

"Yes," Brightwing said. "Why wouldn't I be?"

"I don't know." But the whole world abruptly tasted wrong. He supposed it was because the combatants had unleashed too much magic that day, enough to scrape and chip at the fundamental underpinnings of matter, force, time, and space. Reality was sick with it, and a magic-user like himself could feel its distress.

But reality and he would have to cope. The battle wasn't over.

The ground rumbled, heaving up and down like the surface of the sea. Some powerful spellcaster had apparently decided to conjure an earthquake, and as far as Aoth was concerned, it was a good idea. The tremors knocked down many of Hezass Nymar's warriors and threw their ranks into disarray. In flight, the griffon riders were unaffected.

"Kill them!" Aoth bellowed. Brightwing dived at Nymar. Aoth had been trying to get at the whoreson ever since their two forces engaged, and now he saw his chance. His comrades plunged at other targets.

As Brightwing plummeted, talons outstretched, and Nymar scrambled to his feet and lifted his shield, Aoth noticed the scarf wrapped around the tharchion's throat. Suddenly he had a hunch why Nymar had switched sides again. It cooled his hatred, but didn't shake his resolve. The fire priest was still an enemy commander and still needed to die.

"Break off!" Bareris shouted, his voice magically amplified so everyone could hear. "Fly higher! High as you can!"

Brightwing flapped her wings and started to climb. Aoth turned this way and that, trying to determine what had alarmed his friend, then gasped.

A wall of azure fire, or something that resembled flame even though it burned without fuel, heat, or smoke, was sweeping across the ground, and across the army of Lapendrar, from the south. Aoth saw that it killed everyone it touched, but no two victims in the same way. Bones and organs erupted from a legionnaire's mouth as he turned inside out. One of Kossuth's monks dissolved in a puff of sparkling dust. A knight and his horse melted into a single screaming tangle of flesh. Nymar froze into a statue of cloudy crystal.

The blue flames towered high enough to engulf many of the griffon riders. They shredded one man and his mount and plucked the heads and limbs from another pair. Then, despite Brightwing's desperate attempt to rise above it, the fire took her and Aoth as well. Pain stabbed into his eyes and he screamed.

•• •• •• •• •• •• •• •• •• •• •• •• ••

By sheer good luck, Xingax had wandered behind his hillgiant zombie when the blast flared and roared at the center of the northern army, and his hulking servant shielded him. It collapsed, a flayed and blackened ruin, and when he looked over the top of what remained of it, he wondered for a moment if the explosion had destroyed Szass Tam as well.

But obviously not, for the lich clambered up from the ground. He was surely hurt, though. Previously, despite his withered fingers and the occasional whiff of decay emanating from him, he could have passed for a living man. Now, with all the flesh seared and scoured from his face and hands, his eyes melted in their sockets, his undead nature was plain for all to see. The hem of his tattered robe was on fire, but he didn't seem to notice.

"Master," Xingax said, "what happened?"

Szass Tam oriented on him without difficulty. A lich didn't need eyes to see. "Can you still transport both of us through space?" he croaked.

Xingax didn't see why not. Such instantaneous travel was a natural ability for him. "Yes."

"Then take us inside the Keep of Sorrows. If So-Kehur and Muthoth accomplished their task, we should be as safe there as anywhere, and I don't want to risk jumping any farther."

"As you command," Xingax said. "But what in the name of the Abyss is happening?"

"We don't have time for an explanation," the necromancer replied. "Suffice it to say, we need to employ your talents, because I can't trust mine anymore. Not for the moment, anyway."

•• •• •• •• •• •• •• •• •• •• •• •• •• ••

Szass Tam vanished, seemingly vaporized by some sort of explosion, although Malark assumed the archmage hadn't really perished as easily as that. Dmitra had fainted, which was better than if she'd remained under the lich's spell and kept trying to murder her own officer. The kraken-things had slowed their irresistible advance and weren't smashing at the soldiers of Eltabbar as relentlessly as before. A few colossi were even pounding at one another.

It all looked like good news, but Malark couldn't rejoice because he didn't understand any of it. Nor would he, so long as he was stuck amid the clamorous, milling confusion that was Dmitra's army. He needed to oversee the situation from the air.

But he couldn't leave his liege lady stretched insensible on the ground. He picked her up, draped her over his shoulder, and trotted toward the place where he'd left his horse tied.

Another tremor shook the earth. He staggered, caught his balance, and scurried on.

•• •• •• •• •• •• •• •• •• •• •• •• •• ••

The agony in Aoth's face abated, and he felt the steady bunching and releasing of Brightwing's muscles beneath him. Somehow both he and the griffon had survived the power that had killed so many others.

He realized that in response to the pain, he'd reflexively shut his eyes. He opened them, then cried out in dismay.

"What's wrong?" Brightwing asked. When he was slow to answer, she joined her mind to his to determine for herself. Then she hastily broke the link again. She had to if she was to see where she was going, because her master had gone blind.

But it wasn't ordinary blindness. He could still see something. In fact, he had the muddled impression he could see a great deal. But he couldn't make sense of it, and the effort was painful, like looking at the sun. His head throbbed, and, straining to hold in a whimper, he shut his eyes once more.

"I'll carry you to a healer," Brightwing said.

"Wait! The legion. Look around. Did anyone else survive?"

"Some."

"Bareris?"

"Yes."

"Then I need to put him in charge before—"

Brightwing's pinions cracked like whips and her body rolled. Aoth realized she was maneuvering to contend with an adversary or dodging an actual attack. An instant later, the air turned deathly cold, as if a blast of frost were streaking by.

"What is it?" asked Aoth.

"One of those big shadow-bats," the griffon said. "I'll see if I can tear up its wing bad enough that it can't fly." She hurtled forward, jolting Aoth back against the high cantle of his saddle.

If their assailant was a nightwing, she had no hope of defeating it by herself. Aoth had to help. But how could he, when he couldn't see?

By borrowing her senses, of course, just as he had many times. He should have thought of it immediately, but the inexplicable onslaught of the blue flame and his sudden blindness had robbed him of his wits.

By the time he tapped into Brightwing's consciousness, she'd nearly closed on her opponent. At the last possible instant, the bat-thing whirled itself away from her talons and struck with its fangs. The griffon dodged in her turn, but only by plunging lower, ceding the nightwing the advantage of height. Brightwing streaked through the air at top speed to get away from it.

"Turn around as soon as you can," Aoth said. "I can't target it unless you're looking at it."

"You won't be able to target it if it bites your head off," Brightwing growled, but she wheeled just heartbeats later.

He saw the nightwing was close, and swooping closer. He aimed his spear at it and rattled off an incantation. As he did, he could tell that something else was wrong.

When he cast a spell, he could sense the elements meshing like machinery in a mill, and feel the power leap from their interaction. But though he'd recited the words of command with the necessary precision, the magic's structure was out of balance. The components were tangling, jamming, and producing nothing but a useless stink and shimmer. Meanwhile, the bat-thing had nearly closed the distance. Brightwing waited as long as she dared, then swooped in an attempt to pass safely beneath it.

Aoth had emptied his spear's reservoir of stored spells over the course of the day's fighting. But he could still charge the weapon with destructive force. Or he hoped he could. For all he knew, even that simple operation had become impossible.

He spoke the proper word, and to his relief, he felt power flow and collect in the point of the spear. Then Brightwing hurtled under the shadow creature, and he couldn't see it anymore. He thrust blindly, and the spear bit into its target. The magic discharged in a crackle.

"Did I kill it?" he asked.

Before Brightwing could answer, agony ripped through her body, beginning in her chest. Linked to her mind, Aoth endured a measure of it as well. His muscles clenched and his mouth stretched into a snarl. Brightwing floundered in flight, and for a moment, Aoth feared she was about to die. Then the pain abated as her extraordinary hardiness shook off the effect of the supernatural attack.

"Does that answer your question?" she rasped.

She turned, and he could see the nightwing for himself. The thing wasn't flying as fast or as deftly as before. But it was still pursuing.

For want of a better plan, he tried another spell, and felt it taking something like the proper form. But he was straining against a resistance, as if he were forcing together puzzle pieces that weren't truly mates.

It worked, though. A cloud of vapor sprang into existence directly in front of the bat-thing, so close that the creature couldn't avoid it. It hurtled in and the corrosive mist burned its murky substance ragged, in some places searing holes completely through.

The creature fell, then flapped its tattered wings and climbed at Aoth and Brightwing.

But then Bareris and Mirror dived in on the entity's flank. The bard ripped the nightwing's head with a thunderous shout. The ghost closed and slashed with his phosphorescent blade. The bat-thing plummeted once more, and this time unraveled into wisps of darkness.

Bareris and Mirror ascended to reach Aoth, who tried to look at them with his own eyes. Maybe his blindness had been temporary. Maybe it was gone.

Then he clamped his eyes shut again as though flinching from overwhelming glare. Although, beneath the unnaturally darkened sky, glare couldn't possibly be the problem.

Bareris's face had become a lean, hard mask over the years, betraying little except a hunger to kill his enemies. Yet now he gaped in surprise.

"What?" Aoth asked. "What did you see?"

"The blue flame," Bareris answered. "It's in your eyes."

•• •• •• •• •• •• •• •• •• •• •• ••

Terrified and disoriented, Dmitra thrashed. A steely arm wrapped around her chest and immobilized her.

"Easy," Malark said. "You're safe now, but you don't want to flail around and fall."

When she looked around, she saw that he was right. She was sitting in front of him on his flying horse, high in the air. His other arm encircled her waist to hold her in the saddle.

"I apologize if this seems unduly familiar," Malark said, "but I had no other way of carrying you out of the thick of battle. Do you remember what happened?"

The question brought memory flooding back. She gasped.

"Szass Tam disappeared in a blaze of fire," Malark said. "He isn't controlling you anymore."

"That's not it," she said. "His influence was . . . unpleasant, but it's over. I'm unsettled because the Lady of Mysteries is dead."

"Do you mean the goddess of magic?" he asked, sounding more intrigued than alarmed. But then, he wasn't a magic-user, and didn't understand the implications.

"Yes. And for the moment, her destruction taints the well from which all mages draw their power."

"Your enchantments made this horse," Malark said. "It isn't going to dissolve out from underneath us, is it?"

She smiled, appreciating his unruffled practicality. It steadied her in moments of stress, not that she would ever admit such a thing. "It seems to be all right."

"I'm glad. If we're not in imminent danger of falling, may I suggest you take advantage of our elevation to look at what the goddess's death has done to our battle?"

It was a sound suggestion. But the charm that enabled her to see like an owl, cast when Szass Tam shrouded the field in darkness, had run its course. She murmured the incantation once again.

It was a petty spell for an illusionist of her abilities, and she was accustomed to casting it with unthinking ease, the way a master carpenter would hammer a nail. But she felt the forces twisting out of her control. She had to concentrate to bind them into the proper pattern.

When her vision sharpened, a secret, timid part of her wished it hadn't, for now she could see how Mystra's death had infected the world. Dislodged by recurring earth tremors, avalanches thundered down the sheer cliffs on the First Escarpment. In the distance, curtains of blue fire swept across the landscape, sometimes cutting crevasses, sometimes lifting and sculpting the plain into hills and ridges.

The upheaval was vast and bizarre enough to transfix any observer with terror and awe, but Dmitra could afford neither. She had an army to salvage, if she could. With effort, she narrowed her focus from the widespread devastation to the chaos directly below.

Before Mystra's death and the mayhem that followed, Szass Tam had been on the verge of victory. Now Dmitra doubted that any living creature on either side even cared about winning. Combatants of all kinds were simply struggling to survive, for the wounding of magic had smashed a conflict in which thaumaturgy had played a dominant role into deadly confusion.

Some of Szass Tam's undead warriors remained under the control of the necromancers, and, with their living comrades, were attempting to withdraw into the Keep of Sorrows. But others had slipped their leashes. Mindless zombies and skeletons stood motionless. Gibbering and baying to one another, a pack of hunchbacked ghouls loped away into the darkness. Gigantic hounds, composed of corpses fused together and three times as tall as a man, lunged and snapped at the wizards who chanted desperately to reestablish dominance. Each bite tore a mage to shreds, and when swallowed, a wizard's mangled substance was added to his slayer's body.

Meanwhile, the southerners faced the same sort of chaos. Demonic archers—gaunt, hairless, and gray, possessed of four arms and drawing two bows each—abruptly turned and shot their shafts into three of Nevron's conjurors. An entity with scarlet skin and black-feathered wings swung its greatsword thrice and killed an orc with every stroke.

Half the kraken-things sprawled motionless. The others dragged themselves erratically around, striking at southerner and northerner, at the living, the undead, and devils, indiscriminately.

"We have to try to disengage at least some of our troops from this mess," Dmitra said. And for such a withdrawal to have any chance of success, she would have to command it. She was reasonably certain her fellow zulkirs had already fled.

"We'll try to find Dimon and Nymia Focar," Malark said. Responding to his unspoken will, his horse galloped toward the ground as if running down an invisible ramp.

chapter three

30 Tarsakh–8 Mirtul, the Year of Blue Fire

The door squeaked open, and Szass Tam turned in his chair. Azhir Kren and Homen Odesseiron faltered, their eyes widening. Their consternation was silly, really. As tharchions, they were accustomed to eyeless skull faces and skeletal extremities. They commanded entire legions of soldiers of that sort. But their master had always presented himself in the semblance of a living man, and though they knew better, perhaps they'd preferred to think of him that way. If so, it was their misfortune, because the truth of his condition was suddenly unavoidable.

"It's nothing," Szass Tam said. "I'll reconstitute the flesh when it's convenient." And when he was sure he could perform the delicate process without the magic slipping out of his control. "Don't bother kneeling. Sit by the fire, and help yourselves to the wine."

"Thank you, Your Omnipotence," Azhir said. Skinny and sharp-featured, the governor of Gauros had doffed her plate armor, but still wore the sweat-stained quilted under-padding.

"We're crowded," Homen said, "but all the troops have a place to sleep." An eccentric fellow with a perpetually glum and skeptical expression, trained as both soldier and mage, he wore the broadsword appropriate for a tharchion of Surthay, and also a wand sheathed on the opposite hip. "The healers are tending to the wounded, and we can feed everyone for a while. Nular Zurn stocked sufficient food for the living, and the ghouls can scavenge corpses off the battlefield."

"Good," Szass Tam said.

Homen took a breath. "Master, if I may ask, what happened? We were winning, and then . . ." He waved his hand as if he didn't know how to describe the immolation that had overtaken them.

Szass Tam wasn't sure he could, either. He disliked admitting that all sorcery, including his own, was crippled. But Azhir and Homen were two of his ablest generals, and they needed to comprehend in order to give good advice and make sound decisions.

But because it would do no good and might shake their faith in him, he didn't admit that he should have known what was coming—that Yaphyll's prophecy had revealed the event, if only he'd had the wit to interpret it. The white queen had been Mystra, the black one, Shar, goddess of the night, and the assassin, Cyric, god of murder. The fall of the city, the collapse of the cavern, and the agonies of the tree referred to the ordered structures of magic crumbling into chaos.

Now that he'd had a chance to reflect, he thought he might even understand how Yaphyll's initial prediction of victory had so resoundingly failed to come true. It would have, if the world to which it pertained had endured. But Mystra's demise was a discontinuity, the birth of a new reality, where the rules were different and certainties were warped.

In touch with that terrible tomorrow, Yaphyll had seized some of the blue fire—enough to break the hold of Thakorsil's

Seat and negate the power of the Death Moon Orb. Szass Tam supposed he was lucky it hadn't empowered her to do worse.

By the time he finished his abridged explanation, Azhir and Homen were gawking at him. He felt a twinge of disappointment. He understood that since they were mortal and not archmages, he could scarcely have expected them to share his own perspective, but it was still irksome to see two of his chief lieutenants looking so flummoxed and dismayed.

People, even the best of them, were such flawed and inadequate creations.

"What does this mean for all of us?" Homen asked.

"Well," Szass Tam said, "plainly, we failed to win the overwhelming victory we anticipated, and now we're facing some unexpected problems. But we took the Keep of Sorrows. That's something."

"If the ground doesn't crumble beneath it and cast it all the way down into Priador," Azhir said.

"Portions of the cliffs are still collapsing," Szass Tam said, "but I examined the granite beneath the castle. It will hold."

"That's good to know." Homen drained his silver cup. "But when I asked what this all meant, I was asking about . . . the whole world, I suppose. Is everybody going to die?"

Szass Tam snorted. "Of course not. Do you imagine the gods are necessary to the existence of the universe? They're not. They're simply spirits, more powerful than the imps that conjurors summon and command, but much the same otherwise. Deities have died before, goddesses of magic have died, and the cosmos survived. As it will again. As for us, we simply must weather a period of adversity."

"How do we do that?" Azhir asked.

"My thought," Szass Tam said, "is that we must garrison the Keep of Shadows. It's too valuable to abandon. It can play a vital role when we go back on the offensive."

"But you don't intend to continue attacking now," Homen said.

"No. We need to withdraw the majority of our forces back into the north, to rebuild our strength and lay new plans. But you two are the soldiers. If you care to recommend a more aggressive course, I'm willing to listen."

Azhir and Homen exchanged glances. "No, Master," the latter said. "Your idea seems the most prudent."

"Good. Then let's sort out the details."

.. ..

Bareris sang a charm of healing, plucking the accompaniment on the strings of his yarting. Mirror, currently a smeared reflection of the bard, hovered silently beside him.

Aoth had been escorted to a dark tent, and sat with bandages wrapped around his eyes. He opened them from time to time and glimpsed the world for just a moment, even though a man with normal vision wouldn't have seen through the bandages or in the dark. Then sight turned against him, jabbing pain into his head, and he had no choice but to flinch away from it.

He felt a cool, tingling caress on his face, a sign that the song was trying to heal him. Bards too were reportedly having difficulty casting spells, but not as much as wizards.

Still, Aoth doubted the charm would be any more effective than the prayers of the priests who had sought to help him already, and at the end of the song, he was proven right. Another peek brought another sickening spasm, and he gritted his teeth and hissed.

"I'm sorry," Bareris said. "I don't know anything else to try."

"It's all right," Aoth said, although it was anything but. He felt a pang of resentment and struggled to quell it, for there was no reason to take out his frustrations on his friend. He could scarcely blame Bareris for failing to deliver what even accomplished clerics could not achieve.

"At least," Bareris said, "you can see through Brightwing's eyes."

"Yes, that solves everything. I just have to live the rest of my life outdoors."

"No, you have to resign yourself to being a blind man indoors, at least until your friends find a way to restore you. But outside, you'll be whole. You'll be able to fly, cast spells, and fight the same as always."

"No. I won't. It's clumsy when your sight isn't centered in your own eyes. It throws off everything in relation to your hands and body."

"In time, you'll learn—"

"Stop! Please, just stop. How are the men and the griffons?"

"The army's still in disarray, and we left much of the baggage train behind when we ran. But I made sure our company got its fair share of what food there is, and of the healers' attentions."

"Good. The Griffon Legion's yours now, what's left of it. I'm sure Nymia will proclaim you captain."

"If she does, I'll accept, but only until you're ready to resume your duties."

"That's good of you to say." Aoth opened his eyes. He'd found that, even though he knew the discomfort that would follow, the urge periodically became irresistible. An instant later, he stiffened.

Because he saw two Barerises, the figures superimposed. One—the real one, presumably—sat on a campstool, cradling his yarting in his lap. Smirking, the illusory one dangled a marionette and twitched the strings to make it dance. The puppet was thick in the torso, clad in the trappings of a griffon rider, and clutched a spear in its hand.

A throb of pain closed Aoth's eyes again, but it wasn't as

overwhelming as usual. He was so shocked, so appalled, that it blunted his physical distress.

He took a deep breath. "I've told you, this blindness isn't like normal blindness."

"Yes," Bareris said.

"I'm beginning to sense that at certain moments, it may even turn into the opposite of blindness. It may reveal things that normal eyes can't see."

"Really? Well, then that's good, isn't it?"

Aoth felt a crazy impulse to laugh. "Perhaps it is, if it shows the truth. You can help me determine if it did. I was ready to desert, and you talked me out of it. Remember?"

Bareris hesitated. "Yes."

"Did you seek to persuade me as any man might try to influence another, or did you use your voice to lay an enchantment on me?"

This time Bareris sat mute for several heartbeats, a silence as damning as any confession. "I did it to save your honor," he said at last, "and because I knew you'd feel like a coward if you left."

"Liar! You did it because *you* wanted me, and the riders who would follow my lead, to stay and fight. For ten years, I've been your only friend. I've sought out your company when everyone else shunned your bitterness and your obsession. But you never truly felt friendship for me, did you? I was just a resource you could exploit in persuit of your mad vendetta."

"It's not mad."

"Yes, it is! You aren't Szass Tam's equal, fighting a duel with him. You're just one soldier in the army his peers have fielded against him. Even if the other zulkirs defeat him, it won't be your triumph or your revenge. Your part in it will be miniscule. But you can't see that. Even though you're just a pawn, you had to try to push your fellow pawns around on the game board, and as a result, I'm crippled!"

"Maybe not forever. Don't give up hope."

Aoth knew precisely where his spear was. He could grab it without looking. He sprang up from his stool and only then opened his eyes, using his instant of clear and painless vision to aim the weapon at Bareris's chest.

The earth bucked beneath his feet and pitched him forward, spoiling what should have been the sudden accuracy of his attack. Vision became unbearable and his eyes squeezed shut. He toppled to his knees and the spear completed its thrust without any resistance.

"If you'll allow it," Bareris said, "I'll help you up and back into your seat."

"No." Aoth realized he didn't want to kill the bard anymore, but he didn't want anything else from him, either. "Just get out and stay away from me."

.. ..

Bareris panted as if he'd just run for miles. His guts churned and his eyes stung.

"He swore an oath to serve the tharchion and the zulkirs," he said, "and so did I. I was right to stop him."

He was talking to himself, but to his surprise, Mirror saw fit to answer. "You deceived him," said the ghost. "You broke the code of our brotherhood."

"There isn't any brotherhood!" Bareris snapped. "You're remembering something from your own time, getting it confused with what's happening now, so don't prattle about what you don't understand!"

His retort silenced Mirror. But as the spirit melted back into the shadows, he shed Bareris's appearance as if it were a badge of shame.

"What about a taste of the red?" a rough voice whispered.

Startled, Tammith turned to behold a short, swarthy legionnaire who'd opened his tunic to accommodate her. She'd known she was brooding, but she must have been truly preoccupied for the soldier to sidle up to her unnoticed, her keen senses notwithstanding.

Those senses drank him in, the warmth and sweaty scent of his living body and the tick of the pulse in his neck. It made her crave what he offered even though she wasn't really thirsty, and the pleasure would provide a few moments of relief from the thoughts tumbling round and round in her head.

"All right." She opened the purse laced to her sword belt, gave him a coin, then looked for a place to go. Big as it was, the Keep of Sorrows was full to overflowing with the northern army, but a staircase leading up to a tower door cast a slanted shadow to shield them from curious eyes.

As they kneeled down together, voices struck up a farmer's song about planting and plowing, which echoed through the baileys and stone-walled passageways of the fortress. Today was Greengrass, the festival held to mark the beginning of spring. Some folk evidently meant to observe it even if Thay had little to celebrate in the way of fertile fields, clean rain, and warm, bright sunlight.

Tammith slipped her fangs into the legionnaire's jugular and drank, giving herself over to the wet salty heat and the gratification it afforded. It lay within her power to make the experience just as pleasurable for her prey, but she didn't bother. Still, the legionnaire shuddered and sighed, and she realized he was one of those victims who found being drained inherently erotic.

He should be paying me, she thought with a flicker of amusement.

The tryst was enjoyable while it lasted, but brought her no closer to a decision. She sent her dazed, grinning supper on his way, prowled through an archway, and spotted Xingax riding piggyback on a giant zombie at the other end of the courtyard.

"Daughter!" he cried. "Good evening!"

Reluctantly, she advanced to meet him.

"Good news," Xingax said. "I'm going home. It's no surprise, of course. I assumed Szass Tam would need me there to help rebuild his strength, but I'm still delighted. Perhaps you can come along and command my guards."

Tammith's upper lip wanted to rise, and her canines, to lengthen, but she made herself smile instead. "I believe you made me so I could charge into the fiercest battles, not stand sentry waiting for foes who, in all likelihood, would never find their way to me."

"I suppose you're right," Xingax said, "but maybe you can at least escort me to the sanctuary, and then I can send you back again. I'll ask Szass Tam about it." He leaned over the hulking zombie's shoulder, reached down, and stroked her cheek with the hand that was shriveled, twisted, and malodorous with rot. Her skin crawled. Then his mount carried him on his way.

If I have to travel with him, Tammith thought, he'll know. He isn't a necromancer himself, not precisely, but he, or one of the wizards in his train, will figure it out.

Then they'd change her back, and she wondered why she'd needed to ponder for so long to realize that would be unendurable.

As the singers struck up another song, she made her way to a sally port and peered around. As far as she could tell, nobody was watching her. She dissolved into mist and oozed through the crack beneath the secondary gate.

She drifted across the battlefield with its carpet of contorted, stinking corpses. The crows had retired for the night, but the rats were feasting. Most of the enormous squid-things had stopped moving, but three of them were still crawling aimlessly around.

When she reached the far side of the leviathans, she judged she'd put enough distance between herself and the castle to risk changing from fog to a swarm of bats. It was unlikely that a sentry would notice her in that guise, either, and her wings would carry her faster than vapor could flow.

Just as she finished shifting, a creature big as an ogre pounced out of nowhere. Its head was a blend of man and wolf, with crimson eyes shining above the lupine muzzle. Dark scales covered its naked body. It had four hands and snatched with two of them, catching a bat each time. Its grip crushed and its claws pierced, and even those beasts that were still free floundered with the shared pain.

"Turn into a woman," Tsagoth said, "and I'll let them go."

She didn't have to. She could survive the loss of some of the creatures that comprised herself. But it would weaken her, and she was reluctant to allow that when she knew Tsagoth could keep pace with her however she chose to flee.

She knew because their abilities were similar. He was a blood fiend, an undead demon who preyed on living tanar'ri in the same way that vampires hunted mortal men and women.

She flowed from one guise to another, and he released the captive bats to blend with the rest of her substance. She shifted her feet, but subtly; she didn't want him to see she was ready to fight. But he evidently noticed anyway, because his leer stretched wider.

"You should have fled," he said, "as soon as the blue fire came, and you realized the enchantments compelling your obedience had withered away."

"Probably so." Irredeemably feral and in some cases stupid to their cores, a number of ghouls and lesser wraiths had bolted instantly. She, however, had long ago acquired military discipline, and during those first moments, it had constrained her as effectively as magic. Only later had she recognized that escape was an option for her as well.

"Now you've missed your chance," Tsagoth continued. "The necromancers understand that they may not have complete control over even those undead who obediently followed them into the keep. They charged me to watch for those who try to stray."

"Good dog," Tammith said.

Tsagoth bared his fangs. "Do you really think it wise to mock me? Your powers are just a debased and feeble echo of mine. I can destroy you in an instant if I choose. But I'd just as soon reason with you."

Tammith shrugged. "Reason away, then." At least a conversation would give her time to ponder tactics.

"You hate our masters," he said. "I understand. So do I. But you thrive in their service. You're a celebrated warrior, and Szass Tam promises you'll be a rich noblewoman after he wins the war."

"I don't want gold or station. I want my freedom."

"Your freedom to do what and go where? Where, except in Szass Tam's orbit, is there a place for a creature like you? And even if it were possible for you to escape me, where could you be safe from the other hunters the lich would send after you?"

"I don't know yet, but I'll figure it out."

"You understand, the blue fires are still raging back and forth across the world destroying all they touch. The earthquakes are still shaking towns to rubble. It's the worst possible time to forsake your allies and strike out on your own."

"Or the best. The necromancers may decide they have more important things to think about than chasing after me."

"At least return to the castle and ponder a while longer. Don't act recklessly."

"I don't have 'a while longer.'" She smiled. "You truly don't want to fight me, do you? Because you sympathize with me. You wish you could do what I'm doing."

He glared as if she'd insulted him even more egregiously than before. "I don't sympathize with anyone, least of all one of your puny kind! But of course, I've tried to break my own bonds. It's like a vile joke that the blue fire liberated common ghouls and spectres and left a blood fiend in his chains."

"Try again," Tammith said. "Don't fight me. Change into your bat guise and fly away with me."

"I can't." Suddenly, he sprang at her.

Fortunately, she was ready. She whirled out of the way and drew her sword, then cut at Tsagoth as he lunged by.

The enchanted blade bit deep into Tsagoth's back, staggering him. She ripped it free and slashed again.

Tsagoth spun back around to face her. His left arm swept downward to meet her blade. The weapon sliced his wrist, but it was only a nick, and the block kept the sword from cutting another gash in his torso.

At the same time, he raked at her with his upper hands. She recoiled, and his claws tore through her sturdy leather jerkin to score the flesh beneath. If she hadn't snatched herself backward, great chunks of flesh would have been torn away.

She leaped farther back, simultaneously extending her sword to spit him if he charged. He didn't, and they started circling.

He gazed into her eyes and sent the force of his psyche stabbing at her like a poniard. She felt a kind of jolt, but nothing that froze her in place or crushed her will to resist. She tried the same tactic on him, with a similar lack of success.

Her wounds itched as they closed. The cut on Tsagoth's wrist was already gone, and no doubt the more serious wound on his back was healing too. In theory, they could duel the night away, each suffering but never quite succumbing to an endless succession of ghastly injuries. Until the sun rose, when she'd burn and he wouldn't.

But it was unlikely to come to that. As he'd boasted, he was the stronger, and if she couldn't beat him quickly, he was apt to wear her into helplessness well before dawn.

He murmured a word and ragged flares of power in a dazzling array of colors exploded from a central point like a garish flower blooming in a single instant. Tammith was close enough that the leading edge of the blast washed over her and seared her like acid.

Even as she staggered, she realized her foe had wounded her but likewise given her an opportunity. Fighting in a war of wizards, she'd seen this same attack, and understood how it worked when it achieved its full effect. Perhaps she could convince Tsagoth that it had done so. It all depended on her skill at pantomime.

She fell on her rump as if her mind and body were reacting too slowly for her to catch her balance. She dropped her jaw in what she hoped was a convincing expression of surprised dismay and started to rise, all with the same exaggerated lethargy.

Tsagoth sprang at her, all four hands poised to snatch and rend. She waited until the last instant, then abandoned her pretence of sluggishness and thrust the point of her sword at his chest.

She knew the ruse had fooled him when he failed to defend himself in time. The blade plunged into his heart.

He kept clawing at her, but for a moment, the shock of the injury made his efforts clumsy, and except for a scratch down the side of her face, she was unharmed. She tore her sword free and slashed open his belly. Guts came sliding out.

He plunged his talons into her shoulder and nearly tore her arm off. It wasn't her sword arm, but it might be next time, or he might manage something even worse, because his wounds were no longer slowing him.

She had to finish this exchange quickly. One sword couldn't parry four sets of talons for long. She dodged out of his way, swung the blade high, and sheared into his luminous scarlet eyes. Then she broke apart into bats, localizing the injury of her mangled shoulder in one crippled, expendable specimen.

The bats flew in the general direction of the Keep of Sorrows, the weak one trailing behind the others. She made sure their wings rustled audibly.

Tsagoth peered after her. Two red gleams appeared above his muzzle as his eyes reformed. Tammith could only hope they couldn't yet see as well as before, and that the desire to catch her and hurt her had pushed every other thought out of his head.

He vanished and instantly reappeared in her path, hands raised to rip the bats out of the air. He didn't realize that by shifting through space as he had, he'd placed himself directly in front of one of the squid-things that still showed signs of animation. Now, if the giant would only react!

It did. Trailing filthy tatters of mummy wrappings, a gigantic tentacle rose and slammed down on top of the blood fiend's head, smashing him to the ground. Then it coiled around him, picked him up, and squeezed. Bones cracked and their jagged ends jabbed through his scaly hide.

Ready to dodge, Tammith waited to see if the leviathan would strike at her, too, but it didn't. A scattered swarm of bats evidently wasn't as provocative a target as a nine-foot-tall undead demon.

She wasn't certain that even the squid-thing could destroy Tsagoth, but she was confident he wouldn't pursue her any time soon. As she swirled upward, she pondered one of the questions her adversary had posed: Where, indeed, could she go now?

•• •• •• •• •• •• •• •• •• •• •• •• ••

Situated at a juncture of secondary roads, Zolum was a humdrum farmer's market of a town. As far as Dmitra could recall, she'd never visited the place before, and she felt none the poorer for it.

But at the moment, it possessed two attractions. Even for battle-weary legions, it was only a few days' march east of the Keep of Sorrows, and it was still standing. No wave of blue flame had obliterated it, nor had any earthquake knocked it down. So the council's army had crowded in, compelling the burghers to billet soldiers who ate their larders bare.

As Zolum was second-rate, so too was the hall of its autharch with its flickering oil lamps, plain oak floor, and simple cloth banners, devoid of gems or magical enhancements. In other circumstances, some of Dmitra's fellow dignitaries might have sneered at the chamber's provincial appointments, or groused about a lack of luxuries. Not now, though. Everyone had more important things to think about.

Which was not to suggest that everyone was frightened or downcast. His nimbus of flame burning brightly, Iphegor Nath looked excited, and Malark smiled as if life were merely a play staged for his diversion, and the plot had just taken an amusing turn.

A soldier led Aoth Fezim and helped him to a chair. The captain wore a dark bandage wrapped around his eyes.

It was a pity about his blinding. He was a good officer. Still, he couldn't command the Griffon Legion as he was.

The most interesting thing about him at that moment was that he was an anomaly. The blue fire had injured but not killed him, and since the zulkirs needed a better understanding of that enigmatic force, Dmitra had a mind to vivisect him and see what could be learned. Although it could wait until he was in one place and his legion in another. Supposedly, the men liked him, so why distress them and perhaps undermine their morale when a modicum of tact could avoid it?

The autharch kept a little brass gong beside his seat at the big round table, presumably to command everyone's attention and silence, and Dmitra clanged it. The assembly fell silent, and the others turned to look at her. "Your Omnipotences," she said, "Your Omniscience, Saers, and Captains. Not long ago, we believed ourselves on the brink of defeat. But fate intervened, and now we have another chance."

Samas Kul snorted. Although no one had set out food in the hall, he had grease on his full, ruddy lips and a half-eaten leg of duck in his blubbery hand. "Another chance. Is that what we're calling it?"

Dmitra smiled. "What would you call it?"

"Considering that we have reports of whole cities and fiefs burned or melted away, of the land itself tortured into new shapes, I'd call it a disaster."

"That," said Iphegor, "is because you don't understand what's happening." He raked the company with the gaze of his lambent orange eyes. "What you take to be a calamity is actually an occasion for great rejoicing and great resolve. Kossuth has always promised that one day the multiverse would catch fire, and that much of it would perish. It's our task to make sure it's the debased and polluted portions that burn, so that we'll dwell in a purer, nobler world thereafter."

"Nonsense," Dimon said. The tharchion of Tyraturos had even fairer skin than most Mulans, and blue veins snaked like rivers across his shaven crown. He was a priest of Bane, god of darkness, as well as a soldier, and wore the black gauntlet emblematic of his order.

Iphegor pivoted to glare at him. "What did you say?"

"I said you're talking nonsense. This blue stuff isn't really fire, and your god and his prophecies had nothing to do with its coming. It's here because Shar and Cyric killed Mystra. We know that much even if we know precious little more, so you might as well stop trying to convince us that the crisis means we ought to exalt your faith above all others."

"You see only the surface of things," Iphegor replied. "Look deeper."

"That's always good advice," Dmitra said, hoping to avert an argument between the two clerics, "whatever god one follows. We need to weigh our options and choose the one that will leave us in the strongest position when the disturbances end."

"Assuming they ever do," Lallara said.

"They will," Dmitra said, trying her best to sound certain of it. "The question is, what shall we do in the meantime?"

"Make peace," Lauzoril said.

"No!" someone exclaimed. Turning, Dmitra saw that it was Bareris Anskuld. She wondered briefly why he'd remained on the other end of the room from Aoth. They generally sat together if they both attended a council, and it seemed odd that he wouldn't be at his comrade's side in the moment of his misfortune.

Prim and clerkish though he was, Lauzoril was also a zulkir, and unaccustomed to being interrupted by his inferiors. He gave Bareris a flinty stare. "Another such outburst and I'll feed you to your own damn griffons."

With a visible effort, Bareris clamped down on his emotions. "Master, I apologize."

"As is proper," Lallara said. "But I might have produced an outburst myself, if you hadn't beaten me to it."

"I hate Szass Tam as much as any of you," Lauzoril said. "But the truth is, we've all been fighting for ten years, with neither side able to gain and keep the upper hand. As a result, Thay was on its way to ruin even before the blue fires came. Now the realm truly stands on the verge of annihilation. All of us who possess true power should work together to salvage what we can. Otherwise, there may be nothing left for anyone to rule."

"Are you talking about reestablishing the council as it once was?" Zola Sethrakt asked, her voice cracking. She was a youthful-looking woman, comely in an affected, angular sort of way, who never went anywhere without a profusion of bone and jet ornaments swinging from her neck and sliding on her arms. As a result, she could scarcely breathe without clattering. "I'm the zulkir of Necromancy now!"

"Rest assured," Lauzoril said, "you will always enjoy a place of high honor."

"Every order has the right to elect its own zulkir, and mine chose me!" Zola screeched.

"The dregs of your order elected you," Lallara snapped, "after the lich led all the competent necromancers into the north. So I suggest you pay careful heed to whatever your seniors on the council advise, and graciously accept any decision this body may happen to reach. Otherwise, if we do invite Szass Tam back, and he resents you spending the last ten years in his chair, you can contend with his displeasure without any support from the rest of us."

Nevron scowled. It made his face almost as forbidding as the tattooed demonic visages visible on his neck and the backs of his hands. "Then you agree with Lauzoril?"

"No," Lallara said, "at least, not yet. But I concede that for once, his idea is worth discussing."

"So do I," Samas said.

"I would, too," Dmitra said, "if—"

"If you didn't know Szass Tam better than the rest of us," Lallara said. "By all the fiends in all the Hells, will we ever have a conversation without you harping on that same observation?"

"I apologize if it's become tiresome," Dmitra said, "but I repeat it because it's both pertinent and true. I don't claim I truly understand Szass Tam. None of us do. But I have some sense of the way his thoughts run, and I assure you, it's a waste of time even to consider making peace. Having begun this war, he'll see it through to the end, no matter the cost. If he indicated otherwise, it would be a ruse."

"We could play that game, too," Samas said. "Pretend we believe he desires peace, exploit his talents to help manage the current crisis, then turn on him later."

"Remember how this all started," Nevron said. "The assassinations and other maneuvers that nearly won him his regency without even needing to fight a war, and then tell me you're confident you could play as cleverly. I'm not sure I could. I'd rather have the bastard as my open enemy raising armies against me in the north than give him free run of the south."

"Well said, Your Omnipotence," Iphegor said. "The Lord of Flames wants us to fight, and cauterize the vileness that is Szass Tam from the face of Faerûn."

Dimon made a sour face. "As I've already explained, His Omniscience is mistaken if he truly believes that his deity, who is, to speak frankly, merely the prince of the fire elementals, has any sort of special role or significance in the current situation. But though his premises are faulty, his conclusion is valid. Speaking as a hierophant of the Black Hand, I too advise relentless aggression until we lay our enemy low, for such is the creed of Bane. It's how men achieve glory in this life and the one that follows."

"It's how Red Wizards commonly conduct themselves, also," Dmitra said, "and it's an approach that's served me well. So I oppose the idea of sending any sort of emissary to Szass Tam."

Samas heaved a sigh. "I suppose I do, too. He'd probably just change our envoys into ghosts and zombies and add them to his legions."

One by one, the remaining zulkirs rejected the notion of suing for peace. Zola looked relieved when it became clear how the informal vote was leaning.

At the end of it all, Lauzoril pursed his pale, thin lips. "So be it, then. Perhaps it was a bad idea. But surely we all agree that, even if we're resolved to remain at war, we can't prosecute it aggressively at the moment. According to Goodman Springhill's spies, Szass Tam has retreated north with the greater part of his army, and we should retire to our own strongholds, to rebuild our strength and determine how to overcome the current impediment to our spellcasting."

Bareris lifted his hand. "If Your Omnipotence has finished, may I speak to that point?"

"You're here to offer your opinion," Dmitra said, "so long as you do it courteously."

"Thank you, Mistress," said the bard. "I'm well aware that I lack the wisdom of a zulkir, a tharchion, or a high priest. I'm just a junior officer. But I have learned a little about war during my years of service, and it seems to me that now is the *perfect* time to launch a new campaign against Szass Tam."

Lauzoril shook his head. "How can that be, when our forces are crippled?"

"Because, Master, such things are relative, and the lich is *more* crippled. For the moment, wizardry has lost a measure of its power. That means, in the battles to come, men-at-arms and priestly magic will play a decisive role, and who has more of both? You do—you zulkirs who control the populous south and the sea trade that enables you to hire sellswords from abroad. Whereas the majority of Szass Tam's troops are undead, constrained to serve through sorcery, and when the blue fires came, he lost the use of a good many of them."

Malark nodded. "My agents confirm it."

"So I respectfully suggest you press your advantage," Bareris said, "before Szass Tam figures out how to neutralize it."

Nevron grunted. "I see the sense in what you recommend, but the world is in turmoil. I doubt we understand a tenth part of what's happening. We certainly don't know how to extinguish or turn back the blue fires. Do you think an army can march and fight under such conditions?"

"Yes," Bareris said, "and why shouldn't it try? What do you have to lose? The blue fire is no more likely to consume a legion on the march than one hiding in its barracks. It can spring up anywhere, with no warning."

Malark fingered the birthmark on his chin. "The disruptions have damaged my network of spotters and scouts. But some of my agents are still on the job, and even with impaired magic, I'm optimistic that they can relay information quickly enough for it to be of use. If a wave of blue flame is flowing across the countryside, perhaps I can warn an army in the field in time for it to get out of the way."

"That's encouraging," Dmitra said. "Having heard the advice of our tharchions and their subordinates, I now believe we ought to fight the northerners as aggressively as we can. What do the rest of you think?"

Samas shook his head. It made his jowls and chins wobble. "I don't know . . ."

Lallara sneered. "No one is requiring you to go yourself."

The fat man seemed to swell like a toad and his blotchy face bloomed even redder. "Are you questioning my courage? I fought at the Keep of Sorrows, the same as you!"

"Yes, you did," Dmitra said, "and none of us doubts the bravery or loyalty of any of the zulkirs." It was, of course, a preposterous statement, at least with regard to their alleged fidelity, but it might serve to steer the discussion back into productive channels. "I understand your misgivings. Truth be told, I share them. But I also know we're fighting for our lives against a powerful, brilliant adversary, and we must take advantage of every opportunity."

Samas snorted. "I seem to remember you saying much the same thing before we marched a critical portion of our strength into Szass Tam's trap. But all right. Let's see if we can finally bring this stupid war to an end."

One by one, the other zulkirs concurred. "So—specifically, what will be our strategy?" Lauzoril asked. "Do we take back the Keep of Sorrows?"

The silver stud in her nostril gleaming in the lamplight, Nymia Focar cleared her throat. "Master, that wouldn't be my advice. Reclaiming the fortress would require a lengthy siege, if it can be done at all, and we want to accomplish something quickly, before Szass Tam regains the full measure of his arcane powers."

"What would that something be?" Nevron asked. "Is it time to assault High Thay itself?"

Dimon shook his head. "No, Your Omnipotence, I wouldn't recommend that, either. It would be even more difficult and take longer than getting back into the keep. So my advice is to ignore the fortress but reclaim the rest of Lapendrar. It should be easy enough with Hezass Nymar and his legions dead. Next, retake your lost territories in northern Eltabbar, and conquer as much of Delhumide as you can. Once you do that, you'll have the Thaymount surrounded, cut off from the Keep of Sorrows and Surthay and Gauros as well."

"I like that," Dmitra remarked. Then, from the corner of her eye, she glimpsed an unfamiliar figure standing just inside the door. Startled, she jerked around in that direction.

•• •• •• •• •• •• •• •• •• •• •• •• •• ••

Bareris looked where everyone else was looking, then cried out in astonishment.

Tammith had somehow slipped past a locked door without an assembly of the greatest wizards in the world noticing until she was fully inside. Tammith, clad in the somber mail and trappings of a champion or captain of Szass Tam's host, her pretty face, though dark in life, now whiter than white in contrast to all that black. Tammith, whom he'd destroyed ten years ago, or so he'd always believed.

Iphegor Nath jumped up from his chair, overturning it to bang against the floor. He raised his hand and scarlet flame burst from it.

Bareris leaped up, too, without knowing what he intended, or why.

Tammith dropped to her knees. "I come as a peaceful supplicant!"

That was enough to persuade Iphegor to hesitate. He had plenty of reason to despise and distrust the undead, but not quite enough to lash out when one humbled herself before him. Even now, such creatures were considered to have their legitimate place in the proper Thayan order of things. Most of the vampires and dread warriors in the realm served Szass Tam, but thanks to the labors of Zola Sethrakt and her subordinates, the lords of the south commanded some as well.

"It appears," said Dmitra Flass, "that everyone can safely be seated." She fixed her gaze on Tammith. "I see what you are, blood-drinker. But who are you?"

"My name is Tammith Iltazyarra. Until Szass Tam and his lieutenants lost control of me and I deserted, I commanded the Silent Company. Perhaps you've heard of it."

Bareris ached to hear her speak. Her voice was sweet and familiar, yet cold and flat, a travesty of the one he remembered.

"Yes," Dmitra said. "You've given us a good deal of trouble over the years."

"Then perhaps," Tammith said, "I can atone for it now. I want revenge on Szass Tam for forcing me to serve him, and the only way I'll get it is to fight for the council."

"That sounds plausible," Lallara said. "But then, if the lich sent an impostor to mislead us and spy on us, I imagine he would give her a persuasive tale to tell."

"Your Omnipotence," said Bareris, "I know Tammi . . . Captain Iltazyarra." Although if she still remembered him, at least with any vestige of emotion, no one could have known from her demeanor. "I mean, I did when she was alive, and I can vouch that she didn't accept her transformation or induction into Szass Tam's army willingly."

"That's fine," said Samas Kul, "but how do we know she isn't acting under coercion now? The blue fire didn't free all of the lich's puppets."

"Zola Sethrakt is the zulkir of Necromancy," Lauzoril said, "and I'm the realm's greatest enchanter. Even with our abilities diminished, we should be able to determine whether her spirit is free or not."

"But what," asked Iphegor Nath, "if she came to embrace her condition and her station during her years of service to the lich? It's plain from her stature and features that she was born Rashemi. Szass Tam gave her immortality, supernatural abilities, and high rank, and by some accounts, drinking blood is a carnal pleasure surpassing any the living can imagine. Perhaps she eventually decided she didn't have it so bad."

"Your Omniscience," Tammith gritted, "if you believe that, then, for all your wisdom, you comprehend very little of what it truly means to have your life stripped away from you, with only thirst and servitude left in its place."

"If Szass Tam doesn't have her spirit chained up tight," Zola said, "then it doesn't matter what she truly feels. I can bind her to serve me."

Tammith rose so swiftly that the eye could scarcely track the motion. "No, Mistress. With all respect, I'll never submit to another such shackle. If you try to impose it, you'll have to destroy me."

And me, Bareris realized. He'd stand with her, crazy and suicidal though it would be.

"I hope you realize," Dmitra said, "that even with our magic impaired, we can destroy you. If we all exert our powers against you, you won't last an instant."

"I understand," Tammith said. "But then you'll forfeit the chance to strike a crippling blow against your real enemy."

"Meaning what?" Nevron asked.

"I heard you discussing strategy before I sneaked in." Tammith smiled. "Vampires have keen ears. Your plan is good, but it could be better. Szass Tam lost many of his warriors to the blue fire. Now Xingax will labor to create replacements. But if we attack his manufactory, we can prevent it, and keep the northern armies weak."

"I take it," Dmitra said, "that you know where Xingax currently has his lair, and how we can get at it?"

Tammith inclined her head.

·· ·· ·· ·· ·· ·· ·· ·· ·· ·· ·· ··

Bareris positioned himself beside a pale marble statue of a robed wizard and struck up a song about a starfish that decided it belonged in the sky. The ballad detailed its comical misadventures as it doggedly tried to clamber up into the heavens and take its place among the other luminaries. The sculpted wizard seemed to frown as if he disapproved of levity.

Bareris disapproved of it, too, or at least had long ago abandoned the habit, and the merry lyrics and rollicking tune felt strange coming out of his mouth. In fact, for some reason, they hurt.

But Tammith had always laughed at the song when the two of them were young, and at length, huge bats swooped out of the darkness. Bareris recoiled a step in spite of himself.

The bats swirled and melted together to become a woman. She'd removed her armor and wore a mannish leather jerkin and breeches. He wondered if she ever opted for skirts anymore.

"Of all the songs you ever wrote," she said, "I always liked that one the best."

He swallowed. "After the council of war, you just wandered off with Zola Sethrakt. You didn't even speak to me."

"And so you thought to flush me out with a tune. Here I am. What do you want?"

"For one thing, to say I'm sorry for what I did in the Keep of Thazar."

"I'm sorry it didn't take."

"Don't say that. You have your freedom now."

"But I'm still dead."

"No. Xingax laid a curse on you, but curses can be broken."

"By whom? Your zulkirs, whose magic is crippled, and to whom I'm more useful as a vampire?"

He shook his head. "I don't understand. You came here of your own volition, and yet you're so bitter and cold. You act as if you don't even want to see me."

"I didn't think I would. I didn't see it myself, but I heard reports that the blue fire burned most of the Griffon Legion out of the air."

"You're saying you hoped I was dead?"

"Yes."

"I don't believe you."

"I don't hate you, and I don't blame you any longer for failing to rescue me. But I want my existence to be easy, and it's easier when I don't have to look at things that remind me of what I've lost."

"Perhaps you haven't lost as much as you think."

She laughed. "Oh, believe me, I have. And even if I were still capable of loving the boy I adored when I was a child, where is he? Long gone, I think, poisoned by hatred and regret."

"I thought so, too, until you appeared before me."

"It will be easier for you if you realize nothing has actually changed. Bareris and Tammith are dead. We're merely their ghosts."

He shook his head. "You can't avoid me. You're going after Xingax, and I am, too."

"We can hunt together. Just don't prattle of things that neither one of us is capable of feeling or being any longer."

"All right. If that's what you want."

"It is. Good night." She turned away.

"Wait."

She pivoted to look at him.

"I took care of your father and brother. I sent money. But they're both dead. Your father drank so much it poisoned him, and Ral caught a pox."

He didn't know why he told her so brusquely, as if he were trying to match her coldness. Perhaps he wanted to hurt her, or to force her to betray soft human emotion, but if so, she disappointed him. She merely shrugged.

chapter four

10–26 Mirtul, the Year of Blue Fire

Over the years, Aoth had all but covered himself in tattoos, repositories of minor enchantments that could be invoked when needed. So he was accustomed to the recurrent sting of the needle. Normally, it wouldn't even have bothered him to have the sharp point playing around his eyes, and over the eyelids themselves.

This time, however, he felt a flare of pain like the touch of a hot coal. He jerked back in his chair. "What in the name of the Black Hand was that?"

"I'm sorry, sir," the tattooist said. "My art has become difficult lately, just like any other form of sorcery."

"Then try being careful!"

"Yes, sir." The artist hesitated. "Do you want me to continue?"

Aoth realized it was a good question. Did he want the wretch to go on etching sigils of health and clear vision around his eyes, even though the magic might conceivably twist awry and create an entirely different effect?

"Yes," he said. Because the tattooist had reportedly restored sight to the blind on two previous occasions, and with the priests unable to cure him, Aoth didn't know what else to try.

The needle pricked his eyelid again, this time without creating searing heat. Then Brightwing screeched.

The griffon was just outside. Aoth reached out with his mind and looked through her eyes at a legionnaire. The fellow had Brightwing's saddle in his hands, and was holding it up in front of him as if he hoped to use it as a shield.

Aoth pushed the tattooist away, jumped up, strode across the room—he'd grown sufficiently familiar with the layout of his billet to avoid running into the furnishings—and threw open the front door. "What's going on?" he said.

"This idiot thinks he can take me away!" Brightwing snarled.

To the legionnaire, Brightwing's utterance was just a feral shriek, and he reacted by taking a step backward. "Sorry to disturb you, Captain," he said, "but there are orders to round up all the griffons whose riders are dead or disabled and give them to legionnaires who are fit but lost their mounts, or else take the animals along for spares. Do you see?"

Aoth understood. As the war ground on, exacting a constant toll in men and beasts, it was standard procedure. But if he lost Brightwing, he'd lose a piece of his own spirit and all the sight he had left. Bareris knew that, but he evidently wanted her anyway. It was more proof of what a false friend and callous bastard he was.

"I'm a war mage," said Aoth, "and Brightwing is my familiar. She won't carry any rider but me."

"I don't know anything about that, sir. I have my orders—"

"I'm still your commander, even if I am injured!"

"Yes, sir, but this order comes from Nymia Focar herself."

"It's a misunderstanding," Bareris said. When Brightwing turned her head, Aoth could see the bard hurrying down the path.

The soldier frowned. "Sir, with all respect, she spoke to me herself. She told me to make sure I collected Captain Fezim's griffon."

"But later on," Bareris said, "she spoke to me." Aoth could feel the subtle magic of persuasion flowing like honey in the bard's voice. "She told me she'd changed her mind, and Captain Fezim should keep his mount. So you can go on your way and forget all about it."

"Well," said the legionnaire, sounding a little dazed, "in that case . . ." He put the saddle back on the stoop, saluted, and strolled away.

"Someone made a list of all the griffons to be collected," Bareris said to Aoth. "I happened to glance at it, saw that Brightwing was included, and came as fast as I could."

Aoth grunted. Courtesy indicated that he ought to say thank you, but he'd have preferred to stick a dagger in his own guts.

Bareris frowned. "You didn't think I'd send someone to take her, did you?"

The question made Aoth's muscles clench. "Is that a reproach? Why in the name of every god wouldn't I believe that, considering how you betrayed me before?"

"As the soldier said, the tharchion gave the order. I assume she did because she knew I wouldn't. Even if you don't believe that." Bareris frowned. "Although, valuable as griffons are, there's something odd about her concerning herself with a single mount."

It seemed strange to Aoth as well, but he didn't want to prolong the conversation to speculate. "I'm going back inside."

Bareris's mouth tightened. "Fine." He turned away.

Aoth felt moisture on his face. He supposed it was blood from the needle pricks, beading and dripping. He resisted the impulse to wipe it away for fear of marring the tattooist's work.

•• •• •• •• •• •• •• •• •• •• •• •• •• •• ••

As the army of Pyarados prepared to march, dozens of tasks and details demanded Bareris's attention. He had to see to his own gear and mount as well as those of his entire company. Procure provisions in a hungry land at winter's end. And review the intelligence Malark's agents provided, and plot strategy with Nymia, Tammith, and the rest of the officers.

It left him precious few moments even to eat and sleep, but from time to time, late at night, he prowled through the house where he'd taken up temporary residence, looking for Mirror and periodically calling his name. The members of the household—a draper, his wife, three children, and a pair of apprentices—made themselves scarce at such moments, and were leery of him in general.

But he didn't care if they thought he was crazy. He just wanted to find the ghost.

Even more than Aoth, Mirror had been Bareris's constant companion for the past ten years. Often, the ghost faded so close to the brink of nonexistence that no one else could detect him. Even cats failed to bristle and hiss at his presence. But Bareris had always been able to feel him as a sort of cold, aching void hovering nearby.

Lately, he couldn't. Mirror had abandoned him shortly after his falling out with the newly blinded Aoth, and had not yet returned.

On the eve of the army's departure, he began hunting in the attic and finished in the cellar, where cobwebs drooped from the ceiling, mice had nested in the filthy, shredded remains of a stray bolt of cloth, and the shadows were black beyond the reach of his candle. It looked like a fine location for a haunting, but if Mirror was lurking there, he chose to ignore Bareris's call.

"Nymia wanted to take Brightwing," Bareris persisted. "I made sure she'll stay with Aoth. He has a tattoo sorcerer working to heal his eyes. It's possible he'll see again."

Still, no reply came, and abruptly Bareris felt ridiculous, babbling to what was, in all likelihood, an empty space.

"To the Abyss with you, then," he said. "I don't care what's become of you. I don't need you." He wheeled and tramped up the groaning stairs.

•• •• •• •• •• •• •• •• •• •• •• •• •• ••

The conjuration chamber shook. Grimoires fell from their shelves, racks of jars and bottles clattered, and the piece of red chalk that was attempting to inscribe an intricate magic circle on the floor hitched sideways, spoiling the geometric precision the sigil demanded.

Szass Tam sighed. The earth tremors jolting all Faerûn had turned out to be particularly potent and persistent in High Thay with its volcanic peaks. The entire castle had been rocking and shuddering ever since his return from the Keep of Sorrows, and although the inconvenience was the least of the ills Mystra's death had engendered, it vexed him nonetheless.

He waved a skeletal hand, and the half-completed figure vanished as if it had never been. He animated a different stick of chalk and set it to recreating the drawing.

This time, the chalk managed to complete the circle without the earth playing pranks. Szass Tam took his place in the center, summoned one of his favorite staves into his hand, and recited a lengthy incantation.

A magical structure, invisible to normal sight but manifest to an archmage, took shape before him, then started to slump and deform. He froze it in its proper shape by speaking certain words of power with extra emphasis, and through the sheer insistence of his will.

At the end, his construct wavered into overt existence as a murky oval suspended in midair. Szass Tam said, "You are my window. Show me the Weave."

Had he given the same command before the advent of the blue fires, the oval would have revealed an endless iridescent web reflective of the magic that infused and connected all things, and the interplay of forces that held it all in equilibrium. Now he beheld scraps of burning crystal tumbling through an endless void. Even for a lich, the sight was nauseating, although Szass Tam couldn't define exactly why.

What he did know was that the Weave showed no sign of reforming. Perhaps it would eventually, if a new deity of magic arose, but since Szass Tam had no idea how or when such an ascension might occur, the possibility failed to ease his mind.

"You are my window," he said. "Show me the Shadow Weave."

As its name suggested, the Shadow Weave was the dark reflection and antithesis of its counterpart. It hadn't partaken of Mystra's life in the same way the Weave had, and Szass Tam had conjectured that it might reconstitute more quickly in the wake of her passing.

If so, it could serve as a source of power. For certain practitioners of an alternative form of sorcery called shadow magic, it always had. Despite his erudition and curiosity, Szass Tam had never learned a great deal about the mysteries of shadow. Conventional thaumaturgy had proved such an inexhaustible well of precious and fascinating secrets that he simply hadn't gotten around to it. But he was willing to learn now if it would ameliorate the current crisis.

But it didn't appear that there was anything left to learn. The Shadow Weave, too, remained in pieces, the fragments falling endlessly through darkness and burning with a dim flame whose radiance was somehow a mockery of true light.

He grimaced. With both structures annihilated, it was no wonder wizardry was crippled.

Yet it was hardly useless. It could still evoke and transform, summon and bind—some of the time. If he could figure out why it worked when it did, and why it failed on other occasions, perhaps he'd know how to make it reliable again.

"You are my window," rasped an unfamiliar voice, startling him from his musings. "Show me the one peeping at magic's corpse. I wish to know if he laughs or weeps."

The interior of the oval rippled and flowed, and an entity appeared. In certain respects, Szass Tam might almost have been gazing at his own reflection, for the creature, too, possessed a grinning skull face and naked bones for hands. But instead of a handsome red velvet robe, it wore dark, rotting cerements, and in place of a staff, it carried a scythe.

The weapon enabled Szass Tam to identify the creature, for its blade was blacker than anything made of matter—a long, curved, movable wound in the fabric of reality. Only entropic reapers, undead destroyers in the service of primordial chaos, carried scythes like that.

Formidable as they were, no reaper should have sensed Szass Tam's ritual in progress, let alone been able to subvert the magic to its own ends. It was another disquieting indication of just how diminished his powers actually were.

But diminished or not, he needed to reestablish control. "You are my window," he said, "and I now close you."

Nothing happened.

"Do you see the beauty?" the reaper asked, and even though it was speaking from another universe, Szass Tam caught a whiff of its cold, stinking breath. "It's the beginning of the end of all structure, all limitation, or so we pray."

Ironically, Szass Tam did see, but he wasn't inclined to chat about it. "I am Szass Tam, whose name inspires fear in every world, and I don't tolerate interlopers in my sanctum. Will you leave, or must I punish you?"

"I see you're a great wizard," said the reaper, "but are you great on behalf of chaos, or great in the service of order?"

"It isn't your place to try to take my measure."

"You're mistaken. It's exactly my place, although I admit, the task is difficult. You sow chaos with every move you make, and yet I sense the goal of all your scheming is law transcendent."

Szass Tam felt an unaccustomed pang of genuine alarm. Exactly how much did the reaper perceive? Too much, he feared, for him to rest easy if he merely drove it from his presence. "You are my window," Szass Tam said, "and you will open wide. Wide enough to pass my enemy through."

The reaper took a stride and entered the mortal realm. Having made up its mind that Szass Tam was a considerable force for order, it had no choice but to try to slay him.

But now that Szass Tam had drawn it within range of his most potent magic, he had no intention of giving it a fair chance to do so. He flourished his staff and spoke a word of command.

A form like an eagle made of dazzling white light leaped from the end of the staff, the visible manifestation of a spell crafted specifically to annihilate undead. The blazing raptor plunged its talons into the reaper's naked rib cage and disappeared, leaving the skeletal assassin unharmed. Like so many spells that Szass Tam had attempted of late, the magic had twisted awry.

Its ragged black cerements swirling around it, the reaper swung its scythe. Szass Tam leaped out of range and the dark blade streaked by him, leaving ripples of distortion in its wake.

Szass Tam spun his staff through another pass. Eight orbs of blue-white light flew from the weapon, accompanied by the smell of thunderstorms. The spheres struck the reaper in quick succession, each discharging its power with a blinding flash and a crackle.

The servant of chaos stumbled backward, and portions of its filthy cerements caught fire. But the barrage didn't blast it to splinters as it should have. As soon as it ended, the thing rushed in for another strike.

Szass Tam attempted another retreat and backed into a worktable. The scythe spun at him and he hurled himself to the side. The black blade sheared through a bronze statuette of Set, a serpent-headed Mulhorandi god of magic. The stroke liquefied it, and it splashed into droplets and spatters.

As he scrambled backward, distancing himself from the reaper, Szass Tam could only infer that the random fluctuations in mystical forces had rendered his staff and its stored magic useless. He had no way of knowing if any of his other spells would work any better, or even if he'd have the chance of find out. Evoking an effect from the ether required more time and precision than releasing one already stored, and an aggressive attacker like the reaper could make it impossible for a wizard to conjure successfully.

As the creature rounded on him, he focused his thoughts on the red chalk. It was still enchanted, and still responsive to his unspoken will. He bade it hurtle at the reaper to scribble on its bony face and crown.

With luck, the unexpected harassment would distract the reaper for a precious moment, until it decided that the chalk was insignificant. Without waiting to see if the trick would work, Szass Tam reached for one of his many pockets. He snatched out a tiny ball of compressed bat droppings and sulfur, flourished it, and rattled off the first words of an incantation.

The reaper stopped swiping at the chalk and charged its animator. That was unfortunate. It meant Szass Tam wouldn't be able to smite the creature with the crude magic he was creating without catching himself in the effect. But he didn't abandon the effort. He had to put the reaper down before it hit him with its scythe.

A spark streaked from his outstretched hand and hit the reaper's sternum. It exploded into a blast of crimson fire.

The detonation threw Szass Tam backward and the heat seared his body, particularly the parts that still had flesh. But liches were preternaturally resistant to harm, and he also carried a ward against flames. Thus, though the blast tore much of his robe away, it left his limbs in place. In fact, it didn't even stun him.

He reeled, caught his balance, and came on guard in a wizard's fighting stance, staff gripped to conjure, strike, or parry as needed. As it turned out, he didn't need to do anything. When the blaze subsided, scraps of bone and tatters of burning garments littered the floor. Only the scythe remained intact, its blade warping and melting the granite on which it rested.

Szass Tam drew a deep breath. Without actually needing to breathe, he couldn't truly feel winded, but even after centuries of undeath, the old, useless habits of mortality sometimes manifested.

That had been too close, and it infuriated him. An archmage should have little trouble coping with an entropic reaper, fearsome as the creatures were to lesser folk, and yet the entity might easily have slain him.

But there was no point in bemoaning his weakness. He'd do better to ponder what he'd discovered.

When intricate magic had failed, his instincts had prompted him to resort to a basic evocation of elemental force. That succeeded, and he thought he knew why. The Red Wizards had developed their art to a level lesser mages could scarcely imagine. Their spells incorporated all sorts of sophisticated shortcuts and enhancements. But those features achieved their efficacy by exploiting the subtle interplay of the forces comprising the Weave.

With the Weave annihilated, those same mechanisms had become a hindrance. Szass Tam's spells could no longer tap into all the elements they required to work. Trying to perform magic that way was like attempting to carry water in a bucket with a hole in the bottom.

Of course, most enchantments took advantage of the Weave to one degree or another, and until the realm of magic stabilized, even a basic spell might run afoul of the same problem. But it wouldn't happen as often.

So long as Szass Tam acted in accordance with this new limitation, he might be able to function effectively. And if he shared his insights with his necromancers, they too—

He sighed. No. For the most part, they couldn't, not anytime soon, because they weren't immortal archmages with his breadth and depth of learning. Most of them had only ever studied Thayan thaumaturgy, and it would take time to retrain them. By then, his rivals, wielding the brute strength of their legions, might gain such a decisive advantage that even sorcery couldn't counter it.

He had to find another way to stave off defeat, and after a time, an idea occurred to him. It would require another divination, and he summoned a blue crystal globe into his hand. For the time being, he'd had his fill of opening windows into the infinite.

·· ·· ·· ·· ·· ·· ·· ·· ·· ·· ·· ·· ·· ··

The world of mortal men in general, and of warriors in particular, was good for Mirror. It filled him like water filled a cup, or perhaps it unblocked a spring of essence that welled up inside him. Either way, it dulled the ache of emptiness.

Yet despite its solace, he sometimes felt obliged to let go of it. He needed to step into a place that, he'd posited, on one of the rare occasions when his thoughts were clear enough for such conjectures, existed only within himself. In effect, he turned himself inside out like a pocket.

Whatever and wherever the place was, it was dangerous, for so far as he'd ever discovered, nothing existed there but a cold whisper of wind that rubbed away at everything his commerce with the material world had given him. For that reason, he never stayed long. He opened himself to its corrosive power then hastily retreated, like a man fingering a sore tooth then snatching his hand away.

Yet now he tarried, for instinct told him there truly was something to find, something the living world could never provide. And though he had no idea what it was, if he recovered it, perhaps he could mend an ill and wash away dishonor.

So he took a stride and then another, fading with every pace.

•• •• •• •• •• •• •• •• •• •• •• •• ••

The wings of her many bodies beating, Tammith peered into the darkness. She, Bareris, and a half dozen griffon riders were scouting ahead of the combined hosts of Eltabbar, Tyraturos, and Pyarados, looking for signs of the enemy, the blue fire, or any hazards the flames might have created.

It had certainly passed that way, scouring away vegetation and sculpting the earth into spires and arches. Eviscerated, virtually pulverized, the remains of a herd of cattle littered a field. A single survivor dragged itself along, lowing piteously.

Even for a vampire, it was unpleasant to see nature herself tormented in this fashion. Baring her many fangs, Tammith sought to snarl the feeling away.

A griffon screeched. "What's that?" its rider called.

It's just Solzepar, fool, Tammith thought, right where it's supposed to be. She could make out the dark shape of the town below, at the point where the road north from Zolum intersected the great highway called the Eastern Way.

On first inspection, it looked as if the wave of blue fire had missed Solzepar, for there was the town, still standing. Then a great crashing and crunching sounded from the midst of the shops and houses. It was like the start of another earthquake, but few of the structures and trees were swaying.

An island of earth and rock within the city rose from its surroundings like a cork popping out of a bottle. A wooden house straddled the edge and the separation tore it in two. The half that ascended disintegrated, raining boards and furniture onto the part below.

The chunk of earth rose high before slowing to a stop, and Tammith saw it was the latest addition to an archipelago of small floating islands ripped from the town below. A number of them supported buildings that were still intact.

The vampire realized she'd done the griffon rider an injustice by deeming him a fool. It was this prodigy, not the mere sighting of Solzepar, that had elicited his outcry.

Bareris climbed high enough to inspect the islands from above. Tammith and the other scouts followed. No lights burned in any of the houses—nor, she realized, in any of the parts of Solzepar that remained earthbound—and she didn't see anyone moving around.

"Fall back and descend," Bareris ordered. He seemed to speak in a normal tone, but his bardic skills projected his voice across the sky.

The scouts touched down several hundred paces from the edge of the town, in a field where the new spring grass had taken on a crystalline appearance, gleaming in the moonlight. Averse to having such uncanny stuff beneath its feet, one griffon clawed chunks of earth away.

Tammith's bats whirled around one another, and she shifted

to human form. When she did, Bareris's appearance stung her somehow. He looked haggard, fierce, and sad at the same time. She reminded herself she didn't care. Creatures like her were incapable of it.

"Well," Bareris said, "we see them. The question is, what to make of them? Captain Iltazyarra, did you hear anything about floating rocks before you fled the Keep of Sorrows?"

"No," she said.

"That's too bad. Malark's people haven't reported anything about them, either."

"We know the blue fire passed this way," another soldier said, unclipping a waterskin from his saddle. "Maybe it went through Solzepar, changed the ground somehow, and now we get . . . this."

"That's a reasonable guess," Bareris said, "for it certainly seems as if the flame can do anything. But up until now, everything that has been changed or destroyed has been affected immediately, at least as far as we know. But we have to consider the possibility that a contingent of necromancers is creating hanging islands."

"Because they know our army is coming this way," Tammith said.

"Yes. And since we would pass under their aerial stronghold, the enemy could rain destruction on our heads."

The soldier who'd spoken before wiped his mouth and stuck the stopper back in his waterskin. "If we're worried about it, the army can just steer clear of them."

"We can," Bareris said, "but only by leaving the road, which slows the march. The tharchions won't do that unless it's proven to be necessary. It's our job to determine whether it is."

"Does that mean prowling around on top of the rocks?" another warrior asked.

"Yes," Bareris said, "but maybe not all of them. One of the

larger fragments has a walled stone house on it, grander and more defensible than the buildings on any of the others. It's the structure I'd occupy if I were going to install myself up there, and it's where we'll begin our search. Up!" He kicked his mount in the flanks, and it spread its wings and sprang into the air.

They all climbed above the island, then spiraled down toward it. When they landed in the courtyard, symbols graven above the door became visible, stylized representations of a lightning bolt, a snowflake, and other emblems of elemental forces with a hand hovering above as if to manipulate them all. The place was, or had been, a chapterhouse of the Order of Evocation.

"This," said Bareris, "looks like an ideal place for necromancers to set up shop." He swung himself off his griffon and his subordinates dismounted. Tammith changed to her human form.

Bareris climbed the steps to the sharply arched door and tried the handle. "Locked," he said.

"Perhaps by enchantment," Tammith said.

"With luck, it won't matter." He sang, and his magic set sparkling motes dancing in the air. Tammith remembered how amazed he'd been the first time he'd sung and produced not merely melody but a green shimmer and the scent of pine, the moment when he'd discovered he was a true bard. Once they realized what it meant, she'd felt just as elated.

She wished she'd died then, or during one of the happy times that followed. Any time, really, before he made up his mind to sail away and seek his fortune.

He twisted the handle and the door creaked open on blackness. He drew his sword and sang luminescence into the blade. The steel shined with a white light brighter and steadier than the flicker of any torch.

"Come on," he said.

"Let me take the lead," Tammith said. "My senses are sharper, and I can withstand attacks that would kill a mortal."

He scowled as if he found the suggestion distasteful, but he said, "All right. Just don't range too far ahead. We're stronger if we stay together."

Beyond the door was a spacious entry hall, its appointments reflecting the luxury Red Wizards took for granted. The walls rose the full three-story height of the house, to one railed gallery, then another, and finally to a stained-glass skylight.

Nothing moved—nothing but the intruders and their long black shadows flowing across the walls. The house remained silent. But Tammith smelled tears, mucus, sweat, and the sour stink of fear. It was the way her prey often smelled when they realized she was about to feed on them.

"Someone's here," she said. She led her companions up two flights of stairs to the upper gallery, then opened the door to a small, sparsely furnished chamber with a narrow bed. A servant's quarters, or perhaps an apprentice's. The thump of a racing heart led her to the wooden chest by the wall.

The box wasn't very big. The lanky Mulan boy in the patched red robe surely hadn't found it easy to fold himself compactly enough to fit inside. When Tammith lifted the lid, he yelped and goggled up at her.

"Easy," Tammith said, "we're friends, here to help you."

"It's true," Bareris said, stepping beside her. "We serve the council, not Szass Tam. Come out of there." He reached to help the lad up.

Instead of taking the proffered hand, the boy pulled his own in closer to his chest. "I can't. It isn't safe. I haven't heard them in a while, but I know they're still here."

Bareris shot a glance at one of his men. The legionnaire nodded and positioned himself at the door.

"It's all right," Tammith told the apprentice, "we'll protect you. Please, stand up." She locked eyes with him and stabbed with the force of her will.

The youth's resistance crumbled, and he suffered her to lift him out of the chest. Still, his eyes rolled and he trembled, so frightened her powers couldn't numb him.

"Tell us who you're hiding from," Bareris said. "Is it northerners?"

"Northerners?" The apprentice shook his head.

"Who, then?" Bareris persisted. "Does this have something to do with the blue fire?"

The boy closed his eyes and tears oozed out from under the lids. "Yes. Some of the folk ran away, but the wizards cast the runes and said the flames would miss the town. They laughed at the people who ran!"

"But the flames didn't miss," Tammith said.

"No. I don't know if the wave split in two or what, but suddenly the fires were here. Some of the mages translated themselves away to safety, but most of us didn't know how. Travel magic's not a part of evocation. And those who knew didn't bother to carry the rest.

"It hurt when the wave swept through. It was like drowning in pain and glare. But afterward, everything seemed the same, and we laughed and cheered, even after we realized no one else was rushing into the streets to do the same. Because we'd survived, even if the rest of Solzepar hadn't. We decided the wards bound into the foundations of the house had saved us."

"But they hadn't," Bareris said.

"No," the novice said. "In time, it occurred to us that we ought to let our superiors know we were still alive, but that the rest of the town was likely dead. We had an enchanted mirror in our library that allowed us to communicate from afar, and we all gathered around it. And that was when the spells came alive."

Tammith didn't understand. Judging from Bareris's frown, he didn't either. "What spells?" he asked.

"The spells in the scrolls and books on the shelves," the

apprentice said. "I don't know how else to put it. They jumped out all at once, crazy jagged forms whirling around us, all flashing or rimmed with blue. Then one of them, some sort of frost, poured itself into Mistress Kranna's eyes."

"You mean it possessed her?" Bareris asked. "That doesn't make sense. Spells aren't demons. They're just . . . formulae."

"But it did," the novice said, "and as soon as she was a person and the spell both, she grabbed Master Zaras and he fell down. I think the shock of the cold stopped his heart. Then a shadow squirmed into his ear, and he got up again and reached to hurt someone else.

"Half of us were either changed or dead and changed in less time than it takes to tell it. I ran and hid. That's all I know."

"What about this piece of ground, and the others like it, rising into the air?" Tammith asked.

"What? What are you talking about?"

She realized he truly had no idea. He'd been in the chest when the phenomenon began. "You'll see in due course," she said. "For now, don't worry about it."

"We're leaving," Bareris said.

"Without searching the rest of the building or any of the other islands?" she asked.

"Yes. We've seen and heard enough to know what's happening here, and it's not the enemy laying a trap for us. It's the lingering effect of the blue fire tainting the earth. We'll tell the tharchions, and they can decide what to do about it. We don't need—"

"Something's coming," said the sentry at the door.

Tammith rushed to his side and looked down the gallery. Most likely the sentry could only perceive a shadow shuffling in the gloom, but a vampire's eyes saw more clearly. It was a Red Wizard approaching, lurching and flopping as if half his bones were broken.

Yet somehow he contrived to hobble faster, even as he

started to shudder. A whine arose, not from his throat, but from all of him. Tammith inferred that he had absorbed a sound-producing magic, and the power was manifesting. Tongues of blue fire licked around his body.

She stepped onto the walkway, stared into his eyes, and tried to stifle his will. It was no use. Perhaps he had some sort of sentience remaining, but she couldn't even feel his mind, let alone grab hold of it.

The droning abruptly swelled into a deafening roar. The gallery shook, and focused noise smashed into Tammith like a battering ram, flinging her onto her back.

She felt broken bones, and her muscles were pulped. She'd heal in a few moments, but she might not have them. The whine rose in another crescendo.

Bareris scrambled onto the balcony and sang at their foe. The wizard below flailed and collapsed. The power of the bard's voice had dissolved the possessing force inside him.

Bareris crouched over Tammith. "Can you walk?" he asked, and she barely understood the words. The howling attack had nearly deafened her. But her ears would recover as quickly as the rest of her.

"Yes," she said.

"Then get up." He hauled her to her feet. "We're going now. If we can believe the apprentice, there are more of those things, and I likely won't find it as easy to put down the ones inhabited by something other than sound."

As they started their scurry back to the staircase, she saw that they were leaving the sentry behind. Peering around the doorframe, he'd caught only the fringe of the attack sent at her, but it had been sufficient to snap his neck.

The young evoker kept balking as if he'd rather retreat to the illusory safety of the chest. A legionnaire cursed him and shoved him along.

"I should have sensed the creatures," Tammith said, drawing her sword. Her leg throbbed when it took her weight, but the next step was better.

"Not if they were undetectable," Bareris said. "It's a big building, and those things were keeping quiet." He halted abruptly, causing some soldiers to bump into the comrades in front of them.

Shrouded in a wavering blue glow, a robed woman strode along the second-floor gallery. She was in position to block the stairs connecting the lower walkway with their own.

A second staircase lay farther away, but when Tammith peered in that direction, she saw other glowing blue figures, on her level and the ones below. The patrol couldn't avoid confrontation by doubling back. It would only cost them precious time.

Bareris turned to his men. "Get to the top of the stairs, and make a lot of noise. Your job is to keep the mages looking up the steps." He pivoted to Tammith. "You and I will fly or drop down to the next level and hit the wizard while she's distracted."

"I understand," she said. As the soldiers tramped on, speaking loudly, she broke apart into bats and Bareris sang a charm.

She flew out under the skylight. Bareris swung himself over the balcony and plummeted. For an instant, it appeared he'd run afoul of the malaise that rendered magic unreliable, but then the enchantment he'd cast slowed his descent.

Tammith swooped down beside the female wizard. From a distance, the evoker had seemed adequately clad in the usual robe, but in fact, the garment had burned to tatters. So had the skin and flesh beneath, corroded by a fluid seeping from within. The same process shrouded the woman in eye-stinging vapor and charred her footsteps into the floor.

Tammith had no desire to bring any part of her body into contact with the acid or the blue flames flowing across the wizard's form. Better to use her blade. She flew behind the possessed woman, then jerked her several bodies into one.

The wizard evidently heard the flutter of wings or sensed the threat somehow, because she pivoted, but by that time, Tammith was ready for her. She drove her sword into the woman's torso.

Though the evoker collapsed to her knees, the stroke didn't kill or cripple her. She opened her mouth wide, and, guessing what was about to happen, Tammith leaped high into the air. Because she had, the torrent of acidic spew caught only her legs, dissolving pieces of armor and boot and searing the flesh beneath.

Pain flared, and kept burning when she landed in a pool of the corrosive liquid, which immediately started eating through the soles of her boots and into her feet. Unfortunately, she had nowhere else to plant them if she wanted to remain within striking distance of her foe. She cut the evoker again, then Bareris floated down into view. He grabbed the railing at the foot of the steps, heaved himself onto the stairs behind the possessed woman, and drove his glowing sword into her spine.

It took several more blows to finish the evoker, but at last she toppled forward onto her face. Bareris peered at Tammith. "Are you all right?"

"Stop asking me that!" she snapped. "You cut my head off and chopped it to pieces. If that didn't destroy me—" Something shifted in his stony face. Perhaps it was the slightest suggestion of a wince. At any rate, it made her falter. "Never mind. We have to keep moving."

"You're right." He looked to the top of the stairs and waved his arm, urging his men onward.

The scouts made it almost to the ground level before anything else maneuvered into position to attack them. But then luminous blue shadows darted across the floor below, moving to block the door.

Bareris shouted, "Everybody out! Get on your griffons and fly!" He sang five syllables and leaped like a grasshopper.

The prodigious jump carried him out onto the floor to intercept the possessed wizards before they could cut off the patrol's escape. He plainly hoped to keep them occupied long enough for everyone else to flee into the courtyard.

Tammith intended to do exactly that, for like any vampire, she cared first and always about her own well-being. Besides, even if she had felt the slightest twinge of regret at abandoning Bareris, he was commanding this venture, and she was supposed to follow his orders.

Instead, she rushed down and positioned herself beside him.

Another female evoker threw a blast of freezing cold from her outstretched hands, but even though it hit Tammith squarely, it wasn't more than she could bear. Snarling, she slashed at the possessed woman until she toppled.

Next came a wizard with yellow flame hissing from his mouth and nostrils, the true fire leaping amid tongues of eerie blue. His hands were burning, too, and he grabbed hold of her sword arm long enough to brand the print of his fingers into her flesh. She pulled free and gutted him.

The remaining evokers maneuvered to encircle their foes. Bareris shifted so he and Tammith could fight back to back. He started singing another spell.

Tammith's arm ached. With her next opponents already edging in, she didn't have time to wait for it to mend. She shifted her sword to her left hand.

She could see at least a dozen transformed evokers remaining, and experienced a cold, pragmatic urge to flee. If she dissolved into mist, it was doubtful her foes could do anything to detain her.

But she stayed in her human body and made a cut at a creature with eyes like prisms.

Bareris's voice soared through the concluding phrase of his spell. Vibrato throbbing, he held the final note, and then, to Tammith's surprise, his hand gripped her shoulder. She just had time to realize that he'd needed to turn his back on the enemy to do so, and then the world seemed to shatter and reform around them. A cool breeze blew, and above their heads, the night sky glittered with stars.

She realized he'd shifted them a short distance through space, away from their foes and into the courtyard. He ran toward his griffon, and she split apart into bats.

・・　・・　・・　・・　・・　・・　・・　・・　・・　・・　・・

Brightwing liked the quarters—she refused to think of them as "stables"—that the zulkirs had reserved for griffons in the great Central Citadel of Bezantur. They were spacious, airy, and clean, with rough stonework and irregular arches intended to resemble the caverns her kind inhabited in the wild. The food was tasty and plentiful, too—a side of fresh horse carried in by two servants who kept a wary eye on her and moved slowly, to avoid arousing her predatory instincts, she assumed.

But their presence darkened her mood. If all were well, Aoth would personally have made sure she had everything she needed. Unfortunately, that was impossible when he could only see what she saw.

But only humans fretted over things they couldn't change. She pushed worry aside and tore into the bloody meat, bones snapping in her beak.

When she'd devoured half of it, pain ripped through her guts. She screamed, and drops of blood flew out with the sound.

・・　・・　・・　・・　・・　・・　・・　・・　・・　・・　・・

Aoth reached to take hold of the bottle and bumped it off balance instead. He snatched and managed to grab it before it toppled over.

He scowled and wondered why he was bothering to pour the tart wine into a goblet anyway. Easier to just hang onto the bottle and swig from that. He tossed the cup away. It clanked twice—once, he assumed, against the wall, and a second time when it hit the floor. It made a smooth rumbling sound as it rolled.

Then Brightwing shrieked. He was too far away to hear the anguished cry with his ears, but it stabbed through his mind. His belly cramped.

The griffon was hurt or ill, and the problem was in her guts. He recited a charm to purge himself of the befuddlements of intoxication. His wits sharpened, and for a moment, his limbs felt almost painfully sensitive. He groped for his spear, rose, and started for the door.

The latch clicked and the hinges squealed before he made it across the room. "Captain Fezim," said a baritone voice. "Our orders are to escort you to Lauzoril."

Aoth felt a surge of hope. Because the blue fire had afflicted him with a kind of curse, the zulkir of Enchantment might be the best person to cure him. Indeed, Nymia Focar had said she was ordering him to Bezantur instead of sending him home to Pyarados precisely so wise and powerful folk like Lauzoril and Iphegor Nath could try to help him. But until that moment, they hadn't taken any notice of him.

Still, he couldn't neglect Brightwing's distress. "I've been waiting for this for days," he said, "but I can't meet with His Omnipotence right now. Something has happened to my griffon."

"I'm sorry, Captain," the other man said, "but we must all do as the zulkir commands."

"Lauzoril doesn't know the situation. He wouldn't want us to let such a valuable creature come to harm. I don't know precisely what ails her, but it's serious. We need to find a healer skilled in ministering to animals. Then I'll go to His Omnipotence."

"I'm sorry, sir, but you need to go now. Tell Lauzoril about the beast. That might be the fastest way to get help for it, anyway."

As the man spoke, the floorboards creaked almost inaudibly, and metal clinked. Aoth caught a whiff of the oil soldiers used to preserve their mail and weapons. His imagination conjured up the image of armed men creeping into the room.

It didn't make sense. Aoth was a loyal servant of the council of zulkirs. Why would anyone believe that force might be required to bring him into Lauzoril's presence? Yet he was all but certain that several armed men had come for him.

Curse it, he had to know what was really happening! He opened his eyes.

As usual, the black bandage wrapped around his head proved scarcely any impediment to his altered sight. Five legionnaires had entered the room, a human speaking from the doorway and four blood orcs creeping up on him. One of the latter held a set of manacles.

The other three held their empty hands poised to grab him. But for a heartbeat, something painted the semblance of knives into their grips, just as he had seen Bareris dangling a marionette.

Though he couldn't understand the reason, the message seemed clear. If he allowed them to take him, he was as good as dead.

Vision turned to pressure. Soon it would be agony, but he could bear it for another heartbeat. The tattoos had produced that much benefit, anyway. He made note of the exact positions of the orcs, then closed his eyes.

He pivoted and thrust the butt of the spear at the midsection of the orc farthest to the right. Mail clashed as the spear jammed into something solid. Aoth whirled, swung his weapon, and bashed the orc on his left flank.

With luck, that at least balked the two that had been on the verge of seizing him. He reversed the spear, presenting the point, and retreated, meanwhile thrusting and sweeping the weapon through a defensive pattern.

"Why are you doing this?" he asked.

"Please stop fighting," said the soldier in the doorway. "I give you my word, you're panicking over nothing. We only want to help you."

If he wouldn't tell the truth, he was of no use. In fact, Aoth realized, he was dangerous. His babble could mask the sound of the orcs sneaking up on their quarry once again.

Aoth spoke a word of command and discharged magic from the spear. He'd emptied the weapon's reservoir of spells at the Keep of Sorrows, but even though his magic failed as often as not, he had recharged it since. It had given him something to do while he waited for healing, and kept him from feeling quite so helpless.

Now he just had to hope the spell would manifest properly, and when he heard the legionnaires thump down on the floor, a couple of them snoring, it was clear that it had.

He listened intently, just in case the spell hadn't put all his foes to sleep, and probed with the spear as he made his way to the door. Nothing tried to interfere with him, and in due course, he reached the threshold.

He stepped over the man lying there, wondered what to do next, and felt his anxiety ratchet up. What could he do when he didn't understand what was happening? When he was a blind man trapped in a sprawling fortress garrisoned with hundreds of men-at-arms?

Then he realized his course was clear. He'd defied the guards to help Brightwing, and that was still what he had to attempt. Spear extended to feel his way, he headed for the griffons' aerie.

** ** ** ** ** ** ** ** ** ** ** ** ** **

Sensing a presence, Bareris turned. Tammith was looking down at him. The light of the campfire tinged her ivory face with gold and caught in her dark eyes.

"You aren't sleeping," she said.

"No."

"What did the tharchions say? Will the army march straight through Solzepar?"

"They were still talking about it when they dismissed me, but my sense was, probably so."

"I imagine it will be all right. For all we know, it's safer to go somewhere the blue flame's already been than someplace it hasn't yet visited." She hesitated. "May I share your fire?"

"If you like."

She sat down across from him. Wrapped in a blanket on the ground not far behind her, a legionnaire shifted restlessly and mumbled, as though he sensed the presence of something predatory and unnatural lurking close.

"I want to ask you something," Tammith said.

"Go on, then," Bareris replied.

"In the chapterhouse, you meant to sacrifice yourself so everyone else could escape."

He shrugged. "I just played rearguard. I hoped to keep myself alive until everyone else was clear, then sing myself to safety. Which is how it worked out."

It occurred to him that if he'd been capable of playing the same trick on the trail to the cursed ruins of Delhumide a decade before, he might well have succeeded in rescuing her. But the spell was one of many he'd mastered in the years since.

"But you're the commander of the Griffon Legion now, and so your life is more important than that of a common soldier. In your position, many officers would have ordered some of their underlings to hold back the evokers, and never mind that ordinary legionnaires wouldn't have had any hope of survival."

"Not all folk see things as clearly as Thayan captains and patricians. Maybe I picked up some foolish habits of thought while I was away."

In fact, he knew he had—from Eurid, Storik, and the other mercenaries of the Black Badger Company. It was the first time he'd thought of them in a while, for he tried not to. They'd been his faithful friends, and at the time, he'd cherished them and reveled in the exploits they shared. But ultimately he'd learned that his sojourn with them had destroyed his life and Tammith's, too, and that made it impossible to remember them without regret. He realized the vampire's presence was stirring up all sorts of emotions and recollections he generally sought to bury.

"I was harsh that night we talked in the garden," she said, "and I snapped at you after we killed the wizard who'd merged with the acid magic. I wondered if . . ."

He peered at her in surprise. "If I was so distraught that I was trying to commit suicide?"

"Well, yes."

"No. I've never done such a thing. It doesn't seem to be in my nature. Otherwise, I would have let you kill me back in Thazar Keep."

"I'm glad to hear it."

He shook his head. "Does it even matter to you?"

"I fought beside you in that chapterhouse, didn't I, at some risk to myself. I'm harder to slay than a mortal, but not indestructible."

"Is that why you're here? Are you waiting for me to thank you?"

"No! I just wanted you to understand. When I pushed you away before . . . I told you, I want things to be easy. If you craved cherries but they made you sick, would it be easier to live under the cherry tree or a day's ride away from it?"

He sighed. "I understand, and you were right. I don't know how you could tell, but I'm not the same Bareris you knew." He thought of his attempt to control Aoth and what had come of it, and it seemed to him only the latest in an endless chain of failures and shameful acts.

She glanced to the east, watchful for signs of dawn. "I may have been right," she said, "but I now see that what I said wasn't the whole truth. Because, while it's painful to see you and talk to you, it's another kind of torment to keep my distance, too."

His throat was dry, and he swallowed. "What's the answer, then?"

"We're not the young sweethearts anymore, nor will we ever again be. Vampires can't love anyone or anything. But I believe we share a common thirst for revenge, even now, at what feels like the end of the world."

"Yes." Indeed, as he contemplated the bleak, fierce thing the necromancers had made of her, his anger was like a hot stone inside him.

"Then it makes sense for us to stand together. Perhaps, if we try, we can learn to be easy with one another and esteem one another as comrades."

Comrades. It seemed like the bitterest word ever spoken, but he nodded, shook her hand when she offered it, and tried not to wince at the corpselike chill of her flesh.

"If we're to be friends," he said, "then you must tell me something. How did you decide just by looking at me that I'd changed so completely? Do you have the power to peer into my soul?"

She smiled. "Not so much. But when was the last time you looked at yourself in a mirror, or better still, caught a whiff of yourself? The boy I remember tried hard to look like a Mulan noble. You managed to keep yourself clean and your head shaved even growing up in the middle of a shantytown."

"I can't imagine going back to shaving my scalp. Once you give it up, you realize it's a lot of trouble." But maybe he'd find a comb.

•• •• •• •• •• •• •• •• •• •• •• •• •• ••

Mirror dimly recalled that one of his companions had given him that name, but no longer understood why. In fact, he wasn't even certain who they were. He couldn't remember their names or their faces.

That was because he was wearing away to nothing.

Yet he knew he had to persevere, even if he'd entirely forgotten the reason. The sense of obligation endured.

So he walked on through a void devoid of both light and darkness. Either would have defined it, and it rejected definition. He trudged until he forgot how it felt to have legs striding beneath him. With that memory forfeit, he melted into a formless point of view drifting onward, impelled by nothing more than the will to proceed.

I'm almost gone, he thought. I'm not strong enough, and I'm not going to make it. But if that was true, so be it. Defeat couldn't strip a man of his honor. Surrender could. Someone wise and kind had told him that, someone he'd loved like a second father. He could almost see the old man's face.

He suddenly realized he was thinking more clearly, and possessed limbs and a shape once again. Then a torch-lit hall sprang into existence around him, appearing from left to right as though a colossal artist had created it with a single stroke of his paintbrush. In the center of the floor was a huge round table with high-backed chairs, each seat inlaid with a name and coat of arms.

Mirror realized that if he looked, he'd find his own true name and device. With luck, he might even recognize them. Then he glimpsed a towering figure from the corner of his eye. He pivoted, looked at it straight on, and realized he had something infinitely more important to discover.

Half again as tall as Mirror himself, the figure was a golden statue of a handsome, smiling man brandishing a mace in one hand and cradling an orb in the other. Rubies studded the sculpted folds of his clothing. Mirror ran forward and threw himself to his knees before the sacred image.

Warmth, fond as a mother's touch, enfolded him. *You found your way back,* said a voice in his mind.

Tears spilled from Mirror's eyes. "Lord, I'm ashamed. I can't remember your name."

And maybe you never will. It doesn't matter. You're still my true and faithful knight.

•• •• •• •• •• •• •• •• •• •• •• •• •• ••

Since coming to the Central Citadel, Aoth had visited the griffons' aerie at least twice a day. He'd made a point of learning the way so he could walk there by himself, without needing a guide.

Yet in his haste, he'd gone wrong. He should have reached Brightwing by now, but he hadn't, and as he groped his way along a wall, his surroundings seemed completely unfamiliar.

He opened his eyes, but had to close them again immediately. Despite his resolve to use them sparingly, he'd overtaxed them, and for the moment vision was unbearable and useless. He couldn't even tell whether he was indoors or out.

Somewhere nearby, somebody shouted, the noise echoing through the hollow stone spaces of the fortress. Aoth couldn't quite make out the words. He wondered if the legionnaires he'd put to sleep had awakened. If so, maybe the manhunt had begun.

I'm sorry, my friend, Aoth thought. *I couldn't even reach you to sit with you while you die.*

"Captain," said a voice.

Startled, Aoth whirled toward the sound and aimed his spear at it. On the verge of hurling fire from the point, he belatedly recognized Mirror, as much by the chill and intimation of sickness radiating from him as the hollow timbre of his speech.

The ghost's disquieting nature notwithstanding, he and Aoth had been comrades for ten years, and the war mage was loath to lash out at him without cause. But neither could he simply assume that Mirror, who generally functioned as an agent of the zulkirs, hadn't come to kill or detain him. "What do you want?" he panted.

"To help you," Mirror said.

Aoth hesitated. Then, scowling, he decided to take the ghost at his word. "Then take me to Brightwing. We may have to dodge legionnaires along the way. For some reason, Lauzoril wants to kill me. I think he had Brightwing poisoned so I couldn't summon her to protect me."

"Your steed will have to wait. I need to help you now, while I still remember what to do."

"The way to help is to get me to Brightwing."

"I need to heal your eyes first."

Aoth felt a jolt of astonishment. "Can you do that?"

"I think so. After Bareris betrayed our bonds of fellowship, I had to set things right. And I sensed that I could, if I could only remember more of who and what I was."

"Did you?"

"Yes, when I went into the emptiness. I remembered I was a knight pledged to a god, who blessed me with special gifts."

"A paladin, you mean?" Thay had no such champions, because it didn't worship the deities who raised them up. But Aoth had heard about them.

Mirror hesitated as if he didn't recognize the term. "Perhaps. The important thing is that my touch could heal, and I believe it still can. Let me use it to cure your sight."

Aoth shook his head. *Maybe* the ghost with his addled, broken mind had remembered something real. *Maybe* he truly had possessed a talent for healing. That didn't mean he still had it. Every wizard knew that undead creatures partook of the very essence of blight and ill, and Aoth had witnessed many times how Mirror's mere touch could wither and corrupt. The sword with which he wrought such havoc in battle wasn't even a weapon as such, just a conduit for the cancerous power inside him.

Yet even so, and rather to his own surprise, Aoth felt a sudden inclination to trust Mirror. Perhaps it was because his plight was so hopeless that, if the spirit's suggestion didn't work, it was scarcely likely to matter anyway.

"All right. Let's do it." Aoth pulled off the bandage, then felt the ambient sense of malaise thicken as Mirror came closer. Freezing cold, excruciating as the touch of a white-hot iron, stabbed down on each of his eyelids. He bore it for a heartbeat or two, then screamed, recoiled, and clapped his hands to his face.

"Damn you!" he croaked. He wondered if he looked older, the way Urhur Hahpet had after the ghost slid his insubstantial fingers into his torso.

"Try your eyes now," Mirror said, unfazed by his anguished reproach.

The suggestion seemed so ridiculous that it left Aoth at a loss for words. He was still trying to frame a suitably bitter retort when he realized that his eyes didn't hurt anymore.

And since they didn't, he supposed he could muster the fortitude to test them. He warily cracked them open, then gasped. Seeing wasn't the least bit painful, and somehow he could already tell it never would be again.

Indeed, vision was a richer experience than ever before.

Wandering blind, he'd blundered into the covered walkway connecting two baileys. No lamps or torches burned in the passage, yet the gloom didn't obscure his vision. He could make out subtle variations of blackness in the painted stone wall beside him and complex patterns in the dusty cobbles beneath his feet. He could only liken the experience to borrowing Brightwing's keen aquiline eyes, but in truth, he was seeing even better now than he had then.

He realized he'd been seeing in this godlike fashion ever since the blue fire swept over him, but the torrent of sheer detail had overwhelmed him. Now he could assimilate it with the same unthinking ease that ordinary people processed normal perceptions.

He turned to the wavering shadow that was Mirror. "You did it!"

"My brothers always said I had a considerable gift. Sometimes I could help the sick when even the wisest priests had failed. Or I think I could." Mirror's voice trailed off as if his memory was crumbling away, and his murky form became vaguer still.

Aoth wondered if the act of healing, so contrary to the normal attributes of a ghost, had drained his benefactor of strength. He prayed not. "Don't disappear! Stay with me! If you can cure blindness, you should be able to cure a poisoning, too. We're going to Brightwing."

This late at night, no one was working in the griffons' aerie. Aoth felt a surge of anguish to see his familiar crumpled on her side, eyes glazed and oblivious, blood and vomit pooled around her beak. He reached out with his mind but found no trace of hers. She was still breathing, though.

"Hurry!" he said, but Mirror just stood in place. "Please!"

"I'm trying to remember," Mirror said, and still he didn't move. Finally, when Aoth felt he was on the brink of screaming, the ghost flowed forward, kneeled beside the griffon, whispered, and stroked her head and neck. His intangible hand sank ever so slightly into her plumage.

Brightwing thrashed, then leaped to her feet and swiped with her talons. Thanks to spells Aoth had cast long ago, her claws were capable of shredding a spirit, but Mirror avoided them with a leap backward.

"Easy!" Aoth cried. "Mirror just saved your life, or at least I hope so. How are you?"

"My belly hurts." Brightwing took a breath. "So does my head, and my mouth burns." She spat. "But I think I'll be all right."

Aoth's eyes brimmed with tears. He hoped he wouldn't shed them, because the griffon would only jeer if he did.

"We're going to find the vermin who poisoned me," she continued, "and then I'm going to eat *them*."

The vengeful declaration served to remind Aoth that they were still in trouble. "I'd like to watch you do it, but we can't fight the whole Central Citadel."

"Would we have to?" Brightwing's voice took on an unaccustomed querulous note. "What's happening?"

"People suddenly want to kill me, and they knew it would be easier if you were out of the way. So they tried to separate us back in Zolum, and when that didn't work, they fed you tainted meat."

Brightwing snorted. "I should have realized that, as usual, you're to blame for any unpleasantness that comes my way. All right, if it's like that, saddle me and we'll flee the city."

It was good advice, especially considering that Aoth had intended to run off anyway, until Bareris tampered with his mind. So it surprised him to realize just how reluctant he was to go.

Deserting because he wanted to was one thing. Fleeing because he feared for his life would leave him feeling baffled and defeated. It would also mean he could never command the

Griffon Legion again. He'd never aspired to do so, and in the years since his elevation, he'd honestly believed he didn't enjoy the responsibility. But after blindness rendered him unfit to lead, he discovered he missed it. Indeed, he'd felt guilty and worthless because he couldn't look out for his men anymore.

"Besides . . . since I don't understand why this is happening," he said, "I don't know how just badly people want to kill me. It may be badly enough to hunt us down if we try to run. I also have misgivings about fleeing when earthquakes and tides of blue fire are ripping the world apart. It doesn't seem a promising time to try to build a new life in some foreign land."

"Then what will we do?" Brightwing asked.

"You'll stay here with Mirror and be quiet. I'll talk to Lauzoril and try to straighten things out."

"That's assuming that he or his minions don't strike you down on sight."

"I think I know who can prevent it, if only I can reach him."

Brightwing snorted. "It sounds stupid to me, but when has that ever stopped you?" She cocked her head. "Say, you aren't wearing your blindfold."

•• •• •• •• •• •• •• •• •• •• •• •• ••

Perhaps it was Malark's imagination, but the ash shaft of the spear seemed to shudder in his grip as though it resented resting in any hand but its master's. He wondered if that could possibly be true, if the weapon was in some sense alive and aware. Perhaps he'd have a chance to ask Aoth about it later, but for now, they had a more urgent matter to address.

Malark hadn't expected to see his comrade again, because he'd heard what fate Dmitra had decreed for him. And although it wasn't the death he would have chosen for Aoth, there hadn't been a reason to intervene. But when, with his lambent blue eyes uncovered and obviously no longer blind, the war mage slipped into Malark's apartments, it was plain the situation had altered.

A small, flat-faced goblin guard used its apelike arms to open the red metal door to Lauzoril's conjuration chamber. When Aoth saw what waited on the other side, he stopped short. Malark didn't blame him.

The room beyond the threshold was the sort of arcane workroom familiar to them both after years spent at the beck and call of wizards. The steady white glow of enchanted spherical lamps illuminated racks of staves and ceremonial swords, a stylized wall painting of a tree that, as Dmitra had once explained, represented the multiverse, and an intricate pentacle inlaid in jet and carnelian on the floor. A thurible suffused the air with the bitter scent of myrrh.

The surprise was the steel table with sturdy buckled straps to immobilize a man, gutters to drain away his blood, and an assortment of probes, forceps, and knives to pick and slice at him. A healer might conceivably have used such equipment. So did a number of the interrogators in Malark's employ.

"Steady!" he whispered. "It's too late to run. They'll only kill you if you try." As if to demonstrate that he was right, a pair of blood orc guards and a Red Wizard of Enchantment advanced to take charge of Aoth.

Aoth strode into the chamber, and Malark followed a pace behind him. An orc reached to seize hold of Aoth's arm. Shifting, the griffon rider evaded the creature's hand and shoved it into its fellow. The pair got tangled up and fell down together.

The Red Wizard jumped back a step and lifted a fist with a pearl ring on the forefinger. Brightness seethed inside the milky stone. Malark interposed himself between the enchanter and Aoth and gave the former a glare and a shake of his head.

Flummoxed if not intimidated, the wizard hesitated.

By then, Lauzoril's other minions were scrambling to intercept Aoth, but they were too slow. He had time to march up to the zulkir and drop to his knees without anyone coercing him. Malark did the same.

Lauzoril frowned. It was a pinched little frown, just as all his smiles were grudging little smiles. "Well," he said, "it's taken half the night, but someone finally caught him."

"No, Your Omnipotence," Malark said, "I didn't. As you surely observed, Captain Fezim obeys your summons of his own volition. Neither I nor anyone else had to force him."

"He resisted the escort I sent to fetch him," Lauzoril said.

"That was a misunderstanding," Malark said. "You'll note, he extricated himself from the situation without seriously hurting anyone. He's too loyal a legionnaire to rob you of the use of any of your servants, even in a moment of alarm and confusion."

"Good." Lauzoril shifted his gaze to Aoth. "Captain, if you are the man your companion claims you are, a faithful soldier willing to give his life in the service of his liege lords, then permit the orcs to secure you on the table, and I'll undertake to make what follows as painless as is practical. Refuse, and my enchantments will compel you."

"Master," Malark said, "may I respectfully ask why you're doing this?"

"Don't you know? It was your mistress's idea."

"No, Master," Malark lied, "she didn't confide in me."

"Then I suppose I can explain. She suggested I examine the griffon rider with all the tools at my disposal and see what I can discover about the blue flame."

"I assume she recommended this while Captain Fezim was blind and unable to perform his usual duties."

"Well, yes."

"Your Omnipotence has surely observed that he has now recovered his sight."

"Of course. I'm not a dunce. But his eyes are still glowing, and I still think it may prove worthwhile to study him."

"I respectfully suggest that my mistress would disagree."

"Then it's too bad she's in Eltabbar this evening, isn't it? Otherwise you could run and ask her. Not that I would feel obliged to accede to her notions if they ran counter to my own."

"No, Your Omnipotence, of course not. It's only that Captain Fezim is one of Nymia Focar's ablest officers—"

Lauzoril snorted. "He's just a soldier. Another such commands the Griffon Legion now, and I imagine he'll do every bit as well. Better, probably, considering he's Mulan."

"You're correct, Bareris Anskuld is also a fine soldier, but—"

A trace of color tinged Lauzoril's cheeks. "Goodman Springhill, your prattle wearies me. If you persist, I'm apt to decide you aren't just tiresome but insolent, and then, you may rest assured, your affiliation with Dmitra Flass won't shield you from my displeasure."

Malark noticed his mouth was dry.

He wasn't afraid to die. But it was entirely possible the archmage had something else in mind. The art of Enchantment lent itself to punishments that crippled and degraded both body and mind but left the victim alive. And despite his prim demeanor, Lauzoril had as sophisticated a sense of cruelty as any other zulkir.

Yet Malark intended to try the wizard's patience for at least a little longer, even though he himself wasn't entirely sure of the reason. Maybe he was simply stubborn, or averse to losing an argument.

"I understand, Master," he said, "but I think I'd be remiss in my responsibilities if I didn't at least point out that Captain Fezim isn't the only creature infected with blue fire. We've received reports of others, and I assume that if you vivisected them, the bodies would yield the same information."

"I remember those reports," Lauzoril said. "The other creatures have become dangerous monstrosities."

"Still, my agents can trap an assortment of them," Malark said. "It will just take a bit of doing. It will delay your investigations a little, but that could work to your advantage. It will give you a chance to involve Mistress Lallara."

"To what end?" Lauzoril asked.

"I shouldn't even presume to speculate," Malark said. "After all, you know everything there is to know about the supernatural, while I know virtually nothing. But I wonder—if the blue fire can get inside a person or animal, generally with hideous results, maybe it can jump from one living being to another. Maybe it would even try to invade you when you cut into the creature. If so, you might want the defensive spells of the zulkir of Abjuration to make sure the power didn't possess you."

"Ridiculous," Lauzoril snapped. "I too am a zulkir. I don't need that shrew or anyone else to protect me. However"—he took a breath—"if a legionnaire is fit for duty, perhaps it would be improvident to sacrifice him when an altered pig or some such would serve just as well. Captain Fezim, you're dismissed. Go away and take this . . . jabberer with you."

"Yes, Your Omnipotence." Aoth held his head high and maintained a proper military bearing until the goblin closed the crimson door behind him and Malark. Then his squat, broad-shouldered frame slumped so completely that for a moment it looked as if his legs might give way beneath him. "By the Flame," he sighed. "By the Pure Flame. I didn't think you were going to convince him."

"To be honest," Malark said, "neither did I. I'm still not sure which argument did the trick. Probably the last. For all their might, zulkirs aren't eager to risk their own skins, particularly when they don't understand the peril. That's how they live long enough to become zulkirs, I suppose. Here, take this." He gave Aoth his spear.

The war mage gripped his shoulder. "I won't forget this."

Malark smiled. "I was glad to help." Aoth had killed a great many men in his time. It felt right to set him free to slaughter more, and to seek an end more befitting such a warrior.

chapter five

29 Mirtul–2 Kythorn, the Year of Blue Fire

Like many orcs, Neske Horthor would have taken offense at the suggestion that she'd ever felt "pity." But it took only a dash of brains to recognize that the prisoners had it hard, marching on short rations day after day with whips slicing into their backs and fear gnawing at their nerves. It was no wonder that one occasionally dropped dead, succumbing to exhaustion, fever, or pure despair.

Such a child had keeled over that day, whereupon Neske halted the march long enough to dress the corpse. It was wrong of her, she supposed. She should have carried the body on to Xingax. But he'd never know about it unless somebody tattled, and Khazisk wouldn't. She and the necromancer had worked together long enough to come to an understanding.

She pulled her skewer back from the campfire, inspected the chunks of fragrant, blackened meat impaled on it, and offered it to Khazisk, sitting cross-legged beside her with the sweep of his red robe pooled around him. "Try it. It's good."

The wizard's narrow, supercilious face screwed up as she'd known it would. "Thank you, no."

She laughed. "You do all sorts of nasty things with rotten bodies. I've watched you. But your stomach rolls over at the prospect of fresh meat, just because it happens to come from your own kind. If you had any sense, you'd realize that's the most nourishing kind of food."

"You're saying you eat orc?"

"Every chance I get." She bit the top piece of juicy meat from the skewer. It was too hot, and seared the roof of her mouth, but she wolfed it down anyway. "You know, it's a puzzle."

"What is?"

"Our real enemies, the ones we're at war with, are in the south. Yet our masters have us sneaking in and out of Thesk, raiding villages and capturing the peasants."

"You mean paradox, not puzzle."

She rolled her eyes. He loved to correct her speech. "Whatever it is, it's stupid."

"Not really. Xingax will turn our captives into potent weapons of war. The result is a net gain in the strength of our legions."

"Maybe." Neske tore another bite of child flesh off the stick. "But when Szass Tam is king, will anyone remember that this chore was important and we did it well? Or will all the rewards go to the warriors who stormed Bezantur and chopped off Nevron and Dmitra Flass's heads?"

"As far as I'm concerned," Khazisk said, "our fellow soldiers are welcome to such opportunities. You and I are better off here in the north. If I never see one of the council's warriors—"

A ram's-horn bugle bleated. On the western edge of the camp, a sentry was sounding the alarm.

Trained reflex made Neske snatch for the targe that lay beside her and leap to her feet. But though her body knew what to do, her mind lagged a step behind, mired in perplexity. It would have made sense if an attack had come while she and her comrades were across the border in Thesk, or even during the trek through Surthay and Eltabbar. But once the slave takers finished the climb up the Third Escarpment into High Thay, they should have been safe.

"Look up!" someone shouted. Neske did, and made out winged shadows sweeping across the sky.

"Griffon riders," Khazisk said. He stood up and brandished his staff over his head. The pole was a gleaming white, whittled down from a dragon's leg bone, or so he claimed. He chanted words that, even though she couldn't understand them, filled Neske with an instinctual revulsion. A carrion stink filled the air.

But that was all that happened. The magic failed.

Khazisk cursed and began again. Four syllables into the spell, an arrow punched into the center of his forehead. He toppled backward.

Neske decided she needed her bow and quiver, not her scimitar and shield. She pivoted toward the place where she'd set the rest of her gear. Then the world seemed to skip somehow, and she was lying on her belly. When she tried to stand, and pain ripped through her back, she understood that an arrow had found her, too.

•• •• •• •• •• •• •• •• •• •• •• •• •• ••

Griffon riders were trained to hit their targets even when their mounts were swooping through the air, and the first flights of arrows did an admirable job of softening up the enemy on the ground. Then the orcs started shooting back.

Bareris was confident his troops would prevail in a duel of archery. But possibly not before the orcs managed to kill a griffon or two, and their masters with them when the stricken beasts plummeted to earth. Better to prevent that by ending the battle quickly.

"Dive!" he said, projecting his voice so every legionnaire would hear. He nudged the back of Murder's feathery neck, and the griffon hurtled toward the ground.

An arrow streaked past Bareris's head. Then Murder slammed down on top of an orc, his momentum snapping its bones, his talons piercing it. The sudden stop jolted Bareris, but his tack was designed to cushion such shocks, and a decade of aerial combat had taught him how to brace himself.

Another orc charged with an axe raised over its head. Murder twisted his neck and snapped at the warrior, biting through boiled-leather armor and tearing its chest apart before it could strike. Bareris looked around but couldn't find another foe within reach of his sword.

In fact, opponents were in short supply all across the battlefield. Orcs were no match for griffons, and the animals were quickly ripping them apart.

That didn't mean everything was under control. Some of the prisoners were cowering amid the carnage, but others were scrambling into the darkness.

Bareris kicked Murder's flanks, and the griffon lashed his wings and sprang into the air. Bareris flew the beast over several fleeing Theskians, then plunged down to block their path. They froze.

"You can't run away," he said. He'd never had the opportunity to learn Damaran, the language of Thesk, but bardic magic would make it sound as if he had. "My comrades and I will kill you if you try. Turn around and go back to the campfires."

The gaunt, haggard folk with their rags and whip scars stared at him. Were they so desperate for freedom that they'd attempt a dash past a griffon and the swordsman astride his back?

A huge wolf padded out of the darkness and stationed itself at Murder's side. It bared its fangs and growled at the captives.

The two beasts made an uncanny pair. Murder was terrible in his ferocity, but his was the clean savagery of nature's predators. The wolf, on the other hand, gave off a palpable feel of the uncanny, of corruption and destruction fouler than death, and perhaps it was the sheer horror of its presence that made the Theskians quail, then turn and scurry back the way they'd come.

Bareris kicked Murder into the air to look for other escapees. He and his companions couldn't be certain they'd collected them all, but they rounded up most of them. Afterward, he set down and dismounted, and the wolf melted back into Tammith.

"So far, so good," she said.

"Thanks to you," he said, and it was true. In times past, even a flying company couldn't foray onto the Plateau of Ruthammar without encountering swift and overwhelming resistance. But Tammith knew how to evade the scrutiny of the watchers overseeing the approaches.

Someone would discover their intrusion soon enough. But if they finished their business quickly and withdrew, they might be all right.

She gave him a smile. "You're too kind."

Bareris lifted his hand to stroke her cheek, then caught himself. Something knotted in his chest.

Ever since they'd agreed to treat one another cordially, as comrades, the same thing had happened to him over and over again. It felt like the most natural thing in the world to have her at his side. It warmed him as nothing had in ten years.

Then he would remember that nothing was really the same. He'd lost her and could never have her again. In truth, she'd even lost herself. By her own admission, she was only a husk, a vile parody of the sweet, generous girl he'd loved. And the realization brought a stab of anguish.

Perhaps she noticed the aborted caress, and perhaps it made her uncomfortable. She turned away, toward the huddled captives.

"Looking for your supper?" he asked. Even as he spoke, he felt shame at the spite in his tone. He had no right to be angry with her. Her condition was his fault, not hers.

"No," she said. "I'm all right for now. I was just thinking. For all these wretches know, they've simply passed from the hands of one band of marauders to those of another."

"Haven't they?"

"Well, at least we don't mean to turn them into zombies. It might comfort them to know that."

He shook his head. "If we tried to make them our willing collaborators, they'd be actors playing a role, and perhaps not convincingly. It's better if they don't think anything has changed."

"I suppose. They're likely to die anyway, aren't they, even if they survive in Xingax's fortress. Because they'll still be stuck in the center of Szass Tam's domain. We certainly aren't going to fly them home."

"Would you, if you could?"

She sneered, whether at the suggestion or herself, he wasn't sure. "I doubt it. What are they to me? It's just . . . seeing them reminds me of when I was one of the slaves being marched into Xingax's clutches, and you were the gallant young fool striving to rescue me. Now we're the drovers flogging the thralls along. It makes you think, is all."

"What are you thinking?"

"Oh, I suppose that the wrongs that the world inflicts on us all can never be set right. They can only be avenged. Perhaps I will slake my thirst after all." She strode away.

The stronghold stood among the desolate foothills of the Thaymount. It presented the façade of an imposing keep, with massive gates at ground level and little round windows and arrow loops above. But it had no other walls, or at least none visible from the outside, because its builder had carved it into the face of a cliff.

Supposedly, he'd been a conjuror, and Tammith winced to think how much trouble someone must have had evicting him from this seemingly impregnable redoubt after Szass Tam and the council went to war. But the lich's servants had managed it, and afterward, Xingax moved in. Now that his existence and endeavors were no longer a secret, he could work more effectively in the center of the realm than in a remote fastness in the Sunrise Mountains.

The conjuror had made efforts to cultivate the approaches to his private retreat, but now the hillsides were going to brush and scrub—pallid, twisted plants altered by the spillover of necromantic energies from within the citadel. Tammith wished the wizard had left the land barren, because she had a nagging sense that something was shadowing her, her comrades, and the captives through the thick and tangled growth. But, her keen senses notwithstanding, she couldn't tell exactly where or what it was.

Maybe it was just an animal, or one of Xingax's escaped or discarded experiments, and perhaps it didn't matter anyway. If it was a sentinel, the impostors had fooled it, or it would have acted already. If it was anything else, it was unlikely to slink too close to the pale stone gates looming dead ahead.

"We have captives," Bareris called, his face shadowed and his long hair covered by the cowl of his cloak. Tammith tugged the scarf she'd wrapped around the lower portion of her face up another fraction, because it was possible the sentries knew the captain of the Silent Company had deserted.

"What's the sign?" someone shouted back. Tammith couldn't see him, but knew he was speaking from a hidden observation port above the gate.

"Mother love," Bareris answered, and Tammith waited to see if the sign was still valid, or if their luck was so foul that Xingax had changed it. She doubted he had. He claimed to be an aborted demigod, and certainly looked like an aborted *something*. The password was his sardonic jape at the parent who'd torn him prematurely from her womb, or permitted someone else to do the deed.

The white stone gates groaned open to reveal what amounted to a barbican, even though it didn't project out from the body of the citadel. It was a passageway with murder holes in the ceiling, arrow loops in the walls, and a single exit at the far end.

In other words, the passage was a killing box, but only if soldiers had positioned themselves to do the killing. The orc and human warriors inside the torchlit space didn't look as if they suspected anything amiss. The valves at the end stood open, and the portcullis was up.

The Theskians balked at entering, and Bareris's men shoved and whipped them onward. An orc, its left profile tattooed with jagged black thunderbolts and its jutting tusks banded with gold, swaggered around inspecting the captives. Tammith wondered if it was looking for someone to rape, like the guard who'd accosted Yuldra and her when they were prisoners.

Whatever was in its mind, it abruptly pivoted and peered at her. "Hey," it said, "I know you."

She met its gaze and sought to smother its will with her own. "No, you don't."

The orc blinked and stumbled back a step. "No," it mumbled, "I don't." It started to wander off, and she turned away from it.

At once it bawled, "This is the vampire that ran off!" She pivoted around to see the creature pointing at her. She hadn't succeeded in clouding its mind after all. It had only pretended she had.

Well, perhaps the memory of that little victory would warm its spirit in the afterlife. She sprang at it, punched it in the face, and felt its skull shatter. The blow hurled it backward and down. Tammith whirled and cast about, trying to assess the situation.

The orc's comrades had no doubt heard it yell, but they were slow to react. Bareris's warriors were not, and cut down Xingax's guards before the latter could even draw weapons.

The problem was the captives, terrified and confused by the outbreak of hostilities, scurrying to stay clear of leaping blades or bolting back the way they'd come. They clogged the passageway and made it difficult for the invading force to reach the far end.

Tammith dissolved into bats and flew over the heads of battling warriors and panicky Theskians. Meanwhile, the gates ahead of her swung inward. She hurtled through the remaining space and discovered zombies pushing the panels shut.

Bat bites had little effect on animated corpses, so, as fast as she could, she pulled herself into human guise, suffering a flash of pain for her haste. She drew her sword and started cutting.

As the last zombie collapsed, she glimpsed motion from the corner of her eye. Two more dead men, gray skin flaking, jaws slack, were fumbling to release the brake on the windlass and drop the portcullis. She charged and slashed them to pieces. Then she looked around, seeking the person who'd commanded them, but he'd retreated.

He could have fled in a number of directions. Half a dozen arches opened on this spacious central hall. Stairs ascended to a gallery, where other doorways granted access to the chambers beyond.

Yellow eyes gleaming, several dread warriors ran out onto the balcony and laid arrows on their bows. Even from her distance, she felt the magical virulence seething in the barbed points. She could have made herself impervious to the shafts by turning to mist, but mist couldn't keep the gates open and the portcullis raised. She poised herself to dodge.

Then a Burning Brazier armed with a chain peered warily through the half-open gate. He spotted the dread warriors and brandished his weapon at them. The links clattered and burst into flames. The dead men exploded into a roaring blaze that burned them to ash in an instant.

The brassy notes of a glaur horn echoed down the passageway at Tammith's back. The attacking force had secured the gate, and Bareris was calling the griffons, and the riders who'd stayed with them, down from the sky.

•• •• •• •• •• •• •• •• •• •• •• •• •• •• ••

Squirming on his padded chair, the cushions, though recently replaced, already stained and stinking with the effluvia of his decaying body, Xingax squinted down at the Red Wizard laboring in the conjuration chamber below the balcony. Squinting didn't bring the scene below into sharper focus, so he closed the myopic eye he'd possessed since birth and looked through the one he'd appropriated from Ysval's corpse. That was better.

It would have been better still if he could have hovered at his assistant's side, but that wasn't practical. His mere proximity was toxic to the living. Although perhaps the idiot chanting and flourishing his athame deserved a dose of poison, because he was useless.

But no, that wasn't fair. Much as Xingax wished he could blame the human for botching the ritual, the fellow had performed each successive revision competently enough. The problem was that the laws of magic were changing, and as a result, Xingax found himself unable to exploit them as cunningly as before.

The fact distressed him. He lacked the natural aptitude to practice necromancy to any great effect, but he deemed himself Faerûn's greatest inventor of necromantic spells, greater in that regard than even Szass Tam, though he had more discretion than to tell his master so. It was his pride and his passion, the deepest delight of a being forever barred from many of the joys natural creatures took for granted.

What if he couldn't work out the new rules? Or what if the balance of mystical forces never stabilized, and therefore no constant, reliable principles ever crystallized? Then he would never again be the sage and brilliant creator. The possibility was terrible to contemplate. So much so that, while he understood he ought to be concerned about more tangible misfortunes—with magic crippled, Szass Tam could lose the war, or cast him off as useless, or blue fire could destroy all Thay and him with it—he could scarcely find it within himself to care about them.

The wizard shouted the climactic words of the incantation. He gashed his forehead with the ritual dagger, swiped at the welling blood with his fingertips, and spattered scarlet droplets across the object of his spell.

For a moment, nothing happened, and Xingax felt his mood sour even further. Then glazed eyes rolled from side to side. A leathery tongue slid over rows of jagged fangs to lick gray, withered lips, but couldn't moisten them.

Something writhed beneath trailing whiskers the color of tarnished brass. Protruding from the ragged neck, tangled guts and veins slithered and clutched to heave the entity across the floor.

The colossal severed head had belonged to a cloud giant sorcerer, and if the reanimation had worked properly, it should still possess arcane powers akin to those it wielded in life. Xingax was suddenly confident that it had worked. By all the lords in shadow, he was still a master of his particular art and always would be, no matter how many deities assassinated one another.

Elsewhere in the fortress, a glaur blared. The unexpected sound extinguished Xingax's jubilation like a splash of water snuffing a candle. His retainers didn't use horns.

An instant later, the door to the chamber below him banged open, and a hunched, shriveled ghoul with foxfire eyes lunged through. The creature faltered when it saw the swollen disembodied head shifting around, but only for a moment.

"Enemies!" it cried, in a voice like a jackal's snarl.

Xingax scowled. He'd believed he'd escaped the battlefields of Szass Tam's war, but it seemed that somehow, conflict had followed him home. "Outside the gates?" he asked.

"No, Master, already inside! I think they tricked the guards!"

That was unexpected, and serious enough to give Xingax a pang of genuine apprehension, because the fortress was lightly garrisoned. It didn't require an abundance of soldiers to control the prisoners awaiting transformation, and no one had expected it would need to repel a siege.

Still, he assured himself, he could cope if he kept a clear head. "Tell everyone to contain the intruders in the central hall," he said to the ghoul, then shifted his gaze to the bloody-faced necromancer. "You woke the giant's head, and it will obey you. Get it into battle."

As his minions scurried to obey him, Xingax sought to enter a light trance. Anxiety made it more difficult than usual, but he managed. He sent his awareness soaring outside the fortress to find his watchdog.

It was hard to imagine that his foes could have slain the creature, let alone have done so without making enough commotion to rouse the citadel, and in fact, it was still creeping through the brush. Evidently, the southerners' "trick," whatever it had been, had fooled it as completely as the legionnaires protecting the gate.

Well, it wasn't too late for the beast to avert calamity, for it was one of the most formidable beings Xingax had ever created, so much so that he'd almost felt guilty withholding it from the legions. But he hadn't survived as long as he had without giving some thought to his own personal protection. Besides, an artist was entitled to retain possession of one or two masterpieces, wasn't he?

He touched the entity's mind, and it bounded toward the fortress.

·· ·· ·· ·· ·· ·· ·· ·· ·· ·· ·· ·· ·· ··

Bareris stood in the gate and waved the griffons and their riders into the entryway. In that enclosed space, the distinctive smell of the beasts, half fur and half feathers, was enough to make his eyes water.

Murder furled his wings and touched down on the ground. Bareris hadn't expected any harm to befall his mount while they were apart. Still, it was good to see the animal hale and ready to fight.

So far, he thought, everything was going well. Then a huge shape crashed out of the brush.

At that moment, Bareris could see in the dark like an orc. It was one of several charms he'd laid on himself just prior to approaching the fortress. Thus, he beheld the oncoming beast clearly. It resembled a dead and rotting dragon, with a saurian head, four legs, and a tail. But the neck was too short, and it had no wings. Tentacles writhed from its shoulders, and weeping sores the size of saucers dotted its mottled, charcoal-colored body. Frozen with shock, Bareris wondered how such an immense creature had managed to conceal itself.

His paralysis lasted only a heartbeat, but as fast as the behemoth was charging, that could have doomed him and his companions. But as it happened, a dozen fleeing Theskians were between the lizard-thing and the cliff face, and it paused to slaughter them. Tentacles picked them up and squeezed, and the flesh of those so grappled flowed like molten wax. Clawed feet stamped others to pulp, and gnashing jaws chewed the rest to pieces.

Bareris saw that all the soldiers couldn't squeeze into the passage in time to escape the behemoth, nor did this disorganized clump of men and griffons have any hope of turning and fighting it effectively. "You!" he shouted, gesturing to everyone still outside, "get in the air and shoot the thing! Everyone else, stand clear of the gates and push them shut!"

The legionnaires scrambled to obey. To his relief, the heavy stone leaves swung easily on their hinges, and the bar slid just as readily in its greased brackets.

As soon as it was in position, the gates boomed and jolted. A few moments later, the same thing happened, and a crack appeared in the bar.

"It won't hold!" a griffon rider cried.

"No," Bareris said, "it won't. Everyone—through the corridor and out the other end!" They pounded down the entryway and he brought up the rear.

When he emerged into the central hall, he found what he expected. Xingax's guards had positioned themselves to keep the attackers from advancing any farther. A motley assortment of orc, goblin, gnoll, and human soldiers, Red Wizards, zombies, and more formidable undead blocked every doorway and threw missiles and spells from the gallery overhead.

In other words, the intruders were encircled and the defenders held the high ground, but the southerners had such a significant advantage in numbers that it ought not to have mattered. But the monstrosity outside changed everything.

"Shut these gates!" he shouted to the men who'd sprinted in ahead of him. "Drop the portcullis!"

With blood smeared down the length of her sword and on her lips and chin, Tammith hurried up to him. "What's wrong?" she asked.

"The creature Xingax kept outside is coming for us," he replied. "Why didn't you warn me about it?"

"I didn't know about it," she said. "I haven't been here in three years. He must have animated it since my last visit. What is it?"

"I don't know. But it's bad, and we won't be able to keep it out. Most of us will have to turn and fight it, but not everyone can, or the rest of Xingax's servants will tear us apart from behind. I want you to take charge of holding them in check."

"I will," she said.

The interior gates rumbled shut, and the portcullis clanged down. "Something big is coming up behind us!" Bareris shouted. "I need all our spellcasters to hit it as soon as it comes into sight, and all our griffons to swarm on it the instant it knocks down the portcullis. We're going to destroy it while it's still in the entryway, with the walls confining it."

His troops scurried to prepare to attack as he'd ordered. Across the chamber and overhead, blood orc sergeants bellowed, exhorting their own men to greater efforts now that so many of the foe had turned their backs.

The secondary gates crashed three times, then shattered into shards. At once the southern mages and priests hurled their power at the horror lurching from the wreckage. Thanks to the gaps between the steel bars, the portcullis didn't stop flares or beams of mystical energy.

Blasts of Kossuth's fire charred patches of the creature's reptilian mask. Darts of blue light pierced it. A dazzling, sizzling lightning bolt stabbed into its breast, but failed even to leave a mark. Bareris hammered it with a shout. The Red Wizard of Evocation beside him pointed an ivory wand, spat a word of command, then cursed when nothing happened.

The lizard-thing kept coming, and smashed through the portcullis as though that barrier were as flimsy as a cobweb. But the twisted remains of the grillwork tangled around its feet, hampering it, and at that moment, while the back half of its body still lay inside the entryway, the griffons and their riders launched themselves at it. Bareris swung himself onto Murder's back and rushed to join the fray.

Beaks, talons, spears, and swords tore oozing, reeking undead flesh. A tentacle snaked past Bareris and Murder to wrap around another griffon and its master. It squeezed so hard that the legionnaire's body all but flattened with a crackle of snapping bone, and some of the beast's insides popped out of its gaping maw.

Murder bit and clawed the tentacle, severing it. Bareris turned his steed toward the lizard-thing's flank. The seeping chancres scarring the behemoth's hide shuddered and bubbled, and then something exploded out of them to darken the air like smoke.

The discharge was all around Bareris before he could make out what it was—a cloud of locusts, or something like them. The vermin crawled on him, biting and stinging. The pain was excruciating, and was surely worse for Murder, who lacked the protection of armor. The griffon snapped a few of his tormentors out of the air, but that could bring no relief when dozens of the vile things were clinging to his plumage and fur.

It wouldn't help Bareris to flail with his sword, either. He struggled to resist the panicky impulse, focus past his pain, and muster the concentration necessary for magic. When he started singing the spell, a locust sought to clamber into his mouth, but he swiped it away.

Power chimed through the air, and coolness tingled over his body. The locusts sprang away, repelled by the ward he'd conjured.

Murder was bloody all over, but still ambulatory and game to fight. Bareris peered around and saw that not everyone had fared as well. Some griffons and their masters had fallen. Another mount, mad with agony, rolled over and over to crush the locusts clinging to it. In the process, it crushed the man in the saddle as well.

But the flying vermin weren't unstoppable. Burning Braziers threw fan-shaped blasts of fire that charred swarms of the things from the air. Meanwhile, the lizard-thing had taken so many grievous wounds that its decaying, cadaverous form appeared on the verge of collapse. Its hide rippled and oozed, trying to seal a breach that revealed splintered bone beneath.

Bareris resolved that it wouldn't get the time it needed to heal. It was going to perish right now, before it could hurt anybody else. He urged Murder forward, and with a sweep of his wings, the griffon leaped high into the air, aiming for the creature's head. Other southerners, possessed of the same furious resolve, rushed the behemoth.

Suffusing the air all around it almost as completely as the insects had, slime sprayed from the lizard-thing's sores. Men and griffons shrieked as the effluvia spattered them.

Murder had jumped above the behemoth's head, and his body shielded Bareris from the stinking barrage. The globs ate holes in his armor and boots and blistered the flesh beneath, but it was nothing compared to what befell the griffon, who melted into smoking grease and bone.

The corrosive pus also dissolved the cinch securing Murder's saddle. It tumbled off the dead mount's back, and Bareris tumbled with it. He sang a word of command and his plummet slowed. He and the saddle landed with a bump.

He kicked his feet out of the stirrups, clambered to his feet, and charged. A few others did the same, and he wondered how they'd survived the acidic spray.

A huge foot stamped down, and he dodged out from underneath. The lizard-thing's jaws hurtled at him, and he jumped to avoid those as well. That put him close to his adversary's putrid breast, and he thrust his sword in again and again, seeking its heart.

His companions struck at other portions of the behemoth's body. Bursts of holy flame danced on its back. Finally, it slumped over sideways.

Bareris drove in his blade several more times, making sure the mammoth carcass was truly inert. Then he pivoted to survey the battle.

The lizard-thing had slaughtered a good many soldiers and griffons, but not enough to cripple the attack. Nor had the rest of Xingax's minions succeeded in destroying their enemies. Tammith and the handful of legionnaires under her direction had prevented it.

In fact, the furious efforts of the resistance were flagging as Xingax's living, sentient servants paused to gawk. Bareris realized that they'd believed the lizard-thing invincible, and were amazed and terrified to see it perish.

He grinned, struck up a song to spark courage in his allies and plant dread in the hearts of his adversaries, and picked up a dead man's bow and quiver. His own had burned to uselessness along with Murder's tack. He shot at enemies up on the gallery until he spotted something that made his guts clench in hatred.

•• •• •• •• •• •• •• •• •• •• •• •• •• ••

When the undead reptile-thing fell, its slayers turned to engage the rest of their foes, which absolved Tammith of the obligation to defend their rear. That was a relief, for she much preferred to attack. She gathered some legionnaires into a wedge, charged one of the doorways, and smashed through the shield wall erected by Xingax's warriors. After that, it was easy to cut them down.

Where next? she wondered. Then fingers gripped her shoulder.

Baring her fangs, she whirled, dislodging the hand, then saw it was Bareris who'd had the poor judgment to slip up from behind and surprise her. His burns, visible through the gaps where something had dissolved portions of his armor, looked nasty, but they didn't appear to bother him. Maybe he was so full of battle rage that it blocked the pain.

"What is it?" she asked.

"I know where Xingax is," he said. "In a doorway in the center of the eastern galley."

Trying not to be obvious about it, she glanced in that direction. "I see one of those giant zombies he likes to ride, but not him. You think he's on top of it, but invisible?"

"Yes. It's just standing there. What other reason could there be for withholding such a strong fighter from the battle? And look. Along every other section of the gallery, the enemy has undead and living soldiers jumbled together. There, it's all dread warriors and their ilk. Why? Because proximity to Xingax sickens live men, and he can't afford to weaken his own defenders.

"I'm going to deal with him before he screws up the courage to take an active role in this battle. I assume you want to help me."

She smiled. "Oh, yes."

He grinned at her, and for a moment she caught a glimpse of the youth who'd once taken delight in surprising her and making her laugh. "Then stand ready and watch this." He raised his hand, swept it down, and started singing.

Several Burning Braziers oriented on the walkway Bareris

had pointed out. One read a final syllable from a scroll, which flared and burned to ash in his grip. The others brandished fists or rattled chains sheathed in flame, and Tammith's skin crawled and stung at the sacred power gathering in the air. When it manifested, the dread warriors and ghouls in front of the giant zombie blew apart in a booming explosion.

Bareris gave Tammith a gentle push, telling her it was her time to attack. As she dissolved into bats, he vanished.

When she flew upward, she spied him again, barely visible behind the gray, hulking form of the giant zombie. He'd shifted himself through space to attack Xingax from behind. He swung his sword in a high arc, aiming for the unseen rider on the hideous steed's back.

Even above the din of battle, she heard Xingax scream like an infant in distress. It was the sweetest music Bareris had ever made.

The giant zombie lurched around and swiped at Bareris, who retreated out of range. Wavering into visibility, Xingax hurled ice crystals from Ysval's blackened, oversized hand. Bareris twisted, but couldn't dodge all of the barrage.

Yet when he sprang back, cut into the zombie's knee, yanked his sword free, and whirled it upward for another slash at Xingax, Tammith could see it hadn't hurt him much, nor had the poison haze that shrouded his opponent. He'd prepared for this confrontation, enhancing his natural capabilities with his songs, and for all she knew, talismans and potions. She felt a thrill of pride to see how well he was faring.

It was a puny little flicker of emotion, an almost indiscernible fleck of flotsam in the torrent of hatred and rage she felt for Xingax. She whirled her bats together and set her human feet down amid the cinders and bits of blackened bone that were all that remained of the dread warriors. Even through her boots, the residue of divine power stung her soles.

She jumped, caught Xingax by the neck, and dragged him from his perch. Bareris could destroy the giant zombie, and she'd slaughter its master. She pulled her sword back for a thrust.

Twisting to face her, Xingax sneered, and she felt vibration through the fingers she held clamped in his putrid flesh. Then she couldn't feel anything, and realized he meant to shift through space or between worlds to escape her.

But an instant later, when his form congealed again, she realized he couldn't. He'd temporarily lost the ability. His twisted little mouth dropped open in dismay, and she drove her blade into his guts.

It didn't finish him. It didn't even stun him, stop him from floating weightless in the air, or keep him from clawing at her face. But that was all right. She wanted him to succumb slowly, because she'd relish every instant of his destruction. She twisted her head and his talons scored her cheek but missed her eyes. She jerked the sword free for another attack.

"Stop!" a deep voice grated.

Tammith froze, and she realized some enchantment had taken hold of her. She strained against it, and her sword arm twitched. She was breaking free.

"Stop!" Xingax said. From the moment of her rebirth as a vampire, he'd been able to command her. She'd believed the blight on wizardry had set her free, but apparently her liberation wasn't as complete as she'd imagined. Xingax was able to muster at least a shadow of his old coercive power, and it combined with the psychic assault she was already fighting to tilt the balance against her. Her body locked into complete rigidity, and Xingax clawed at her hand until flesh and bones came apart and he was able to pull free of her grip.

Something snaked around her. When it lifted her off the balcony, it turned her, and she beheld the creature that had crept up behind her.

Once it sat atop a giant's shoulders. Now the severed head was a swollen, misshapen thing with rows of jagged fangs in its oversized mouth. Some of the guts and blood vessels protruding from the neck hole had wrapped around her. Others had plastered themselves to the wall above the doorways, allowing it to crawl along the vertical surface like a fly.

"You're a bad, ungrateful daughter!" Xingax shrilled. "I gave you everything!"

The crawling head's trailing tendrils lifted Tammith toward its jaws. Change to mist, she told herself. Then it can't hurt you or hold on to you. But she couldn't transform.

Her captor turned her body. She realized it was positioning her so it could nip her head off.

Then Bareris sprang onto the balcony. He must have finished slaying the giant zombie, clearing away the obstacle that stood between him and the rest of the combat.

He struck at Xingax before the maker of undead realized he was there. His sword crunched into the bulbous skull, and Xingax dropped from the air onto the gallery floor. Bareris instantly pivoted toward the crawling head and Tammith.

But Xingax was still conscious. He grabbed Bareris's leg with his nighthaunt hand, sinking the claws deep into his calf, and pointed with the stunted, withered one. Tammith felt malignant power burn through the air.

Bareris cried out and arched his back, but he didn't fall. After a moment, as the agony abated, he pivoted and cut until Xingax stopped moving, and he could pull free of the long bloody claws.

He hobbled toward Tammith and the thing that clutched her tightly. The giant's head howled, a shriek as full of murderous force as Xingax's final attack, but Bareris sang a fierce, sustained, vibrating note that shielded him from harm.

The crawling head lashed at him with lengths of artery and

intestine. Hampered by his torn, bleeding leg, Bareris defended as best he could. At the same time, the creature positioned Tammith's neck between its rows of teeth.

Once more, she struggled against her intangible fetters. Perhaps Xingax's death had weakened them, because her limbs jerked. Bonds of ropy flesh still held her, but nothing else did.

But she was out of time to shapeshift. She strained with all her inhuman strength, heaved her arms free, and braced her sword to prop the head's jaws open.

Heedless of the grievous wound it thus inflicted in the roof of its mouth, the horror snapped its fangs shut. A fiery pain through her neck told Tammith her head had come loose from her body.

She fought to defy terror's grip, to remember that she'd survived this same mutilation before. Then a rippling peristalsis tumbled her head inside the creature, depositing it in some manner of sac. In the darkness, fleshy strands nudged at her scalp, brow, and cheeks, then, biting or stinging, anchored themselves like lampreys.

Her consciousness faded. Despite the layers of bone and flesh around her, she heard Bareris bellow a thunderous battle cry, felt the crawling head jerk in reaction, and then her mind guttered out completely.

chapter six

2–21 Kythorn, the Year of Blue Fire

Bareris's shout tore flesh from the giant's head and splintered the bone beneath. At instant later, a Burning Brazier blasted the creature with flame. It lost its grip on the wall and crashed down on the gallery, where it lay blackened, smoking, and still.

Fast as he could, Bareris limped toward it, and a yellow-eyed dread warrior placed itself in his path. He had to slay it, and then the ghoul that took its place. It reminded him that, although all he truly cared about was breaking open the giant's head, he still had a battle to win.

In fact, it didn't take long. When the crawling head perished, the defenders' last hope of victory perished with it, and they began to turn and run.

Bareris cast about, found a fallen battle-axe, and chopped the colossal skull apart. For a time, he was terrified that Tammith's head had completely dissolved inside it, but he finally found it within a sac of leathery flesh.

It didn't move. Not the mouth, not the eyes. Even when he yanked loose the tendrils that had attached themselves to it and lifted it free, it looked as dead as the putrid mass that had imprisoned it. Bareris shuddered and felt a howl building inside him.

Behind him, someone cleared his throat. He turned to see one of the Burning Braziers. Though far advanced in the mysteries of his order, the priest was a relatively young man of Mulan stock.

"Forgive me, Captain," he said, "but you still have work to do."

Bareris took a breath. "Yes." He proffered the head. "You're the best healer we have. Help her."

The Brazier hesitated. "Captain . . ."

"That's an order!"

The priest accepted the head. "I'll try."

Limping, using a spear for a cane, Bareris oversaw the securing of the fortress. The chambers echoed with the chanted prayers of the priests. The flashes of fire they conjured gilded the walls. Their power would so purify the place that no one could ever practice necromancy there again.

Meanwhile, the southern wizards plundered the necromancers' libraries and stores of mystical equipment. The warriors of the Griffon Legion hunted down and killed the enemies cowering in dark corners. Finally it was done, and Bareris rushed to find out what had become of Tammith.

The Burning Brazier had taken her to a small room so he could work undisturbed. There she lay atop a table, her form—white skin, black clothing and armor, raven hair, and dark dried gore—ghostly and vague in the glow of a single oil lamp. But even the feeble light revealed the ragged discontinuity that circled her neck like a choker and the mottling of ugly wounds on her face.

Bareris could tell by looking at her that nothing had changed. Still, he turned to the cleric and asked, "How is she?"

The fire priest hesitated, then said, "She's dead, sir. She was dead when you last saw her and she's still dead now."

"She can't be. She survived decapitation before."

"If so, then I surmise that when the giant thing bit off her head and began the process of combining it with its own substance, the injury was qualitatively different. At any rate, she hasn't moved, and the two . . . pieces of her don't show any signs of growing together."

"Did you try to encourage the healing with your magic?"

"Yes, Captain, just as you ordered. Even though healing prayers, which channel the cosmic principles of health and vitality, are unlikely to help a being whose existence embodied malignancy and a perversion of the natural order."

You're glad she's dead, Bareris thought, and trembled with the urge to knock the Burning Brazier down. Instead, he said, "Thank you for trying. Go help the other priests with their tasks."

"I'm sorry I couldn't bring her back. But I can perform the rites to cremate the body with the proper reverence and commend her spirit to Kossuth."

"Perhaps later."

"I can also tend you. Your leg needs attention, and unless I'm very much mistaken, you're still feeling sick and weak from Xingax's mystical attack. Let me—"

"Are you deaf? I told you to get out!"

The Brazier studied Bareris's face, then nodded, turned on his heel, and left Bareris alone with Tammith's body and the gloom.

Bareris sang his own charms of healing, even though they were no more effective than the spells the priests employed for the same purpose. He sang until he exhausted his magic, and she didn't stir.

Then he sang the tale of the starfish that aspired to be a star, and other songs she'd loved when they were young. Perhaps he hoped they'd entice her spirit back from the void where even magic had failed, but she still didn't move.

That's it, then, he thought. I tried, but all I could do was say good-bye. The music was my farewell.

Perhaps her destruction was for the best, for truly, she'd perished ten years ago. The cold, implacable killer that remained was a mockery of the Tammith he'd loved. She'd known it herself. She'd wanted to die, even if she never quite said it.

Perhaps it was even better for him. He'd pined for her every day, but when she miraculously returned to him, it had only initiated a different kind of torment. Then he had to contemplate what his failure had made of her, and hold back from touching her and pouring out his heart.

Yes. Perhaps. But how could he stand to lose her again?

Maybe he didn't have to, because there was one measure he had not tried. For a vampire, blood was life, and many tales told that they particularly craved the blood of those they loved, or had loved prior to their rebirths.

He unbuckled his sword belt, pulled off his armor, and rolled up the sleeve of his shirt. He drew his knife and poised the blade at his wrist.

I'm mad to do this, he thought. I have no reason to think it will work, and the Brazier was right. I'm still weak from Xingax's death magic, and I've already lost a good deal of blood. Shedding more is apt to kill me.

Yet still he sliced into the vein.

The blood welled forth. It looked black in the dim light. He poised his wrist over Tammith's mouth and let it drip in.

Nothing happened. For a moment he felt she was actively resisting him, and even though he knew the idea was crazy, it evoked a spasm of anger nonetheless.

He smeared gore across his own lips, then decided that wasn't good enough. He scratched them with the point of the knife so fresh blood would keep trickling forth. Then he bent down and kissed Tammith, moving with exquisite care to make sure he didn't jostle her head away from her body.

.. ..

Tammith woke to fiery pain in her neck, gentle nuzzling pressure on her lips, and the coppery tang of blood in her mouth. She couldn't see, or remember where she was or what had happened.

She only knew her thirst was overwhelming, and whatever was feeding her blood was doing it too slowly to suit her. She tried to grab it, but her arms refused to obey her. In fact, she realized, she couldn't feel them, or anything else below the agony in her neck.

Because, she abruptly recalled, Xingax's creation had bitten her head off. She wondered if her body was nearby, and experienced a pang of fear that it wasn't, or that even if it was, this time, she wouldn't fuse back together. Then, as if to soothe her anxiety, she felt flesh and bone growing and flowing to reassemble her neck. Her body announced itself with a stab of agony in the mangled hand Xingax had clawed apart.

Absolute blackness flowered into blurry patches of light and shadow as the infusion of blood returned the use of her eyes. As her vision sharpened, she saw Bareris restoring her. Resurrecting her with bloody kisses.

She returned the next one, and he drew back to regard her with joyous incredulity. His smile stabbed shame and sorrow into her. Don't be happy, she thought. I ruined you. I'm going to be the death of you. Then another surge of thirst washed such notions away.

She pulled him down to her and sucked and licked at his lips. They still weren't yielding enough blood, and she felt as if he were teasing her. As soon as she was sure she'd regained sufficient strength, and that vigorous motion wouldn't break her into two pieces again, she sought a better source.

When she cast about, she saw that he'd slashed his wrist, and it had bled copiously enough to spatter gore all over him, her, and the table on which she lay. But she realized his arm wouldn't satisfy her either. She wanted a more intimate connection. Because this time, the thirst wasn't just a craving for blood, but rather a melding of passions.

She shifted her mouth to the side of his neck, slipped her fangs into the pulsing vein, and tore at his garments. When he realized what she was doing, he ripped at hers as well.

Fiercely, they ground their bodies together. Excitement carried her higher and higher, and after a time, she felt the frantic hammering of his heart, struggling to keep him alive despite the extreme demands he was placing on it.

Good. Let it burst. Let him die. His death was a part of the exultation she sought.

Yet at the same time, the prospect of destroying him was intolerable.

Once, her vampiric instincts would have ruled her in any such situation. They were no less potent now, but she'd had a decade to learn self-control. Though it was as difficult as anything she'd ever done, she withdrew her fangs from his neck, licked the double wound to close it, and contented herself with a lesser consummation.

He blacked out at the same moment, and sprawled atop her like a dead man. She squirmed out from under him, dashed to the door, and screamed for a healer.

•• •• •• •• •• •• •• •• •• •• •• •• ••

When Bareris's eyes fluttered open, he found that someone had carried him to a proper bed. Tammith sat beside him, holding his hand, her fingers cool as usual. She was fully clad again.

"Water," he croaked.

"I knew you'd want it." Easily as a mother shifting a small child, she lifted him up and held a cup to his lips. The cold liquid tasted of iron.

"Thank you."

"How are you?" she asked.

"Weak, but all right, I think."

"I fetched a healer as soon as we . . . finished." She lowered her eyes and it occurred to him that he hadn't expected her to look shy ever again.

Bareris chuckled and it made him cough. "I must have presented an interesting tableau for his inspection—clothing in disarray, cut wrist, cut lips, blood everywhere."

Tammith smiled back. "Especially since I was half naked and bloody, too, and I still have this." She held up her left hand for his inspection. It had begun to regenerate, but was still bone, tendon, and little else.

It hurt him to see it. "By the Harp!"

"Don't worry about it. It will likely finish healing the next time I drink blood."

"I should probably hold off on that for a little while."

She frowned. "I don't mean yours."

"Well, I realize it can't be me every time. Sometimes it will just be supper."

"You saved me, and I'm grateful. But what we did together is an abomination."

"It didn't feel abominable."

"I drank too much. I nearly killed you."

"I know."

"It would be like that every time, the thirst pushing me, infecting me with a pure cruel wish to see you die."

"I trust you."

"Then you're an idiot!"

"Maybe. And you were right. We aren't the people we once were. We're lesser, tarnished things. And so we can never again possess a love like the one we had before. Yet a bond remains between the people we've become, and why shouldn't we have that? Why shouldn't we see where it takes us, and enjoy whatever happiness it can provide? What would be the point of doing anything else?"

"To save your life."

"I haven't cared about that since Thazar Keep."

"I do." She sighed. "But if you reach out for me, I won't turn you away."

•• •• •• •• •• •• •• •• •• •• •• •• •• ••

A tap on the door roused Malark from poring over the latest dispatches, and made him realize his eyes were dry and burning. He rubbed them and called, "Come in."

A skinny, freckle-faced boy entered, balancing a tray with one hand while using the other to manage the door. Was it suppertime already? It must be, because the sky beyond the window was red, and the spicy aroma of the roast pork made Malark's stomach gurgle.

The boy looked around. The room was spacious and adequately furnished, but maps, books, ledgers, and heaps of parchment covered almost every horizontal surface.

Malark shifted a stack of paper onto the floor, clearing the corner of a table. "You can set it here."

"Yes, sir." The servant placed the tray as requested, then turned as something caught his eye. Head cocked forward, he stepped closer to the largest map in the chamber, a representation of Thay and neighboring lands painted on a tabletop. A person could scrawl notes on it with chalk or set miniature figures atop it to represent armies and fleets, and Malark had done both. The southern tokens were pewter, and the northern, brass.

He could understand why the display might intrigue a child, but the servant had no business scrutinizing state secrets. "You'd better run along now," Malark said.

The boy shifted a little pewter griffon. "You're well informed. I can add a few lines to the story the map tells, but only a few. Your griffon riders destroyed the north's primary manufactory for the creation of undead and then withdrew successfully from High Thay."

He picked up a stick of turquoise chalk. "Just last night, blue fire melted Anhaurz, killing all within." He drew an X through the city. "The ruins have a weird beauty about them."

He set down the chalk, rubbed his fingertips together to brush off the dust, and moved a pair of ships. "Thessaloni Canos and her men made it to the Wizard's Reach and secured both Escalant and Laothkund for the council.

"In short, it's the same story everywhere. Despite the inconveniences of waves of blue flame, earthquakes, wizardry misbehaving, and dangerous new animals rampaging around, southern armies are winning victory after victory, and I give much of the credit to you, Goodman Springhill, and your network of agents."

Malark swallowed. "Who are you?"

"Oh, I think you know. Once, I spoke with you and your comrades in a grove. I offered you my patronage, and you spurned me."

"Szass Tam."

"Say it softly, if you please, or better still, don't repeat it again at all. I'll tell you something I'd admit to few others. I'm not the mage I was before Mystra died and the Death Moon Orb blew up in my face. I've yet to recover the full measure of my strength, and I'm not eager to fight the entire Central Citadel. It was difficult enough just sneaking in here despite the wards Lallara and Iphegor Nath set to keep creatures like me out."

"Why did you?"

The boy grinned widely enough to reveal he was missing a molar on the upper left. "I've already told you, more or less. For ten years, you've played a key role in the war. If I'd realized just how important you were going to be, perhaps I would have killed you that evening in the wood. But I imagined it beneath me to destroy a person like you—meaning a man with no command of magic—with my own hands, especially when I'd entered your camp under sign of truce. Vanity and scruples are terrible things. They can cause all sorts of problems."

Malark didn't have to glance around the room. He already knew where everything was, including his enchanted cudgels, hanging on a peg by the door. It seemed likely he was going to need them. He knew better than to batter the chill, poisonous flesh of a lich with his bare hands, even when the undead wizard had cloaked himself in the semblance of a living child.

Of course, even if he reached the batons, no sane person would give a shaved copper for his chances. It seemed that Death had forgiven his sins at last and stood ready to usher him into the blackness. He felt a thrill of anticipation.

"Please," Szass Tam said, "don't spring into action like the hero of some tawdry play." It startled Malark that the necromancer knew he was about to move. "I've never had the opportunity to study the fighting system you employ, and no doubt it would be interesting. But I'd prefer you not make a commotion, and I promise, there's no need. If I'd wanted to kill you, I could simply have poisoned your supper. Feel free to eat it, by the way. No point letting it get cold."

Malark felt out of his depth. It wasn't a feeling to which he was accustomed, nor one he enjoyed. "If I'm such a stone in your buskin, then why wouldn't you want to murder me?"

"Because it wouldn't accomplish anything. Before she ascended to greater things, Dmitra was a brilliant spymaster in her own right. If I eliminated you, she'd just pick up where you left off. What I need to do is bring you over to my side."

"As you mentioned, I've already refused your offer of patronage."

"So you did, and I daresay the events of the ensuing decade have given you no cause to regret it. Ordinary folk deplore the widespread loss of life the war produces, but a worshiper of Death must revel in it, and in the destruction produced by the blue fire as well. You must feel as giddy as a lad at his first carnival."

Malark took a breath. "I'm impressed. You've discovered something I haven't confided to anyone in a while."

"Actually, monk of the Long Death, I've discovered everything. In desperation, with all my schemes unraveling, I employed divination to learn more about my adversaries. I don't mean Dmitra and the other zulkirs. I long ago learned all their sordid little secrets. I focused on those among their lieutenants who've done the most to hamper me."

"If you really know everything about me, you know I regard the undead as affronts to the natural order of things. That's why I'd never come over to your side, no matter what you offered."

The boy grinned. "Never say never. If you'll consent to hear it, I'd like to share a story. Along the way, it will answer a question that's perplexed you for ten years. Why did I murder Druxus Rhym?"

The tale went on for a long time. The patch of sky beyond the window turned black. Stars flowered there, and shadow enfolded the chamber.

By the time he finished, Malark's heart was pounding. He swallowed and asked, "Will it work?"

"I admit—Druxus doubted it, but I attribute that to a failure of imagination, because his own analysis suggested it would. I believe it will, and I'm generally considered the greatest wizard in Thay, which is to say, in the most magically advanced realm in all Faerûn. Of course, the only way to know for certain is to try. Will you help me put it to the test?"

chapter seven

26 Kythorn–11 Flamerule, the Year of Blue Fire

Nymia Focar ran her gaze over the mounted knights lined up before her, their lances rising straight and high, their fierce chargers standing submissive to their masters' wills, with scarcely a snort, a head toss, or the stamp of a hoof. She could scarcely help noticing which of the faces framed in the steel helms were particularly handsome, or wondering who might prove exceptionally virile if summoned to her tent. A woman had her appetites.

But Nymia indulged them at night. It was morning now, and she had an army to lead to its next engagement. If the gods continued to smile on her, that would yield its own satisfactions.

After the host that marched north from Zolum divided, she'd led her troops up the narrow strip of flatland between Lake Thaylambar and the foothills of the Sunrise Mountains, then west into Delhumide. So far, she'd encountered only feeble resistance, and had high hopes of taking Umratharos before Midsummer.

Satisfied with her inspection, she waved her arm, wheeled her destrier, and rode toward the road. Hooves clattered and harnesses jingled as her horsemen started after her, and a phalanx of spearmen took a first marching stride in unison. Griffons shrieked and lashed their wings, taking to the air.

Then a black bird swooped down from the sky, its plumage glinting in the morning sunlight. Nymia reined in her steed and raised her hand. Her army stumbled to a halt.

Many army commanders used pigeons as messenger birds, and accordingly, their foes watched for the creatures and shot them. That was the reason that Dmitra Flass—or her outlander lieutenant—had trained ravens to perform the same task. The birds had a touch of magic in them, and weren't limited to flying to and fro from set locations. They could locate an army in the field or even a specific individual.

One of Nymia's aides held out his arm. The raven landed on his wrist like a falcon. He untied the miniature leather scroll case on the bird's leg and proffered it to Nymia.

She unscrewed the cap and magic swelled the tube to its natural size. She shook out the parchment and unrolled it.

The message read:

> *As you are surely aware, Kethin Hur was not present at the battle for the Keep of Sorrows, nor is he participating in the present campaign. He claims his strength is needed to guard his southern border and make sure the Mulhorandi don't invade while we Thayans are busy fighting one another. But my sources report signs he's secretly massing troops in the northernmost lands of his domain.*
>
> *The council wouldn't approve of me telling you this. They want you focused on laying waste to Szass Tam's territories. But I thought you should know. In days to come, remember who did you a favor.*

Malark Springhill had neither signed the message nor spelled out the reason Nymia ought to be concerned, but he hadn't needed to. She understood. While she was busy fighting in the North, Kethin Hur, the governor of Thazalhar, meant to raid into Pyarados, pillaging and perhaps even seizing land.

Grasping and treacherous though he was, he wouldn't have dared attempt such a thing in peacetime. But amid the chaos spawned by war, blue fire, and earthquakes, he was all too likely to succeed.

Nymia had to thwart the whoreson. But could she, when the zulkirs themselves had ordered her north?

She wished Aoth were present to counsel her. Over the years, he'd offered consistently good advice, and she'd regretted sending him to Bezantur for vivisection. But his life hadn't seemed worth an argument with Dmitra Flass.

What might he say if he were with her? Maybe that a high-ranking officer had no choice but to follow the commands of her masters, but enjoyed some discretion as to precisely *how* to obey. If Nymia split her army in two and left a portion of it to fight in Delhumide, she could maintain she'd prosecuted her part in the master strategy with all due diligence.

And if that wasn't good enough for the zulkirs, she'd say she was sick, had needed to return to Pyarados, and could hardly travel without a proper escort. Or, she could claim she had reason to believe Kethin Hur had aligned himself with Szass Tam. By the Black Flame, that might even be true! It made more sense than if he'd decided to raid a neighboring tharch without a powerful ally backing his play.

Anyway, she'd solve today's problem today, and figure out how to appease the council later. Because for her, the real point of the war wasn't to decide if one archmage or several would rule Thay, but to protect her own station and possessions. Nothing else mattered half as much.

She spent most of the morning dividing her army and its provisions in two and instructing Baiyen Tabar, who looked less than eager to assume command of the troops she was leaving behind. In truth, Nymia didn't blame him. He wouldn't have enough men to be confident of accomplishing the tasks the zulkirs had set him—or rather, her.

But she could scarcely acknowledge she might be abandoning him to defeat and destruction. Instead she promised rich rewards for the victories she professed to be certain he would win. She pledged, too, to return as soon as she could, then marched the best of her warriors south.

·· ·· ·· ·· ·· ·· ·· ·· ·· ·· ·· ·· ··

The sky was the color of slate as the Gray Archers, or what was left of them, laid their comrade on the pyre. Cremation wasn't one of their customs, but during their years in Thay, they'd learned not to bury anyone even if he hadn't perished at the hands of a vampire or something similar. With the power of necromancy rampant in the land, the corpse was all too likely to dig its way out of the grave and start slaughtering its former friends.

"Damn it," Darvin Redfox whispered, "we can't even send our dead to the Foehammer in the way they would wish."

Taller than he and snub-nosed, her chestnut hair gathered in a long braid, Lureene Pinehill was both his lieutenant and his lover, but generally didn't allow the intimate side of their relationship to show in her public behavior. Now, however, she gave his hand a surreptitious squeeze. "Tempus will welcome him anyway."

"I hope so." The torch dropped onto the oil-doused wood, and flame crackled upward. "And the rest of us, too, when our time comes."

"That won't be anytime soon. The sickness has run its course.

Evendur was the first case in several days, and he'll also be the last. You'll see."

"I hope so," Darvin repeated. To take back Nothos, a mostly ruinous town in northern Lapendrar, the mercenary company had needed to destroy a garrison of necromancers and dread warriors. With the wizards' magic weakened, the Gray Archers succeeded, but afterward, sickness broke out among the ranks, possibly a result of close contact with the undead.

"I think you're tired," Lureene said.

"I am. Tired of fighting ghouls and wraiths, and of serving lords who traffic with demons and feel only contempt for anyone who isn't both Thayan and Mulan."

"Do you want to seek employment elsewhere? I'm sure someone is fighting a war in some other part of Faerûn."

"I'd love it, but how would we get there? With the earth shaking and the blue fires burning, it's difficult enough to march overland. Can you imagine how dangerous it must be to travel by sea? No, we're stuck here." He spat. "People say the world's ending. If so, I guess it doesn't matter anyway."

"When the funeral's over, you're coming to my tent. I know how to brighten your mood."

But it seemed she wouldn't have the chance. When the fire had had its way with the dead Gray Archer, and the company priest finished the final prayer, several of the men accosted Darvin. He inferred that they too must have been conferring in hushed voices as they watched the body burn.

"Captain." Squinting Aelthas said, "Sir. Sorry to bother you, but the money didn't come again today."

"I know," Darvin said. He'd been assured their pay would follow them north, but it was a tenday late.

"You know we're not shirkers or cowards, Captain. We've followed you into all nine kinds of Hell. But if the council of zulkirs isn't going to pay us, what's the point?"

Darvin groped for the right words to persuade the men to be patient. Then, it was as if something turned over in his head, and he decided he was out of patience himself. "Fortunately, there's an easy remedy," he said. "Collect our wages from the town."

Lureene pivoted toward him, her brown eyes narrowed. "Are you sure that's wise? By the looks of it, this place has been sacked already."

"Then the people should be used to it."

"I don't think we're supposed to mistreat them. The zulkirs want Lapendrar—"

"We're not mistreating them. We're charging a fair price for ridding their settlement of undead. Now stop blathering and organize the collection!"

Her mouth tightened. "Yes, sir."

He felt a pang of guilt for snarling at her, but he'd never been one for apologies, and so he didn't tell her he was sorry. Not even late that night, when a burgher had broken her arm with a club and the riot was well under way.

•• •• •• •• •• •• •• •• •• •• •• •• •• ••

The dead griffon scarcely had any flesh left, let alone feathers. Yet its rattling wings carried it through the air, because that was the unnatural nature of undeath.

Bareris was no necromancer. But over the years, as his bardic powers increased and his mood grew ever bleaker, he'd discovered that his music could reanimate dead bodies. With mounts in scarce supply, he'd used the talent back in Xingax's stronghold to create one more. It was carrying Tammith, too, strapped to its skeletal form and shrouded in black cloth to ward her from the sun.

He peered through the gathering twilight at the plains of Tyraturos stretched below. Soon it would be time to set down and make camp, and Tammith would wake. He smiled at the prospect of seeing and touching her again. His throat tingled.

Then he spied a deep gorge splitting the earth, and the legionnaires milling around on the far side of it. Their banners bore the eight-pointed crimson star device of the council, as well as the Black Hand of Bane.

Dimon's troops, more than likely. Evidently they'd been heading north and had been unpleasantly surprised to find the chasm barring the way.

Clearly, they wouldn't be marching any farther until morning, and Bareris supposed he and his men might as well share their camp. Using magic to project his voice, he called to them that he and his companions were Nymia Focar's men, then blew a signal on his trumpet to convey the same message.

Meanwhile, his undead steed carried him over the wound in the earth. When he was directly above it, he gasped.

Something huge was climbing out of the depths, a mass of writhing tentacles with bulging eyes and circular orifices, alternately expanding and puckering, down the length of the arms. Blue fire flickered around it and allowed it to sink the tips of its arms into the stony wall, which they penetrated as easily as a knife cutting butter.

It was the most grotesque thing Bareris had ever seen. He couldn't even tell what sort of creature it had been before the blue flame transformed it. Perhaps it hadn't been alive at all. Maybe the wave of chaotic power had made it out of rock, earth, and air, or nothing at all.

Whatever it was, it had nearly reached the top of the crevasse, and by ill fortune, none of the legionnaires were looking over the edge. Bareris bellowed a warning.

It came too late. The creature heaved itself over the edge of the rim and flailed its tentacles. The blows bashed men to the ground or hurled them through the air. But more often than not, what actually killed them was the blue flame playing around the entity's body. When it touched them, they melted.

Bareris hoped that after slaying its first several victims, the creature would stop to slurp up the remains. It didn't. Motivated by fury rather than hunger, it crawled toward more of Dimon's soldiers.

It was fast, too. Panicking, jamming and tangling together, knocking one another down, some legionnaires might escape, but not many.

Bareris sang a song of lethargy. The creature slowed, moving more sluggishly than before.

"Hit it!" he called to the other griffon riders. "But stay high enough that it can't snatch you out of the air."

His men loosed arrows. The Burning Braziers hurled sprays of fire, or conjured flying hammers wreathed in yellow flame. He slammed the creature with the force of a thunderous shout.

Was any of it doing the beast harm? The thing was so bizarre that he couldn't tell. But the barrage distracted it. It left off pursuing the men on the ground to grope impotently at the attackers harassing it from on high.

Or perhaps not so impotently after all. Without warning, it shot up into the air.

If it could fly all along, Bareris wondered why it had climbed to the top of the chasm. It made no sense, but then, nothing associated with the blue fire did.

He wheeled his mount to keep beyond the creature's reach, but the skeletal griffon didn't respond quickly enough. A tentacle whipped around its neck, shattering naked vertebrae, and hung there in a loop. Blue fire ran up the arm toward the steed and its rider as though following a trail of oil.

Bareris chanted words of power, unclipped the strap holding Tammith to the saddle, and grabbed hold of her shroud. The azure flame leaped at him just as he sang the final note. The world seemed to break apart, and then he was standing on the ground with his legs still spread as though straddling a mount. Tammith fell to the ground at his feet, her weight jerking his hand down with her. The folds of the shroud separated. Smoke billowed forth, and Bareris cried out in horror.

But Tammith wasn't burning up. The sun had already dropped out of sight, and she'd turned to mist to extricate herself from her cloth cocoon. The swirls of fog congealed into human form.

"What's going on?" Tammith asked.

Bareris pointed. "That."

The creature had scattered the griffon riders. Perhaps thinking that now they'd leave it alone, it plummeted, and jolted the earth when it slammed down. It then heaved itself toward him, Tammith, and Dimon's men, crawling and lashing its tentacles as fast as it had originally. The curse of slowness had worn off.

Tammith smiled, revealing upper canines extending into fangs. "I'll stop it."

"No. Stay back. The blue fire can destroy anything, even a vampire."

"Then I'll make sure it doesn't touch me." She exploded into a cloud of bats.

The winged beasts hurled themselves at the oncoming giant. Dodging the sweeps of its tentacles, they caught hold of them in their claws and sank their fangs into them. Bareris couldn't tell if the immense horror had any blood for them to suck, but he was sure Tammith was using the cold malignancy of her touch in an effort to drain its life away.

He, too, did his best to kill it. He wanted to charge and fight near her with his sword, but the better tactic was to stand back and use magic. So he battered the horror with shout after shout and spell after spell.

As Tammith had promised, at first the bats took flight whenever blue flame flowed or leaped close to them, but then she failed to notice a flare until it was too late. The blaze engulfed a bat, and it burst in a sort of fiery splash. Bareris winced.

Then the gigantic creature collapsed, its dozens of arms flopping to the ground and beginning to liquefy. A putrid stench suffused the air.

Bareris hadn't been able to tell which attacks had truly hurt it, and he couldn't tell which had killed it, either. Perhaps none of them. Possibly the beast had borne some fundamental flaw in its anatomy that kept it from living very long.

The surviving bats took flight from the rotting tangle, then whirled together. Tammith wasn't marked or bleeding, but she stumbled.

Bareris ran to her. "Are you all right?"

She nodded. "I will be. That was close. When the fire took a portion of me, it felt as if it was going to jump to all my bodies. But somehow I pushed it back."

"You really didn't have to charge and attack."

"As far as that's concerned, when you moved us, you didn't have to drop us between the creature and the soldiers of Tyraturos. Neither one of us is responsible for looking after them."

"I suppose that's true." They each had acted as instinct prompted, which suggested that, whatever she believed, not all her urges were selfish and cruel.

The captain of Dimon's legionnaires came trotting up to them. He hadn't observed the final phase of the fight in any detail, and he stopped short when he noticed Tammith's alabaster skin, the subtle luminescence in her dark eyes, and the fangs still furrowing her lower lip. Before the war, he might have felt a personal aversion to vampires, but he would have accepted their presence in the army as a matter of course. Now, he feared that any such creature served Szass Tam.

"It's all right," Bareris said, investing his voice with a dash of magic to calm and convince. "Captain Iltazyarra is on our side."

The other commander took a breath. "Of course. Please, forgive my moment of confusion. To tell you the truth, I'm still rattled from seeing that beast tear into us. I don't know what we would have done if you griffon riders hadn't happened by."

You would have died, Bareris thought. "We were glad to help."

"Can you help some more? I've got soldiers who fled and are still running, not realizing the creature is dead. Can your fellows catch up with them and herd them back?"

"Of course."

"Thank you." The officer shook his head. "By the Hand, what a mess! This route was supposed to be clear. A wave of blue flame must have carved the gorge and created the beast just a short time ago."

Bareris frowned, then shrugged. "I suppose."

•• •• •• •• •• •• •• •• •• •• •• •• ••

Long before his superiors in the Order of Conjuration commanded him to serve with the army, Thamas Napret had become accustomed to the groans and whimpers of injured men. A Red Wizard couldn't climb the ladder of his hierarchy without hearing such noises frequently.

Yet now they seemed like a reproach, and distracted him from his contemplation of the stars. He rose, picked up his staff with its inlaid runes of gold, and walked away from the camp.

He didn't go far. Some of Szass Tam's warriors might still be lurking around, and even if not, wild kobolds and goblins sometimes crept down from the Sunrise Mountains to forage and raid in the wooded hills of Gauros. He put a few paces between himself and the nearest of his associates, then sat down on ground carpeted with dry pine needles, crossed his legs, and sank into a meditative trance. Perhaps the gods—assuming that any were left alive—would reveal how things had gone so horribly wrong.

Dmitra Flass had ordered their small band to inflict as much harm on Gauros as possible, and in truth, it didn't take a huge army to burn farms and villages and overrun tax stations in the sparsely settled tharch, especially when Azhir Kren and the majority of her troops were fighting elsewhere. The ability to move fast and vanish into the forests kept the southerners safe from retaliation.

Or at least it had for a while. Then a force of howling blood orcs and yellow-eyed dread warriors descended on them under cover of night. Taken by surprise, Thamas and his allies had nonetheless managed to repel the attackers, but they'd lost half their number in the process, with several more likely to succumb to their wounds before the end of the night.

It shouldn't have happened. They'd covered their tracks and hidden themselves well, as always. Even skilled manhunters—

Thamas sensed rather than heard a presence at his back, and twisted his head around. Gothog Dyernina and two soldiers had crept up behind him. Gothog was half Rashemi and half orc, as his pointed ears and protruding lower canines attested. As far as Thamas was concerned, such creatures had no business commanding, but as the war killed Mulan officers, it provided opportunities for the lower orders to rise from the ranks, and over time, he'd gotten used to Gothog, too.

Which didn't mean he wanted the lout interrupting him when he was trying to concentrate. "What is it?" he asked.

"I want to know," Gothog said, "why you didn't warn me the enemy was coming."

"Because I'm not a diviner," Thamas said. "I'd like to know why your scouts and sentries didn't spot them."

"Right," Gothog said, "you're a conjuror. But it didn't do us a lot of good during the fight, did it? At first, you didn't do anything. Then, when you finally whistled up that big three-headed snake, it attacked our own men."

"It destroyed several of our foes first, and I sent it back to the Abyss as soon as I lost control. I explained this to you. The mystical forces in the cosmos are out of balance. Until that changes, wizardry won't be as reliable as it ought to be."

Gothog grunted. "Maybe that was the problem, or maybe you didn't really want to fight."

"Are you stupid? Why wouldn't I, when the northerners were trying to kill me, too?"

"Were they?"

Thamas decided he no longer felt comfortable sitting on the ground with the half-orc and the legionnaires looming over him. He drew himself to his feet. "Exactly what are you insinuating?"

"Maybe the enemy found us because someone called them to us. Maybe it was you."

"That's ridiculous! Where did you come up with such an idea?"

"A magus wouldn't have much trouble passing messages to the enemy. You have spells that let you talk over distances. You'd only need to sneak off by yourself for a moment, and here you are again, alone among the trees."

"Did I look like I was doing anything sinister? I was just sitting!"

"I don't take much pleasure in this." Gothog took hold of the leather-wrapped hilt of his scimitar, and the blade whispered out of the scabbard. The other soldiers readied their broadswords. "You always made it plain you think I'm dirt, but you helped me win gold and a captaincy, too. I wish you were still helping. The Horde Leader knows, we'll likely need a sorcerer's help to get us out of Gauros alive. But I can't trust you anymore." He and his companions stepped forward, spreading out as they did so.

Thamas stood frozen, losing a precious moment to shock and bewilderment. Then he hastily retreated. "This is crazy! I'm no traitor, and besides, I'm a Red Wizard! You scum can't touch me!"

"Oh, I think I've just been handed the authority," Gothog said, "but you're right, why put it to the test? I'll just say you died fighting Azhir Kren's warriors, and nobody will ever know any different."

You're the one who's about to die, Thamas thought. You should have struck me down before I realized I was in danger.

Because he'd long ago prepared for a moment of ultimate peril like this. He needed only to speak a name and a certain alkilith, a formless demon made of oozing filth, would appear to serve him for thirteen of his heartbeats.

"Shleeshee!" he cried. Magic whined through the air, and he sensed power shifting in his staff, making the top half feel heavier than the bottom. Then the pole exploded. Splinters stung his cheek and forehead, and he flinched.

Nothing else happened.

Thamas whirled, ran, and smashed into the trunk of a pine tree he hadn't realized was directly behind him. He rebounded, then a blade bit into his back.

•• •• •• •• •• •• •• •• •• •• •• •• ••

Malark sauntered among the rooftop mews, inspecting them. From a certain perspective, it was a waste of time. He knew he'd find the cages clean and the food and water bowls filled. But the stooped, white-haired Rashemi who took care of the ravens liked to have his diligence perceived and commended.

"Everything looks fine," Malark said. He tossed a silver coin, and the aged servant caught it deftly. "Go have some breakfast, and a bottle of wine later on."

The Rashemi grinned, bowed, and withdrew. Humming, Malark took out the first of the scroll cases he'd brought to the roof and touched it with an ebony wand. He reflected that one of the nice things about magic was that one often needn't be a wizard to use an enchanted tool.

The wand shrank the leather tube to a fraction of its former size. Malark opened a cage, removed a raven, set it on a perch, and fed it a scrap of fresh meat. Then he tied the tiny scroll tube to its foot. Well accustomed to the process, the bird suffered it without protest, merely cocking its head and regarding its master with a black and beady eye.

Malark was sure he was alone on the roof. Even so, he took a glance around before whispering, "Find Szass Tam."

The raven spread its wings and took flight, soaring over the spires and battlements of the Central Citadel, then the myriad houses and temples beyond.

Malark shrank another scroll and bade a raven carry it to Kethin Hur. Then footsteps echoed in the stairwell, and Aoth climbed onto the roof. The glow of his azure eyes in their framework of fresh tattooing was more noticeable in dim light, but perceptible even now.

"Good morning," Malark called. "You look well."

Aoth smiled. "A lot better than I would if not for you."

Malark waved a dismissive hand. "You already thanked me for that. We don't have to keep talking about it."

"If you say so."

"Did you come to watch the sun rise over Loviatar's Manor? If so, you're doomed to disappointment. It's another gray day."

"Another gray and hungry year, I imagine, unless the zulkirs can finally wrest control of the weather away from Szass Tam.

But to answer your question, no. I came for a couple of those." He nodded toward the box of scrolls.

Malark's awareness sharpened, and he began to breathe slowly and deeply, as the Monks of the Long Death trained themselves to breathe in the moments prior to combat. "I don't follow."

"Before Nymia promoted me, Brightwing and I carried a lot of messages. We might as well carry some more."

Feeling relieved, Malark smiled. "You're bored hanging around Bezantur?"

"Yes. Really, I'm itching to take back command of my legion, but I can't do that until several pieces of it return from their various errands." His mouth twisted. "If they return."

"I admit, much of the news, as it filters in, isn't as good as we'd hoped."

"It was for a little while, but now we hear of defeat after defeat and setback after setback. You're the spymaster. Do you understand what's going wrong?"

Malark shrugged. "We knew it would be perilous for our armies to take the field under current conditions. And that the necromancers were still formidable even with their powers weakened. But I still believe the decision to take the offensive was a sound one. We still have reason to hope for victory."

"I'm glad to hear you think so. Now, will you trust me with a dispatch or two?"

"Certainly." Fortunately, many of them were inconsequential. Malark didn't really think Aoth would succumb to idle curiosity, open a message, and read it along the way. Though far from stupid, the griffon rider was also a straightforward fellow with ingrained habits of military discipline. But it was best to be safe.

Malark looked down and rummaged in the box of scrolls. Aoth gasped.

Once more poised to kill if necessary, Malark turned around. "Are you all right?"

"Yes," Aoth said. "My eyes just gave me a twinge." He rubbed them. "They still ache every once in a while."

"Are you sure you want to take on this duty?"

"Oh, yes." The war mage hesitated. "But I'll tell you what. To start with, give me something that's going to Pyarados. It's a short trip there and back."

chapter eight

19 Flamerule–14 Eleasias, the Year of Blue Fire

Wearing a murky, wavering semblance of his true face, Mirror trailed Bareris into the griffons' aerie. Now that the bard had returned, the ghost meant to resume his practice of following him around.

Bareris saluted and stood at attention, and Aoth left him that way for a long breath. Eventually, he said, "I'm taking back command of the Griffon Legion."

"Of course." Bareris smiled. "If you recall, I predicted you would."

"Cordial words can't mend our friendship," Aoth snapped. "Not even if you sweeten them with magic."

Bareris's mouth twisted. "I wasn't. I won't do that ever again. I was wrong to do it before, and I'm ready to leave the legion if that's what you'd prefer."

"Does anything remain for you to leave?" Aoth waved his spear at the many vacant cavelike stalls and the wounded griffons occupying others. The sharp smell of the salves used to treat the animals' gashes and burns blended with the normal cat-and-bird stink of the aerie.

"Captain, it's true I lost mounts and riders. But we succeeded in killing Xingax and destroying his manufactory."

"Which is all that matters, isn't it? Your revenge."

"I won't deny feeling that way. But destroying Xingax was the task our masters set me."

Aoth sighed and felt a little of his anger seep out of him. "You're right, it was. And fortunately, you didn't take the whole of the legion with you to High Thay. Maybe, when the rest return from Delhumide, it will turn out there are enough left to lead. But considering the tidings of late, I wouldn't count on it."

Bareris frowned. "It is much worse than I thought it would be. I understood the hazards, but still, I never imagined the campaign would go so badly."

"Has it occurred to you that there might be a reason? A reason beyond the obvious, I mean."

"What are you talking about?"

Aoth took a breath. "When I was blind, I told you I occasionally glimpsed things invisible to normal sight. Now that I can see properly again, that's even more true. I can see in the dark, or through a blindfold. When an illusionist casts a glamer, I see it, but I also see through it."

"That . . . sounds useful."

"Once in a while, I also see signs. After you tampered with my mind, I saw you dangling a puppet made in my image, and when the guards came to march me to my death—"

"Someone ordered your death?"

Aoth waved the interruption away. "I saw knives in their hands. Not long ago, I saw Malark's face turn into a naked skull."

Bareris hesitated. "And you thought, a skull to signify

allegiance to Szass Tam, or that Malark's a deadly menace to our cause? Mightn't it simply mean that he's a skilled fighter and assassin? You and I have seen the proof of that, time after time."

"Yes. So this new sight of mine didn't need to conjure a phantasm to tell me."

"You're assuming you understand how it works, and that it works efficiently. You could be mistaken."

"Maybe."

"Why would Malark, of all people, turn traitor ten years in? He stood with us when we defied Szass Tam himself. He kept the lich from taking Bezantur in the first tendays of the war."

"I don't know. I've always trusted him, and I'd like to go on doing it. I mentioned I was nearly killed. The zulkirs hit on the idea of vivisecting me to learn more about the blue fire. I wouldn't be here if Malark hadn't interceded. I feel like a filthy traitor myself just for suspecting him of treachery."

"But you saw his face turn into a skull."

"That's only part of it. Short of a zulkir, who's the one person who, if he turned traitor, could do the most to ruin our campaign? Our spymaster, the grand collector of information and disseminator of orders and intelligence. He could reveal all our plans and the disposition of our forces to Szass Tam. Steer our troops into ambuscades, or into the path of the blue fire. Sow rivalry and mistrust among our officers. Kossuth knows, they're all jealous of their positions as it is."

Bareris fingered his chin. "I'm still not convinced, but we did run into an interesting situation on the flight home."

"What?"

"Some of Dimon's troops expected to march over clear terrain, but instead found their way blocked by a new chasm and an abomination that climbed out of it. They assumed that the blue fire had passed by recently. But the griffon riders had spent the day flying high enough to see a long way, and we hadn't spotted any blue flame."

"So it's possible Malark deliberately guided Dimon's soldiers into difficulty."

"I suppose. But why are you telling me this? Take your suspicions to the zulkirs."

Aoth scowled. "I can't. I mean, I won't accuse a friend unless I'm certain. I especially don't want to do it when it's my sight that put my thoughts running in this direction."

"I understand. You barely escaped being vivisected. If they learned that you've acquired extraordinary abilities, they might insist on slicing you up after all."

"Yes. And if that weren't bad enough, I also have to recognize that Dmitra Flass values Malark, trusts him as much as any zulkir ever trusts anyone. She has reason. He saved her life at the Keep of Sorrows."

"So you can't denounce Malark, at least not yet, but you can't forget what you've seen, either. You'll need proof, and you must be telling me because you want my help. Why? I mean, why me?"

It was a good question. Aoth supposed it was because even though Bareris had betrayed him once, in the decade leading up to that moment of treachery, he'd been as faithful a comrade as anyone could want. No matter how grim and morose he became, how utterly indifferent to his own well-being, he'd always given his utmost when Aoth needed him.

But Aoth didn't want to acknowledge that out loud. "I'm asking you because you owe me," he said. And that was true as well.

"I do," Bareris said, "and of course I'll help you, even to spy on another friend. But I hope you turn out to be wrong."

"So do I." Aoth hesitated and tried to rein in his curiosity, but didn't quite manage it. "You're . . . different. This Tammith. Even changed, she's what you need?"

Bareris smiled a smile that conveyed happiness and rue in equal measure. "In life, she was a river. Undeath has dried her to a trickle. But after ten years in the desert, a man will weep with gratitude at any taste of water."

•• •• •• •• •• •• •• •• •• •• •• •• •• ••

Pyras Autorian, tharchion of the Thaymount, had a meadow outside his castle walls. Working under Szass Tam's supervision, twenty necromancers drew a broad and intricate pattern in yellow powder on the flat, grassy field, then set the stuff on fire to burn the design into the ground.

Long-necked and weak-chinned, Pyras watched the process from a chair his slaves had fetched. An awning protected his pasty skin from the feeble sunlight leaking through the cloud cover. He plainly wanted to ask what was going on, but couldn't quite muster the nerve.

His restlessness amused Szass Tam, but that wasn't the reason he opted not to explain. Though timid and dull-witted, Pyras had served him to the best of his ability for a long while. It would be shabby to repay him with an explanation that would only make him more uncomfortable.

The necromancers positioned and consecrated the altar stones inside the pattern with meticulous care. By the time they finished, the sun had set.

Szass Tam turned to Pyras. "Now," he said, "we need the slaves."

He focused his will, and after a moment, dread warriors marched a score of naked slaves out of the castle gate and over the drawbridge. The zombies' amber eyes shone in the gloom.

When the thralls beheld the pentacle and altar stones, and realized what lay in store, some tried to run. Dread warriors clubbed them senseless and dragged them onward.

Pyras cleared his throat. "You know, Master, slaves are valuable."

Szass Tam wished he could offer a reassuring smile, but he was still lacking a face capable of such nuances. "I promise that in days to come, you won't regret the loss. Now I must ask you to excuse me. It's time for me to take a more active role."

He rose and walked to the center of the mystic figure, while dread warriors shackled weeping slaves on top of stones, and the necromancers took up their ritual daggers. When the zombies finished their task, they cleared out. The wizards looked to Szass Tam like a choir awaiting a downbeat from its conductor.

He called a staff of frigid petrified shadow into his bony hands, raised it high, and spoke the initial words of the lengthy incantation. Chanting in unison, the lesser Red Wizards supplied the counterpoint and made the first cuts.

The slaves screamed louder. Szass Tam amplified his voice to keep it audible above the din. His followers needed to synchronize their declarations with him. If the timing was off, the ritual could escape his control, with fatal consequences.

In fact, that could happen anyway. His powers were diminished, wizardry itself had become slippery and undependable, and he was undertaking something he'd never attempted before.

If even a zulkir felt a hint of apprehension, he could only imagine how nervous the lesser wizards must be. Since the ritual had nothing to do with necromancy, they must truly feel they were treading on alien, treacherous ground. Yet no one could have read it in their demeanors, and he was proud of their discipline.

Gradually, shadow flowed, and a sickly green shimmer danced in the air. Disembodied voices whispered and sniggered, and a vile metallic taste filled Szass Tam's mouth. Invisible but perceptible to the wise, a metaphysical structure took form, a little at a time, like a stone hall constructed without mortar. Szass Tam could feel that the slightest misstep would bring it crashing down. But it didn't fall—the elements were in perfect balance.

Perceiving what he perceived, his assistants smiled. Then triumph turned to puzzlement when the slaves expired, their killers recited the last lines they'd been schooled to say, and nothing happened. The power they'd raised was like a bow, bent but not released.

"Don't worry," Szass Tam said. "We simply haven't finished. Unlock the fetters and push the corpses off the altars."

The Red Wizards did as instructed, and when they were done, he concentrated fiercely, focusing every iota of his will-power. "Now, shackle yourselves to the stones and lie quietly. I'll come around to lock down the hand you can't secure for yourselves."

He'd long ago laid enchantments of obedience on these particular followers. Yet the disorder arising from Mystra's death could conceivably break those bonds, and if even one of the necromancers tried to fight or flee, his exertions would spoil the ritual.

Fortunately, it didn't come to that. Some of the mages made choking sounds or flailed, others shuddered as if in the throes of a seizure as they tried to resist. But in the end, they all shackled themselves to the gory stones. Szass Tam completed the task of restraining them, then drew an athame into his hand and commenced butchering them.

By the time he finished, he had blood all over the front of his robe. He turned to Pyras, who looked on with goggling eyes.

"Come into the circle," Szass Tam said.

Pyras stood and advanced, trembling and stumbling. He too was mind-bound, and had no choice.

Szass Tam met him halfway, took his arm, and conducted him to the center of the circle. "We won't bother with fetters," he said, because Pyras was no Red Wizard, just a weak-willed wretch who had no hope of squirming free of his master's psychic grip.

"Please," Pyras whispered, tears sliding from his eyes, "I'm loyal. I always have been."

"I know," Szass Tam said. "I'm grateful for your fidelity, and I apologize. If it's any consolation, your sacrifice will serve the best of causes, and I'll make it go as quickly as I can." He slit open Pyras's gold-buttoned velvet doublet and silk shirt.

Szass Tam sensed it when the tharchion's heart stopped beating, and felt the man's anguished spirit fleeing his ruined body. The magic he'd worked so assiduously to create finally discharged an instant later.

A sudden sense of overwhelming wrongness and malice impressed itself on his mystical awareness and bashed his mind into momentary confusion.

Then the moon and stars disappeared, and Pyras's castle, too. Darkness sealed the pentacle away from the rest of the world like a black fist closing around it.

And then Bane appeared. His form was murky, but Szass Tam could make out dark armor, the infamous jeweled gauntlet, and the glint of eyes.

On first inspection, the Lord of Darkness appeared no more terrible than some of the spectres Szass Tam had commanded in his time. Yet an aura of vast power and cruel intelligence emanated from him, and the lich felt a sudden urge to abase himself.

Annoyed, he quashed the impulse. Bane is simply a spirit, he told himself. I've trafficked with hundreds and this is just one more.

"How dare you summon me?" said the god. His bass voice was soft and mellifluous, but some hidden undertone pained the ears.

"I invited you," Szass Tam replied, "by sacrificing twenty men and women in the prime of their lives, twenty accomplished necromancers I can ill spare, and one of Thay's wealthiest and most powerful nobles."

Bane sneered, although how Szass Tam knew that, he couldn't say, for he couldn't make out a twist of lip in the smudge of shadow that was the deity's face. "Say, rather, twenty slaves, twenty charlatans whose magic had largely forsaken them, and a half-witted, cowardly toady."

"That is another way of looking at it, but my perspective is as valid as yours. I tendered the gift at a moment when I had every reason to fear the magic would wriggle out of my grip and destroy me. I hoped that even a god would appreciate such a compliment."

"I might," said Bane, "if it came from one of my worshipers, but that you have never been."

"Yet I've always supported the church of the Black Hand."

"But no more than you've supported the churches of Kossuth, Mask, Umberlee, and even Cyric. You played each against the other, making sure that none ever achieved preeminence in Thay, and thus, that none will ever undermine the rule of the Red Wizards."

"I concede the point. That is how it used to be. But now Thay is a different place, and I have more urgent concerns."

"As do I. Far more urgent than chatting with an impudent magus with no claim on my consideration. With Mystra slain, the higher worlds are in turmoil. My place is there. Open the door to the Barrens."

"As soon as we finish our talk."

Bane didn't lift his fist in its shell of gems and dark metal, nor did he grow any bigger than Szass Tam himself. Yet suddenly the Black Hand gave off a sense of profound and immediate menace, even as, in some indefinable but unmistakable fashion, he loomed taller than a giant. "Do you imagine," he asked, "that your puny summoning can hold me here?"

"For a while."

"Then die a true death," said Bane. "Die and be nothing."

Darkness seethed around Szass Tam and took the form of shadowy hands with long claws. Some gripped him, seeking to immobilize him, some pummeled him, and the rest hooked their talons in his body and ripped strips of flesh away.

The pain was excruciating. He forced himself to focus past it and speak the words of command to activate the talismans of protection concealed around his person.

The grip of the dark hands grew feeble. He wrenched himself away from them, and they faded into nothingness.

His now-tattered robe flapping around him, Szass Tam brandished his staff. Tendrils of gleaming ice coiled around Bane like vines climbing a tree. Spikes sprouted from them to push against the shadowstuff that was his body.

For a moment, the god seemed surprised, perhaps even slightly disconcerted, as a grown man might be if a child slapped him. Then he jerked the hand with the gauntlet over his head, shattering his bonds.

"You see how it is," Szass Tam said. "Yes, you can break free, and quite possibly destroy me in the process. But you'll have to work at it, and I might even bloody your nose before you finish. It will be less trouble and take less of your time to grant me the parley I seek."

The Black Lord snorted. "What is it you want, dead man?"

"Help winning my war. My rivals currently hold the upper hand. I have a new aide who's doing a brilliant job of keeping them from making the most of their opportunities, but he can't turn the conflict around by himself."

"I won't lend you an army of devils. I wouldn't even give them to the Zhentarim, or any of the other folk who have already rendered me their service. With the old order shattered, I'll have my own wars to win."

"I understand. That's not what I'm asking for."

"What, then?"

"First, teach me everything you can about the nature of magic as it exists today."

"I'm not the god of wizardry, and the nature of the arcane has yet to stabilize. It continues to alter even as we speak."

"But you are a god, and I'm sure you understand things I don't. I'll take whatever you can give me."

"What else do you want?"

"I've emptied the tombs and graveyards of the north. I've slaughtered many of its slaves and peasants and even some of my own living soldiers. Which is to say, I'm running short of raw material on which my necromancers can practice their art."

"What a shame."

"Isn't it? Yet it needn't be a disaster. This ancient land is still full of dead bodies. It's just that they've decayed so utterly as to be indistinguishable from the soil in which they lie. But a highly skilled necromancer could still call something forth—if he were capable of recognizing the exact patch of ground containing the remains."

"And so you want me to give you that ability as well."

"Yes, and I fear there's more."

Bane laughed. Though musical, the sound was even more hurtful than his speech, and Szass Tam stiffened. "You don't lack for gall, necromancer."

"So people often told me. When I was climbing up the hierarchy of my order, I mean. Once you become a zulkir, people stop critiquing your character to your face. Anyway, you're probably aware that I share a psychic bond with many of the sorcerers under my command, and that I have a limited ability to be in multiple places simultaneously."

"Yes."

"I need my powers augmented, so I can direct my wizards more efficiently. Otherwise, I won't be able to turn a fresh supply of corpse dust into warriors fast enough to do me any good."

"Anything else?"

"Just one thing, the obvious. Currently the Church of Bane supports my fellow zulkirs. It would help if you instructed your priests to back me instead."

"Dead man, just for amusement's sake, let's imagine I might be willing to grant you all these extravagant favors. What could you possibly offer of comparable worth?"

"Thay. When I'm its sole sovereign, you'll be the only god worshiped within its borders."

"I've explained. With the higher worlds entering an era of strife and chaos, Faerûn, let alone this little piece of it, is of little concern to me."

Szass Tam stared at the sheen of eyes in Bane's murky face. "I don't believe you. We inhabitants of the physical plane may seem like grubs and ants to the gods, but you need us. Our worship gives you strength."

"Yet I reject your terms."

Szass Tam sighed. "Then how about this? After I make myself master of Thay, give me one thousand years to enjoy the fruits of my victory, and then you can take my soul. I'll be your bonds-man forever after, in this world or wherever you decide to have me labor on your behalf."

Bane laughed. "Do you think so highly of yourself as to imagine that appreciably sweetens the bargain? The addition of one tiny soul, due a millennium hence?"

"It's not a prodigiously long time in the context of your eternal existence, and I am Szass Tam. Jeer and scoff at me all you like, but I know you're wise enough to understand what that means. You could scour your 'higher worlds' from one end to the other without finding a vassal who will further your schemes half as well."

Bane laughed again. "I'm tempted to accept this bargain. Then, in days to come, to make you the lowliest of my slaves, performing the most painful and degrading duties, just to punish your arrogance as it deserves."

"If you want to waste my talents, that will be your prerogative. Now, will you make a pact with me or not?"

"Do you know . . . I believe I will, but the terms must change in one respect. My priests and other worshipers will continue to aid the council."

"Because that way, no matter who wins, you and your creed will enjoy the favor of the victors. Very shrewd. All right, it's a bargain. Give me knowledge and power and I'll make do without your clerics."

"I warn you, you're asking for more than you were ever meant to hold, and jamming it inside you all at once will exacerbate the stress. Your mind may break apart."

"That I doubt."

"We'll see." His arm a blur of motion, Bane whipped the back of his jeweled gauntlet against Szass Tam's face.

Bone cracked, but the initial numbing shock of impact didn't give way to pain. That was because a sensation like a discordant scream stabbed into Szass Tam's mind, and it was so intense as to eclipse mere physical distress.

It howled on and on until he began to fear that, as Bane had warned, he might not be able to bear it. Then it resolved from a grating shriek into harmony. His inner self seemed to vibrate to it, but no longer felt as if it might tear apart. Rather, the sensation was exhilarating.

He realized he'd fallen, and picked himself up off the ground. He looked around for Bane, but the Black Hand had taken his leave. The dark barrier had dissolved, and the stars shined overhead.

Szass Tam's face gave him a belated twinge. Now confident of his ability to perform the delicate manipulations, he mended the bone, regenerated flesh and skin, and even regrew his beard. He started to heal the rest of his wounds as well, realized he could now rid his hands of any trace of blemish, but then, on a whim, left the fingers withered. He was used to them that way.

He could feel that, while the new knowledge was his to keep, the prodigious mystical strength Bane had lent him would gradually fade. He needed to exploit it immediately if it was to carry him to victory. Yet as he sent his thoughts soaring to link with the minds of his followers, he had time to grin at the reflection that even a so-called god with all his alleged omniscience could be gulled into making a disastrously bad bargain.

* * * * * * * * * * * * * * *

Perched on Brightwing's back, Aoth surveyed an expanse of sky, and his preternaturally keen vision discerned all sorts of things. Subtle variations in the grayness of the clouds. Sparrows. Vultures circling. A white gull that had strayed too far north of the seashore. But no ravens.

A cold drizzle started falling, further souring his mood. "Will ravens fly in this?" he asked.

"They might," Brightwing said, "if it doesn't get any harder."

"Wonderful." That meant he and the griffon had to keep flying in it, too.

Proving Malark's treachery, if in fact he was a traitor, seemed simple enough in principle. One need only show a discrepancy between the intelligence the spymaster received and the information he supplied to the zulkirs or the commanders in the field. Or between the orders the council gave him to transmit and those he actually sent along.

The trick was identifying those contradictions. Aoth was a high-ranking officer, and Bareris likewise occupied a position of trust, but even so, they had no right or apparent reason to review every secret message that found its way to Malark, or that he sent in turn. Nor were they informed of the outcome every time the zulkirs conferred, or when one of the archmages acted unilaterally.

Since they doubted their ability to spy on Malark and remain undetected while he waited on his superiors and read and prepared his scrolls, that left Aoth and his fellow conspirators to hunt messenger birds on the wing, but not near the Central Citadel or anywhere over Bezantur, where they might have had some reasonable hope of finding them. They had to seek them in the vastness of the countryside, and hope that if they did manage to kill one, its message would prove duplicitous, and they'd know enough to recognize the treason when they saw it.

"Curse it, anyway," Aoth growled. "I'm working with the false friend who betrayed me to trip up the true one who saved my life, and I'm doing it to serve the masters who wanted to cut me to pieces. What in Kossuth's name is wrong with me?"

"I've been wondering that for years," Brightwing said. "We can still desert if you'd rather."

Aoth sighed. "No, I've lost the inclination. Walking away from a long, slow grind of a stalemate is one thing, because what does it matter if you're there or not? But for a little while, after the blue fires came, it seemed the south might actually win, and now it looks as if Szass Tam might defeat us for good and all. Either way, the war feels different, and running off would seem more cowardly."

"Is that supposed to be an example of human reason at work? Because to a griffon, it makes no sense."

Aoth tried to frame a retort, then sat up straight in the saddle when he spotted a fleck of black in the distance. Before the blue flame infected his eyes, he wouldn't have been able to see it at all. Now he thought he could discern a brown wrapping bound to a yellow foot.

"There," he said.

"Where?" Brightwing asked.

He married his mind to hers, sharing his vision. "To the right, above the abandoned vineyard."

"Got it." She raised one wing, dipped the other, turned, and hurtled in the proper direction.

The raven saw them coming and fled. Perhaps, in its animal way, it wondered why they were troubling it, for such a small bird should have been beneath the notice of such a large predator.

A war mage would have no trouble bringing a raven down, but Aoth had to make sure he did it in a way that wouldn't destroy the message it carried. He recited a spell, brandished his spear, and a cloud of greenish vapor materialized around the bird. It convulsed, fell, and smashed against the ground.

Brightwing landed beside it. Aoth dismounted and picked up the broken carcass. For a moment, he felt like a bully, using powerful sorcery to kill such a fragile, defenseless creature.

He opened the tiny scroll case and it swelled to its full size. He shook out the document inside, unfurled it, and read it. A chill oozed up his spine.

"Is it anything?" Brightwing asked.

"Yes." He rolled up the parchment again. "We need to get back to the city."

•• •• •• •• •• •• •• •• •• •• •• •• •• ••

Dmitra Flass kept a garden in the heart of the grim black fortress that was the Central Citadel, and the rosebuds blazed in voluptuous shades of crimson and gold despite the droughts, tainted rains, and plant-killing pests of the past ten years. Perhaps, Malark thought, it was illusion that kept the flowers bright and the grass thick and verdant at all times.

Whatever the truth of the matter, when his schedule allowed, as it did that evening, he liked to stroll and meditate here. He headed for a favorite bower, and then Aoth stepped onto the path ahead of him.

Aoth was carrying his spear, had his falchion strapped across his back, and wore mail, but none of that was unusual. It was the deliberate way he moved and the grim set of his square, tattooed face that betrayed his intentions.

A pity. Malark had known someone would discover his treason eventually, but he'd hoped for more time.

Had Aoth come alone? It was possible, but Malark doubted it. It seemed more likely that someone else was sneaking through the trees and bushes to strike him down from behind if he resisted arrest. He listened, trying to pinpoint the location of that hypothetical threat, meanwhile giving the war mage a smile. "Good evening. How are your eyes?"

"I know about your treason," Aoth said. "I got my hands on one of the scrolls you wrote."

"This is some sort of misunderstanding."

"Don't insult my intelligence."

"You're right. I should know better, and I apologize." Malark had never had any reason to doubt the acuity of his hearing, but he still couldn't detect anyone creeping up on him. Maybe no one was. On the other hand, if Aoth had enlisted Mirror's aid, the ghost wouldn't make any noise unless he wanted to. "Can I appeal to friendship and gratitude instead?"

"No. I hate this, but I mean to do my duty. Curse it all, why would you turn traitor now, when we actually had a chance of winning? What can Szass Tam give you that Dmitra Flass wouldn't?"

Malark sighed. "It's complicated."

"Have it your way. I'm sure it will all come out during your interrogation. Will you accompany me peacefully? It might go a little easier for you if you cooperate."

"All right. Take me to Dmitra."

"No. She's fond of you. Of course, she's also a zulkir, and I doubt mere sentiment would cloud her judgment sufficiently for you to talk your way out of trouble, but I figured, why risk it? I showed the proof of your guilt to Nevron, and he's the one who ordered your arrest. He'll question you first, and involve the rest of the council when he sees fit."

"All right." Malark took a step forward. "But indulge my curiosity. Tell me what aroused your suspicions." Sometimes people had trouble talking and focusing on an opponent at the same time, and if he could distract Aoth, maybe he could spring and attack without provoking a blaze of arcane power from the head of the spear.

Or maybe not. Malark rarely met a warrior whose prowess he truly respected, but the commander of the Griffon Legion was one of the few.

Which meant this confrontation could quite possibly end in a fitting death for one of them. But the prospect made Malark feel an unaccustomed ambivalence. He still wanted to die, but he also wanted to share in what was to come.

"Sorry," Aoth said. "I don't care to answer that question." He leveled the spear and stepped off the path, making way for his prisoner to move in front of him, and then, off to Malark's right, something brushed in the grass.

At last Malark knew the approximate position of another adversary, and this one might be less formidable than Aoth. He pivoted and charged toward the faint noise.

He felt a pang of surprise when he saw Bareris. He'd thought the bard and war mage had had a falling out, but apparently they'd patched things up. From a certain perspective, that was unfortunate, for Bareris too was a fighter to be reckoned with.

Happily though, Malark's sudden move caught both griffon riders by surprise. Aoth hurled a blast of flame from his spear, but it only roared through the space his target had just vacated. Bareris extended his sword, but his timing was off. Malark brushed the blade aside with one hand, stepped in, and struck at Bareris's chest with the heel of the other.

Bareris jerked back from the blow, which kept it from landing with full force. Instead of smashing splinters of rib into his lung and heart, it simply sent him staggering backward.

Malark sprinted to the door in the garden's east wall, then glanced back. The closest foes were Mirror, who looked like a wavering semblance of Bareris, and a huge wolf that could only be Tammith Iltazyarra. Aoth and the bard were farther back, the former circling, trying to reach a position from which he could cast another spell without a tree or his allies blocking the line to the target, and the latter still doubled over, gasping and pressing a hand to his chest.

The odds against Malark were even longer than he'd initially guessed. Still, since he'd broken out of the noose that had been closing around him, maybe he had a chance. Szass Tam had given him a charm to use when the moment came to make his escape, but had also made it clear that he must be particular as to how he employed it. Otherwise, the effect could prove as deadly to him as to his pursuers.

Now, he judged, was the moment. He opened a hidden pocket on his belt, snatched forth a black pearl, threw it, and spun around. He jerked the handle of the door and found it locked. He kicked it off its hinges and dashed onward.

•• •• •• •• •• •• •• •• •• •• •• •• •• •• ••

Tammith understood that Bareris and Aoth hoped to take their friend into custody without hurting him or depriving him of his dignity. That was why they hadn't blasted him with spells the instant they found him, or brought a squad of legionnaires along. The part of her that still remembered fondness and compassion made her feel that she might have done the same, even as her vampire side scorned her comrades as fools.

Now she no longer felt any such ambivalence. Malark's break for freedom had suppressed what passed for her humanity and fired her predatory instincts. As she raced after him, all she wanted in the world was to rip his legs out from under him, tear him with her fangs, and guzzle his blood. Indeed, it was going to take all the self-control she could muster to stop short of killing him, but Nevron wanted him alive.

Certain the barrier would delay him long enough for her to close with him, she grinned a lupine grin when he scrambled to the locked door. Then he threw a dark bead or stone.

Since it landed in grass, it shouldn't have shattered. It did anyway, and shadow boiled out of it, separating into ragged, floating figures that moaned and gibbered as they advanced.

Tammith felt a dullness numbing her mind and exerted her will to banish it. Only after she succeeded could she think coherently enough to recognize the entities: allips, the mad, vengeful spirits of suicides. A particularly nasty rearguard to cover Malark's retreat.

She melted from she-wolf to woman, because the touch of an allip was venomous. If she had to fight the things, she preferred to do it with the superior reach her sword afforded.

Bareris started singing, probably to counter the hypnotic effect of the allips' babble. Tammith drew her blade, and then a pair of the spirits closed with her.

Fangs bared, she slashed at one and the sword whizzed all the way through it without any tangible resistance. The weapon was enchanted, but she sensed that the stroke hadn't hurt her foe. Well, perhaps the next one would.

The allips whirled around her, groaning and keening. She cut and thrust, and perhaps their murky forms began to fray, but it was difficult to tell for certain. She dodged and ducked to avoid their scrabbling, raking fingers.

But it was hard to avoid every strike when the entities were attacking from two sides, and eventually, one landed a blow from behind. Or so she assumed, for she didn't see it, nor did she feel localized pain or a shock of impact as such. Rather, she experienced a sudden disruption of thought, followed by confusion, fear, and a sense of filthy violation.

It was like having Xingax in her head again, and it drove her to fury. Screaming, she laid around her until her attackers dissolved into nothingness and their ghastly voices fell silent.

She turned, surveying the battle. Malark had broken the locked door and fled. Still singing, Bareris was holding his own against two remaining allips, and Mirror was exchanging blows with another.

Aoth, however, was having problems. Half a dozen of the crazed, vicious spirits had swarmed on him, and, plainly hurt, he was stumbling around in the middle of them jabbing desperately with his spear. A spell would likely have served him better, but perhaps he was already too addled to cast one.

It occurred to her that Aoth was Bareris's friend, and that she could rush to his aid. But he was nothing to her, and the prey responsible for fouling her own mind was getting away. She dissolved into bats and flew in pursuit.

•• •• •• •• •• •• •• •• •• •• •• •• ••

Though Mirror hadn't consciously tried to summon his targe when the allip engaged him, it had materialized on his arm anyway, and served him well. A wooden or steel shield would likely have proved all but useless, but he, his ethereal opponent, and his armor were all made of the same refined essence of darkness and pain.

He thrust his blade into his adversary's murky, demented features, and it gave a last mad gabble and withered from existence. That freed him to help Aoth.

But when he turned toward the war mage, he saw that it might already be too late to succor him. Aoth staggered and fell, the spear flying from his grip. The allips sprang on top of him and clawed like famished ghouls ripping at a corpse.

Mirror could leap to Aoth in an instant, but he couldn't strike half a dozen blows quickly enough to keep one of the allips from giving the griffon rider his death. But he could attempt something else, because communion with his god had partly restored him. At times, he thought more clearly, and he could now invoke the holy powers he'd wielded in life.

That didn't mean he was eager to do so, because as he'd discovered when healing Aoth's eyes, there was a fundamental discrepancy between the divine champion he'd once been and the tainted shadow that remained of him. When he channeled the power of his deity, he was like a snowman trying to handle fire.

Yet if his faith was strong, his master would protect him. He raised his sword and called to that which he no longer understood or could even name, but which he loved and trusted nonetheless.

A radiance like daylight blazed from his blade. The allips cringed from it, floating away from the fallen Aoth.

Mirror charged them and cut at the nearest. Now shrouded in blur to hamper an opponent's aim, Bareris rushed to stand beside him. Fighting in concert, the two companions slashed the remaining allips into evaporating wisps of murk, then hurried over to Aoth.

Mirror didn't trust himself to examine the war mage. After repelling the allips, he felt too hollow, too close to dissolving into mindless ache and malice, and in such a condition, his touch or even proximity might further injure a wounded man. "How is he?" he asked.

Bareris kneeled, stripped off his leather gauntlet, and worked his fingertips under the mail to feel for Aoth's pulse. "At least his heart is beating."

•• •• •• •• •• •• •• •• •• •• •• •• •• ••

Malark sprinted through the labyrinth of corridors, chambers, and courtyards that was the Central Citadel. He was reasonably hopeful of escaping. Even if it didn't kill his adversaries, Szass Tam's gift would at least provide him a fair head start, and thanks to his training in the monastery, he could run faster and longer than most anyone he'd ever known.

The question was, where should he run? His horse offered the fastest way out of the city, but he suspected Aoth and Bareris had posted guards at the stable should he elude them in the garden.

Better, he thought, to procure a cloak and hood to throw on over his expensive courtier's clothing, then slip out of the fortress. He'd worry about a quick way north later. If worse came to worst, he could run the entire distance about as fast as an ordinary horse could carry him.

He plunged into another area open to the sky, an octagonal paved yard with a phosphorescent statue of the late Aznar Thrul, staff raised high, the bronze folds of his robe streaming as if windblown, towering in the center. Then something fluttered overhead.

Malark surmised it was a bat's wing—Tammith Iltazyarra's wing. He tried to spring aside, but to no avail. Something furry bumped down on top of his head.

The bat was so light that the impact didn't hurt. It did sting, however, when the creature hooked its claws into his scalp and ripped at his forehead with its fangs.

The bite sent an icy shock of sickness through his frame. He lifted a hand to tear his attacker away, and a second bat lit on the extremity and sank its teeth into his index finger. A third landed on his back, and, clinging to his doublet, climbed toward his neck.

He threw himself down on his back and crushed the creature before it could reach its goal, then whipped his arm and smashed the bat on his hand against the paving stones, dislodging it. He grabbed the one on his head, yanked it free, and wrung it like a washcloth.

Others descended on him. He rolled out from underneath them, sprang to his feet, and when they wheeled in pursuit, met them with stabs of his stiffened fingers. He hit one, and then they flew away from him, swirled together, and became a pallid woman in black armor, a sword extended in her hand. Despite the harm he'd inflicted on the bats, Malark couldn't see any sign of it in the way she carried herself. Still, it was possible she'd been injured.

"Perhaps you assumed," he said, playing for a little more time to steady his breathing, "that I couldn't hurt you without an enchanted weapon." He had the monks' esoteric disciplines to thank for it that he could. "Otherwise you might not have come at me as a flock of bats. You would have opted for something less delicate."

She glided closer. "That was the only mistake I'm going to make."

"Everything you've done since the Keep of Sorrows has been a mistake. You know Szass Tam, and now you've had a chance to take the measure of his rivals. Surely you recognize that none of them is a match for him. He may have encountered setbacks of late, but he's still going to win." He edged sideways and she turned to compensate.

"So help me escape and come back with me," Malark continued. "If I plead your case, the lich will forgive you. You'll command your followers just as you did before."

She glared and showed him her fangs. "I don't want anything to be as it was before, because I was a slave, with my mind in chains. Maybe you don't know what that's like, spymaster, but you will. With the Silent Company lost to me, I need some new progeny to do my bidding, and I'm going to start with you."

His mouth tightened. "Captain, it's conceivable you may kill me, but I swear by everything I hold sacred that I will never allow you to make me undead."

"It's always either funny or sad when people make vows they have no hope of keeping. In your case, I'd have to say funny." She sprang at him.

He twisted aside, hooked her ankle with his foot, and jerked her leg out from underneath her. She lurched forward. He snapped a kick into her kidney and chopped at the nape of her neck with the blade of his hand.

She planted her front foot and recovered her balance, but her upper body was still canted forward. That should have kept her from even perceiving the strike at her neck, let alone reacting quickly enough to counter it. But she twisted at the waist, grabbed Malark's wrist, and ripped the back of his hand with her fangs.

Her bite was frigid poison, and another wave of light-headed weakness almost buckled his knees. He shouted to focus his strength, and she thrust the point of her sword at his midsection.

Fortunately, she was still in her awkward crouch, and they were too close together for her to use the long blade easily. It gave him just enough time to twist his arm free of her grip and her fangs and fling himself backward. Her thrust fell short by the length of a finger.

Tammith Iltazyarra straightened up and returned to a conventional swordsman's stance. She had his blood smeared across her mouth. More of it ran down from his torn hand, and dripped from the wounds in his brow to sting his eyes and blind them. He wiped them and willed the bleeding to stop. It didn't quite, but at least it diminished.

Tammith stared into his eyes and stabbed with her will, trying to hypnotize him. But his psyche proved too strong, and he struck back with a kick to her knee. She snatched her leg out of the way and cut at his torso. He dropped low, and the stroke whizzed over his head.

The combatants resumed circling, exchanged another set of attacks and then another. Still, neither could land a decisive blow.

It was plain to Malark that he was more skillful. Unfortunately, Tammith's preternatural strength helped to make up the difference, as did her sword, armor, indefatigability, and resilience. In theory, the naked hands of a monk could hurt her, but it was difficult to strike to great effect when mere pain appeared unable to slow her for more than an instant, and she no longer required the use of most of her internal organs.

Yet Malark had to finish the duel quickly. He couldn't linger, sparring, until her allies caught up or until someone came to investigate the commotion. It was time to take a chance.

She stepped forward, then back, or at least it was supposed to look that way. In reality, her lead foot hitched backward, but the other stayed in place. She was trying to throw off his sense of distance, to make him perceive her as farther away than she actually was.

He advanced as if the trick had deceived him. She lunged, her sword extended to pierce his guts.

Using both hands, he grabbed the blade. It cut him instantly. With her inhuman strength, his adversary needed only to yank it backward to slice him to the bone, sever tendons, and possibly even shear his fingers off.

He hammered a kick into her midsection. The shock locked her up and weakened her grip. He jerked the weapon free.

By doing so, he cut himself more deeply, but it didn't matter. He didn't care about the pain—wouldn't even really feel it until he chose to allow it—and his fingers were still able to clasp the hilt.

Employing both hands, he seized it in an overhand grip like a dagger, swung it over his head, lunged, bellowed, and struck. It was a clumsy way to wield a sword, but the only way to attack with the point and achieve the forceful downward arc he required.

The point crunched through her mail, pierced her heart, popped out her back, and stabbed into the pavement beneath her toppling form, nailing her to the ground.

A wooden stake would have been better. It would have paralyzed her. But at least the enchanted sword had her shrieking, thrashing, and fumbling impotently at the blade. In another moment, she might collect herself sufficiently to realize she could free herself by dissolving into mist, but he didn't give her the chance. He gouged her eyes from their sockets, then drove in bone-shattering blows until her neck broke and her head was lopsided.

He stepped back, regarded his handiwork, and felt a pang of loathing that had nothing to do with the harm she'd done to him. She was an abomination, an affront to Death, and he ought to do his utmost to slay her, not leave her to recover as she unquestionably would. But it wasn't practical. In fact, considering that she'd survived repeated beheadings, it might not even be possible.

He'd cleared her out of his way, and that would have to do. He turned and ran on.

chapter nine

21 Eleasias–15 Eleint, the Year of Blue Fire

Aoth peered at the faces looking back at him. At first he didn't recall them. He only had a sense that he should. Then one, a ferocious countenance comprised of beak, feathers, and piercing eyes, evoked a flood of memories and associations. "Brightwing," he croaked.

The griffon snorted. "Finally. Now maybe I can have my lair all to myself again." She nipped through the rope securing Aoth's left wrist to the frame of the cot.

He saw that his associates had actually tied him to a bed in the griffon's pungent stall. Shafts of moonlight fell through the high windows. Tammith's skin was white as bone in the pale illumination. Mirror was a faceless smudge.

"How are you?" Bareris asked.

"I'm not crazy anymore, if that's what you mean."

"Do you remember what happened to you?"

"Part of it." Some kind of spirits had attacked him, not spilling his blood but seemingly ripping away pieces of his inner self. He'd fallen unconscious, and when he awoke, he was like a cornered animal. He didn't recognize anyone or understand anything. He thought everyone was trying to hurt him, and fought back savagely.

The healers had tried to help him, but at first their magic hadn't had any effect. Then someone had hit on the idea of housing him with his familiar, in the hope that proximity to the creature with whom he shared a psychic bond would exert a restorative effect.

Maybe it had, for afterward, he grew calmer. He still didn't recognize his companions, but sometimes his fire-kissed eyes saw that they meant to help and not harm him. During those intervals he was willing to swallow the water, food, and medicines they brought, and to suffer the chanted prayers and healing touch of a priest without screaming, thrashing, or trying to bite him.

The recollection of his mad and feral state brought a surge of shame and horror, as well as fear that he might relapse. Sensing the tenor of his thoughts, Brightwing grunted. "Don't worry, you're your normal self again, for what little that's worth. I can tell."

"Thank you. I suppose."

The griffon bit through the other wrist restraint. His limbs stiff, Aoth sat up and started untying the remains of his bonds. His minders had used soft rope, but even so, his struggles had rubbed stinging galls into his wrists and ankles.

As he dropped the last piece of rope to the floor, the final bit of the jumbled puzzle locked into place. "Malark!" he said. "Did you get him?"

"No," Bareris said.

"Curse it! Why did I bring you into this in the first place? What good are you?"

Even as he spoke, Aoth realized he was being unfair. But he didn't care. He'd been crippled and humiliated twice, once by blindness and once by madness, an enemy had escaped, and the false friend who'd tampered with his mind was a convenient outlet for his frustrations.

Bareris frowned. "I'm sorry Malark got away. But at least you unmasked him. He can't do any further harm."

"You offered to leave the Griffon Legion," Aoth replied. "It's time for you to do that."

"No," Mirror said.

Aoth turned his head just in time to see the ghost's blur of a face sharpen into a kind of shadow-sketch of his former self—a lean, melancholy visage, an aquiline nose, and a mustache.

"I know I owe you," Aoth said, "and I know you've taken Bareris for your friend. May he prove more loyal to you than he did to me. But—"

"We champions of the order are one," Mirror said. "What stains one man's honor tarnishes us all, and by the same token, a companion can atone for his brother's sin. I helped you. Accordingly, our code requires you to forgive Bareris."

Aoth shook his head. "We aren't your ancient fellowship of paladins or whatever it was. I'm a Thayan, and we don't think that way."

"We are who we are," Mirror said, "and you are who you are."

Even by the ghost's standards, it was a cryptic if not meaningless declaration, yet it evoked a twinge of muddled, irrational guilt, and since Aoth was truly the injured party, he resented it. "The whoreson doesn't even care whether I forgive him or not. If you understand anything about him, you know he only cares about his woman."

"That isn't true," Tammith said. Her voice had an odd undercurrent to it, as if echoing some buried sorrow or shame. "He always valued his friends, even when grief and rage blinded him to his own feelings, and now his sight is clearer."

Aoth glowered at Bareris. "Why are you standing mute while others plead for you? You're the bard, full of golden words and clever arguments."

"I already told you I'm sorry," Bareris said, "and I truly want your forgiveness. But I won't plead for something to which I have no right. Hold a grudge if you think you should. Sometimes a wrong is bitter enough that a man must. Nobody knows that better than I."

Brightwing spread her rustling wings, then gave them an irritated snap. "Either forgive him or kill him. Whatever will stop all this maudlin blather."

Aoth sighed. "I'm just getting up off my sickbed. I'll need a bath and a meal before I feel up to killing anyone." He shifted his gaze to Bareris. "So stay in the legion if you'd rather."

Bareris smiled. "I would. Thank you."

"What's been going on while I was insane?"

"The zulkirs are convening another council of war. You recovered just in time to attend."

"Lucky me."

＊＊ ＊＊ ＊＊ ＊＊ ＊＊ ＊＊ ＊＊ ＊＊ ＊＊ ＊＊ ＊＊ ＊＊

Nevron gazed at his fellow zulkirs—prissy, bloodless Lauzoril, gross, bloated Samas Kul perpetually stuffing food in his mouth, and all the rest—and suffered a spasm of loathing for each and every one of them.

Nothing unusual in that. He despised the vast majority of puny, muddled human beings. In general, he preferred the company of demons and devils. Even the least of them tended to be purer, grander, and certainly less prone to hypocrisy than the average mortal. He often entertained the fancy of abandoning the blighted realm that Thay had become and seeking a new destiny in the higher worlds. What a glorious adventure that would be!

But it could also prove to be a short one. Nevron was a zulkir and confident of his own mystical prowess. But he also comprehended, as only a conjuror could, what awesome powers walked the Blood Rift, the Barrens, and similar realities. He would have to confront them with comparable capabilities if he was to establish himself as a prince among the baatezu or tanar'ri.

Which, he supposed, was why he tarried where he was, learning and inventing new spells, crafting and acquiring new talismans, and impressing new entities into his service. It was the most intelligent strategy, so long as he had the judgment to recognize when he'd accumulated enough. Otherwise, preparation could become procrastination.

Dmitra Flass clapped her hands together to call the assembly to order. The percussive sound didn't seem louder than normal, but was somehow more commanding, as if she'd used her illusionist abilities to enhance it in some subtle way. They were all gradually figuring out how to make their spells reliable in the dreary new world Mystra's death had spawned.

The company fell silent, zulkirs and lesser folk alike, but the response seemed slower and more grudging than on previous occasions. Nevron wondered if Dmitra perceived the challenge apparent in the rancorous stares of several of her peers.

"We're here—" she began.

"To decide our next move," Lallara snapped. "We know. You don't have to begin every council by harping on the obvious."

"In fact," Nevron said, "you don't have to begin them at all." A fiend bound in the iron bracelet he wore around his left wrist whispered to him, encouraging him, as it often did when he said or did anything that smacked of malice or conflict.

Dmitra arched an eyebrow, or rather, the smooth stretch of skin where an eyebrow would be if she hadn't long ago removed it. "Someone must preside, and we seem to have slipped into the habit of letting the task fall to me."

"Well, perhaps we should slip out of it," Lallara said. "I'm not fighting Szass Tam just to see someone else set herself above me."

"That was never my intention," Dmitra said.

Nevron sneered. "Of course not. But it's inevitable that the one who presides over our deliberations exerts a degree of leadership, and perhaps you aren't the best choice for the role, considering the damage Malark Springhill did."

Dmitra sighed. "We all opted to trust Malark."

"But he was your servant," Nevron said, "and thus, your responsibility."

Dmitra waved a dismissive hand adorned with ruby rings and long crimson nails. "Fine. You guide the discussion. What does it matter, so long as we confer to some intelligent purpose?"

Her quick acquiescence caught Nevron by surprise, and the spirit in the bracelet sniggered at his fleeting confusion. Through an exertion of will, he afflicted it with pain, and the laugh became a scream, another sound that only he could hear.

"As you wish," he said. Since she'd plainly wanted to preside herself, Lallara gave him a glower, not that it differed appreciably from her usual clamp-mouthed, venomous expression. "This is the situation. We've sent a host of messengers—ravens, griffon riders, spirits, and others—racing around to countermand the false orders and refute the fraudulent intelligence Malark Springhill transmitted, and to find out exactly what lies he disseminated."

Dmitra smiled her radiant smile. "Thanks be to the High One," she drawled, "that the zulkir of Conjuration isn't wasting our time harping on the obvious."

The devil Nevron carried in the heavy silver ring on his left thumb murmured to him, imploring him to unleash it to punish the bitch for her mockery, and he wished that it were practical. Yes, he was saying what everyone already knew, but he had to launch the discussion somehow, didn't he?

"Once we determined what falsehoods Springhill uttered," he continued, "we could try to figure out why. The reason for some of it was obvious. He steered companies into traps, or to destinations that served no military purpose, or sowed suspicion and disaffection in the ranks. But he also sought to shift all our forces off the plain where the road heads up the Third Escarpment to Thralgard Keep."

His wobbling chins speckled with sugar glaze, Samas Kul swallowed a mouthful of pastry. "Szass Tam's army just retreated into High Thay. This makes it sound like they're ready to come down again."

"Which doesn't make a lot of sense," Lauzoril said. "He withdrew because the disaster at the Keep of Sorrows weakened him even more than us. Granted, with Springhill's aid, he's managed to stall and hurt us since, but not so severely as to shift the balance back in his favor."

"I wouldn't think so," Nevron said. "However . . ." he turned his gaze on Nymia Focar.

The tharchion of Pyarados looked uncomfortable at becoming the center of attention, and that was as it should be. Her withdrawal from Delhumide had been one of the more damaging missteps of the past several tendays.

She cleared her throat. "My flying scouts confirm that Szass Tam is massing troops in and around Thralgard Keep."

"Perhaps," Lauzoril said, "the necromancers are simply protecting the route we'd need to use if we tried to climb up after them."

"I doubt it," Dmitra said. "The original garrison at Thralgard was already adequate for that purpose."

The zulkir of Enchantment frowned and made a tent of his long, pale fingers. "Let's say you're correct. What's Szass Tam's objective?"

"Eltabbar, most likely," Dmitra said, plainly referring to the capital city of her tharch. "He's tried to take it repeatedly, because it hinders him moving troops in and out of High Thay, and because it poses a constant threat to any enemy host fighting in the lands to the south of it."

"Can Eltabbar withstand another siege?" Nevron asked. A demon, a spirit of war caged in an amulet dangling on his chest, stirred restlessly at the thought of such battle. Its agitation made the bronze medallion grow warm, and sent a sort of shiver across the psychic link that it shared with Nevron.

"A short one, perhaps," Dmitra said. "Last year's harvests were so meager that we don't have a great deal of food stored away, and, going by past experience, the necromancers will seed the lake with lacedons to make fishing hazardous. But in any case, I don't want to defend against a siege. I want to meet Szass Tam's legions as they descend from the heights."

"Because the road down is narrow," said Thessaloni Canos, "and they can come only a few at a time." Tall even for a Mulan woman, the governor of the island tharch known as the Alaor and Thay's most capable admiral, she had a pleasant face, hooded green eyes, and weather-beaten skin. She wore scale armor and ornaments of coral, pearl, and scrimshaw, and her tattooing followed the same aquatic motif.

Dmitra gave Thessaloni a smile and a nod. "Exactly so. Obviously, it would be even better if the necromancers were clambering uphill, but we should still enjoy a tactical advantage."

Samas Kul grunted. It made his jowls quiver. "What happened to isolating High Thay and its legions? I liked that plan."

Lauzoril pursed his lips. "I don't suppose you can isolate them if they're absolutely resolved to come down. Not until you push them back up again."

"We could if we destroyed the roads that connect the Plateau of Ruthammar with the lands below," Samas said. "I've been pondering the problem. The evokers could send a vibration through the cliffs to break them apart, or the conjurors could summon a host of earth elementals."

"But we won't," Nevron said. "We won't attempt anything that ambitious and accordingly hazardous while sorcery is unreliable. If you think it's a good idea, then you transmuters give it a try. Turn the slopes under the roads into air. Just don't whine to me when the magic rebounds on you and obliterates your followers instead."

Samas pouted. "All right. If you think it's impractical, I withdraw the suggestion."

"The question we need to answer," Nevron said, "is why would Szass Tam make this particular move now? Why does he imagine it will work? Does he believe he can march his army down the Third Escarpment without us noticing?"

Aoth Fezim lifted his hand.

The griffon rider had botched the attempt to apprehend Malark Springhill, but he was also the man who'd discovered the spymaster's treason in the first place. Nevron supposed that on the whole, he was less useless than many of the weaklings and imbeciles assembled in the council chamber. "Yes, Captain?"

"I guarantee you, Your Omnipotence, the necromancers see our scouts in the air. They realize they can't head down without us knowing. What they hope is that they can bring up troops from the Keep of Sorrows to secure the base of the descent, or, if we get there first, to attack our flank while we're trying to kill the warriors coming down from the heights."

"I see that," Lauzoril said. "Still, why attempt such a risky ploy now? Szass Tam can't possibly have rebuilt his strength already."

"Desperation?" Dmitra said. "He is weaker now than at any time since the war began, and Eltabbar is a big city. If he takes it, he can slaughter the populace and turn them into walking dead to replace the troops he's lost."

Lallara laughed a nasty laugh. "Didn't we already sing this song earlier this year? Oh joy, oh joy, through impatience, desperation, or whatever, the lich has miscalculated at last. Let's commit our strength and crush him. Except that it didn't turn out that way. We walked into a snare, and only the coming of the blue fire saved us from utter defeat."

"No one respects Szass Tam's brilliance more than I," Dmitra said. "But we can't be afraid to try to outthink him, nor to act decisively when we see an opportunity."

"I'm not afraid," Lallara snapped. "But we lost plenty of men at the Keep of Sorrows, and more when your servant wrecked the subsequent campaign. Perhaps it's time to assume a defensive posture and rebuild our own strength."

"It's already summer," Dmitra said. "In essence, you're talking about finishing out the year with another series of inconsequential moves and countermoves. While Thay starves and the necromancers rebuild their own legions with warriors who have no need to eat. While the realm burns and shakes to pieces, and we do nothing to arrest the destruction because we're too busy prosecuting a war we're unable to end."

"We don't know," Samas said, "how much longer the blue fires will burn and the earth will shudder. It could all stop tomorrow."

"And it might not."

"I think," Nevron said, "that we should allow Szass Tam to squander resources he can ill afford in what will surely prove a futile attempt to take Eltabbar." And if by chance the lich did overwhelm it, at least the loss would injure Dmitra more than the rest of them. "Meanwhile, we'll retake the rest of the tharch, lay waste to Delhumide, and relieve the city if necessary."

"I concur," Lauzoril said.

"So do I," Lallara said. "For once, let's not do the stupid thing."

Samas Kul nodded. "Once we pacify the far north, we can bring all our strength to bear to deal with the armies of High Thay and the Keep of Sorrows."

As Nevron had assumed they would, Zola Sethrakt and Kumed Hahpret chimed in to support the majority point of view. With luck, it meant that henceforth, he would exert the greatest influence over the council, and he gave Dmitra a gloating smile. She responded with a slight and somehow condescending shake of her head, as if to convey that he was a fool to worry about precedence when it was essential that they make the right decision.

For a moment, he felt a pang of foreboding, but the feeling faded quickly. He and the others *were* making the right decision. She was the one who was misguided, and even if she weren't, a man's own position and power were never irrelevant to any deliberation.

"It seems we have a plan," he said. "It only remains—"

A shimmer of yellow flame crawling on his crown and shoulders, Iphegor Nath rose from his seat. "I've already explained," he said, "that the Firelord wishes us to assail the necromancers relentlessly."

"As we will," Nevron said, "but guided by a prudent strategy."

"If you mean to pass up an opportunity to smash the legions of High Thay—"

"They'll die before the walls of Eltabbar," Nevron said. "Now then. We always benefit from your wisdom, Your Omniscience, but the rulers of Thay have made their decision. That means your role is to determine how your church can best support our strategy."

"Is that my role, also?" asked a sardonic masculine voice. Nevron turned his head to see Dimon stand up.

The tharchion's utterance caught Nevron off guard. Iphegor Nath was at least the head of a church that had proved an invaluable resource in the struggle against the necromancers. It was understandable, if not forgivable, if he sometimes addressed the zulkirs as an equal. Dimon was a lesser priest of a different faith and a governor, beholden to the council for his military rank. It was absurdly reckless for him to take an insolent tone.

"If I were you, Tharchion," Nevron said, "I'd sit back down and hold my tongue."

"No," Dimon said. "I don't believe I will."

"So be it," Nevron said. He released the entity bound in his silver thumb ring like a falconer tossing a goshawk into the air.

The devil was an advespa, a black wasp the size of a bear, with a hideous travesty of a woman's face and scarlet striations on its lower body. Beating so fast they were only a blur, its wings droned, and even the other zulkirs recoiled in their chairs. Its body cast a smear of reflection in the polished surface below it as the thing shot down the length of the long red table.

But Dimon didn't cringe. Rather, the pale priest with the twisting blue veins vivid in his shaven crown laughed and stretched out the hand wearing the black gauntlet.

It seemed a useless gesture, an attack easily evaded by a creature as nimble as an advespa on the wing. But Dimon somehow contrived to seize the devil at the point where its head fused with its thorax, and to hold on to it.

The advespa's raking, gouging claws ripped his face, vestments, and the flesh beneath. Its abdomen rocked back and forth like a pendulum, repeatedly driving its stinger into the cleric's chest.

Dimon kept on laughing and squeezing the juncture of his

attacker's head and body, sinking his fingers deeper and deeper. Until the creature convulsed, he jerked his arm back, and the advespa's head with its antennae, mandibles, and harpy face ripped away from the rest of it. The carcass thumped down on the tabletop in a splash of steaming ichor.

Dimon's reedy Mulan frame became bulkier, and flowing darkness stained him. In other circumstances, Nevron might have assumed it was the effect of the poison the wasp devil had injected. But the blackness tinged tattered clothing as well as torn flesh, and even if it hadn't, all the bound spirits Nevron kept ready to hand were clamoring, some terrified, some transported by demented ecstasy.

In another few moments, Dimon was virtually all shadow, although Nevron could make out a glint of eyes, the gleam of the jewels now encrusting the gauntlet, and the static curves of clothing turned to plate. "Do you know me?" the tharchion asked, and though his voice was soft and mellow, something about it lanced pain into a listener's ears.

Nevron took a breath. "You're Bane, Lord of Darkness." He rose, but resisted the craven urge to bow or kneel, prudent as it might have been. He'd decided long ago that a true archmage must never abase himself before anyone or anything, self-proclaimed deities included. Much as he hated Szass Tam, it was the one point on which they'd always agreed.

"Yes, I am," said Bane. "You mages have done a fair job of sealing your citadel against spiritual entities you don't summon yourselves, but you can't lock out a god, and the bond I share with my faithful servant provided a convenient way in." He stroked his temple—Dimon's temple—rather like a man petting a dog.

"To what do we owe the honor of your presence?" Nevron asked.

"I'm tired of your sad little war," the Black Hand said. "It drags on battle after battle, year after year, ruining a realm we gods of shadow raised up to dominate the east."

Lauzoril rose from his seat. When it splashed, the advespa's inky gore had spattered his scarlet robes. "Great Lord, we're doing our best to bring the conflict to a conclusion."

"Then your best is pathetic," said Bane. "Seven archmages against one, seven orders of wizardry against one, the rich and populous south against the poor and empty north, and still, Szass Tam holds you in check for a decade."

"It isn't that simple," Lauzoril said. "At the moment, we don't have a zulkir of Divination, and over time, wizards of every order have defected . . ." His voice trailed off as he realized that it might not be an ideal moment for his usual practice of fussy, argumentative nitpicking.

Dmitra rose. "Great One, we accept your rebuke. Will you instruct us how we might do better?"

Bane smiled. Nevron couldn't see the expression, but he could feel it, and although it conveyed no threat in any immediate sense, something about it was disquieting even to a man accustomed to trafficking with the most hideous denizens of the higher worlds.

"You already know the answer," said the god, "for you proposed it yourself. Fight Szass Tam when he descends from High Thay, and that will settle the war. All the northern tharchs will lay down their arms if you slay their overlord."

Nevron felt a strange mix of disgust and hope. Ever since Dmitra's ascension to the rank of zulkir, he'd chafed under her pretensions to leadership. The revelation of Malark Springhill's treason had called her judgment into question, and he'd exploited the situation to pull her off her pedestal and claim the chieftain's role for himself.

But only for a tantalizing moment, because this meddling god had lifted her up again. Nevron could see it in the expressions of the other zulkirs. Arrogant though they were, when a deity invaded their council chamber to recommend they reverse a decision, it made an impression.

And there was no point swimming against the tide, especially if it would carry them all to victory. "Lord Bane," Nevron said, "I'm sure I speak for everyone when I say we'll do as you direct. We pray you'll give us your blessing and your aid."

"Wherever men shed one another's blood," and Bane, "there will you find me."

The darkness suffusing the Black Hand's form drained away, and then he was merely Dimon once again. The wounds the advespa had given him hadn't bled while he was possessed, but they gushed blood now, and he pitched forward. His head cracked against the edge of the table, then he crumpled to the floor.

Her black and white ornaments clinking, Zola Sethrakt shifted her chair to take a better look at the fallen priest. "He's dead," she said, and Nevron supposed that, worthless as she often proved to be, she was necromancer enough to be right about that, anyway.

•• •• •• •• •• •• •• •• •• •• •• •• •• ••

After scouting throughout the morning, surveying the way ahead for the troops on the ground, Aoth, Bareris, and Mirror lit on a floating island to rest. The griffon riders dismounted, and Aoth peered over the edge of the floating chunk of soil and rock at a landscape of chasms, ridges, and twisting, leaning spires of stone stretched out far below. The earthbound portion of the council's legions struggled over the difficult terrain like a column of ants. Even with his fire-touched eyes, he couldn't see anything else moving.

He'd imagined that over the course of the past decade,

he'd seen his homeland reduced to a wasteland, but he'd been mistaken. *This* was a wasteland, viewed through a lens of nightmare.

"It looks as if we already fought the war to a bitter end," he murmured, "or the gods waged a final, world-killing war of their own. Like we're an army of ghosts, damned to march through an empty land forever."

Strands of his blond hair stirring in the wind, Bareris smiled. "You should leave morbid flights of fancy to us bards."

Aoth grunted. "I'm just getting over being insane. I'm entitled to be a little moody."

"Fair enough. Still, the war isn't over, but it soon will be. According to you, Bane said so himself."

"That's right, but he never came right out and promised we were going to win it, or that he was going to do anything out of the ordinary to help us. What he did was let his own priest drop dead when he was through wearing him like a festival mask. I felt awe when he manifested among us—how could you not? But even so, I don't know that I trust him."

Bareris shook his head. "I wish I'd seen him. I'm sure it would have given me inspiration for a dozen songs. But if you don't trust the Black Hand, put your faith in Kossuth, or our own prowess."

"Because we're so mighty? That army marching down there is big, but not as big as it was last summer."

"If we're mightier than Szass Tam's legions, that's all that matters. And despite your grumbling, I guess we both believe the south can win, because otherwise, why stay and risk our necks? You've considered running, and I confess, now that I have Tammith back, I have, too."

"Since I recovered my sight, I've thought of many reasons to stay, but I'm not sure that any of them make sense, or is the *real* reason. Maybe I'm still here simply because it's my fate."

"Or perhaps those magical eyes of yours peeked into the future and saw Aoth the tharchion, lounging on a golden couch with concubines feeding him apricots."

Aoth's lips twitched into a smile. "Maybe." It seemed unlikely, but he appreciated his friend attempting to brighten his mood.

And he supposed Bareris truly was his friend. He'd agreed to allow him to remain in the Griffon Legion to stop everyone blathering at him, but he hadn't believed he could ever feel as easy with the bard as he had before. Yet it hadn't taken him long to slip back into old habits of camaraderie.

Perhaps it was because, since Tammith's return, Bareris truly seemed a changed man. Or maybe Aoth simply lacked the knack for clinging to old hatreds and grudges, because he hadn't come to resent serving under Nymia, either. He didn't actually trust her, but then, he never had.

He chuckled. "Maybe it's true, what folk have told me all my life. Maybe I'm really not much of a Mulan. I'm definitely not made of the same stuff as Nevron or Lallara."

Bareris cocked his head. "What are you talking about?"

"It's not important. Ready to go?"

They flew onward. A line of blue fire glimmered far to the east.

•• •• •• •• •• •• •• •• •• •• •• •• •• •• ••

Bareris woke from the foulest of nightmares, the one in which, as he had in real life, he beheaded Tammith and hacked her skull to pieces.

For a moment, he was the man he'd been until recently, anguished and bereft. Then he remembered that Tammith was back. He stopped gasping, his heartbeat slowed, and he rolled over in bed to face her.

She was gone.

The army had reached Tyraturos at midday. Part of the city lay in ruins, its once-teeming barracoons, markets, and caravanserais largely empty. Hunger and disease marked the faces of the people in the streets. But even so, it had been a relief just to see that the place was still here. No tide of blue flame had melted it away, nor had any earthquake knocked it flat.

Bareris had secured lodging at an inn, where the proprietor's obsequious desire to please masked a dogged determination to sell travelers every conceivable amenity at inflated prices. Since that was just as it would have been in better times, Bareris found it heartening as well. As he drifted off to sleep, he decided he'd told Aoth the truth: Their homeland was wounded but still lived. They could still save it.

But no such comforting reflections came to him now. Rather, Tammith's absence filled him with foreboding.

He told himself his anxiety was absurd. Tammith was a nocturnal creature. It made sense that she'd grow restless simply lying next to him after he fell asleep.

Still, his instincts told him to find her. He pulled on his clothes, buckled on his weapons, and plucked a tuft of bloodhound fur from one of the pockets sewn into his sword belt. He swept it through an arcane pass, sang a charm, then turned in a circle.

The magic gave him a sort of painless twinge when he was facing southwest. If she was in that direction, it meant she'd left the inn. He did likewise, striding through the rows of legionnaires snoring in the common room.

Selûne had already forsaken the sky, clouds masked the stars, and the streets were all but lightless. Bareris crooned a second spell to give himself owl eyes. Yet even so, at first all he saw was a man in ragged clothing, a beggar, most likely, sprinting. Then a shadow pounced on the fellow from above, dashing him to the ground. When the dark figure lifted its head and its black tresses parted to reveal its alabaster face, Bareris saw that it was Tammith. At once she skittered back up the side of a building like a spider. The beggar peered wildly around, but failed to spot her, and, judging by appearances, he had only the vaguest idea of what was happening to him. Shaking, whimpering, he climbed to his feet and ran again. Tammith crawled above him, keeping pace.

"Stop!" Bareris shouted. "Leave him alone!"

Tammith leaped down on the beggar and grappled him from behind. He tried to tear himself free, and she dug her slim white fingers into him until the pain paralyzed him. She peered at Bareris over her captive's shoulder. "What's wrong?" she asked.

"You shouldn't hurt him," Bareris said. "He's a subject of the zulkirs, not one of Szass Tam's rebels."

"He's a Rashemi pauper, and I'm a captain in the council's legions. I can do anything I want to him, and no one will care."

He knew she was right, but it was ghastly to see her this way. "You started out as a Rashemi pauper, and you've endured mistreatment in your time."

She laughed, exposing her extended fangs. "All the more reason to make sure that from now on, I'm the snake and not the rabbit."

He gazed into her dark yet chatoyant eyes. "Please. As a kindness to me, let the poor man go."

She glared, then shoved the man away. He staggered, caught his balance, and bolted.

"Thank you." Bareris walked toward her. "If you need blood, you're welcome to more of mine." His throat tingled in anticipation.

"No. It wouldn't be safe. In fact, you shouldn't come any closer or touch me."

He kept walking. "You won't hurt me. But if you don't want to drink from me, use one of the prisoners."

She shook her head. "You don't understand. It's not that I'm thirsty. I want to hunt."

Apparently, he thought, that involved playing with her prey like a cat with a mouse, and murdering the unfortunate wretch at the end of it, but he kept the observation to himself. He didn't want to reproach her and feed the shame he sensed seething inside her. "We'll be fighting soon. Then you'll have plenty of people to kill."

"The problem is that I *want* to kill."

"It's not a problem for me. We acknowledged that we've both changed, but we also agreed we can still love one another."

"You believe that because you don't truly comprehend. You imagine that at bottom, I'm still the same girl you loved when we were young. The bloodthirst is like a fever that recurs from time to time, and can be managed when it does. But the vampire is my true self. Everything that reminds you of times past, everything human, is just a surface, like glaze on a pot. That's why, when Aoth was in danger, I couldn't find it in myself to care, even though he's your friend. I need to go away before I hurt you."

"No." He took her hand. She shuddered, but didn't jerk it away. "The fact that you don't want to harm me shows who you really are."

"What I really am is *dead*. We so-called *un*dead feel the weight of that truth every moment of our existence, no matter how much blood we drink or how frantically we mimic the passions and ambitions of the living to convince ourselves otherwise."

"Not dead—merely changed, and after the war, we'll scour all Faerûn to find a way to change you back. For all we know, the answer is waiting for us in one of Szass Tam's grimoires.

Anyway, no matter how long it takes, I'll stay with you and help you govern your urges, and you won't ever turn on me. We'll be together and we'll be happy."

She sobbed and threw her arms around him. "I'm going to be the death of you."

He stroked her hair. "I know better."

•• •• •• •• •• •• •• •• •• •• •• •• •• •• ••

Murmuring words of power, Dmitra formed a huge griffon, its fur scarlet and its feathers a gleaming copper, out of magic and imagination. It was a compliment to the riders who would escort her aloft, and no one could deny they deserved it. The Griffon Legion had fought valiantly for ten years, as the depletion of its ranks and the lean, haggard faces of the survivors attested.

Because wizardry had grown fickle, the spell began to warp. The transparent, partially materialized griffon grew deformed, one leg and one wing shortening to stubs, a fecal stink filled the air, and Dmitra felt the sudden imbalance of forces like the throb of a toothache.

She chanted more vehemently, demanding that the cosmos bow to her will. The red griffon flowed back into the shape she intended, became opaque, and started moving. It shook out its wings and the feathers rustled.

Dmitra swung herself onto its back and it sprang into the air. Her bodyguard followed her skyward.

For a pleasant change, the heavens were mostly blue and the sun was shining. The Third Escarpment towered to the west, with the gray walls and turrets of Thralgard Keep guarding the summit and the road switchbacking its way down the crags. Some of Szass Tam's troops—living orcs and zombies, most likely, creatures that could bear daylight even if they disliked it—had begun the lengthy descent.

To the south, the force from the Keep of Sorrows stood in its battle lines. The council had arranged its infantry in what amounted to a three-sided box, with one side facing the bottom of the zigzagging road, one opposing the enemy on the plain, and the third placed to prevent the warriors from the keep from flanking them. Reserves—horsemen, mostly—waited inside the box to rush where they were needed.

Dmitra looked over at Aoth Fezim. Employing a petty charm that would enable them to talk without strain despite the space separating them, she asked, "What do you think?"

Aoth hesitated. "Well, Your Omnipotence, we can be glad of a couple things. We reached the bottom of the road and got ourselves in formation before the necromancers actually did come down, and before the troops from the Keep of Sorrows got here to claim the ground ahead of us. Also, it's still a decent field for fighting. No blue fire has washed through to carve it into ridges and chasms."

"What are you not glad about?" she asked.

"Ideally, you never want the foe coming at you from two directions at once." Aoth stroked the feathers on his griffon's neck. "Also, as the warriors from High Thay come down the road, they'll be like men on the battlements of a castle. They'll have the advantage of height, and rain arrows and magic down on us."

Dmitra smiled. "So remind me again why it's a cunning scheme for us to make a stand here."

"Because you said so, Your Omnipotence, and then a god appeared to second your opinion."

"True. But do you see any additional reasons for optimism?"

"Yes. We outnumber the enemy, and Szass Tam won't have many bowmen on the slopes. Undead archers do exist, but the necromancers design most of their creations for close combat.

And since they'll most likely attack at night, so they can use all their troops, the darkness will spoil the aim of even a dread warrior or an orc beyond a certain distance.

"Also," Aoth continued, "we're going to harry them as they come down. We griffon riders will handle part of it. The bastards won't have the advantage of height on us. And I'm told you Red Wizards will make the descent as hellish as possible. You'll conjure hail and wind, and send demons to tear the ghouls apart as they creep along."

"That all sounds promising. But I wonder if we might fare even better if we attacked the force from the Keep of Sorrows immediately."

"I wouldn't, Mistress. You can't be sure how long it will take the warriors from Thralgard to come down the road, so you can't be certain of defeating the troops from the Keep of Sorrows and getting your men back into formation fast enough to meet them. Szass Tam may have brought his men up from the south hoping he could use them to lure us out of position."

She nodded. "True, and even if we did manage to win the first battle and reform our lines in time, we'd already be tired heading into the next confrontation. Better, then, to hold where we are."

"I think so, Your Omnipotence.

"You know, if I were Szass Tam, now that we're down here eager to receive him, I'd simply decline the invitation. He doesn't have to advance. Even the force from the Keep of Sorrows isn't quite committed. They could scurry back to their fortress to fight another day.

"But I guess Szass Tam will come. The Black Hand promised he would. I just don't see why he should, and that worries me."

Despite Bane's assurances, Dmitra realized it troubled her as well.

•• •• •• •• •• •• •• •• •• •• •• •• •• ••

The orders Szass Tam's lieutenant had given to Harl Zorgar sounded simple enough: Hurry his band of blood orcs down the mountainside until they found a place that provided a suitable platform for shooting down at the southerners, and where the road was wide enough for the rest of the army to continue descending while they did it.

But it wasn't simple. The steep, zigzagging highway was sufficiently wide for caravans, but nowhere truly broad enough to accommodate an army attempting to traverse it in a fraction of the time that safety or sanity would require. Often, the constant pressure from behind shoved Harl along too relentlessly even to look for a suitable archer's loft. It was all he could do to keep his feet, avoid being trampled, and keep his warriors together. If he hadn't been able to bellow as loud as only a blood orc sergeant could, he wouldn't have had much hope of accomplishing the latter.

Then a white bolt of lightning leaped up from the ground to strike on the slopes below. The southerners had started fighting, and after that, everything became even more dangerous and confused. Finally, when he'd nearly blundered past it, Harl spied a place where the road bulged outward in a sort of overhang. It even had a low parapet of rough, piled stone to protect bowmen from missiles flying up from below, and to keep the warriors streaming along behind them from jostling them over the edge.

"Here!" he roared. "Here, you fatherless, chicken-hearted bastards! Come here!"

His followers had to struggle through the press, but, one and two at a time, they shoved their way to him, fell in line, and strung their yew bows.

He counted to make sure he had everybody, came up one

short, and realized that at this point he could do nothing about it. He strung his own bow and looked out at the empty space before him and the ground below. The griffon riders, he decided. "Shoot the griffons!"

He heard a strangled cry. From the corner of his eye, he saw one of his archers topple forward over the parapet.

He pivoted just in time to see a murky ghost drive its insubstantial scimitar into a second orc's torso. For a moment, it looked like the ghost of an orc itself, and then it melted into the semblance of a human with a beak of a nose and a long mustache. A round shield appeared on its arm, and its curved blade straightened.

Frozen with shock, Harl didn't understand where it could have come from. Then he saw that its intangible feet were in the ground. Perhaps it had hidden in the rock.

The ghost cut down another archer, and that jarred Harl out of his immobility. "Necromancer!" he bellowed. "We need a necromancer!" But no Red Wizard appeared to intervene.

Another orc fell. His mouth dry, Harl realized that if anybody was going to save the rest of the archers, it would have to be him. He wore an enchanted blade, which meant he had at least a forlorn hope of slaying a ghost.

He dropped his bow, drew his scimitar, screamed a war cry, and charged.

The ghost shifted out of his way and stabbed him in the side. A ghastly chill burned through him. He staggered on, and the top of the parapet banged him just below the knee. He pitched over it and plummeted.

•• •• •• •• •• •• •• •• •• •• •• •• •• ••

The dread warrior no longer recalled the name it had borne as a living man. Sometimes it didn't even remember it had ever had one. But in its fashion, it still understood the ways of war, and it knew it and its companions were taking a big chance charging at the jutting spears and overlapping shields of the enemy.

But it didn't care, because it was incapable of fear. It simply wished to kill or perish. Either would satisfy the cold, irrational urges that were all that remained of its emotions.

Arrows thudded into the gray, withered zombies on either side, and a few of them fell. Priests spun burning chains and called to their god, and other dead men burst into flame.

Their numbers diminished, the rest ran on. The dread warrior threw itself at the enemy. Spears jabbed at it, and one punched into it despite its coat of mail. But it didn't catch it anywhere that could destroy, cripple, or immobilize it. It simply pierced its side, near the kidney, and the dread warrior tore free with a wrenching twist of its body.

Then it smashed at the southerners with its battleaxe. They caught the blows on their shields, but the force jolted them backward, indenting the battle line. The dread warrior lunged into the breach and kept chopping.

It killed two foes. The legionnaires were no match for it now that it had penetrated their protective wall, and their spears were awkward weapons in close quarters.

Then a black-haired woman with alabaster skin scrambled out of the darkness. "Keep the line!" she cried, revealing the fangs of a vampire. "I'll deal with this thing!"

The dread warrior cut at her neck, and she ducked beneath the blow. Her sword sliced her opponent behind the knee.

It didn't hurt. Nothing ever did. But suddenly the dead man's leg wouldn't support it anymore, and it pitched sideways.

Her sword split its skull before it even finished falling. As its awareness faded, it heard cheering, and realized the first assault had failed.

It was, Bareris reflected, regrettable that all the warriors of High Thay didn't have to use the road to descend to the plain below. But as ever, Szass Tam had his share of flying servants.

Bareris's new griffon, Winddancer, beat his wings, climbed above the flapping rectangle that was a skin kite, caught the undead in his talons, and ripped it apart with claw and beak. Bareris hadn't noticed the creature closing with them. He was glad his steed had.

Then something else swooped down the cliff face from on high. Its form was shadowy, and even with augmented sight, Bareris could barely make out its twisted skull face in the dark. But every griffon rider in the vicinity knew of it instantly, because it screamed, and its keening evoked a surge of unreasoning panic. The legionnaires' winged mounts wheeled and fled.

Bareris quashed his own terror by sheer force of will, then started singing a battle anthem to purge the emotion from the minds of his comrades and their steeds. Even then, Winddancer still wouldn't fly nearer to the deathshrieker, as such wailing phantoms were called, until Bareris crooned words of encouragement directed specifically at him.

As they hurtled toward it, the deathshrieker oriented on them, and its cry focused on them as well. It stabbed pain in Bareris's ears, beat at him like a hammer, and triggered a fresh spasm of terror and confusion. He defended with his own voice, singing a shield to block raw violence and pain, adding steadiness and clarity to counter fear and madness.

After what seemed an eternity, the deathshrieker's wail faded, leaving Bareris and his mount unharmed. He sang a charm to cloak Winddancer and himself in a deceptive blur, and then another spell that made the roar of the battle fall silent.

He rarely considered casting an enchantment of silence on

himself, because it would prevent him from using any more magic. But over the past ten years, he'd learned a good deal about Szass Tam's more exotic undead servants, including the fact that silence wounded a deathshrieker.

Winddancer carried him close enough to strike, and Bareris pierced his foe with the point of his spear. While the enchanted weapon likely hurt the phantom, it was the absolute quiet that made it convulse.

It tried to flee from the excruciating silence, but Winddancer stayed with it. The griffon had shaken off his dread, and now his savage nature ruled him. He wanted revenge on the adversary that had hurt and discomfited him.

Bareris kept thrusting with the spear. Finally the death-shrieker turned to fight and plunged the intangible fingertips of one raking hand into Winddancer's beak. The griffon froze and began to fall, but at the same instant, Bareris drove his spear into the spirit's torso again. The deathshrieker withered from existence. Its jaws gaped wide as if it was voicing a final virulent wail, but if so, the silence warded its foes from the effect. Winddancer lashed her wings and arrested her fall.

Twisting in the saddle, Bareris looked around and didn't see any immediate threats. Good. He and Winddancer could use a few moments to catch their breath, and if his aura of quiet dropped away during the respite, so much the better. It was only a hindrance now.

He urged his mount higher for a better look at the progress of the battle. At first, he liked what he saw. Despite everyone's best efforts, some of the High Thayans on the road were reaching the field at the base of it, but only to encounter overwhelming resistance when they did. Meanwhile, the legionnaires from the Keep of Sorrows assailed the southerners' formation but had failed to break it. Rather, they were beating themselves to death against it like surf smashing to foam on a line of rocks.

Its leathery wings flapping, a sword in one hand and a whip in the other, a gigantic horned demon flew up from the ground. A halo of scarlet flame seethed around its body.

The balor's sudden appearance didn't alarm Bareris. He assumed that a conjuror had summoned it to fight on the council's side, and indeed, the tanar'ri maneuvered close to the crags as though seeking adversaries worthy of its lethal capabilities.

But as it considered where to attack, the wavering red light emanating from it illuminated sections of the road. As a result, Bareris realized for the first time just what a gigantic host of undead was swarming down from the heights.

With wizardry undependable, how had the necromancers created so many new servants? Where had they obtained the corpses? Had they butchered every living person left in High Thay?

This is how it starts, Bareris thought. This is how Szass Tam has always liked to fight. He makes you think you're winning, gets you fully committed, and then the surprises start.

•• •• •• •• •• •• •• •• •• •• •• •• •• ••

So-Kehur and Muthoth had armored themselves in enchantments of protection, and their personal dread-warrior guards stood in front of them in a little semicircular wall of shields, mail, and withered, malodorous flesh. Yet even so, an arrow droned down from on high to stick in the ground a finger-length from the pudgy necromancer's foot.

"We're too close," So-Kehur said. He heard the craven whine in his voice and hated it.

His wand gripped in his good hand, Muthoth, predictably, responded with a sneer. "We have to be this close, or our spells won't reach the enemy."

"What spells?" So-Kehur said, although it wasn't a reasonable comment. After Mystra's death, he'd scarcely been able to turn ale into piss, but when Szass Tam force-fed his followers insights into the changing nature of the arcane, he'd more or less recovered the use of his powers.

But as far as he was concerned, it wasn't worth it. He'd never liked knowing that the lich had constrained his will. It bothered him even though he'd always had better sense than to flout his zulkir's wishes and so rouse the magic. But having Szass Tam shove knowledge straight into his mind was a more overt violation, and thus considerably more odious. Along with a vague but sickening feeling that a wisp of the mage's psyche remained in his head, spying on him and polluting his own fundamental identity, the new lore rode in his consciousness like a stone.

But the howling, crashing terror of the battlefield, with quarrels and arrows flying and men and orcs falling dead on every side, was worse. *I never wanted to be a necromancer in the first place,* So-Kehur thought, *or any kind of wizard. My family pushed me into it. I would have been happy to stay home and manage our estates.*

Horns blared, sounding a distinctive six-note call. "It's time," Muthoth said. He sounded eager.

So-Kehur wasn't, but he knew his fellow mage was right. No matter how frightened he was, he had to start fighting.

He shifted forward and the two guards directly in front of him started to step apart. He clutched their cold, slimy forearms to keep them from exposing him. "I only need a crack to peek through!" he said.

So that was what they gave him. He picked a spot along the enemy's battle line and started chanting.

Stripped of the cunning shortcuts and enhancements that were the craft secrets of the Order of Necromancy, reduced to its most basic elements, the spell seemed an ugly, cumbersome thing. But it worked. A blaze of shadow leaped from his fingertips to slice into two southerners in the front rank. They collapsed, and so did other men behind them.

Muthoth snarled words of fear, and several men in the enemy formation turned tail, shoving and flailing through the ranks of their companions. A sergeant, failing to understand that the afflicted men had fallen victim to a curse, cut one down for a coward and would-be deserter. Muthoth laughed and aimed his wand.

Other flares of power, some luminous, many bursts of shadow, blazed from the ranks of the legionnaires from the Keep of Sorrows, and from up and down the crooked length of the path that climbed to High Thay. When they realized their adversaries were casting more spells than they had before, the council's sorcerers intensified their efforts as well. But as often as not, their magic failed to produce any useful effects, or yielded only feeble ones. Whereas nearly all the necromantic spells performed as they should, and many hit hard.

A pair of Red Wizards—conjurors, judging from the cut of their robes and the talismans they wore—appeared in the mass of soldiery opposite So-Kehur, Muthoth, and the troops surrounding them. They looked old enough to have sons So-Kehur's age, and were likely genuine masters of their diabolical art. Reciting in unison, somehow clearly audible despite the din, they chanted words in some infernal tongue, and So-Kehur cringed at the grating sound and the power he felt gathering inside it.

Muthoth hurled flame from his wand. It burned down some of the council's soldiers, but the conjurors stood unharmed at the center of the blast. They shouted the final syllables of their incantation.

Nothing happened. No entity answered their call, and the sense of massing power dwindled like water gurgling down a drain.

So-Kehur's fear subsided a little, and he realized he'd better not permit the conjurors to try again. He jabbered an incantation of his own. A cloud of toxic vapor materialized around the southern wizards, and they staggered and crumpled to the ground.

I beat them, So-Kehur thought. I was sure they were going to kill me, but I was better than they were. Muthoth grinned at him and clapped him on the shoulder without a trace of mockery or bullying condescension, as if, after all the years of shared danger and effort, they were truly friends at last.

So-Kehur decided the battlefield wasn't *quite* as horrible a place as he'd imagined.

.. ..

Perched on a round platform at the top of Thralgard Keep's highest tower, Szass Tam peered into a scrying mirror to track the battle unfolding in the gulf below. Sometimes he simply beheld the combatants. At other moments, glowing red runes appeared as one or another of the ghosts bound to the looking glass offered commentary.

Lacking mystical talents of his own, Malark sat on a merlon with his feet dangling over the crags and peered down at what he could make out of the struggle. Szass Tam doubted that was a great deal. The night was too dark, and everything was too far away.

"I see more flickers and flashes," Malark said, "than I did a while ago. It's like looking at fireflies, shooting stars, and heat lightning all dancing in a black sky together."

"My wizards," Szass Tam said, "are showing the council what they can actually do."

"Can they do enough? Are you going to win?"

"It might be sufficient, but I'm not finished. The Black Hand lent me even more power than I expected, and I mean to use it."

"Then you're going to raise the force you told me about. Are you sure that's wise?"

Szass Tam chuckled. "Sure? No. How can I be, when, to the best of my knowledge, no magus has ever roused such an entity before? It's possible that Bane understands my ultimate intentions, and gave me the strength to try precisely so I'd overreach and destroy myself. He is a god, after all. I suppose we have to give him credit for a measure of subtlety and discernment."

"Then maybe you should refrain."

"No. Call me smug, but I like my chances. Besides, if I shrink from attempting this, how will I ever muster the courage to perform the greater works to come?"

"Fair enough. Is there anything I can do to help?"

"Thank you, but no."

"In that case . . ." Malark hesitated.

Szass Tam smiled. "You'd like my help to reach the battlefield quickly."

"Yes, if you can spare the magic. So many interesting things are happening below that it would grieve me to stand aloof."

Szass Tam plucked a little carved bone from one of his pockets, swept it through a mystic pass, and whispered an incantation. Shadow swirled in the air overhead and gathered into the form of a gigantic bat.

The beast's rotting wings gave off a carrion stink. It furled them and landed on a merlon, its talons clutching the block of stone.

"It will obey your commands," Szass Tam said, "and carry you wherever you want to go."

"Thank you." Malark swung onto the bat's back and kicked it with his heels. It hopped off the merlon and glided over the battlefield.

Szass Tam hoped Malark would be all right. It was pleasant having a confidant again. At one time, Dmitra had played that part, but he hadn't been able to confide his grandest scheme to her. She wouldn't have reacted well, and he'd assumed that no one ever could. He didn't believe in fate, but even so, it almost seemed like destiny had brought a former monk of the Long Death into his orbit.

But Malark had served his purpose. He didn't actually matter anymore. Szass Tam had far more urgent matters to concern him, and it was time to address them. He summoned one of his favorite staves and raised it over his head.

.. ..

"What's this?" Brightwing asked. Aoth looked where she was facing, then cried out in shock.

A prodigious mass of fog spilled down the cliffs like a slow waterfall. Anguished faces appeared—stretched, twisted, and dissolved amid the vapor. A chorus of faint voices, some moaning, some gibbering, others laughing, emanated from it.

It was some form of undead, though it was far more gigantic than any creation of necromancy Aoth had ever seen. But it wasn't the size of it that dismayed him. It was the enormous might and insatiable hunger his fire-touched eyes saw burning inside it. "We're in trouble," he said.

Brightwing laughed. "No! Look! It's all right."

The fog hung over the crags like a curtain, and where the swirling vapor intersected the road, insubstantial tentacles writhed from the central mass to snatch for the orcs and ghouls scrambling on the slopes. The creatures they engulfed convulsed and dissolved into nothingness.

If the mist-thing simply continued attacking Szass Tam's army, all would be well. But then, though it continued to reach for the occasional luckless northerner like a man plucking berries from a bush, it floated lower.

It splashed at the foot of the crags and drifted outward. Its path carried it across the clump of northerners who'd managed to reach the bottom and keep themselves alive once they got there, but straight at the southern army as well. Panicking, some of the council's legionnaires threw down their weapons and turned to flee.

"Griffon riders!" Aoth bellowed. "Kill it!" He and Brightwing dived at the fog-thing. He pointed his spear and hurled a burst of flame into the heart of it. His men shot arrows.

The entity responded by snatching for them with lengths of its vaporous body. It hadn't reached nearly so far before, and the attack caught Aoth by surprise. A frigid column of shadowy, babbling faces engulfed him.

His thoughts shattered into confusion. He suddenly knew without questioning that his psyche and flesh were about to crumble, and then his attacker would absorb the residue.

Screaming, Brightwing lashed her wings and carried them free of the fog. Gasping, peering around, Aoth saw that other griffon riders hadn't been as lucky. Mired in writhing pillars of murk, they and their mounts disappeared. Meanwhile, as far as he could tell, their assault hadn't injured the mist-entity in the slightest.

It flowed toward the mass of the southern army, devouring men and the conjurors' demonic warriors as it went. Only zombies, skeletons, and golems—mindless things—endured its touch with impunity.

•• •• •• •• •• •• •• •• •• •• •• •• •• ••

Malark sent the zombie bat swooping low over the southern army. It was a reckless thing to do, but no arrows or thunderbolts came flying up to strike him or his steed. The enemy was too busy fighting the force from the Keep of Sorrows and goggling at the fog-thing seething toward them from the foot of the cliff.

Malark spied Dmitra conferring with several illusionists, the lot of them amid a contingent of bodyguards. It was too bad her minions hadn't fled and left her unattended, but he'd cope.

The bat furled its wings and plunged to earth in front of the zulkir and her entourage. Someone cried out, and guards hefted javelins.

Malark swung himself down from his mount. "Your Omnipotence." He bowed.

Dmitra shook her head. "I wondered if you were insane to betray me. Now I know you must be, to do so and then return."

Malark smiled. "I'm sure it looks that way. You're an archmage, and you and your servants have me outnumbered. Even worse, Szass Tam's creation is advancing on our location. If I don't finish my business and get away quickly, it will eat me as readily as it would you."

"What is your business?" Dmitra asked.

"Knowing me for as long as you have, I thought you might have guessed already."

"I have an idea. Did you come to keep me from trying to destroy the creature?"

"Not exactly."

"To switch sides again?"

"No, I'm where I belong. But you, Mistress, were always generous to me in your fashion. I've always liked you. I want to repay your kindness by giving you a better death then you'd suffer with your body and mind breaking apart in the fog-thing's grip. In particular, I hope to spare you the ugliness of undeath, either as one small part of that abomination yonder or as a lich under Szass Tam's control."

Dmitra laughed a little puff of a laugh. "It sounds as if you're challenging me to a duel."

"You could put it that way."

"But that implies some sort of equality where none exists. I'm a zulkir of Thay, and you're a treacherous worm. Kill him!"

Legionnaires threw their javelins. Malark sidestepped some and batted one away with his forearm. He waved the giant bat forward.

The zombie was clumsy crawling on the ground. But its sheer bulk, gnashing fangs, and long flailing wings made it formidable. It bobbed its head and bit the top of a warrior's skull off, and Malark dashed forward.

A soldier tried to thrust a broadsword into his belly. He twisted out of the way, caught his opponent's outstretched arm, and spun him around to slam into one of his comrades. Tangled together, they fell with a clash of armor. One of the lesser illusionists rattled off rhyming words of power, and Malark chopped her across the throat before she could finish. Another stride brought him within striking distance of Dmitra.

She gave him a radiant smile.

He felt himself falling, suffered a pang of alarm, and then his eyes flew open. He realized he'd dreamed of plummeting and then awakened.

Disoriented, he looked around. He and Dmitra were sitting on the roof of a tower in her palace in Eltabbar. A carafe held red wine to fill the golden goblets, trays offered lobster, oysters, beef skewers, grape leaves, figs, sweetmeats, and other delicacies, and a scarlet awning provided shade in the midst of amber sunlight. Slaves hovered at a discreet distance.

Beyond the red marble balustrade and the walls of the castle, the city murmured, its voice arising from teeming streets and bustling markets. To the west, south, and east were green fields, and to the north, Lake Thaylambar, reflecting the clear blue of the sky. Sailboats and galleys dotted the surface.

It occurred to Malark that the vista was as lovely as any he'd seen in all his centuries of protracted life. Then, belatedly, he realized Dmitra was speaking to him. He resolved to pay attention and catch the sense of whatever she was saying, but she reached the end too quickly and then watched him, awaiting his response. He tried to think of something to say, but he was still muddled, and nothing came.

Dmitra laughed. "I thought you dozed off."

"I humbly beg your forgiveness."

"No need. You went without sleep for a tenday to find out what Nevron and his followers are up to. You can go to bed if you like."

He took stock of himself and decided he didn't need to. He didn't feel exhausted so much as bewildered. He remembered spending days without sleep to spy on the Order of Conjuration, but had the crazy sense that it had happened years ago. "Thank you, Your Omnipotence, but I'm all right."

She cocked her head. " 'Your Omnipotence'? Have you promoted me to zulkir? I fear Mythrellan won't approve."

He blinked. "Didn't Mythrellan die during the war?"

"What war?"

"The one the rest of you zulkirs are waging against Szass Tam." The one that had come close to transforming Thay into a desert, although no one could have told it from looking out over Eltabbar on such a warm, clear summer afternoon.

Dmitra shook her head. "I think you must have dreamed a very strange and vivid dream. I, alas, am simply a tharchion. I give my allegiance to Szass Tam, and since you serve me, so do you. There isn't any war among the zulkirs unless you count the usual endless politicking and intrigue to steer the realm in one direction or another."

"I . . . all right."

"I insist you go and rest. I'll have someone escort you." She crooked a finger, and two slaves came scurrying.

He felt a twinge of alarm, but knew that was senseless. The men were just thralls, cowed and subservient. They had no particular reason to hurt him and wouldn't dare to try even if they did. Nor did they possess the weapons or martial skills they'd need to have any hope of succeeding.

He stood and suffered them to close in around him. Dmitra smiled at him from her couch.

Something about her smile was ever so slightly wrong. Perhaps it held a hint of malice or triumph. Whatever it was, it reminded him she was an illusionist, and prompted him to exert his will to try to see clearly.

The world darkened abruptly as the semblance of day she'd created in his mind gave way to the reality of night. The men he'd mistaken for slaves were legionnaires about to plunge their swords into his body.

He thrust his stiffened fingers into their throats, one hand for each, and lunged, bulling his way between them. Dmitra was standing on the other side. Her eyes widened in dismay.

Though he didn't see a telltale glimmer or anything comparable, he had no doubt she had defensive enchantments in place. He bellowed to focus every iota of his strength and spirit, and punched at her heart.

He felt ribs break. The shards had nowhere to go but into the pulsing organ behind them, and she fell backward.

It was a perfect death, for she'd perished wielding the art and guile that defined her. Malark felt the mix of exultation and envy that transported him on such rare occasions.

But he had no time for contemplation. He had other foes to fight. He pounced, grabbed the ruby amulet dangling on the Red Wizard's chest, and gave it a jerk that snapped the illusionist's neck.

•• •• •• •• •• •• •• •• •• •• •• •• ••

Bareris had exhausted his bardic powers, and he had a single arrow left. Seeking an appropriate target, he peered at the ground.

The fog-entity wasn't a logical choice. Even magic didn't seem to hurt it, although given its amorphous nature, it was difficult to be sure. If anyone had wounded it, the steady growth it experienced as it absorbed victim after victim likely offset the damage.

He spied an orc nocking an arrow. Judging from its position on the battlefield, it had come from the Keep of Sorrows. Like the rest of its comrades, it was keeping its distance from the fog-thing. But as the southern army fell back before the entity and its formations disintegrated, the orc and its fellows were shooting foes who blundered within easy reach of their weapons.

Bareris let his own arrow fly before the orc finished aiming. The missile punched into the warrior's neck just above its shoulder, and it staggered. It lost its grip on its bowstring, and its shaft flew wild.

Another orc shouted and pointed, and arrows hurtled up from the ground. Winddancer raised one wing, dipped the other, veered, and dodged the missiles. But one came close enough to tear a feather from the griffon's wing, and Bareris realized his mount was as weary as he was.

It's time to go, he thought, but couldn't make himself give Winddancer the appropriate command. Not yet. He wouldn't flee until he was certain the situation was as bleak as it seemed. He made the griffon climb for a better view of the battleground.

Large as an army itself, the cloud of gibbering, keening faces extruded arms that dissolved one southerner after another, although Bareris wasn't certain why it bothered. All it really needed to do was flow forward and engulf the council's warriors to obliterate them. The dread warriors inside it swung their axes and jabbed with their spears, dispatching anyone lucky or hardy enough to survive the vapor's touch.

Until the fog-thing rippled, churned, and contracted in on itself, uncovering the marching corpses and skeletons. It shrank to a writhing point, then vanished entirely.

Bareris shook his head in amazement. If the thing was gone, perhaps that meant the southern army might yet prevail.

But no. When he studied the field, the last dogged trace of hope withered inside him.

The remnants of the southern army were too few, too disorganized, and too demoralized. They only wanted to run away. Whereas Szass Tam had succeeded in bringing enormous numbers of undead down from the top of the plateau. They and their comrades from the Keep of Sorrows had arranged themselves in well-defined battle lines and in the proper positions to assail their foes from three sides at once.

Aoth had been right to mistrust Bane. The council had lost the battle, and its agents had no choice but to run until the sun rose to slow pursuit. Only those possessed of horses or capable of flight were likely to last that long.

Bareris was grateful that Tammith could fly. Praying she still survived, and that she could somehow find him before dawn, he turned Winddancer south.

chapter ten

16 Eleint–4 Marpenoth, the Year of Blue Fire

Samas Kul impaled a link of venison sausage on his knife, lifted it, and smelled its spicy aroma. His stomach squirmed, and he discovered that even though he hadn't eaten since lunch, and it was now mid-afternoon, he wasn't hungry. The realization startled him, as if he'd looked down at his hands and discovered they'd turned green.

He supposed that last night's debacle was responsible for his loss of appetite. Most of all, the horrible moment when he'd ventured to the front of the battle formation to confront the cloud-thing.

He hadn't wanted to, but he'd judged that only a zulkir could destroy the thing. Because plainly, none of the lesser Red Wizards, nor Burning Braziers hurling gout after gout of fire, were having any luck against it.

So he raised his power and attempted to turn the entity into an enormous lump of stone. But it didn't transform. Rather, it reached out and caught him in a dark, swirling extension of itself, and a terrifying intimation of dissolution ripped through his body and mind alike. He barely managed to cling to sufficient lucidity to activate the magic of the tattoo that whisked him to the Central Citadel.

Looking older than usual, and for once, shaken rather than ill-tempered, Lallara had appeared shortly thereafter, and then other Red Wizards capable of translating themselves across long distances. Samas realized that if they too were forsaking the field, the battle was surely lost, not that he'd had much doubt of it before.

Scowling, Nevron marched into the council chamber and took his seat at the table. He was the last to arrive at a conclave that, the zulkirs had decided, only they would attend, and not all of them at that. Like Yaphyll's, Dmitra Flass's chair was empty. No one knew what had become of her, only that she hadn't transported herself back to Bezantur with the rest of her peers.

"Let's get to it," Nevron growled. "I summoned the high priest of Bane this morning. I thought he might care to explain yesterday to me. The son of a dog sent his regrets. He claims to be ill."

Lauzoril's thin lips twitched into a grim and fleeting smile. "That sounds plausible. Living as he does in a great temple, where would he possibly find a healer?"

"What does this mean?" Samas asked.

"Either that he fears to face my displeasure," Nevron said, "or that he imagines he can flout my commands without consequences."

"When your devils drag him forth screaming," Lallara said, "you can ask him which it is."

"I hope that day will come," Nevron said, "but for now we have graver matters to address. What was that new creation Szass Tam sent against us?"

Zola Sethrakt cleared her throat. The slight stirring made her white and black jewelry clink. "My assistants and I," she said, "have been reading the grimoires and journals the griffon riders took from the sanctuary of the creature called Xingax. In one passage, he describes such an entity, although it doesn't seem that he had any intent of creating one himself. He thought the process would be difficult, and that it might prove even harder to control the thing."

"But obviously," Lallara said, "Szass Tam dared, even with sorcery weakened and unreliable."

"Yes. Xingax called the entity a dream vestige."

Samas snorted. " 'Vestige' seems a puny word to describe anything so dangerous and immense."

"I suppose," Zola replied, "but that's the name he gave it. It's somewhat similar to a creature known as a caller in darkness, which is made of a number of spirits melded together. A dream vestige begins as hundreds of nightmares gathered, combined, and infused with the energies of undeath. It grows by devouring any being possessed of a mind."

"Is it as impervious to magic as it seemed?" Lauzoril asked.

"Not entirely," Zola said. "But even though we could see it, it isn't a physical entity. Intangibility gives even a common wraith a measure of protection, and this creature has strong additional defenses. So, with wizardry diminished. . . ." She shrugged her bony shoulders, and her necklaces and bracelets clattered.

"We're lucky," Samas said, "that it only existed for a while. Maybe Szass Tam will prove incapable of making another, or maybe he'll lose control of it if he does. Maybe it will eat him."

Zola sighed. "I'm sorry, but it didn't cease to exist. A dream vestige can pass back and forth between the physical realm and what I infer is some sort of demiplane of dreams. When Szass Tam judged that it had done all he required, he sent it there."

"To keep it from slipping its leash and getting into mischief," Nevron said, "like a conjuror keeping an elemental in a ring or bottle. I'm familiar with the concept. So, you're telling us he can call the thing forth whenever he feels the need, and that it will grow bigger and stronger every time it kills somebody."

"I'm afraid so."

"Our luck is a wondrous thing," Lallara said. "There are two schools of wizardry, divination and illusion, that make a study of dreams, and those are the two zulkirs we lack. Yaphyll went over to Szass Tam, and Dmitra is missing."

"I suspect," Lallara said, "Dmitra, too, has betrayed us. Remember, at one time, she was Szass Tam's most devoted minion, and she urged us to fight at the base of the cliffs."

"With a god endorsing her point of view," Lauzoril said.

"Are you sure?" Lallara asked. "Dmitra is the zulkir of Illusion. Perhaps she tricked us into believing the Black Hand spoke to us."

"I hope you're wrong," Lauzoril said, "because that would make it Szass Tam and two other zulkirs against the rest of us. But let's stay focused on the lich's new servant. We no longer have a wizard with a special understanding of dreams in our company. But we do have an authority on undeath."

Zola's mouth tightened. "If you're asking me if I know how to stop the creature, Your Omnipotence, I'm sorry, but the answer is no."

Lallara sneered. "Zola Sethrakt at a loss. How astonishing."

"Perhaps," Lauzoril said, "since the dream vestige is a form of undead, the priests can destroy or at least repel it."

"Don't count on it," Nevron said. "I watched Iphegor Nath and a circle of his acolytes try and fail. I detest that arrogant whoreson, but he's the best of his breed. He always has been."

"The Order of Abjuration," Lallara said, "can try to devise a ward to hold the dream vestige back. Although if it can jump back and forth between this world and some astral realm, that makes the task more difficult."

"Perhaps it's time," Lauzoril said, "to ask ourselves whether it even matters if we can devise a defense against the dream entity."

Nevron glowered at him. "Are you suggesting what I think you are?"

"Reluctantly," the zulkir of Enchantment replied, "but someone has to say it. We just lost the greater part of our military strength."

"We have other troops," Nevron said.

"Who are out of position to confront the horde of undead that is surely racing south, and too few to stop it even if they could. Because somehow, Szass Tam has raised a vast new army when it should have been impossible. He and his necromancers also appear to have discovered how to make wizardry reliable again while the solution still eludes us. In short, the lich holds every advantage."

"I don't care," Nevron said.

"Nor does it matter to me," Lauzoril responded, "what your pride obliges you to do. But I don't intend to die struggling to cling to my position in a realm that mostly lies in ruins anyway. Not if the cause is hopeless."

"It may be that Szass Tam would offer us terms," Samas said.

Lallara laughed. "Now that his victory is at hand? He'd butcher you and feed your bloated carcass to his ghouls before you could even blink."

"Even if he was inclined to be merciful," Lauzoril said, "I'd prefer a comfortable life in exile to subservience."

Nevron shook his head. "I won't give up." But for the first time in all their long acquaintance, Samas heard a hint of weakness and doubt in the conjuror's voice.

"No one has to flee yet," Lauzoril said. "We can keep

searching for a way to turn the situation around. But we'll also make preparations to depart, and take comfort in the fact that, whatever resources Szass Tam may possess, he doesn't have ships, and some forms of undead can't cross open water."

"Very well," Nevron said. "I suppose that's reasonable." He turned his glower back on Zola, studying her, and his mouth tightened. He stroked the hideous face tattooed in the palm of one hand and muttered under his breath.

A creature resembling a diseased satyr appeared behind the conjuror's seat. Open sores mottled its emaciated frame. It had horns and a head like a ram, but with seeping crimson eyes and pointed fangs. Its serpentine tail switched back and forth, scraping a cluster of metallic spines on the tip against the floor. It clutched a huge spear in its four-fingered hands. Nevron pointed, and it oriented on Zola.

The necromancer jumped out of her seat. "What are you doing?"

"It's only a bulezau," Nevron said, "not all that powerful for a demon. A true zulkir shouldn't have any trouble defending against it."

The tanar'ri leveled its spear and charged.

Zola shouted a word of power and swept her hand through a mystic pass. Swirls of jagged darkness spun from her fingertips to fill the space between the bulezau and herself. The demon lunged in and stuck fast like an animal caught in brambles. Zola grabbed a bone-and-onyx amulet.

The bulezau vanished from the shadowy trap and appeared behind her. She sensed it, started to turn, but was too slow. It raised its spear high, rammed it into her torso, and the force of the blow smashed her to the floor. The bulezau threw itself on top of her, clawed away hunks of flesh, and stuffed them into its mouth. The rattle of the jewelry on her flailing limbs found a counterpoint in the snapping of her bones.

Samas swallowed and wondered if he would even be hungry at suppertime.

"If this really is the end," Nevron said, "I'll be damned if I meet it in the company of a useless weakling claiming to be my equal and looking to rule our shrunken dominions along with the rest of us."

Samas noticed that Kumed Hahpret had turned an ashen white.

·· ·· ·· ·· ·· ·· ·· ·· ·· ·· ·· ·· ·· ··

If the war had taught the people of Thay anything, it was that horrible entities were apt to come stalking or flying out of the dark. That was why Aoth approached the walls of Mophur wrapped in a pearly conjured glow that also enveloped Brightwing, and with a fluttering banner of the Griffon Legion tied to the end of his spear.

Even so, crossbow bolts flew at him from the battlements. One struck his shoulder with stinging force but glanced off his mail.

"Bareris!" he shouted. The bard was better able to communicate over a distance.

"Stop shooting!" Bareris called. "We fight for the council. Look carefully at Captain Fezim and you'll see."

More quarrels flew. Brightwing screeched in anger. "Go away!" someone yelled.

Aoth flew Brightwing away from the walls and waved his spear for his fellow griffon riders to follow. They landed beside the High Road, near the mounted knights and men-at-arms who'd fled south with them. The griffons were so tired that they didn't even show signs of wanting to eat the horses. Some wounded, heads hanging low, the equines were in even worse shape. One charger toppled sideways, dumping its master on the ground, writhed once, and then lay still.

While he flew, the kiss of the wind had kept Aoth alert, but on the ground, he suddenly felt weary enough to keel over himself. He invoked the magic of a tattoo to clear his head and send a surge of energy into his limbs. It helped, but not a great deal. He'd already used the trick too many times.

"What's wrong?" asked the knight at the head of the column. Aoth tried to recall the man's name and rank, but couldn't dredge them out of his memory.

"Apparently," said Aoth, "the autharch of the city doesn't want to let us in."

"He has to!" said the knight. "Now that it's dark, Szass Tam's creatures will be on our trail again."

"I know," said Aoth. "Bareris and I will talk to him." He found a sycamore growing near the road, chopped off a leafy branch to signal he wanted a parley, and he and the bard walked their griffons toward the city's northern gate. Currently resembling an orc with a longbow, Mirror oozed into visible existence to stride along beside them.

As they came near enough to the gate for Aoth to converse without shouting at the top of his lungs, several figures mounted the crenellated wall-walk at the top of it. The flickering light in the grip of a torchbearer was inadequate to reveal them clearly, but Aoth's fire-infected eyes had no difficulty making them out.

One was Drash Rurith, autharch of the city. Aoth had met him a time or two. Gaunt and wizened, he hobbled with a cane, and looked so frail that one half expected the weight of the sword on his hip to tip him over. But there was nothing feeble or senile in the traplike set of his mouth.

Beside him stood a younger man. Judging from his dark gauntlet and the black pearls and emeralds adorning his vestments, he must be the high priest of Bane's temple in Mophur. Where Drash looked unhappy but resolute, like a person determined to perform some unpleasant task and be done with it, the cleric smirked and had an air of eagerness around him.

The other eight men were guards, some clad in the livery of the city, the rest sporting the fist-and-green-fire emblem of the Black Hand's church.

"Milord autharch," said Aoth, "it's a relief to see you. Your servants apparently doubt my identity, or that we all owe our fealty to the same masters. I come to you with a number of the council's soldiers at my back. We need shelter and food."

"I regret," said Drash, "that Mophur can't assist you. The city is already full to overflowing with country folk who fled here when the war, the earthquakes, or blue fire destroyed their homes. I need all my resources to tend to their needs."

"I understand your situation," said Aoth. "But you can at least spare us water from your wells, and a length of street on which to unroll our bedding."

"I'm afraid not."

"If I must, I demand it in the zulkirs' names."

The high priest spat. "There is only one true zulkir, and his name is Szass Tam."

Aoth stared at Drash. "Does this priest speak for you? Have you switched sides?"

"I only say," the old man replied, "that, to my sorrow, it isn't practical for Mophur to accommodate you at this time."

"You'd better be sure of what you're doing."

"We are," said the priest. "Do you think we don't know that Szass Tam smashed the army of the south? We do! The Lord of Darkness revealed the truth to his servants, and now we understand that the lich's triumph is inevitable, and likewise in accordance with the will of Bane. Those who act to hasten that victory will thrive, those who seek to thwart it will perish, and when Szass Tam claims his regency, the earth will stop trembling and the blue fires will burn out."

"Do you truly find this mad rant convincing?" asked Aoth, still speaking to Drash. "You shouldn't. I actually saw Bane appear to the council and give them his blessing. Kossuth and the other gods of Thay stand with the south as well. I'll admit, we lost a battle beneath the cliffs, but we've lost them before. It doesn't mean we've lost the war."

"I regret," said Drash, "that Mophur cannot help you at this time. I wish you good fortune on the road."

Speaking softly enough that the men above the gate wouldn't hear him, Aoth said, "Can you charm the bastard into letting us in?"

"No," Bareris said. "I pretty much exhausted my magic during the battle. Even if I hadn't, I doubt I could beguile the autharch with the priest standing right there to counter any enchantment I cast."

"I was afraid of that. Curse it, we need what's inside those walls, but I don't know how to get it. I don't have any magic left, either. Knights are pretty much useless in situations like this, especially with their horses dropping dead underneath them. The griffons have a little strength left, enough to fly over the walls. But even if they weren't exhausted, we don't have enough riders with us to take a city. We don't even have any arrows."

"Don't worry about taking the city. Let's take the gate, right now, the three of us."

"Five," Brightwing said.

"We just rode up out of the dark," Bareris said. "Most of the town guards have barely gotten themselves out of bed. They're making their way to the battlements to drive us off if need be, but they aren't there yet. Let's strike before they're ready."

Mirror frowned around his jutting orc tusks. "We stand before this gate under sign of truce."

"The autharch has betrayed his oaths to the council. He isn't an honorable man."

"But we are."

No, thought Aoth, we're Thayan soldiers, not followers of some ancient and asinine code of chivalry. Although in fact, the ghost's objections gave him an irrational twinge of shame. "Our comrades are going to die if we don't get inside these walls. That will weigh heavier on my conscience than sinning against the supposed meaning of this stick in my hand. But I won't ask you to help if you feel otherwise."

Mirror changed from an orc into a murky, twisted semblance of Aoth. "I'll stand with my brothers and seek to atone afterward."

"Then let's do it," said Aoth. He dropped the sycamore branch, and the weary griffons beat their wings and heaved themselves into the air. Sword in hand, Mirror followed.

Someone atop the gate cried out in alarm. Quarrels flew, and Brightwing grunted and stiffened, the sweep of her wings faltering. Because of their empathic link, Aoth felt the stab of pain in her foreleg. "I'm all right!" she snarled.

They plunged down on top of the battlements. She bit, and her beak tore into a guard's torso. Aoth twisted in the saddle and thrust his spear into one of the warriors pledged to Bane. From the sound of it, Bareris, Winddancer, and Mirror had reached the walkway and were doing their own killing, but Aoth was too busy to look around.

Someone roared a battle cry and charged him. It was Drash Rurith, cane discarded and sword in hand. The blade glowed a sickly green, and perhaps the enchantments sealed inside it were feeding the old man strength and agility, for he moved like a hunting cat.

Occupied with another foe, Brightwing couldn't pivot to face Drash. Aoth was on his own. Drash feinted a head cut, slashed at his opponent's chest, and Aoth parried with the shaft of his spear. The impact jolted through his fingers. He struck back with a thrust to the belly, but Drash twisted out of the way, then rushed in again. The head of the spear was behind the autharch now, and he was plainly confident that he could drive his sword into Aoth before the griffon rider could pull his long weapon all the way back for another jab.

But Aoth simply whirled the spear in a horizontal arc as if it were a club, and the shaft took Drash in the side. Teeth gritted, exerting every iota of his strength, Aoth kept shoving, threw the autharch off balance, and pushed him staggering through a crenel and off the walk.

A city guard attacked immediately thereafter. Aoth speared him in the guts, and then had a moment to look around.

What he saw was less than encouraging. His comrades were holding their own for the moment, but other guards were running along the battlements toward the gate, with even more scurrying on the ground just inside it, about to climb the stairs on either side.

"Let's kill the ones down below!" Brightwing snarled.

"I suppose somebody has to," Aoth replied, and she leaped down into the mass of soldiers, smashing two or three to the ground beneath her.

She ripped with beak and talon, and he thrust with his spear. For a few heartbeats, it was all right, but then a blade sliced the same foreleg the crossbow bolt had pierced, and afterward Brightwing couldn't use it to claw or even support her weight.

Sword strokes hit Aoth as well, and though his mail kept them from doing more than bruising the flesh beneath, that luck couldn't hold indefinitely. He heard himself gasping, felt the burning in his heaving chest and the exhaustion weighting his limbs, looked at the feral faces and upraised weapons hemming him in all around, and decided that his time had come. After all the perils they'd survived, he and Brightwing were about to die trying to take a stupid gate in a drab little market town that was supposed to be on their side.

Then scraps of darkness fluttered down from above. They attached themselves to several of Aoth's foes, and he realized they were enormous bats biting and clawing at human prey. Startled by the unexpected assault, the warriors of Mophur broke off their furious assault to flail and fumble at the creatures sucking their blood.

The guards so afflicted either collapsed or turned tail. The bats abandoned them to whirl together and become a pale, raven-haired woman in black mail. Mirror floated down from the top of the gate to stand beside her.

The remaining guards decided they no longer liked the odds. They ran, too.

Tammith nodded to indicate the gates. "Let's get these open."

Aoth climbed out of the saddle. Together, they threw their weight against the enormous bar, and it groaned and slid in its brackets. They swung the leaves open while Brightwing and Mirror guarded their backs.

Aoth peered up at the platform atop the gate. It looked as if the fight had ended there as well, and although he couldn't see the bard from this angle, Bareris must have won it. Otherwise, the surviving guards would be taking steps to kill their foes on the ground and close the gate once more.

"Sound your horn!" Aoth shouted, or at least that was what he intended. The cry emerged as more of a wheeze.

But Bareris evidently heard, for he gave the signal. Griffons soared into the air and winged their way toward the city. Hoofbeats drummed as knights spurred their steeds in the same direction.

His sword gory from point to guard, Bareris jumped from Winddancer to the ground, and then his eyes opened wide. It was only at that moment that he realized Tammith had arrived.

He scrambled out of the saddle and embraced her. "I kept waiting for you to appear. If you hadn't found me by morning, I was going to turn back to search for you."

As Aoth watched them clinging to one another, he felt wistful. He'd never in his life known anything like the fierce obsessive adoration Bareris felt for Tammith, and she for him. The closest he'd ever come had been with Chathi. But she was long dead, and he supposed that meant that on a certain fundamental level he would always be alone.

On the other hand, he didn't have to worry that any of his casual lovers or whores would ever rip his throat out in the throes of passion, so perhaps things balanced out.

In any case, he had more immediate problems to ponder. "I recommend we clear the gate," he said. "Otherwise, the knights are liable to ride us down."

"Right," said Bareris. Everyone moved aside.

"I did my best to find you," Tammith said, "but what's left of the army has broken into countless tiny pieces fleeing south. It took time to find the right piece, especially since I had to lay up by day."

"Are other griffon riders still alive?" asked Aoth.

"I saw some."

"Thanks be to the Lord of Flames for that. And thank you, too, for coming to help me when you did."

"I needed to help," the vampire said, "if we were going to get the gates open. But . . . I wanted to. I cared about what might happen." She sounded like a person who'd just discovered something surprising about herself, although Aoth didn't understand what it was.

The rest of his band of refugees arrived before he could ask. Griffon riders glided down the sky to perch on rooftops, and the horsemen trotted through the gate. The leader of the knights inspected the litter of corpses on the ground, shook his head, and said, "What now?"

"We take what we need," said Aoth, "as fast as we can. Food, water, arrows, and fresh horses. Healing and charms of strength and stamina from any priest or wizard we can find. Then we ride on."

"If we could sleep for just a little while—"

"We can't, because if Szass Tam's legions show up outside the walls, we can't hold Mophur by ourselves, and we can't count on the townsfolk to help us. So we have no choice but to keep moving. Get used to it. We're likely to find people changing allegiance all the way south, or at least in every place that has a shrine to Bane."

.. ..

Bat wings beating, Tsagoth flew over the battlements of Hurkh, and his command—vampires, wraiths, and other undead capable of flight—hurtled after him. No one was stupid enough to shoot at them.

That was as he expected. The town was flying crimson banners adorned with black skulls. The flags glowed with magical phosphorescence to make them stand out against the night sky. The no-doubt hastily sewn cloths didn't precisely duplicate any of Szass Tam's personal emblems, but their message was plain enough.

Tsagoth swooped down into Hurkh's central square and flowed into bipedal form. Some of the vampires did the same, while others melted into wolves. The phantoms hovered, and elsewhere in the city, dogs began to howl.

"Whoever governs this place," Tsagoth shouted at the gates of the town's central keep, "reveal yourself!"

No one inside the fortress responded, although he could sense wretched little humans cowering inside. Rather, the door of a building on the opposite side of the plaza opened.

Constructed of blackened stone, the structure was a temple of Bane, a mass of spires adorned with spikes, jags, and windows narrow as arrow loops. Judging from the black and green gems adorning her dark vestments, the Mulan lady who emerged first looked to be the high priestess. She smiled and strode with a confident air, but the four lesser priests creeping in her wake were pale, wide-eyed, and stank of sweat and fear.

"Good evening," she said. "My name is Unara Anrakh." Up close, she smelled of the myrrh she probably burned during her devotions.

"Are you in charge?" Tsagoth asked.

"For the moment," Unara replied. "Until His Omnipotence Szass Tam appoints a new autharch. The previous one was deaf to the voice of Bane."

Tsagoth grinned. "So you murdered him."

"Should I have allowed him to keep his position and continue giving his fealty to the council? I knew that if I did, you and your comrades would lay siege to Hurkh and put us all to the sword."

Perhaps she believed Hurkh was of greater strategic importance than it actually was. Still, she had a point. "We might have gotten around to it eventually."

"But now there's no need. We pledge our loyalty to Szass Tam and have already begun to serve him. Come visit the Black Hand's altar. See the heads heaped before it. Each belonged to a southern legionnaire. The autharch gave them refuge inside the city walls, and after we killed him, my followers and I disposed of them as well."

"I'm sure it's an impressive display," he said, not caring whether or not she detected his sarcasm. "But I doubt you managed to kill every southern soldier who fled in this direction."

Unara blinked. "That's true. We needed to fly the skull banners so you wouldn't attack us by mistake. But once we started, the southerners stopped coming near the walls."

"Then my company and I need to press on without delay. With luck, we might overtake more southerners before the end of the night. But first we want to feed. I need forty people, one for each of my followers."

The priestess hesitated. "I . . . learned about spectres and similar entities during my training. Do they require nourishment?"

"No. But they have a constant, insatiable drive to hurt and kill, and it's easier to control them if I allow them to gratify it periodically."

"Oh. I see. But as I explained, we've pledged ourselves to Szass Tam, and I promised everyone that it would make us safe."

"Most of you will be, unless you keep trying my patience. Have your guards fetch the forty folk you consider most expendable. Otherwise, I'll simply turn these hounds of mine loose to feed on whatever rabbits they can catch."

As he'd expected, Unara brought slaves and emptied out the town jail to fulfill his requirements. Still, as ghosts plunged their shadowy hands into the flesh of the living, withering their victims, and the occasional vampire, lost to blood lust, chewed a throat to shreds, she periodically winced. Perhaps it had occurred to her that Szass Tam's troops would pass this way again, and eventually all the thralls and captured felons would be gone.

Tsagoth rather enjoyed her discomfiture. Prompted by her god, or so she claimed, she chose to embrace the rule of a lich and the necromancers and undead who carried out his will. Well, here was a first taste of what that would entail.

.. ..

It wasn't the first time Aoth had regretted attaining high rank. With the exception of Mirror, every other member of the ragtag band he'd shepherded south was almost certainly sleeping the sleep of utter exhaustion. He, on the other hand, was standing at attention and saluting.

"By the Great Flame," said Nymia Focar, seated behind a silvery soth-wood desk so highly polished that it gleamed even in the wan daylight shining through the window, "was the journey as hard as your appearance suggests?"

"I'm just tired and dirty. We didn't have to fight south of Mophur. But we had to keep running. I kept hoping we'd reach a place where we could rest for a while and be safe, but we never found it. Some towns and fortresses have gone over to Szass Tam. Some no longer exist, or are in such bad shape that the northerners could overrun them in a heartbeat. Earthquakes knocked the walls down, or they endured some other calamity. Even Tyraturos was no good for us. Dimon naturally favored the church of Bane while he was alive, and the clerics are taking full advantage of the authority he gave them." He gave his head a shake. "Am I rambling? If I am, I'm sorry."

"Don't be. You're making sense." She gestured to a table laden with bottles of wine and a platter of dark brown bread, apples, pears, and white and yellow cheeses. "Take whatever you want, sit down before you fall down, and then give me a full report while you eat."

He generally didn't try to eat and converse with a superior at the same time. He feared it would make him look more graceless and uncouth—more Rashemi—than he did already. But for once he was too starved to worry about it. He poured a goblet of pale amber wine, loaded a plate, and dropped down in a chair.

He fancied that, exhausted and famished though he was, he at least managed to talk between mouthfuls rather than through them. When he finished, Nymia said, "Your report agrees with everyone else's. This situation is bad."

"You didn't see firsthand?"

"I happened to be near a circle of conjurors when they made the decision to abandon the battlefield, and they translated me back to Bezantur along with them. I didn't have to journey overland."

How nice for you, he thought. "I saw a fair number of griffons in the aerie, so a reasonable number of my men must have made it to safety. That's something, anyway."

"It would be more if we were actually safe."

Aoth took another sip of wine. "Don't you think we are? Bezantur's the biggest city in Thay. The walls are high and thick, and whatever strength remains to the south stands ready to man them. Give or take a few companies still wandering around the countryside, maybe unaware that we even lost a major battle in Eltabbar."

Nymia sighed. "I don't know. A year ago, I would have said that even Szass Tam couldn't take Bezantur. But now the south is weaker than ever before, and I'm not just talking about our legions. We lost two more zulkirs. Dmitra Flass didn't return from the battlefield. She died, was taken prisoner, or defected. Then Zola Sethrakt dropped dead. Of wounds sustained in the battle, or so I'm told."

"I admit, that's unfortunate."

"So is the state of the city's food stores. We can't endure a protracted siege. Szass Tam can starve us into submission."

"What are you telling me—that the council wants to surrender?"

"No, but they might flee into exile and abandon mainland Thay to fend for itself. The fleet is in port waiting to carry people of importance away. We legionnaires are likewise prepared to commandeer every other vessel we can lay our hands on."

Aoth felt sick to his stomach. "So that's it? After fighting for ten years, we're just going to run away?"

"Not necessarily. The zulkirs haven't made a final decision." Her lips quirked into a crooked smile. "Nor have I."

"What do you mean?"

"Perhaps it's not too late to slip out of Bezantur, offer my services to Szass Tam, and secure a position of wealth and influence in the Thay to come."

Aoth marveled that she trusted him enough to confide such thoughts to him. Didn't she realize that he knew she'd acquiesced to the zulkirs' plan to vivisect him?

Maybe, he thought with a flicker of wry amusement, she understood him better than he'd ever imagined, well enough to realize her callousness hadn't ignited a thirst for revenge in him. He still wasn't sure why not. Perhaps, with the world falling and burning around him, he simply didn't have the outrage to spare for every disappointment and betrayal.

At any rate, he told her, "Go if you want to. I won't tell. But I won't go with you, either."

"Why not?"

"If I weren't so tired, maybe I could explain it to you. Or to myself. As it is, I just know after coming this far, I don't feel like turning my cloak at the end. Maybe I don't want to be like that whoreson Malark."

"I think you owe it to yourself to think more deeply than that. Even if we assume that the zulkirs can somehow hold this part of the coast, or that Szass Tam won't come after them if they flee into exile, we surely can live grander, richer lives in his new kingdom than in the council's shrunken dominions."

"I wouldn't be certain of that. You see what he's made of Thay already."

"As a tactic. He'll bring back sunshine and green grass after he wins the war."

"You're probably right. But, maybe because I'm so tired, I swear I can hear Malark asking the question he pondered over and over again—why did Szass Tam murder Druxus Rhym?"

Nymia shook her head, and the stud in her nostril caught

a ray of light. "*Now* you're no longer making sense, or at least you're fretting over trivia. He killed Rhym before the war even started. Ten years later, what does it matter why?"

"I suppose it doesn't. Unless it points to the fact that there's still something about Szass Tam's schemes that we don't understand."

"We may not understand everything about his strategy, but you'd have to be an imbecile not to comprehend his objective. He means to be sole ruler of Thay, and once he is, he'll launch wars of conquest and try to make himself emperor of the East."

"Of course. You're right, and I'm blathering. But here's something that isn't blather: Szass Tam has plenty of lords and war leaders who have served him faithfully since the war began. Even if he welcomes you into his host, those others will all be standing in line ahead of you to claim their rewards when the conflict ends. Do you think there'll be a tharch left for you to govern? Or even a town in need of an autharch?"

She sighed. "Probably not. So I suppose I might as well stick where I am. But if only all these wretched zulkirs would destroy each other! Then I'd crown myself queen of Pyarados and appoint you marshal of my legions."

Aoth smiled. "It's a nice dream, High Lady."

•• •• •• •• •• •• •• •• •• •• •• •• ••

As a boy, Bareris had loved the harbor. The sea breeze made a refreshing change from the stinks of the slum in which he lived, travelers sang new songs and told new stories, and the spectacle of the myriad ships with their towering masts, intricate rigging, and banks of oars fed his dreams of finding adventure and wealth in foreign lands. Tammith had liked it too, or perhaps she'd simply liked accompanying him wherever he chose to wander.

As in days past, they strolled beside the water, but everything seemed different than he remembered. The docks didn't bustle by night as they had by day, particularly with legionnaires standing watch to keep ordinary folk away from the piers. The waves were black, not blue and rippling with sunlight, and Tammith's fingers were cold in his.

Still, he was grateful to be here.

Tammith sniffed, her nostrils flaring. He did the same, but could smell only salt air and the leftover stink of the catch the fishermen had brought into port earlier that day. He supposed that she, with her inhumanly keen senses, perceived something more.

"It's a pity," she said.

"What is?"

"This part of the docks used to smell of spices. Now it doesn't."

"You have a good memory."

"When we were paupers' children, we used to imagine a day when we'd be able to afford foods prepared with expensive seasonings and all the other luxuries Bezantur provided for the wealthy. Now we're officers, lords of a sort, and we can have most anything we want. But the war has turned our home into a faded, tired place."

"Do you mind so very much?"

She sighed. "Perhaps I'm simply trying to mind. I don't have a problem with caring too much about things that don't really matter. My difficulty is trying to feel that anything does."

He forced a grin. "You were supposed to say, 'No, I don't mind at all, so long as we're together.'"

Her pale lips quirked into a smile. "That would have been better, wouldn't it? But you have to remember, you're the bard, gifted with a ready wit and golden tongue."

"Perhaps I can use them to coax you behind that pile of crates where you first permitted me to touch you under your shift."

"Bezantur would have to have some lazy dockhands if it's still there after all these years. Anyway, I can't believe you're feeling lickerish again so soon."

"We have sixteen years' worth of lost love to make up for. I assure you, I can couch my lance for another tilt. And you can nibble my neck if you want."

"No!"

Her vehemence surprised him. "You realize, I like it, too."

"That only makes it worse. If we're going to do this—be together—it has to be in the way of a natural man and woman. We need to put perversity behind us."

"All right. If you want it that way. Although you know, there are different sorts of perversity."

She cocked her head. "I suppose you learned of all manner of strange and disgusting practices during your time among the outlanders."

"Well, obviously, I kept myself pure for my beloved, but I could hardly help hearing the lewd stories told around the camp-fire. Storik once swore to me that dwarves like to—"

Tammith pivoted away from him to peer into the dark. "Something's happening," she said.

He looked where she was looking. At first he couldn't see anything. But he heard a muddled sound, and a moment later, the first ranks of what seemed to be a considerable number of folk tramped into the pool of amber glow cast by a hanging lantern. Most of the newcomers carried weapons, either proper ones or tools like axes and chisels that could serve the purpose. Many dangled sacks in their hands, or bore them slung across their shoulders. One fellow pushed a barrow full of bundles. The wheels squeaked and rumbled on the cobblestones.

There'd been a sentry posted at the far end of the street. He must have tried to turn these people back. Bareris wondered how badly the mob had hurt him.

He also wished he and Tammith were wearing armor. Although no one had specifically ordered them to quell unrest and protect the fleet, in an emergency, it was their duty even so.

"I'm going to try to turn them back without fighting," he said. "Don't hurt anyone unless you have to."

Tammith nodded. "My abilities aren't like yours. I can't tamper with so many minds at the same time. But I'll help as much as I'm able."

He crooned a charm that made him appear a shade handsomer and taller, more sympathetic and commanding, in the eyes of anyone who beheld him. Then he smiled and ambled toward the mob as if they were all staunch friends. Tammith kept pace beside him.

"Good evening, Goodmen," he said, infusing his voice with the magic of influence. "What's going on?"

A big man at the front of the pack, a trowel clutched in one fist and both arms banded with tattooed rings, glared at him. "We're taking a ship. Or ships, if we can't all fit on one."

"Why?" Bareris asked.

"Because the blue fire is coming."

"No, it isn't, and if someone told you otherwise, he was simply repeating a baseless rumor. I'm not wearing my insignia at present, but I'm an officer of the Griffon Legion. I hear what the scouts and soothsayers discover, and I give you my word, nobody has seen any blue flame moving toward Bezantur."

"What about Szass Tam?" shrilled a voice rising from farther back in the throng. "Are you going to tell us he isn't coming?"

"No," Bareris said, "he probably is, but even he won't be able to get inside the city walls. No enemy could. You'll be far safer here than trying to sail to some foreign land. The same upheavals that shake the land are raising huge waves at sea. The depths are giving birth to strange new creatures."

"The nobles don't think it's safer to stay," said the man with the trowel. "Everybody knows they're getting ready to sail away and leave us 'lowly Rashemi' behind to die."

"Once again, I give you my word. They haven't made any such decision."

"We're done listening to you, legionnaire. We're going. If you want, you can come along. If not, you'd be wise to step aside."

Since the mason seemed to be a leader of sorts, Bareris targeted an enchantment of persuasion at him specifically. "I won't do that, because I'm trying to save your lives. The ships are well protected. Their crews are sleeping onboard, and the zulkirs have other troops and wizards stationed in the warehouses adjacent to the piers. If you proceed any farther, someone will spot you and sound the alarm. Then all those legionnaires and wizards will rise from their hammocks and bedrolls and slaughter you."

The big man took a deep breath. "Or we'll kill them."

"There are mothers and children at the back of the crowd," Tammith whispered. "I can hear them talking to one another."

"No," said Bareris, still addressing the big man, "you won't. You can't win. I understand you're brave and determined, but the soldiers have armor, superior weapons, and the training to put them to good use. They also have sorcery backing them. If you press on, you can only die, and watch your wives and babies hacked to pieces alongside you. Is that what you want?"

The man with the trowel swallowed. "You said it yourself. At this time of night, most of the soldiers are asleep. If—"

Tammith stepped forward. Her eyes gleamed and she snarled, exposing her extended fangs. A sudden feeling of foulness and menace radiated from her, and even Bareris flinched back a step.

"Idiots!" she cried. "You know what Red Wizards can do. What they *love* to do to anyone who defies them. You know the sort of creatures who fight for them. I'm only the first of many such beings who stand in your way, I could butcher every one of you by myself, and I'm getting bored with your stupidity. Choose now whether you mean to live or die, or I'll choose for you."

For a heartbeat, the mob stood and gaped at her. Then the big man dropped his trowel, and it clanked on the street. He turned and bolted, shoving into the mass of humanity behind him.

When he panicked, so did his fellows. They all ran.

Tammith laughed an ugly little laugh and took a stride after them. Bareris caught her by the forearm.

Fangs still bared, she rounded on him, glared, and then seemed to remember who he was, or perhaps who they were together. The chatoyant sheen left her eyes, and the long pointed canines retracted.

"I'm sorry," she said.

"Don't be. You did that brilliantly."

She smiled. "We did it together. Your magic softened them up, and afterward I thought that if I could throw a scare into the leader, they'd all lose their nerve."

"I'm glad we were able to chase them off before any of them came to grief."

"Believe it or not, so am I. They're just frightened people trying to survive. They don't deserve punishment for that."

Trumpets blew, and someone screamed. Crossbows clacked, discharging their bolts.

"Damn it!" Bareris cried. Prompted by instinct, he dashed toward the water, and Tammith sprinted at his side.

When he looked up and down the boardwalk at the end of the lane, with the docks extending out into the surf beyond, he saw what he'd feared he might. He and Tammith had turned back the troublemakers advancing down one particular street, but those misguided souls had been only one contingent of a far bigger mob converging on the harbor. Emerging from other points, the malcontents were trying to fight their way toward the docked vessels, while lines of legionnaires formed to hold them back. Other soldiers scrambled from the warehouses to reinforce them, and sailors leaped from the decks of their long, sleek ships.

The violence exploding on every side made Bareris and Tammith's little coup in the cause of peace and public order feel like a bitter joke. But there was nothing to do now but stand with their fellow soldiers.

So they did. Whenever possible, Bareris sang songs of fear to force rioters to turn tail before anybody had to kill them. But he still had to bloody his sword, and the necessity sickened him as it seldom had before.

Light and heat flared behind him, and he risked a glance backward. Flames leaped up from the prow of a warship.

It didn't make sense that a rioter had started the fire. None of them were anywhere near it, and besides, they wanted to steal the vessels, not destroy them. Bareris suspected that one of the wizards on his own side was responsible. He'd been trying to hurl flame at the enemy, and because of the problems with sorcery, the spell turned against him.

But that didn't make much sense, either. Bareris had seen his share of battle magic, and incendiary spells usually flew in a straight line. A wizard onboard the ship wouldn't have had such a clear path to the foe. Legionnaires were in the way.

But if someone had been trying to hit the vessel with a flaming arrow or spell, the best way would be to shoot from an elevated position. Squinting, he peered upward.

At first he saw nothing to justify his sudden, half-formed suspicions. But then he spotted a point of light like a firefly. It was an arrowhead, glowing as if the point had just been forged.

He could just make out the dark figure holding the shaft. And other archers creeping around on a warehouse rooftop.

He started a song to shift himself through space. He was only halfway through when one of the black-clad bowmen loosed a shaft. The arrow lodged in the foremast of another ship, and flames instantly roared up the spar. The missiles had to carry a potent enchantment to spark such a prodigious blaze so quickly.

The world shattered into blurry streaks, and then Bareris was standing on the sloping, shingled rooftop. He'd cast the spell to position himself behind the three archers, and moving quickly but silently despite the pitch, he stalked up behind the nearest and drove his sword into his back.

The bowman made a croaking noise as he toppled forward. Despite the clamor rising from the struggle below, it was loud enough to alert his comrades, and they both jerked around in time to see his corpse roll down the slope.

Bareris rushed the nearer of the two remaining archers. He didn't have an arrow on the string, and didn't like his chances of nocking, aiming, and loosing one in time. He threw down his bow and whipped a short sword from its scabbard. The hand gripping the blade was tattooed solid black, a sign of devotion among worshipers of Bane.

Bareris scrambled to close with the man. He wanted to kill him quickly, before the third archer, who was now standing behind him, could attack from that favorable position. But his haste, coupled with the slant of the roof, betrayed him. One foot slipped out from underneath him and he fell. The swordsman stabbed at him.

Bareris slammed down hard, but managed to swing his blade in a frantic parry. Somehow it carried his adversary's thrust safely to the side. Taking advantage of his supine position, he sliced the bowman's hamstring. The man with the black hand yelped and fell. Bareris heaved himself to his knees and cut, shearing into the archer's stomach.

That should take care of him, but what about the third enemy? Bareris twisted around just as the other man's arrow leaped from the bow.

The bard wrenched himself sideways and the shaft hurtled past him. The bowman instantly snatched for another. Bareris sucked in a breath to batter him with a thunderous shout.

But before he could, a cloud of black bats swirled down to rip at the archer from all sides. He collapsed immediately. The bats hadn't shed nearly enough blood to kill, but the cold poison of their touch had stopped his heart.

The bats flew round and round one another and became a woman. "Are you all right?" Tammith asked.

"Yes." He looked up and down the row of roofs and saw other black figures slinking with bows in hand. "But we have problems." He bellowed loud as his magic would permit. "Legionnaires! Look up! At the rooftops!"

Despite the volume he achieved and the power of coercion with which he infused his call, he wasn't certain anyone would heed him. There was too much happening on the ground. But someone paid attention. Arrows and quarrels flew up from the docks and ships, and the dark bowmen started to drop. Bareris heaved a sigh of relief, and then an enormous shadow swept over him.

Black against a black sky, largely visible because it eclipsed the few stars shining through the cloud cover, a nightwing soared above the harbor, while other huge, batlike shadows glided over other parts of the city. Bareris wished again for his brigandine, wished, too, that Winddancer was with him, and that he hadn't already expended so much of his power. But the nightwings didn't dive and attack, and when they wheeled and flew north, he inferred that they'd simply been scouting the city stretched out beneath them.

He was glad he wouldn't have to fight one, but far from overjoyed. If the creatures had ventured here tonight, it could only mean the rest of Szass Tam's host was following close behind.

●● ●● ●● ●● ●● ●● ●● ●● ●● ●● ●● ●●

The Tower of Revelation offended Lallara's sensibilities. As far as she was concerned, a wizard's fortress was meant to hide secrets and provide strong defenses, and the sanctuary of the Order of Divination seemed capable of neither. The acoustics were so excellent that she could hear tiny sounds from two chambers away, and the place sported so many big, costly glass windows that it scarcely seemed to have enough solid stone wall to support its mass. More often than not, the casements stood open to admit the morning breeze and the faint sounds of the city, abnormally quiet, almost holding its breath after last night's insurrection and the sighting of Szass Tam's flying creatures.

But though the citadel made her feel exposed and ill at ease, she was an archmage specializing in protective magic, and perceived that the building had wards in place to foil eavesdroppers and keep assassins from flinging daggers or thunderbolts through the openings. So she supposed she could tolerate it for a while. Certainly it had seemed more expeditious for the zulkirs to go to the diviners than to require the seers to drag the appurtenances of their discipline to the Central Citadel.

Two dozen senior diviners chanted spells to their mirrors and crystal orbs. Light seethed inside the devices, then coalesced into coherent images. Lallara, Nevron, Lauzoril, Samas Kul, and Kumed Hahpret prowled among them, peering at ranks upon marching ranks of dread warriors, packs of loping ghouls, crawling hulks with writhing tentacles like the ones that had reared up out of the ground outside the Keep of Sorrows, and skeletal horses drawing closed wagons.

After a time, Lauzoril said, "You've done well. Thank you."

A diviner with additional eyes tattooed above and below his

real ones said, "To be honest, Your Omnipotence, it wasn't difficult. The necromancers aren't trying to conceal their numbers or their location."

Nevron spat. "No. Why should they? You soothsayers, get out. Your masters need to talk."

If the diviners resented the brusque dismissal, they had better sense than to let on. They filed out docilely.

Samas flopped down on a stool, plucked a silk handkerchief from a pocket of his luxurious scarlet robe, and wiped sweat from his mottled, ruddy face. He looked as if the brief stroll around the chamber had taxed his stamina, and, as on many previous occasions, Lallara felt a pang of disgust at his gross, wheezing immensity.

"How can Szass Tam have such a large army?" the obese transmuter said. "How could the necromancers create so many undead in so short a time?"

"We don't know!" Lallara snapped. "We already discussed it and agreed that we don't understand. Either think of something new to contribute or keep your mouth shut."

Samas glared at her. By the look of him, he was attempting to frame a truly scathing retort, but Lauzoril intervened before he could.

"Let's not take out our frustrations on one another," the zulkir of Enchantment said, his manner that of the stuffy, condescending schoolmaster he was at heart. "We have decisions to make, and we need to make them quickly, because I recognize that tax station." He gestured to a greenish sphere floating in the air. The luminous scene inside it revealed gigantic hounds, their forms composed of mangled corpses twisted together, standing near a roadside keep, its walls a distinctive mosaic of white stones intermingled with black. "The lich's host has nearly reached the First Escarpment."

"How do they travel so fast?" Kumed asked.

"The undead are tireless," Lauzoril said, "and by day, the wagons carry the creatures who can't bear sunlight. And we have no one left in the field to harry the enemy and slow them down."

"The Griffon Legion did it at the start of the war," Samas said.

"The Griffon Legion is a shadow of its former self," Nevron said, "like all our other legions. I don't think they could manage the same trick again. Let's not send them to their deaths until we can accomplish something thereby."

"So," Samas said, "Szass Tam will be here soon. The question is, do we linger to receive him?"

"Yes, damn it!" Nevron snarled. "This is Bezantur! It can withstand a siege."

"Can it?" Lauzoril asked. He waved his hand again, this time in a gesture that encompassed all the globes and mirrors shining on every side, and all the visions of martial and mystical might flickering inside them.

"If it can't," Nevron said, "the four of us—" He stopped short, then gave Kumed a cold smile. "Excuse me, Your Omnipotence, obviously I meant to say, the *five* of us can always transport ourselves to safety."

"In the midst of battle," Lauzoril said, "nothing is certain. It would be difficult to articulate any spell properly with a vampire's fangs buried in one's throat. Besides, if we waited to escape until Szass Tam's army had breached the walls and flooded into the city, we might get away, but it's likely that the ships carrying our treasure and our more useful followers wouldn't. Is that how we want to start our lives in exile?"

Samas looked pained at the mere thought of leaving his vast wealth behind.

"At this point," Lallara said, "we can count ourselves fortunate we even have ships. Only four burned, but we could have lost all of them."

Kumed cleared his throat. "What really happened last night? Who was responsible?"

"The church of Bane," said Lauzoril. "Their agents stirred up the rabble to try to steal the ships to flee the city. The point was to create cover for the Banites to sneak over the rooftops, shoot flaming arrows into the vessels, and so keep us from fleeing."

Kumed attempted a scowl as fierce as Nevron's. "Then we should hang every Banite we can find."

"You won't find the ones who actually pose a threat," Lallara said. "They've gone into hiding."

"Which means they could try again," Samas said, summoning a golden cup into his hand. Lallara caught a whiff of brandy. "For that matter, the mob could rise again, now that the Dreadmasters have put the idea in their heads, and this time succeed in making away with the boats."

"All the more reason," Lauzoril said, "to use them ourselves as quickly as possible."

Nevron shook his head. "Are you really so craven?"

"I'm not surrendering," Lauzoril said. "I intend to spend my time in the Wizard's Reach planning and gathering strength. I'll deal with Szass Tam when the time is right, but that time has yet to arrive. If you disagree, then you're free to try and prove me wrong. Stay in Bezantur and command the defense. Just don't expect me to leave any enchanters, or any of the soldiers we command, behind to fight."

"I'm leaving, too," Lallara said. The admission wounded her pride, but pride was of no use to the dead.

"So am I," said Samas.

"And I," said Kumed, as if anyone cared.

"Then I must come as well," Nevron said. "Plainly, I can't hold the city without you. But curse you all for the gutless weaklings you are!"

He seemed furious enough, but Lallara sensed a histrionic quality to his bitterness. Perhaps, underneath it all, the conjuror was grateful they'd made it impossible for him to stay.

·· ·· ·· ·· ·· ·· ·· ·· ·· ·· ·· ·· ·· ··

His fingers scratching among the feathers atop Winddancer's head, Mirror wafting a chill at his back, Bareris stood at the rail of a barge overloaded with griffons and their riders and watched the zulkirs' fleet set sail. It took a long time for so many vessels to maneuver out of the harbor. The Red Wizards and nobles had laid claim to every trawler, sloop, and cog in port to transport themselves, their troops, their possessions, and favored members of their households.

The city stood in a haze of smoke. As the fleet set forth, evokers had hurled blasts of fire at the piers and the shipyards with their half-completed and half-repaired vessels suspended in dry dock. The idea was to make it as difficult as possible for the necromancers to give chase over the Alambar Sea, and if the conflagrations spread to other parts of the city, the lords who were abandoning it no longer had any reason to care.

The smoke was thick enough to sting their eyes and make them cough. Yet hundreds of folk perched on rooftops, or ventured as close as they could to the water's edge, to watch their masters' departure. Bareris wondered if they were happy or sad to see them go.

He wondered the same about himself. He'd been a warrior for sixteen years. He didn't like losing, and despite all the council's swaggering talk of hiring a mighty host of sellswords and returning to reclaim mainland Thay in a year or two, he judged that was exactly what had happened. He doubted he'd ever lay eyes on the city of his birth again.

It was particularly hard to accept defeat after a ten-year

struggle against Szass Tam. He'd hated the lich ever since he'd discovered that his minions had turned Tammith into a vampire, and he still did.

But that loathing wasn't the passion that ruled his life anymore. His love for Tammith was stronger, and perhaps he ought to regard this final retreat as a blessing. Now they could devote themselves to one another, and to finding a remedy for her condition, without worrying that, in one ghastly fashion or another, war would sunder them yet again.

Yes, it might all be for the best—if the fleet managed to slip away unmolested.

•• •• •• •• •• •• •• •• •• •• •• •• ••

The late Aznar Thrul had commissioned a magnificent pleasure ship for himself. After succeeding the murdered evoker, Samas Kul had looked forward to taking full sybaritic advantage of the vessel, only to discover that he was prone to seasickness. After that she had seldom left her berth.

But now he had a use for her, and he'd invited his fellow zulkirs aboard to enjoy a splendid breakfast and watch Thay fall away behind them. He hoped he wouldn't disgrace himself by needing to rush to the rail. So far, the potion he'd drunk seemed to be doing an adequate job of preventing distress in his guts, but one never knew.

Nevron summoned a demon with the head of a beautiful woman and a body like a small green dragon to carry him between ships. Lallara flew like a bird, and Lauzoril shifted himself through space.

That left only Kumed Hahpret to appear. Samas waited a little longer, then asked if anyone knew where he was.

Nevron smiled. "I'm afraid our young peer won't be joining us. He met with an unfortunate accident before we even set sail.

I myself had to command his underlings to set the port on fire or it wouldn't have gotten done."

Lauzoril inclined his head as if to convey approval. "I suppose the evokers will hold an election."

Nevron snorted. "They can try."

chapter eleven

6–11 Marpenoth, the Year of Blue Fire

It gladdened Szass Tam to see the gates in the high black walls of Bezantur standing open, and the banners of the Order of Necromancy flying from the spires that rose above. He had a sudden foolish urge to spur his infernal steed with its jet black coat, iron hooves, and red eyes, gallop ahead of his army, and enter the city immediately.

It wasn't an entirely mad idea. According to his scouts and seers, no one was left in the city with the will and the power to have any chance of harming him. But he was going to rule Thay in years to come. It would be politic to start out by entering the realm's greatest city with the pomp appropriate to the new "regent."

So he took the time to organize a procession, while his officers chafed at the delay, and he derived a bit of secret amusement from their restlessness. They believed he was wasting precious time, but that was because they didn't understand just how much mystical strength the Black Hand had given him.

He'd already expended a goodly portion of it, and the rest had begun to slip away as he'd known it would. But he fancied he had enough left to bring his war to a satisfactory conclusion.

When everything was ready, he marched his army into the city with Malark Springhill, Homen Odesseiron, and Azhir Kren riding in places of honor just behind him. The streets echoed to the deafening chants that kept the blood orcs striding in unison, and to the huzzahs of the folk who lined the streets and leaned out of windows to wave little red flags and cheer for him.

Sometimes the cheering faltered, and when it swelled again, it had a forced quality to it. Szass Tam suspected that happened when the crowd caught sight of some particularly hideous or uncanny-looking horror, even though he hadn't put a great many of his most alarming servants on display. Some were too gigantic to pass easily through the streets, some were invisible in the afternoon sunlight, and others had to hide from it lest it sear them from existence. Still, enough remained to daunt even a populace that had long ago accustomed itself to the fact that demons and undead served in the ranks of its armies.

Or perhaps the carrion stink of all the dread warriors and ghouls packed together was making people sick to their stomachs.

In any case, Szass Tam was realist enough to understand that few, if any of these supposed well wishers, had yearned to see him crush his rivals, although it was likely a number had prayed for *someone* to win and bring the long war to an end. They were cheering to convince him they'd only served the council because they had no choice, and therefore it would be pointless for their new overlord to punish them.

Comprehending their true motives didn't vex him. He enjoyed the moment because it was a symbol of his victory. He didn't need Bezantur to love him.

Triumphal processions through the city traditionally entered through the northeast gate, followed a circuitous route that took them past the major temples and Red Wizard bastions, and terminated in the plaza north of the Central Citadel. Szass Tam adhered to the custom and found Zekith Shezim waiting to greet him. His eyes and the jagged patterns of his tattooing as dark as his gauntlet and vestments, the high priest of Bane advanced, kneeled, and proffered a ring of iron keys.

They should properly have been keys to the Central Citadel, but Szass Tam, who'd seen the genuine items before, albeit not for ten years, recognized that they weren't. His enemies had probably taken all the real ones when they fled.

No matter. This little ceremony was like the acclamation of the crowd. He could appreciate it for what it was.

He took the keys and said, "Thank you. Now stand, Your Omniscience, and rest assured, a bow will suffice in the future."

Zekith rose stiffly. "Thank you, Your Omnipotence."

Szass Tam smiled. "It occurs to me that I may need a new title. Every zulkir is 'Your Omnipotence.' "

"On the other hand," Malark said, "you're the only one left."

"Not yet," said Szass Tam, "but with luck, soon."

Zekith took a deep breath. "Master, I apologize. I tried to burn the fleet as you directed, but it didn't work out."

"It's all right," Szass Tam said. "When one arrow misses, you shoot another, and happily, my quiver isn't empty yet. Now, I need someone to govern this place. Would you like to be autharch of Bezantur, with more honors to come if you do a good job?"

"I would."

"Then you'll need these." Szass Tam handed back the keys. "Well, not really, but one good piece of mummery deserves another."

"Yes, Your Omnipotence."

"Your first task will be to see to the needs of my troops. Many have requirements and appetites that the citizens of Bezantur may find objectionable. But I want my warriors strong and satisfied that their commander takes good care of them. Up to a point, that means making sure no one interferes with them as they pursue their pleasures, but it would also be nice if the city was still standing tomorrow morning. Do you follow?"

"Yes, Master. I can strike the proper balance."

"Then I leave the matter in your hands. My captains and I are going to look at the harbor." He, Malark, the two tharchions, and an escort rode in that direction.

The waterfront still smelled of smoke, and small fires flickered here and there. The major conflagrations had reduced the vessels in dry dock to black, flaking shells, ready to crumble at a touch. The piers had burned until whatever remained of the walkways collapsed into the sea. Only the support posts remained, sticking up out of the waves.

Malark smiled a crooked smile. "I'm afraid there isn't much harbor left to look at."

Azhir glared at him. "Is that how you acquired your reputation for cleverness? By stating the obvious?"

Szass Tam had already noticed that the tharchion of Gauros resented his newfound amity with a man, who, until recently, had been one of their most troublesome foes. He wished he could convince her that Malark had no interest in usurping her position. Unfortunately, she scarcely would have found an honest explanation of the spymaster's interests reassuring.

"Is this it, then?" Homen asked. He, too, disliked Malark,

but he'd always been more adept at masking his emotions. "I don't see so much as a serviceable rowboat. I suppose we could march west to Thassalen. We might find ships there. But even if the autharch lets us into the city without a fight, by that time, the council will be far away."

"We aren't going to Thassalen," Szass Tam said. He turned to one of the mounted guards. "Tell my wizards to attend me." The warrior saluted and pounded off, his horse's hooves drumming on the pavement.

The mages were no doubt weary from so many days of travel, but they had the good sense to come running. Szass Tam called the necromancers forward and positioned them so as to define the vertices of a complex mystic sigil. Then he took his place at the center.

He summoned a staff made of the fused bones of drowned men, bound with gold salvaged from sunken ships, into his withered hands. He hadn't had occasion to use the rod in over two hundred years, but perceived immediately that it was as potent as ever. He could feel the force inside it pulsing slow and steady as a line of rumbling breakers pounding at a shore.

He linked his consciousness to that of his subordinates. He chanted words of power, and they chorused the responses.

The feeble sunlight faded until it seemed that dusk had arrived early. The air grew cold. Then gray, shriveled heads bobbed to the surface of the harbor as sailors who'd fallen overboard and swimmers who'd ventured too far from shore responded to the necromancers' call. There were scores of them in view, and Szass Tam could sense still others, too far out to be visible but waiting to serve him nonetheless.

Meanwhile, memories of ancient pain and hatred woke in the ooze on the sea floor, and there they would shelter until true night fell. But then, they too would slither forth to do his bidding.

When he'd summoned and bound all he could, Szass Tam changed his incantations and the ritual passes that accompanied them, altering the net that was his magic to gather a different catch. Before, he'd fished for the festering stains left by the deaths of men. Now he trawled for echoes of the extinctions of beasts.

The rotting carcass of a kraken shifted its tentacles and swam upward from the seabed. The bones of a colossal eel tumbled and slid through slime to reassemble its skeleton. Mad with the need for vengeance on wyrm slayers who were long since dust, the ghost of a sea dragon roared, and although no one standing beside the ruined docks could see or hear it, people cringed and cried out nonetheless.

Szass Tam lowered his staff. When the ferrule touched the ground, he suddenly felt so weak that he leaned on the instrument.

It was unexpected. Liches were supposed to be immune to fatigue. But this wasn't ordinary weariness. He truly was nearing the end of the Black Hand's gift of power, and he realized that once it was gone, he'd be weaker than normal for a time. Perhaps it took a portion of his own strength to contain Bane's energies safely until required, and then turn them to their proper purpose.

He was glad the weakness lasted only a moment. It was poor practice for a lord to allow his vassals to catch him looking vulnerable.

"You've raised a fair number of drowned men and dead sea creatures," Malark called. "But not enough, I think, to destroy the council's fleet."

"I'm not done," Szass Tam said.

He dismissed his necromancers. They were too spent to assist any further. Then he called forth any other sorcerers capable of helping with his next effort, which was to say, every Red Wizard who'd defected from the order Mythrellan and Dmitra had commanded in their turns, and anyone else possessing a working knowledge of the same discipline.

He arranged them in a different pattern, then switched the bone staff for one made of moonlight, shadow, shimmering desert air, and fancies plucked from a madman's mind, all bound together. He led his assistants in another series of elaborate, contrapuntal invocations.

Darkness swirled on the water. By degrees, it sculpted itself into solid shapes and froze into solidity, until it became a fleet of warships floating at anchor, their hulls and sails black with scarlet trim and accents.

Szass Tam grinned at Malark, Homen, and Azhir. "I realize we didn't make enough vessels to carry the entire army. But, with the warriors we can take onboard, the ones who'll swim alongside, and those who can fly, do you think we now have sufficient strength to sink our foes?"

Homen smiled. "Your Omnipotence, I believe we do."

The world tilted and spun. Szass Tam staggered. This time, if he was to remain upright, he had to lean heavily on his staff, and not just for a moment either. He growled a word of power whose virtue was to lend stamina to a flagging body and clarity to a beleaguered mind, and his dizziness abated.

Malark, Azhir, and Homen all ran to him, the fleet-footed former monk outdistancing the others. Despite his chagrin at having his appearance of majesty compromised, Szass Tam felt touched by what at least gave the impression of genuine concern. It warmed him in a way that all the cheering in the streets had not, and reminded him that the future, glorious as it would be, would come at a certain poignant cost.

"Are you all right?" Malark asked.

"I'm fine," Szass Tam said.

"Maybe you should rest."

"No. Perhaps I'll want to by and by, but for now, I'm more than strong enough to do what needs doing. Which is raise a storm at sea to slow the council's flight. Our fine new ships, zombie sea serpents, and what have you won't do us any good if we can't catch our quarry."

He turned, scrutinized the sorcerers who waited to assist him, and called forth those with power over the weather.

•• •• •• •• •• •• •• •• •• •• •• ••

Whenever Thessaloni Canos looked around the deck of Samas Kul's floating seraglio, she had to suppress a sneer. She hated the lewd gilded carvings, the companionways broad and easy to negotiate as any staircase on land, and every other detail where the shipwrights had forsaken spare, efficient utility in favor of luxury and opulent display.

But the ridiculous vessel seemed to have become a flagship of sorts. Samas had entertained his fellow zulkirs onboard shortly after setting sail, and that had put them in the habit of gathering here to confer. Thessaloni simply had to make the best of it.

With her trident dangling in her hand, she waited for the mage-lords to arrive, prowling the decks and trying to look past the ship's annoying toys and fripperies and determine how her captain ought to handle her in a fight. How nimbly could the ship maneuver, and how many archers could stand and shoot from the forecastle?

Meanwhile, Aoth Fezim, who'd carried her to the ship on the back of his griffon, descended to the galley, procured two hams, and watched with his luminous blue eyes as his steed snapped them down. Sailors watched, too, curious but keeping their distance as if they feared the beast might eat them next. Cold drizzle spattered down from a charcoal-colored sky, and the sea was choppy. The wind moaned out of the west.

The archwizards all appeared within a few heartbeats of one another. Samas crept on deck looking pale, shaky, and unshaven, as if he'd had a difficult night and had only just risen from his berth. Lauzoril and Lallara simply popped out of nowhere, and Nevron arrived riding a creature resembling a gigantic two-headed canary. When he dismounted, the thing turned into yellow vapor, which flowed into a brass ring on his left hand like steam retreating back into a kettle.

Aoth approached the zulkirs, came to attention, and saluted. Thessaloni climbed down from the bow and did the same. "Masters," she said.

Lallara looked Samas up and down, smirked, and said, "Aren't you treating us to another lavish breakfast this morning? More pork loin with green pepper sauce, perhaps? I do hope that enormous belly isn't queasy."

The transmuter scowled at her. "I hope you know how much I despise you."

"I do. It lifts my spirits whenever I think of it."

"We didn't come here for bickering and japes." Lauzoril turned to Thessaloni. "What's our situation?"

"I'll let Captain Fezim tell you," Thessaloni replied. "He and his men are the ones who've been aloft this morning, scouting."

The short, burly legionnaire cleared his throat. "We lost three ships, either because the storm sank them or because it blew them so far away that we can't locate them."

Nevron shrugged. A smell of smoke and burning clung to him. Thessaloni had first met him aboard a ship under her command, and she recalled how the odor had alarmed her until she realized where it originated. "Three isn't so bad," the conjuror said.

"I agree," Thessaloni said, "but you haven't heard everything yet."

"The storm damaged a number of ships," said Aoth, "and the

crews are making repairs. I'm no mariner, but I'll try to give you the details if you want them.

"The bad weather scattered the fleet as well. It will take some time for it to gather back together. But the really bad news is that the necromancers are chasing us. Somehow, they put their own fleet in the water. They've also got undead sea creatures swimming among their vessels, and skin kites and such flying above them."

"Damn Szass Tam!" Nevron snarled. "Can we make it to the Alaor before he catches up with us?"

"No," Thessaloni said. "The storm blew us east of the islands. The necromancers would intercept us en route."

"I thought we brought the priesthood of Umberlee along with us," Lallara said. "Someone remind me, what use are they, if they can't bend the wind and the tides to our advantage?"

"You Masters obviously comprehend mystical matters far better than I," Thessaloni said, "but as I understand it, Szass Tam's spellcasters are still wrestling with ours for control of the weather, and at the moment, the enemy is having more success than we are."

Lauzoril cocked his head. "Could Szass Tam catch us if we headed farther east and south?"

Thessaloni felt a stab of annoyance at the obvious tenor of his thought and did her best to mask her feelings. "Possibly not, Your Omnipotence. Not soon, anyway."

"But then what?" Lallara asked. "Do we beg for sanctuary in Mulhorand? Do you imagine they love us there, and will give us estates to rule? I think I can guarantee you a chillier reception. We have to reach the Alaor and the colony cities and confirm our mastery of them if we're to have any sort of lives at all."

Thessaloni had never liked Lallara. Why would anyone feel fondness for a woman who went out of her way to be waspish and obnoxious? But she liked her now.

Samas articulated the logical corollary to Lallara's observation. "If that's still our objective, then we need to fight. Can we win?"

"Yes," Thessaloni said.

Lauzoril gave her a skeptical frown. "You seem very sure of yourself."

"I am." It was an exaggeration, but she'd long ago learned that few things were more useless than a captain who dithered and hedged. "Masters, with all respect, over the years I've built you the best navy in eastern Faerûn. Perhaps you've forgotten, because, the Bitch Goddess knows, for the past decade the fleet has had little to do. You've been fighting a land war, and our only tasks have been to intercept smugglers trying to convey supplies and mercenaries to Szass Tam, and to discourage raiders hoping to take advantage of the weakness of a Thay divided against itself."

She smiled. "But by the Bitch's fork, it's a sea war now, and your sailors are eager to prove their mettle. We don't care what fearsome powers Szass Tam possesses, or how many orcs, zombies, and whatnots are riding on his black ships. They're landlubbers, and we're anything but. Give me leave to direct the battle as I see fit, and I promise you victory."

The zulkirs exchanged glances, and then Samas smiled. "That makes me feel a *little* better."

 •• •• •• •• •• •• •• •• •• •• •• •• ••

When she sensed that the sun was gone, Tammith arose from the hold to find the griffon riders trying to saddle their mounts. The beasts were skittish, fractious, and liable to screech and even snap. They were creatures of mountain and hill, and according to Brightwing's grumbling as translated by Aoth, they didn't like the crowding, the rolling deck, the expanses of water to every side, or any other aspect of the sea voyage.

But Brightwing possessed enhanced intelligence and a psychic link with her master, and Bareris had used his music to forge a comparable bond with Winddancer. No doubt for those reasons, the two officers had succeeded in preparing their steeds for battle in advance of the soldiers under their command. Now they stood in the bow gazing west, where the sky was still red with the last traces of sunset. Looking like the champion he'd been in life, Mirror hovered behind them.

Tammith judged that it would be easier to float over the mass of irritable griffons and their riders than to squirm her way through them, so she dissolved into mist. The transformation dulled her senses, but not so much as to rob her of her orientation, particularly with the forbidding pressure of the sea defining the perimeter of the deck as plainly as a set of walls. She flowed over the heads of beasts and legionnaires and congealed into flesh and bone at Bareris's side. He smiled and kissed her, and she resisted the impulse to extend her fangs, nibble his lips, and draw blood to suck.

"I thought I might wake to find you fighting," she said, "or even that the battle was already over."

Bareris grinned. "That's because you haven't fought at sea. It takes at least as long for fleets to maneuver for position as it does with armies on land."

"But it won't be long now," Mirror said. The sword in his scabbard disappeared, then reformed in his hand, the blade lengthening like an icicle. A round shield wavered into existence on his other arm.

Aoth nodded and hefted his spear. "It's time to get into the air."

"I wish I could fly with you," said Tammith to Bareris. "It bothers me that we won't be together."

"That would be my preference, too," he said. "But I'll be most useful riding Winddancer, and we all need to do our best if we're going to smash through Szass Tam's fleet. So—one last fight, and then it's on to the Wizard's Reach and safety."

She smiled. "Yes, on to Escalant. Just be careful."

"I will." He squeezed her hands, and then he and Aoth strode back to their steeds.

The survivors of the Griffon Legion leaped into the sky with a prodigious clatter and snapping of wings. Mirror floated upward to join them on their flight.

•• •• •• •• •• •• •• •• •• •• •• •• •• ••

Night could blind an army or a fleet, sometimes with fatal consequences. Accordingly, the council's spellcasters sought to illuminate the black, heaving surface of the sea by casting enchantments of illumination onto floats, then tossing them overboard. But the results were only intermittently useful. As often as not, the glowing domes revealed only empty stretches of water, and when they showed more, the necromancers were apt to cast counterspells to extinguish them. Nevron donned a horned, red-lacquered devil mask invested with every charm of augmented vision known to the Order of Divination, and it gave him a far superior view of what was transpiring.

It wasn't an especially encouraging view, consisting as it did of dozens of black ships crewed by rotting corpses, gleaming wraiths soaring above the masts, and skeletal leviathans swimming before the bows, all rushing to annihilate the council and its servants. Despite himself, he felt a twinge of fear.

But a true zulkir—as opposed to useless pretenders like Kumed Hahpret and Zola Sethrakt—learned not merely to conceal such weakness but to expunge it as soon as it appeared. Nevron quashed the feeling by reminding himself that it was his destiny to reign as a prince in one of the higher worlds. This little skirmish was merely practice for the infinitely grander battles he would one day fight to win and keep his throne.

When he was certain he was his true self, all foxy cunning and steely resolve, he pivoted toward the other conjurors on the deck. "Now," he said. "Bring forth your servants."

His minions hastened to obey him—some by chanting incantations, some by twisting a ring or gripping an amulet—and demons, devils, and elemental spirits shimmered into view until the deck and the air overhead were thick with them, and the warship reeked of sulfur. An apelike bar-luga slipped free of its summoner's control long enough to grab a sailor and tear his head off.

Most of Nevron's followers had called the entities with whom they'd dealt most frequently—the same spirits they would have summoned on land, and that was all right. Most of the creatures could reach the enemy by flying or translating themselves through space. But Nevron knew how to bring forth and control every extradimensional creature the Order of Conjuration had ever catalogued, and he suspected that denizens of the infernal oceans might prove even more useful in this particular confrontation.

He chanted and, infuriatingly, nothing happened. The blight afflicting magic had ruined his spell. Some of the entities caged in the talismans he carried laughed or shouted taunts. He gave them pain enough to turn their mockery to screams, then repeated the incantation.

Forces wailed and shimmered through the air, and then the patch of sea directly beneath him churned as a school of skulvyns materialized. Lizardlike with black bulging eyes and four whipping tails, the demons raised their heads and looked to him for instructions. Other Red Wizards, sailors, and even spirits started drawling their words and moving with languid slowness as the hindering aura emanating from the swimming creatures took them in its grip.

Nevron told the skulvyns who and what to destroy, then recited a second incantation. A gigantic wastrilith appeared in the sea, its mass displacing enough water to rock the ship. The demon resembled an immense eel with a vaguely humanoid upper body, round amber eyes, and a mouth full of fangs. Nevron didn't have to speak to it out loud, because wastriliths could communicate mind to mind. When it learned what he required of it, it roared with glee and hurtled toward one of the black ships. It reared, spewed, and raked the enemy vessel's main deck with a stream of seawater heated hot enough to scald. Blood orcs screamed.

All right, Nevron thought. It appeared that his wizardry was working properly again, so perhaps it was time to attempt something challenging. His grating words of command cracked the planks under his feet and made the people around him cringe, even though they couldn't understand them. A sailor's nose dripped blood. The spirits locked in Nevron's rings and amulets howled and gibbered in fear.

The myrmixicus's arrival triggered a sort of purely spiritual shock that staggered nearly everyone, as if the mortal world itself were screaming in protest at having to contain such an abomination. Like the wastrilith, the demon resembled an enormous eel but was even bigger. Its head was reptilian. Beneath that were four arms, each wielding a scythe, and below those, six tentacles. Its tail terminated in a lamprey mouth.

Nevron sent it at the black ships, and a zombie kraken swam to intercept it. The undead creature threw its tentacles around the tanar'ri and dragged it toward its beak. Except for making sure that its arms didn't become entangled, the myrmixicus didn't resist. It wanted to close, and when they came together, it hacked savagely, shredding its foe into lumps of carrion.

Then it resumed its swim toward the enemy fleet. A ghostly dragon, a vague shape made of sickly phosphorescence, rose from the depths to challenge it.

Nevron realized the wizards around him had fallen quiet. He looked around and discovered his followers watching the myrmixicus in awe and fascination.

So had he, for a moment, but that wasn't the point. "What's the matter with you?" he shouted. "Do you think this is a pageant being staged for your amusement? Keep conjuring, or you're all going to die!"

•• •• •• •• •• •• •• •• •• •• •• •• •• ••

The ghost of a woman, slain by torture from the look of her, flew at Aoth and Brightwing. The mouth in the phantom's eyeless face gaped as if the hapless soul had died screaming, and burns and puncture wounds mottled the gaunt, naked form from neck to toe. Its limbs flopped as though suspension or the rack had separated the joints.

Aoth tried to throw flame from the head of his spear. Nothing happened.

The ghost reached out to plunge its tattered fingers into his body. Brightwing swooped and passed under the insubstantial figure.

Certain the ghost would give chase, Aoth twisted around in the saddle and tried again to summon flame. To his relief, a fan-shaped blaze of yellow fire leaped from his weapon to sear the spirit.

But though its entire form contorted like a sketch on a sheet of crumpling parchment, it wasn't destroyed by the fire. It kept hurtling forward and thrust its hand into Brightwing's backside just above the leonine tail. She screamed, convulsed, and fell. Anchored to the griffon's body, the ghost snatched at Aoth, its skinny arm stretching like dough.

Aoth jerked his upper body away, leaning over Brightwing's neck, and although it came so near he felt the sickening chill of it, the ghost's hand fell short. He drove his spear into its chest, snarled a word of power, and channeled destructive force into the weapon.

The ghost dissolved. Brightwing spread her wings and arrested her plummet.

"Are you all right?" Aoth asked.

"Yes," Brightwing croaked, her voice more crow than eagle.

He studied the black, suppurating sore where the phantom had wounded her. "Are you sure?"

"I said yes!"

"All right, but let's take a moment to catch our breaths."

The griffon veered, climbed, and carried him to a clear section of sky. Aoth took the opportunity to study the battle raging around and beneath them.

His fire-touched eyes could see nearly everything clearly, even at a distance and in the dark, but at first he wasn't sure he'd be able to make sense of it all. So much was going on.

Swimming devils and zombie leviathans tore at one another.

Archers and crossbowmen shot their shafts. Ballistae threw enormous bolts, and mangonels, stones. Wizards hurled bright, crackling thunderbolts and called down hailstones.

Galleys and cogs maneuvered, seeking the weather gage or some comparable advantage. One vessel drove its ram into the hull of another. Dread warriors flung grappling irons, seeking to catch hold of a nearby ship and drag it close enough to board. Aquatic ghouls tried to clamber onto what had been a fishing boat, with nets still lying around the deck, while legionnaires jabbed at them with spears.

Fighting from one of the largest warships, Iphegor Nath and some of the Burning Braziers alternately hurled holy fire at enemy vessels and at any particularly dangerous undead that wandered within range. Suddenly, quells appeared among them, shifted through space by the wizards in their midst.

Shadowy figures in swirling robes, glowing mystic sigils floating in the air around them, the apparitions were capable of sundering a priest from the source of his power. Warrior monks, the Braziers' protectors, charged the quells with burning chains whirling in their hands.

Aerial combatants soared, wheeled, and swooped around the sky. A balor struck at spectres with its fiery sword and whip. Half a dozen griffon riders loosed arrow after arrow at a skirr, one of the huge, mummified, batlike undead, while dodging and veering to keep clear of fangs and talons.

Gradually, Aoth sorted it all out, or at least he thought he had. It seemed to him that up in the air, neither side had gained the advantage, which meant that the flyers stayed busy with one another. They couldn't do much to exploit their elevated position to threaten the ships below.

The same was true of the swimming horrors. They seemed equally matched, and as long as that held true, they wouldn't pose much danger to either fleet.

But happily, not every part of the battle reflected the same furious, lethal stalemate, with men, orcs, and conjured creatures struggling and perishing without tipping the balance one way or the other. In the ship-to-ship combats, the true heart of the conflict, the council was faring better than its foes.

Szass Tam had as many ships as his rivals, vessels filled with formidable undead monstrosities, but as Thessaloni Canos had predicted, their crews didn't handle them well. The council's vessels came at the enemy ships from behind or amidships, and only grappled them when it was to their advantage.

The necromancers' thaumaturgy was more reliable than that of their fellow Red Wizards, but combined, the powers of the other orders were more versatile. In addition, they had all the priests they'd evacuated from Bezantur—servants of Kossuth, Mask, Cyric, Umberlee, and every other Thayan god except

Bane—backing them up with their own kind of magic.

By the Great Flame, Aoth thought, am I truly seeing this? Has Szass Tam overreached at last? He remembered all the times when the zulkir of Necromancy had feigned weakness to lure his foes, then snapped a trap shut around them, and was afraid to believe what he was seeing.

Then one of the black ships faded into a vague shadow of itself. Another abruptly went flat, like a paper cutout standing upright on the surface of the sea.

At first Aoth surmised that the necromancers aboard the two vessels had activated some sort of defensive enchantments. But then Brightwing said, "What are you peering at?"

"Two of Szass Tam's ships look different. Can't you see it?"

"No."

After another moment, Aoth couldn't, either. The two vessels appeared normal.

But that didn't matter. He suddenly thought he understood the meaning of what he'd observed, and if so, perhaps the council could maintain its edge no matter what tricks Szass Tam held in store.

"Find Lallara," he said.

The zulkir of Abjuration rated an even larger and more formidable ship than Iphegor Nath, and was accordingly easy to locate. When Brightwing dived out of the night sky, voices cried the alarm. Crossbowmen in the high sterncastle raised their weapons, and Red Wizards, their wands and staves. For an instant, Aoth was sure that his eagerness to share his discovery would be the death of him.

Fortunately, Lallara screamed, "Stop, you idiots!" Her minions froze.

Brightwing landed in the sterncastle between the archwizard and the parapet. She did so lightly, but even so, the planking groaned beneath her weight. "Thank you, Mistress," said Aoth.

"What do you want?" Lallara said.

"I've observed something. We wondered where Szass Tam got a fleet, and now I know. He created the black ships with illusion magic. They aren't entirely real."

Lallara spat. "Nonsense. If that were true, I'd be able to tell. Or the diviners would. Or the illusionists. But no one else has discerned such a thing."

Aoth took a breath. "Your Omnipotence, there's something I haven't told you. The blue fire in my eyes gives me absolute clarity of vision. So if I've ever accomplished anything of note in the service of the council, if I've ever given sound advice, then please, heed me now. Because if the black ships are made of illusion—"

"Then a circle of abjurers should be able to cast counterspells to expunge them from existence," Lallara snapped. "I don't need you to instruct me in basic magical theory." She called for several lesser wizards to attend her, and they came scurrying.

Lallara arranged them in a circle with herself at the center, directed their attention to the nearest black ship, and started a long incantation with an intricate structure and rhyme. Her assistants chimed in on the refrain. Aoth, whose system of battle magic concentrated on attacks and was mostly devoid of feats of abjuration, felt lost immediately.

But he had no trouble comprehending the results of their effort. The dark ship abruptly vanished, dumping the dread warriors and necromancers aboard into the sea.

He knew the abjurers wouldn't be able to make all the enemy vessels disappear. Some would prove impervious to their magic, especially if Szass Tam himself had taken part in their creation. Still, Aoth had given his allies a potent new weapon.

"Well done," he said.

Lallara turned and glared at him. "Why are you still here? Your place is with your men, if you're not trying to shirk the fight."

He sighed. "I'm on my way."

"No, wait. Fly to the senior illusionists and tell them what you told me. They may be able to unmake the black ships as well."

·· ·· ·· ·· ·· ·· ·· ·· ·· ·· ·· ·· ·· ·· ·· ··

Standing in the prow of his flagship, his staff of drowned men's bones in his hand, Szass Tam gazed over the water and smiled. "I should have made a greater effort to win Thessaloni Canos over to my side. Or had her assassinated."

"If it's hopeless," Malark said, "I recommend you pull your ships out of combat before you lose any more soldiers. The skeleton sea serpents and their fellows can cover our retreat."

"I think not."

"You've already won the war."

"But if I kill my fellow zulkirs tonight, or failing that, send their treasure and followers to the bottom of the sea, I can rest secure in the knowledge I won't have to fight another. And the battle is far from lost. I'm sure you haven't forgotten the trump up my sleeve."

"Are you still strong enough to use it?"

"Let's find out." Szass Tam focused his awareness on the air above an empty stretch of water and murmured words of power. Frost crept across the railing in front of him, and the remaining flesh on a dread warrior's frame liquefied all at once, leaving it a figure of dripping bone.

·· ·· ·· ·· ·· ·· ·· ·· ·· ·· ·· ·· ·· ·· ·· ··

The roundship's task had been to transport the Griffon Legion, and now that Aoth and his command were in the air, not many soldiers were left aboard. Thus, although the crossbowmen shot at any target of opportunity, the sailors were doing their best to keep the vessel out of the thick of combat.

It was only prudent, but it frustrated Tammith. The smell of blood hung on the wind, enticing her, drying her throat, and causing her fangs to extend. She longed to be on one of the pairs of grappled ships, where she could fight, kill, and drink until her appetites were satisfied.

In lieu of that, she'd obtained her own crossbow, but killing someone at range was a poor substitute for tearing him apart with her sword or fangs, not that she often hit her mark in any case. She possessed preternatural senses and physical prowess, but no training in the use of that particular weapon.

She pulled the trigger, the crossbow clacked, and the bolt flew too low, imbedding itself in the ebony hull of an enemy galley. She hissed and reached for another. Then someone shouted.

Tammith pivoted. A dead man was climbing out of the water onto the stern. A haze hung in the air around it.

She grinned. The zombie had no blood to slake her thirst, but at least she'd have the satisfaction of cutting it up. Or she would if her shipmates didn't dispatch it first, for a single animated corpse shouldn't pose much of a threat. She dropped her crossbow and drew her blade.

The men closest to the undead newcomer stumbled, retched, and fell. Whatever was afflicting them, it rendered them incapable of defense, and, its bare fists striking with bone-shattering force, the creature had no difficulty breaking their backs and skulls. Two crossbow bolts plunged into its torso, but it didn't even seem to notice.

Tammith charged.

The haze surrounding the dead man was cold and wet, and as soon as she entered it, a burning tightness ripped through her chest. She couldn't breathe, as if her lungs were full of water and she was drowning.

But a vampire had no need to breathe. She clamped down on her irrational terror, raised her off hand to signal her comrades to stay away—she doubted she could speak coherently with the choking fullness in her mouth and lungs—and rushed the zombie.

The creature evidently hadn't realized she too was undead, because her immunity to its lethal aura seemed to take it by surprise. When she thrust her sword at its chest, it tried to parry with its forearm, but was too slow. The blade plunged through soft, rotten tissue, scraped a rib, and pierced the heart.

But it wasn't the mortal injury she'd hoped for. Without even faltering, the creature shoved itself farther onto the blade, closing the distance, then whipped a punch at her head. She ducked and scrambled backward, yanking the sword free as she retreated.

For the next few moments, she and the zombie traded attacks. The creature had yet to connect, but as strong as it was, it might only need to hit her once to incapacitate her, and then smash her bones while she was helpless. She cut and pierced it repeatedly, but the wounds weren't slowing it down. In fact, some were starting to close. Her foe possessed a gift of quick healing akin to her own.

It was also inching the duel toward the bow of the ship, and she thought she understood the reason. It wanted to engulf the other mortals in its drowning effect. Then she'd have to slay it quickly if she wanted her allies to survive. She'd need to fight more aggressively and take chances, and that might finally give the creature the opportunity to get its hands on her.

If you want aggression, Tammith thought, I'll give it to you. She exploded into a cloud of bats.

It hurt to transform so quickly, and hurt again when each of her creatures felt the strangling weight of water in its lungs. The bats were more primal, more creatures of instinct, than she was in human form, and a fresh surge of terror threatened to overwhelm them. But the part of her that was shadowy overmind, the guiding consciousness they shared, resisted.

The bats hurtled at the zombie. It caught one in each hand, squeezed and crushed them, and all the survivors felt the death agony, but that couldn't balk them either. Two others landed on the creature's face and clawed out its eyes.

Then all the surviving bats flew away and whirled into a single form again. That didn't quell the pain, but Tammith had to ignore it. Because, orienting on the rustle of wings, her foe lurched around to confront her with slime seething in the orbits of its deliquescing face. Its new eyes had nearly formed already.

She bellowed a battle cry and cut at its neck.

Its head tumbled free of its shoulders. The body collapsed, then crawled after its severed portion. Tammith ran to the head, snatched it up, and hurled it over the rail. The body stopped moving, and the cold, wet haze evaporated.

Tammith surveyed the deck. More men were alive than otherwise, but the survivors were simply standing and gawking. "Get back to your duties!" she rasped. "Sail the ship and watch for other enemies!"

Most of them scrambled to obey, but one youth stayed huddled on the deck, weeping and gasping as if he couldn't catch his breath.

Tammith strode over to him. "Get up. You're all right now."

He just stayed where he'd fallen, his shoulders shaking, and she experienced a spasm of contempt. He was a coward, and useless. Or rather, useful only as a source of blood. If she drained him, the throbbing pain inside her would ease more quickly.

She jerked him to his feet, tilted his head back to expose the throat, and in so doing, got a good look at his tear- and snot-streaked face. He was even younger than she'd imagined, and, judging from his lack of any uniform or insignia, not a member of the zulkirs' navy, just a fisherman's son or trader's cabin boy they'd pressed into service to help with their escape.

Shame rose inside her. It didn't extinguish her thirst, but it counterbalanced it. She stared into the youth's eyes and said, "Calm down. Everything's fine."

He blinked and smiled, then stiffened. A bat far larger than the ones she could become swooped over the deck and then melted into a towering, four-armed figure with crimson eyes and a lupine muzzle. "Good evening, Captain Iltazyarra," Tsagoth said. "I've been hunting you for a while."

.. ..

Aoth watched in dismay as the dream vestige came streaming and boiling from empty air. He could hear its myriad voices moaning and whimpering even from high above.

"You didn't think we were going to get through the fight without seeing that thing again, did you?" Brightwing asked. The undertone of stress in her voice revealed that the wound she'd received from the ghost was still paining her.

"I hoped so, but maybe the zulkirs can handle it this time. I know they talked about how to do it. Our job is to keep our troops away from it." He flew around bellowing a warning, and other griffon riders took up the call in turn.

Although perhaps it wasn't necessary. The dream vestige had manifested just above the water and there it floated still, either because that was where Szass Tam wanted it or because it judged it would catch more prey there. Tentaclelike extrusions groping for any sentient swimming or flying creature unfortunate enough to be within reach, it streamed forward and engulfed one of the council's war galleys. When it flowed on, no one was left on deck.

The Red Wizards and the priests of Bezantur counterattacked with every form of magic at their disposal. Hurtling sparks exploded into blasts of flame at the center of the cloud. Thunderbolts pierced it, and howling winds shoved at it. Two of the largest conjured entities Aoth had ever seen, both eel-like with vaguely human upper bodies, spat their breath weapons, then swam in to rip with fang, claw, and scythe before dissolving in the dream vestige's misty embrace.

Aoth told himself that his allies must be hurting the thing. Whether alive or undead, no being was entirely impervious to harm. But they weren't causing enough damage to stop it.

It devoured the crew of a second ship.

"Take me nearer," said Aoth.

"Are you joking?" Brightwing replied. "If the thing doesn't grab us and eat us, a stray lightning bolt will fry us."

"I trust you to dodge the dangers."

"Thanks so much."

"I need to look at the fog up close. If I do, I might see something nobody else can see."

"I think I liked you better blind." Brightwing furled her wings and dived.

They swooped over Szass Tam's servant with the height of a tall ship's mainmast separating them from the top of the billowing vapor. It wasn't nearly enough separation to keep them safe. Composed of writhing, mewling shadows all ragged and intertwined, columns of mist shot up and lashed at them. Angled upward, a lightning bolt stabbed out of the cloud just in front of them and burned an afterimage across Aoth's vision. An elemental in the form of a towering, roaring waterspout, a rudimentary face repeatedly forming and disappearing in the swirl, rushed toward them. Brightwing veered constantly, striving to evade whatever threat was closest without running straight into another.

When they finished running the gauntlet, they were above the necromancers' fleet, but the threat implicit in that seemed almost trivial compared to what they'd just endured. "Did you get what you wanted?" the griffon asked.

"No," Aoth said. "Do it again, but fly lower."

Brightwing laughed. "Of course. Why not?"

As they skimmed just above its surface, the fog-thing tried even harder to seize them, and since its extrusions didn't have to shoot far, the griffon had less time to dodge. Blasts of flame seared and dazzled them, and Aoth's thoughts threatened to shatter into panic and confusion. The latter resulted from too much magic unleashed in too small a space and in too short a time, straining the foundations of reality itself.

He struggled to ignore the distractions and *look,* although the cloud streaking by just under Brightwing's talons and paws was so palpably vile that he wanted to cringe and avert his gaze. Murky, tangled, inconstant figures crawled over and over one another like a nest of snakes. Mouths gaped and twisted, and shredded fingers clutched and scrabbled.

One of the dream vestige's arms leaped up directly in front of Brightwing. She veered, but Aoth saw that she had little chance of avoiding it. Then an ammizu, a squat, bat-winged devil with a face like a boar, dived at the necromancers' servant and the misty tentacle twisted away from the griffon to snatch for the baatezu.

The shadowy vapor below gave way to black water. In another moment, Aoth and Brightwing hurtled beyond the dream vestige's reach.

"I'm not doing it a third time," Brightwing rasped.

"I wasn't going to ask. Take me back to Lallara."

.. ..

"It seems," Tammith said, "that you're a bad loser."

Tsagoth laughed. "Not really. I rather admire the way you

tricked me. I'm here because Szass Tam ordered me to seek you whenever my other duties permitted. You could consider it a compliment of sorts that he took special notice of your departure." He vanished.

Tammith had been expecting such a trick. She whirled and swung her sword in a horizontal cut at the level of Tsagoth's belly.

But the attack fell short. She assumed he'd position himself close enough to attack instantly, without the necessity of stepping in, but she'd been mistaken.

He sprang at her before she could recover. She flung herself to one side, and three of his snatching hands closed on empty air. The fourth, however, grabbed her shoulder, yanked, and came away with flesh, leather, and lengths of rattling chain clutched in the talons.

She cried out at the burst of pain but couldn't allow it to slow her. Tsagoth pivoted toward her, and she heaved her blade into line. He halted rather than risk impaling himself on her point, and she retreated farther away from him.

She'd kept herself alive for at least another moment, but that was all. She had no hope of winning. She still carried the hurt the zombie had given her, Tsagoth had just injured her a second time, and he overmatched her in any case.

But if she couldn't prevail, she might still survive. She couldn't turn into bats and flee over open water, but he wouldn't be able to harm her if she melted into mist, and so, although the savage part of her protested, she willed the transformation.

Pain stabbed into her back. She lost control of the change, and her form locked into solidity again.

In fact, she lost control of everything and couldn't move at all. Her legs buckled beneath her, dropping her to her knees. She would have fallen farther, but something was holding her up. Her head lolled backward, and then she could see it. At some point,

Tsagoth had used his hypnotic powers on one of the sailors, who now crept forward and thrust a spear into her back.

The mortal had done a good job of it, to penetrate her mail and plunge the lance in deeply enough that the wooden shaft transfixed her heart. That was why she couldn't move, and likely never would again.

Tsagoth advanced and reached for her head, probably to tear or twist it off. Then a thunderous shout staggered the blood fiend and flayed flesh from the upper part of his body. Winddancer and Bareris plunged down on top of him. The griffon's talons impaled Tsagoth, and his momentum smashed him down onto the deck.

Tsagoth heaved himself onto his knees, tumbling his attackers off of him. He scrambled upright, and gathered himself to spring before Winddancer found his footing or Bareris could shift his sword to threaten him. Then Mirror, resembling a sketch of Bareris wrought in smoke and starlight, flew down on his flank. The ghost cut, and his intangible blade sheared into Tsagoth's torso. The blood fiend staggered.

Attacking relentlessly, the newcomers pushed Tsagoth down the deck toward the stern. Bareris slipped off Winddancer's back, ran to Tammith, shoved the unresisting sailor away from her, and, grunting, pulled the spear out of her back.

As soon as he did, her mobility returned. She felt an itching across her body and realized that, with a length of wood jammed in her heart, she'd already started to rot. Now the process was reversing.

Bareris threw the spear over the side. "I have to fight."

She bared her fangs and stood up. "So do I."

She expected him to protest that she ought to keep away from Tsagoth, at least until her wounds closed, but he didn't. Something in her manner must have told him he couldn't dissuade her. He simply turned and advanced on their foe, and she glided after him.

Bareris didn't try to climb on Winddancer's back, nor, biting and clawing, did the griffon need a rider to encourage him to fight. Battling in concert, the four of them—bard, beast, ghost, and vampire—harried Tsagoth, each defending when the blood fiend oriented on him and attacking from the side or rear when their adversary sought to rend a comrade.

By degrees, they slashed Szass Tam's agent into a patchwork of gaping wounds, and dark sores erupted where Mirror's sword had penetrated. The fiend couldn't heal them fast enough, and Tammith prayed that he was too lost to battle rage to realize that his only hope was to translate himself through space to safety.

His wolfish muzzle partly sliced from the rest of his head, he leered at her as if he'd read her mind, as if to promise that he wouldn't leave with the matter between them unresolved. Then he charged her.

That action required him to abandon any attempt at defense, and Bareris, Mirror, and Winddancer all cut deep. But Tsagoth didn't drop, the reckless tactic caught Tammith by surprise, and she couldn't dodge in time. The blood fiend grabbed her and bulled her onward. They smashed through the rail and plummeted into the sea.

•• •• •• •• •• •• •• •• •• •• •• •• •• ••

The circle of abjurers recited the final line of their incantation, and power whined through the air. Some of the shrouds attached to the foremast snapped. But the cloud-thing across the water continued devouring every sentient being it could seize, exactly the same as before.

Aoth was disappointed, but not surprised. Lallara and her subordinates had tried thrice before with the same lack of success.

The zulkir pivoted and lashed the back of her hand across

a female Red Wizard's mouth. Her rings cut, and the younger woman flinched back with bloody lips.

"Useless imbeciles!" Lallara snarled. Then she looked at Aoth, and, to his amazement, gave him a fleeting hint of a smile. It was the first such moment in all his years of service. "There. That made me feel a trifle better, but it didn't help our situation, did it?"

"No, Your Omnipotence. I guess it didn't."

"Then it's time to go. Would you care to accompany us? Perhaps you've earned it, even if this last piece of information—or alleged information—you brought me is worthless, too."

"Mistress, is it possible that if you and the other zulkirs all combined your powers—"

"I think not, and for all we know, the others have already transported themselves to safety."

"Surely it wouldn't take long to find out for certain."

She scowled. "The dream vestige has turned the tide in Szass Tam's favor, and our fleet is going to lose. I don't like it either, but that's the way it is. Now, do you want to live?"

"Yes, Mistress, very much. But I have griffon riders in the sky."

She looked up, then snorted. "By my estimation, not many, not anymore."

"Still." He swung his leg over Brightwing's back.

•• •• •• •• •• •• •• •• •• •• •• •• •• ••

Tammith and Tsagoth splashed down into the dark water, and it paralyzed her as completely as the spear, even as it ate at her like acid. As they sank deeper, the blood fiend clawed and bit at her eroding flesh.

Something else plunged into the sea. Her eyes were burning like the rest of her, but she could make out Winddancer's talons ripping at Tsagoth, and Bareris's sword stabbing repeatedly.

The blood fiend vanished.

The weight of Tammith's mail dragged what was left of her deeper amid a cloud of corruption. Now she was beyond Winddancer's reach. Her fingers corroded to nothing, and her sword fell away.

Bareris dived after her, seized her, and struggled to swim upward. She herself wasn't weighing him down. She scarcely had any weight left. Her mail and his brigandine were the hindrances.

She felt relieved when her chain shirt slipped off the wisp of mush she'd become, and he finally started to make headway toward the air above. She couldn't have borne it if he'd drowned.

But it was too late for her, and probably that was for the best. Now she couldn't hurt him anymore. She wished she could tell him so, and then blackness seemed to rise like a great fish from the gulf beneath her and swallowed everything.

•• •• •• •• •• •• •• •• •• •• •• •• ••

Sopping wet, the wind chilling him, Bareris stood at the rail and stared out at the night. Illuminated by the flickering glow of burning ships and flares of mystic force, the battle raged before him on the sea and in the sky, and he knew he could make sense of it if he wanted. But he couldn't muster any interest.

Why did I swim to the surface? he wondered. What was the point? Why can't I find the courage to dive back in?

Wings snapped and fluttered behind him. He assumed it was Winddancer trying to dry her feathers until Aoth's voice said, "I expected to find you aloft directing the men."

Bareris took a breath, then reluctantly turned to face his comrade. "I was. Then I saw Tsagoth fighting Tammith. He was pressing her hard."

Aoth closed his smoldering eyes as if in pain. Perhaps he'd just realized that Tammith was nowhere to be seen, or maybe he surmised her fate from Bareris's manner. "My friend, I'm truly sorry."

"So am I," Mirror said.

For some reason, their sympathy infuriated Bareris, but he realized in a dim way that he ought not to let his anger show. "Thank you," he said, his voice catching in his throat.

"If I were you," Aoth said, "I'd just want to stand here and grieve. But you can't. The battle's going against us. Lallara's fled already, and maybe the other zulkirs, too. I don't know how many griffon riders are still alive, but we need to collect them and try to lead them to safety. On the wing, if we think land is close enough, and aboard this vessel otherwise."

Bareris drew breath to say, Go without me.

But Mirror spoke first. "I thought we were winning."

"We were," said Aoth, "but then Szass Tam unleashed the dream vestige, and for all their theorizing and preparations, the Red Wizards can't stop it. I thought I'd discovered something that would help them, but it was no use, either."

"What was it?" Mirror asked.

Aoth made a sour face. "The souls that make up the cloud are in torment, tangled together as they are, trapped in a kind of perpetual nightmare, and they hate one another even more than they hate the rest of the world. Much as they hunger to eat the living, they're even more eager to lash out at their fellows, but something about their condition—some binding Szass Tam created, perhaps—prevents it. I hoped knowing that would give the Red Wizards an opening, but . . ." He shrugged.

Bareris wasn't making any effort to attend to Aoth's explanation. The dream vestige no longer interested him, or so he imagined. Yet even so, his friend's words evoked an idea, and an urge to do something more than "stand here and grieve."

"It might be a weakness we can exploit," he said. "I'm going to try."

Aoth scowled. "I told you, Lallara and her circle had the same information, and they couldn't slay the thing. Neither can Iphegor Nath and the other high priests."

"That may be," said Bareris. "But no one weaves magic to spark or twist emotion better than a bard." And he believed at that moment, he understood suffering and hatred as well as any singer ever born.

"Is this just a fancy way of committing suicide?" Aoth demanded. "I ask because it won't end your pain, or send you to rejoin Tammith. You'll be stuck inside that thing, sharing its agony, forever."

"I promise, my goal is to destroy it."

"Let him try," said Mirror to Aoth. "You'd do the same if you believed you had any chance of succeeding."

Aoth snorted. "After watching Lallara abandon the fleet to its fate? Don't count on it." He turned his head toward Bareris. "But all right. I won't stand in your way."

"Thank you." Bareris looked around at some of the surviving sailors and called for them to lower a dinghy. Since the dream vestige wasn't far away, he saw no reason to take Winddancer close enough for the cloud-thing to grab.

"I'll come with you," Mirror said.

"No, you won't. You can't sing spells or row a boat, so you truly would be risking your existence for no reason whatsoever, and that would trouble me."

The ghost lowered his head in acquiescence.

It didn't take the mariners long to put the dinghy in the water, or for Bareris to climb into it. He nodded to his comrades, then rowed toward the dream vestige.

Nothing molested him. Except for mindless things like zombies and their ilk, even Szass Tam's other minions were trying to stay clear of the fog-thing, and so they made no effort to intercept a boat headed toward it.

When he was close enough, he started to sing.

He sang of loving Tammith more than life itself and losing her over and over again. Of hating the world that inflicted such infinite cruelty, and despising himself still more for his failure to shield his beloved from its malice. Of the insupportable need to attain an end. He took rage and grief, guilt and self-loathing, and sought to forge them into a sword to strike a blow against Szass Tam and to aid his friends.

The dream vestige extended a murky arm. He kept singing. The groaning, whispering swirl of shadowy figures engulfed him and hoisted him into the air.

The phantoms slithered around him like pythons trying to crush him. Their jagged fingers scratched and gouged. Shocks of fear and cold jolted him, and he felt some fundamental quality—the boundary that made him a separate entity, perhaps, as opposed to just one more helpless, crazed component of the fog—rotting and dissolving.

Rotting and dissolving as Tammith had, turning to scum and nothingness in his embrace. He focused on that and it gave him the strength to force out another note and another after that, to keep trying to enflame the dream vestige's wrath and self-hatred until they were strong enough to burst any constraint.

•• •• •• •• •• •• •• •• •• •• •• •• •• •• ••

Samas Kul decided it was time to go. But he didn't share his conclusion with the transmuters who'd had the honor of journeying with him aboard his own ship, and they kept hurling spells at the enemy.

They were useful followers. He was genuinely fond of some of them. But they weren't made of gems and gold, and it was their bad luck that a spell of translocation could shift only so much weight.

Hoping that no one would notice his absence for at least a little while, he descended a companionway, murmured a word of opening, and entered his luxurious cabin inside the sterncastle.

A stack of chests stood in the center of the space. They couldn't contain the whole of Samas's liquid assets—the entire ship scarcely sufficed for that. But they did represent a significant portion of them, holding as they did, rare mystical artifacts and his finest gems.

He regretted it bitterly that henceforth, he wouldn't be any sort of sovereign lord. But at least he'd still be the richest man in the East and perhaps all Faerûn.

He removed a scroll from within his robe, unrolled it, and drew breath to read the trigger phrase of the magic bound in the ink and parchment. Then voices clamored overhead.

In itself, that wasn't unusual. People had been yelling all night when some threat or target drew near. But this time, the noise had an excited, almost exuberant quality that piqued his curiosity. He decided it wouldn't hurt to delay his departure long enough to determine what all the fuss was about.

He slipped out of the compartment and felt the locking ward seal it behind him. He walked to the rail to peer across the waves at whatever had manifestly riveted everyone else's attention.

It was the dream vestige. The cloud was churning, thinning, shrinking, drawing in on itself. He recited a rhyme to enhance his vision, and then he could see why. The shadows that comprised it were clawing at one another. To some degree, they always had, but now it mattered. They were ripping each other to bits.

Samas murmured an incantation that would allow him to communicate with Thessaloni Canos aboard her war galley. For a moment, he actually glimpsed her, breathing hard with a bloody cut just beneath her left eye. "Do you see what's happening to the dream vestige?" he asked.

If his voice, sounding from the empty air, startled her, he couldn't tell. She answered immediately, and her manner was crisp. "Yes, Your Omnipotence."

"If the entity shrivels up and dies, can we salvage this situation?"

"Yes."

Feeling like a dauntless warrior in a ballad, Samas squared his shoulders. "All right, then, Tharchion. Let's do it."

.. ..

The fleets battled through the night, and for most of it, Malark couldn't tell who was winning. It was too dark, the conflict was unfolding over too wide an area, and too many of the combatants were entities whose capabilities he didn't understand.

But he realized the truth when Szass Tam stopped brandishing his staff and chanting words of power to flop down atop a coil of rope and slump forward. The lich looked as spent as any mortal laborer after a hard day's toil.

Malark squatted down on the ink black deck beside him. Up close, he noticed that the lich stank of decay more than on any occasion he could recall. "They beat us, didn't they?" he whispered, making sure that no one else would overhear the question.

Szass Tam smiled. "Yes." He nodded toward the east, where the strip of sky just above the horizon was gray instead of black. "Dawn is coming to exert its usual deleterious effect on our troops. I've expended all the power Bane gave me, and my own magic, too. Of course, I could still call any number of arcane weapons and talismans into my hands, but none of them would change the outcome."

"So what do we do?" Malark asked.

"Precisely what you in your wisdom suggested earlier. We withdraw our remaining ships while our swimming and flying warriors cover the retreat." Szass Tam struggled to his feet. Suddenly he held a scroll in his withered fingers. "I'll send shadows of myself to the various captains to inform them of the plan."

"We can communicate with bugle calls," Malark said. "You don't have to strain yourself any further."

"I suppose not," Szass Tam answered. "But I'm their leader and I'd prefer they hear the bad news directly from me, or at least a reasonable facsimile thereof."

•• •• •• •• •• •• •• •• •• •• •• ••

Aoth, Brightwing, and Mirror flew back and forth across the slate gray sea, edged with silver where the wan sunlight caught the crests of the waves. Corpses, arrows, and scraps of charred and shattered timber, the detritus of the battle just concluded, floated everywhere. The council's ships were dots dwindling in the west.

Aoth knew he should give up and return to his own vessel before it sailed farther away. He was exhausted, and through their empathic link, he could feel that Brightwing was wearier still. How could it be otherwise, considering that she was wounded and had carried him around all night?

Yet for once she performed her task without grousing, even though he sensed she considered it futile. Bareris had destroyed the dream vestige, but had almost certainly perished in so doing. It was doubtful his friends could even recover his body. It could have dissolved in the fog-thing's grip, or sunk to the bottom, or a current could have swept it far away.

Aoth was just about to abandon the search when he spied a pale form bobbing in the chop. Responsive to his unspoken will,

Brightwing swooped lower. Bareris was floating face down, but Aoth recognized him anyway, perhaps by the uncommon combination of a lanky Mulan frame and longish hair.

Aoth rattled off an incantation. Bareris floated up out of the water. Brightwing flew past him as slowly as she could, and Aoth snatched hold of him and hauled him onto the griffon's back.

Bareris's ordeal had dissolved his armor and clothing and bleached his skin and hair chalk white. It had also stopped him breathing and stilled his heart.

All his friends could do was carry him back to the roundship and then make ready to give him to the sea all over again, this time with the proper observances and prayers. Aoth couldn't find a priest of Milil, god of song, so one of the Burning Braziers agreed to officiate.

They packed a dingy with inflammables to make a floating pyre, then laid Bareris inside it. They were just about to light it and set it adrift when the bard opened eyes turned black as midnight.

epilogue

18–19 Marpenoth, the Year of Blue Fire

Aoth swallowed a first mouthful of sweet red Sembian wine, sighed, and closed his eyes in appreciation. As far as he was concerned, Escalant wasn't much of a city compared to Bezantur, Eltabbar, or even Pyarados, especially now that it was overrun with refugees. But it had taverns and strong drink, and after a day of trying to help the town accommodate the needs of all the newcomers without exploding into riots, and striving to shore up the port's defenses in case Szass Tam showed up to attack it, those were the amenities he craved.

The common room suddenly fell silent. Aoth opened his eyes. Bareris and Mirror, the latter currently too vague a shadow to resemble anyone in particular, were standing in the doorway, and everyone else was edging away from them.

Aoth didn't share the crowd's instinctive antipathy for walking corpses and ghosts, but he couldn't help wishing that his friends hadn't come looking for him just then. He'd hoped for some time alone to relax. Still, a decent fellow didn't duck his comrades, so he called out to them, rose, grabbed the bottle, and led them outside. Better that than to shroud the whole tavern in gloom and apprehension.

The Wizard's Reach hadn't suffered the filthy weather Szass Tam had inflicted on Thay proper. That was one nice thing about the place. Still, the air was chilly. Autumn had started in earnest. Aoth touched a fingertip to one of his tattoos, and warmth flowed through his limbs.

He and his companions strolled in silence for a time. Other pedestrians gawked but kept their distance. Aoth swigged from the bottle, then offered it to Bareris, who declined it. Maybe he wasn't capable of enjoying wine anymore.

"I owe you an apology," Bareris said at last.

Aoth cocked his head. "You do?"

"You warned me that I was too puny a creature to fancy myself Szass Tam's special enemy, but I resisted the notion. I kept on, even after Mystra died and the blue fires and earthquakes started scourging the world and making our entire war look petty by comparison. That would have convinced any sensible person of his own insignificance, but not me. You were right, and I was wrong."

Aoth grunted. "I never meant to imply that you're anything less than a worthy, capable man." He hesitated. "Or maybe I did. I was angry. But the truth is, you're a good soldier and a good friend, and maybe people like you and me make more of a difference than I thought. We stopped the dream vestige and saved the fleet."

Bareris shook his head. "I failed every time it truly mattered."

"I understand why you think that, but I disagree."

"When she came back to me, she said she hadn't really returned. That the girl I loved was long dead. But it wasn't so.

Every night, the old Tammith grew a little stronger, and the vampire, weaker. I could see it even if she was afraid to believe it. But now. . . ."

Aoth didn't know what else to say.

After three more paces, Bareris said, "I'm leaving Escalant."

"Don't. Now that the zulkirs are here, the place will become more and more like the real Thay, which means that folk will get used to the undead. You'll be better off here than you would be anywhere else."

"I'm going back to the real Thay."

"Damn it, why? To hunt down Tsagoth and hope that somehow, one day, you might be able to inconvenience Szass Tam himself in some minor fashion? To devote *another* ten years to revenge? I thought you just told me you'd realized you were wasting your life."

Bareris smiled a smile that sent a chill oozing up Aoth's spine. "But since the touch of the dream vestige changed me, I no longer have life to waste."

Aoth took a deep breath. He felt like a traitor, but he had to speak his heart. "If you go, I'm not coming with you. It's been ten years for me, too, ten years of risking my life, and while we may have done some notable deeds, I'll be honest with you. Here at the end, I'm not really sure there was a point. All I know is that the fight took my youth, and I don't want it to steal the rest of my days as well. If Szass Tam leaves me alone, I'll leave him alone."

"But I'll accompany you," said Mirror.

"Thank you," Bareris replied, "but I can't ask that. You followed me out of the mountains in the hope that contact with living people would heal your mind. It hasn't, entirely, but it's helped, and if you go back to Thay, you won't have that anymore. We'll have to hide in the shadows and the wilderness, and I'm afraid that everything you've regained will slip away from you."

"Then you'll just have to talk to me and give me things to think about," Mirror said, "because I refuse to let you go alone."

....

When Malark entered Szass Tam's apartments, the lich was frowning at his reflection in a full-length mirror enclosed in a golden frame. From high collar to dragging train, sparkling gems encrusted his robe so thickly that it was hard to discern the crimson velvet beneath.

Malark realized it must be a coronation robe. The lich had proclaimed himself regent long ago, but now that he'd driven his rivals into exile, a second ceremony was in order.

As Malark bowed, Szass Tam asked, "What do you think?"

"Samas Kul himself would envy it."

"Voices of the Abyss, as hideous as that? I'll ask the tailors to attempt something a trifle less gaudy."

Malark proffered a sheaf of papers. "I don't promise this is a comprehensive inventory of every seaworthy vessel and able-bodied mariner on the coast. But it's close."

Szass Tam accepted the parchments and set them on a chair. "Thank you. It's important information, and we'll put it to good use. But I've decided that I'm not going to try to take the Alaor or the Wizard's Reach. Why should I, when I already have all the territory I need?"

"To keep the other zulkirs from starting a new war?"

"Upon further consideration, I've concluded that's unlikely. Their remaining dominions lack the resources, and when we construct our own fleet and build up our coastal defenses, they'll recognize that their prospects have become even more hopeless."

"I still think you'd be safer to kill them."

"Theoretically speaking, you might be right, but after

ten long years of playing chess with them, I begrudge them any more of my time. My instincts tell me the blue fires and earth tremors will subside by the end of the year, and then my real work can begin. Speaking of which, I thought you might appreciate a look at this." Malark somehow missed the instant it appeared, but the lich held a thick, musty-smelling book bound in flaking black leather.

Malark swallowed. "Is that really it?"

Szass Tam smiled. "Yes. The boldest, most brilliant arcane treatise ever written, penned by an unknown genius at the dawn of time and unearthed by Fastrin the Delver when Netheril was young."

personages of thay

LORDS, CAPTAINS, AND OTHER NOTABLES
OF THE COURTS OF THE NORTH

THE REGENT
Szass Tam, zulkir of the Order of Necromancy and pretender
 to the regency of Thay

THE THARCHIONS
Azhir Kren (Gauros)
Hezass Nymar (Lapendrar), also Eternal Flame of the temple
 of Kossuth in Escalant
Homen Odesseiron (Surthay)
Invarri Metron (Delhumide)
Pyras Autorian (Thaymount)

OTHERS
Tammith Iltazyarra, captain of the Silent Company
Xingax, a maker of undead

LORDS, CAPTAINS, AND OTHER NOTABLES
OF THE COURTS OF THE SOUTH

THE ZULKIRS
Dmitra Flass (Illusion), also tharchion of Eltabbar and princess
 of Mulmaster, "the First Princess of Thay"
Kumed Hahpret (Evocation)
Lallara (Abjuration)
Lauzoril (Enchantment)
Nevron (Conjuration)
Samas Kul (Transmutation), also tharchion of Priador and
 Master of the Guild of Foreign Trade

Yaphyll (Divination)
Zola Sethrakt (Necromancy)

THE THARCHIONS

Dimon (Tyraturos), also a priest of Bane
Kethin Hur (Thazalhar)
Nymia Focar (Pyarados)
Thessaloni Canos (the Alaor)

OTHERS

Aoth Fezim, captain of the Griffon Legion of Pyarados
Bareris Anskuld, a lieutenant of the Griffon Legion
Drash Rurith, autharch of Mophur
Iphegor Nath, High Flamelord of the Church of Kossuth
Malark Springhill, spymaster to Dmitra Flass
Nular Zurn, castellan of the Keep of Sorrows
Unara Anrakh, high priestess of the temple of Bane in Hurkh
Zekith Shezim, high priest of the temple of Bane in Bezantur

RavenLoft™
the covenant

RavenLoft's Lords of darkness have always waited for the unwary to find them.

From the autocratic vampire who wrote the memoirs found in *I, Strahd*
to the demon lord and his son whose story is told in *Tapestry of Dark
Souls*, some of the finest horror characters created by some of the most
influential authors of horror and dark fantasy have found their way to
RAVENLOFT, to be trapped there forever.

Laurell K. Hamilton
Death of a Darklord

Christie Golden
Vampire of the Mists

P.N. Elrod
I, Strahd: The Memoirs of a Vampire

Andria Cardarelle
To Sleep With Evil

Elaine Bergstrom
Tapestry of Dark Souls

Tanya Huff
Scholar of Decay

EBERRON

HEIRS OF ASH

RICH WULF

The Legacy . . . an invention of unimaginable power. Rumors say it could save the world—or destroy it. The hunt is on.

Book 1
VOYAGE OF THE MOURNING DAWN

Book 2
FLIGHT OF THE DYING SUN

Book 3
RISE OF THE SEVENTH MOON
November 2007

BLADE OF THE FLAME

TIM WAGGONER

Once an assassin. Now a man of faith. One man searches for peace in a land that knows only blood.

Book 1
THIEVES OF BLOOD

Book 2
FORGE OF THE MINDSLAYERS

Book 3
SEA OF DEATH
February 2008

THE LANTERNLIGHT FILES

PARKER DEWOLF

A man on the run. A city on the watch. Magic on the loose.

Book 1
THE LEFT HAND OF DEATH

Book 2
WHEN NIGHT FALLS
March 2008

Book 3
DEATH COMES EASY
December 2008